Acclaim for V. Romas Burton

"*Fortified* is a riveting, beautifully-written adventure full of intrigue, betrayal, strife, and one woman with enough faith and bravery in her heart to face it all." —CASEY L. BOND, author of *Where Oceans Burn*

"Burton's new book is filled with fast-paced action, her signature faith-based content with hard-hitting themes and characters you want to root for. The story of embracing faith and becoming confident in abilities and self is one that any young person will love. Humor, touching moments, wholesome friendships between young women of different backgrounds, political intrigue, and a burgeoning romance will keep you flipping pages and leave you impatient for the next book. Another fantastic tale, and one I'm eager to follow!" —C. M. BANSCHBACH, award-winning author of *The Wolf Prince*

"For fans of empowered heroines, soulful themes, and gorgeous worldbuilding reminiscent of CJ Redwine, Morgan Busse, and Mary Weber, *Fortified* is the kind of pure romantic fantasy that will leave you swooning. Get ready to meet Devora, a young woman with powers the kingdom hates in a fight for her life, and the secretive hero we've all been waiting for, Captain Blake, who helps her survive and is the most appealing sort of strong, silent, military version of Mr. Darcy type. Political intrigue, unexpected friendships, and the ending—my heart! Read and see for yourself!" —BRITTANY EDEN, author of the *Heartbooks* series

"The depth of this story just left me breathless. Action, romance, intrigue, and characters who linger long after the story is finished! I can't wait for the next installment in *The Legacy Chapters*!" — AJ SKELLY, bestselling author of *The Wolves of Rock Falls* series and *Magik Prep Academy* series

"*Fortified* is an exciting tale of redemption, empathy, doubt and faith. The fast-paced fights and intriguing twists had my head spinning by the end. I'm left waiting on the edge of my seat for the next installment in this new series." —TABITHA CAPLINGER, author of *The Wolf Queen* and *The Chronicle of the Three* series

"What a journey! *Fortified* kept me enthralled from the first page with its rich story world and intriguing twists and turns. Walking alongside Devora as she develops deep relationships, grows in strength and integrity, and triumphs over increasingly difficult circumstances was both emotional and so rewarding. Action, romance, humor, mystery--this book had everything I look for in a fabulous read and more! When can I snag Book Two??" —LAURIE LUCKING, award-winning author of *Common*

"*Fortified* is a well-balanced, character driven story that will hit you in your sweet spot so you won't put it down! Prepare for unexpected twists, well-delivered humor, and an ingenious subthread that makes the story come together in the final moments of the climax. Burton's story is perfect for fans of CJ Redwine who are looking for clean YA fantasy with a meaningful message and deep character growth." —LAURA ZIMMERMAN, award-winning author of *Keen*

"Romas Burton has a way of luring you into the world with enchanting prose and heart-pounding scenarios. *Fortified* kept me flipping pages to find out every one of the characters' secrets. It is a must read for fantasy fans who love a visceral experience with twists and turns around every corner." —CANDICE PEDRAZA YAMNITZ, author of *Unbetrothed*

"With dazzling world building, strong female characters, epic battles, and all the swoon you could want... *Fortified* is the fantasy you need in your life right now!" —Alison Morquecho, The Bookish Camper, Influencer and Book Reviewer

"A truly enthralling tale. Full of heart pounding moments, intriguing characters, and swords! I am eagerly (and impatiently) awaiting the next book." —Aly Shaver, The Little Librarian, Influencer and Book Reviewer

FORTIFIED

Also By V. Romas Burton

Heartmaker Trilogy
Heartmender
Heartbreaker
Heartrender

The Legacy Chapters
Fortified
Justified (coming 2024)

THE LEGACY CHAPTERS
FORTIFIED
Quill & Flame
PUBLISHING HOUSE
V. ROMAS BURTON

To anyone who has been told your dreams are are too big,
they're not.

TENTON
THE FORTRESS
VLACKLEAR ACADEMY
JURO -CAPITOL (MALDOVE PALACE)
BALLEAR
YEKEL
GRENLY

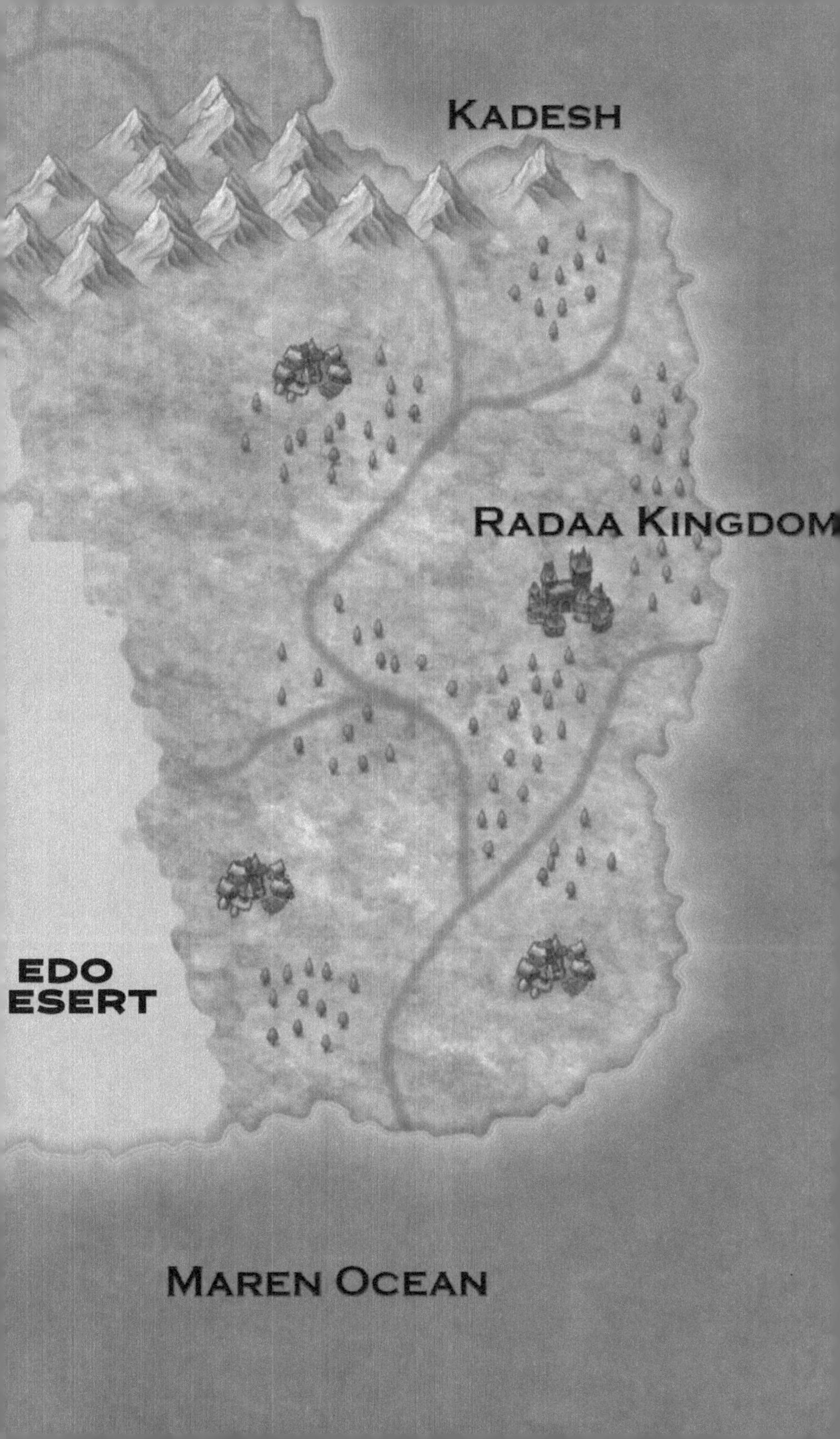

KADESH
RADAA KINGDOM
EDO
ESERT
MAREN OCEAN

LEAD
YOUR
LEGACY.

PROLOGUE

BY THE KING OF TENTON

A PROCLAMATION

*On the Observation of Seers in the Kingdom of Tenton
To continue to strengthen our borders in the face of the
growing rebellion from Kadesh, His Majesty, King Atol
of Juro, hereby orders all Seers of prophetic dreams and
visions to be sent to the Capital for observation. Should
any Seer fail to comply, the sentence will be execution by
hanging.*

*Given at Royal Council at Maldove Palace, the Fifteenth
Day of the Summer Harvest, in the Fourth Year of the King's
Reign*

Tunri save the King.

By the King of Tenton

A Proclamation

On the Observation of Seers in the

Kingdom of Tenton

To continue to strengthen our borders in the

face of the growing rebellion from Kadesh,

His Majesty, King Atol of Juro, hereby

orders all Seers of prophetic dreams and

visions to be sent to the Capital for

observation. Should any Seer fail to comply,

the sentence will be execution by hanging.

Given at Royal Council at Maldove Palace, the

Fifteenth Day of the Summer Harvest, in the

Fourth Year of the King's Reign

Tunri save the King.

Chapter One

Grenly, Southern Region, Tenton

The steaming cup of tea looked like cow dung. Lady Devora Medee brought it to her face and sniffed. Gagging, she pulled the brown sludge away, covering her nose and mouth with her hand. As always, it smelled like cow dung, too. Devora pinched her nose. She'd endured the same horrible tea for years, but the process of swallowing it never got easier.

Squeezing her eyes shut, Devora threw back the disgusting blend, choking before forcing it down her throat. The effects of the suppressing tea blend would last for three weeks, but all she wanted to do was scrape the rotten taste from her tongue.

A warm morning breeze twisted around her ebony braid. Placing the cup down, Devora refocused on the stones in front of her. Five shining pebbles glimmered against the flat rooftop of her home, the governor's mansion. As she settled herself back on the rooftop, Devora lifted her olive-toned hand. The rocks levitated from the stark-white stone before assembling into a flawlessly balanced cairn.

Perfect, as always, she mused, enjoying the rainbow of colors winking back at her.

She had been categorizing her stones—lifting them with the power in her blood—the same way since she was a child: blue, yellow, green, red, purple. From the day she received her pouch of pebbles, Devora had mastered the simple categorization quickly. But now was when it counted the most.

"Devora, my dove, are you joining me today?" Mama called from the open window below. Her delicate sing-song voice rivaled the twittering birds. From her tall, slim frame to her angelic laugh, Mama was ever the perfect example of a governor's wife.

Devora stifled a groan as she rolled her eyes. Visiting Lower Grenly was the only outing her parents ever allowed—besides the prayer vigil held every two weeks. Devora pursed her lips, thinking of Victoria Drazier, the councilman's eldest daughter, and her birthday celebration. Apparently, it was the party of the year, and Devora wasn't allowed to attend. Just like all the other parties over the last sixteen years of her life. Didn't Mama realize she wanted to go to fabulous parties, not fraternize with peasants?

"Not today, Mama," Devora called as she leaned over the edge of the roof. Her braid hung over her shoulder as she watched Mama stick her head out the window below. Devora sighed and leaned back. She swiped her palm over the stones. They clattered across the roof, threatening to roll over the edge. She peeked back over the edge. Mama was glaring up at her. Biting her lip, Devora quickly came up with a believable excuse. Lifting her hands, she replied, "I need to keep practicing for my Categorization Call tonight."

Upon birth, every citizen in Tenton received the same pouch of stones and a list of categories from King Atol and Queen Leza. When a citizen wanted to categorize, they would simply prick their finger and add a drop of blood to each stone in their pouch. Only then would they be able to practice the different color patterns provided by the kingdom.

The significance of the stones thrummed against Devora's mind as she recited her daily lessons:

Blue for the sky and sea, which made trades possible for thee;

Yellow for the sun that shines down from up above;

Green for the plants, we thank them for their nourishment;

Red for blood, purple for unity; we thank King Atol for helping us live in harmony.

Devora rubbed her temples, despising the silly poem. But she knew she needed it to pass her Categorization Call. Once a citizen turned sixteen, they recited the chant and performed five categorizations in front of the king's Categorizer. The color pattern of stones that repeated three times would place the participant in the job they were destined to do for life.

"All right, my dove. Don't forget to say your prayers to Tunri. Especially today." Disappointment clung to Mama's voice as she pulled her head back through the window. The wooden door to their home opened and shut.

Devora gave a sidelong glance to the prayer scroll lying atop her stack of war tactic textbooks and that week's news from the battlefront. A crisp lavender ribbon, the Medee family color, tied the prayers shut. Huffing, Devora ignored the scrolls and focused on the empty clay cup that held the obnoxious tea sludge. Why should she pray to Tunri? What had He done other than give her the curse that kept her confined to the house drinking horrible tea blends to keep her visions at bay?

With her sandaled foot, Devora kicked the prayers off the roof and stood, peering out into the jungles of Grenly. A warm wind rustled the branches of the tall trees, shaking their thick, wide leaves with vigor.

Even as a child, Devora had big dreams. Dreams that were bigger than the small citadel of Grenly. She had been preparing to leave this hot, humid city for years, and now it was finally time. With another flick of her wrist, the stones stacked again in the perfect categorization for Vlacklear Academy.

Scooping up the stones, Devora dropped them into her pocket. She straightened her lavender sash then hauled herself off the roof. Extending her arm, she quickly latched onto the familiar vine that spiraled to the ground. With a wild grin, Devora swung off the thick tendril and started running the moment her sandals hit the hard soil.

It was almost midday and she needed to see her love. Never did she feel freer than when she snuck out of the house to meet Tristan. No stinky teas. No forced prayers to a god who didn't listen. And no age-old edicts threatening to take her life.

The crinkled note Tristan sent a week ago sat in her dress pocket as she plastered herself against the wall surrounding Grenly. Though the wall protected the citadel from the dangerous jungle, beyond the stone wall was the only privacy she and Tristan could get. Another vine brushed her arm, encouraging her to climb to her few moments of freedom.

Grasping the thick emerald plant, Devora shimmied up the wall and climbed down the other side. Once she landed, she shielded her eyes from the late morning sun before surveying her surroundings. The tall trees of the jungle waved back at her, their branches heavy with succulent fruits.

Sighing, Devora leaned against the wall and waited. Tristan was late.

As usual.

They had been meeting at this same spot at the same time for the last six months. Devora fiddled with the end of her purple sash, remembering how she was instantly drawn to Tristan's bulky muscles when she first noticed him at the jeweler's shop on her birthday months ago.

Grinning, Devora took the note out from her pocket. Although she'd memorized its contents, she still enjoyed reading the rushed, slanted script.

My dearest honeybee,

Devora stifled the squeal wanting to escape her throat. She darted a glance into the jungle, not wanting to encourage any animals to find her. After a few moments without any animal visitors, Devora hugged the letter to her chest and started reading again.

My dearest honeybee,

Words cannot describe the pain I feel in not having seen you for weeks. Meet me at our spot just before noon.

Longingly yours,

Tristan

Devora bit her lip to contain her excitement as she folded the note and tucked it back in her pocket. Steadying her breaths, she smoothed the flyaway hairs from her braid and straightened her stance. Only a few more minutes and she would be with her love. And everything would be perfect.

Two strong arms wrapped around her waist from behind and held her close.

"Right on time, as usual," Tristan whispered, nuzzling into her neck.

The aroma of apples and honey swirled around her, jumbling her insides. Turning to face him, Devora roamed her gaze over Tristan's angular features. From his wavy chestnut hair to his sun-kissed skin, Devora couldn't think of anyone she desired more. Though he was only two years older than her, Tristan's jaw was sharp and his muscles thick. Devora absentmindedly ran her hands over his biceps, thrilling her nerves. But what captivated her most were his dark blue eyes. Her heart almost leaped out of her chest every time she gazed into their depths.

Tristan reached out and skimmed her cheek with his thumb. Devora's lids fluttered closed, enjoying his silky-smooth skin against her own. Leaning into his hand, she melted into Tristan's chest, her heart higher than a cloud.

"How's your day been, honeybee?" he whispered into her hair.

Pleasant chills raced across Devora's skin as she breathed in his scent, her thoughts melting to mush.

"Good, now that you're here," she murmured into his chest. "Mama asked me to go to Lower Grenly. Again."

Tristan pulled back, his elegant brow furrowed in concern. "Did you?"

Devora scrunched her nose. "Of course not. Why would you ask such a silly question?" Shaking her head, Devora trailed her fingers across Tristan's soft black academy uniform.

"Good," he replied, bringing her closer. "You're the governor's daughter and will be attending the most acclaimed academy in Tenton. There's no point in subjecting yourself to those of lesser birth. Especially if you plan on taking your father's place one day."

Devora nodded in agreement. But somehow, when Tristan said it out loud, it sounded horrible. Ignoring her conscience, Devora lifted her head and wrapped her arms around Tristan's neck. He was only a few inches taller than her, so she could easily look him in the eye.

"How about you? Did you spend all day thinking about me?" She playfully batted her eyelashes at him.

Tristan stiffened slightly, then eased into his reply. "Always, my honeybee." He gave her a peck on the cheek. "My workload at the academy has been brutal, which is why I haven't been able to visit as often." He paused, then added, "I did hear some news about Tenton needing more soldiers at the front. There are rumors that the king is going to make some decree about a mandatory draft for male citizens or something." Tristan waved his hand in the air like it was nothing of importance.

The warm tingles beneath Devora's skin froze and she stepped away. "Why would the king order a draft? Is the Fortress running out of criminals to use?"

Her mind reeled with the news. *Would they take Tristan? Would they take Papa?*

Years ago, King Atol moved the military academy to the Fortress, the once-prison-now-military-academy, to train the prisoners into soldiers instead of bleeding Tenton's male citizens dry. Each prisoner was assigned a five-year commitment. When that was complete, if the prisoner was still alive, they would be pardoned.

"It's nothing to worry about, honeybee," Tristan assured, grabbing Devora's waist, pulling her back into his arms. "Everything will be fine. They'd be stupid to pick students from Vlacklear first, so I'll be okay. And you're a woman. In the twenty years Tenton has fought with Kadesh, Tenton has never drafted women." He brushed a stray hair out of her face and kissed her forehead. "Plus, your tutor said you have the highest marks in all of Grenly, right? Your mind won't be wasted at the Fortress." He tapped her nose.

"True," Devora agreed, knowing she was smarter than every inmate in the prison.

Yet as she placed her hands on the smooth ebony fabric of Tristan's uniform again, the topic of the Fortress wouldn't leave her mind.

What would happen if the king forced a man from each household to fight? Tristan already had a brother that was in the military. So, Tristan would be fine. But Papa? He was the only male in their home.

What would Mama and I do if he were drafted?

Devora ran her fingers along the golden crest embroidered onto Tristan's chest. Maybe there would be a way around it. Tristan mentioned that his older brother was a high-ranking officer in His Majesty's Army. Maybe, if Papa had to go, Tristan could talk to his brother and make an exception. She heard that other governors had been drafted in the past and she couldn't allow that to happen to Papa.

"What's the matter?" Tristan asked, noting her long silence. He traced her jaw with his thumb. "Are you worried about your Categorization Call tonight?"

Devora snorted. "Not at all. I've been practicing the pattern for Vlacklear since I was a child."

Tristan flitted the end of her braid between his fingers. "I know you'll do great. You'll be joining me at Vlacklear before you know it."

Tristan had been at Vlacklear for two years already, learning everything he could to prepare to run for a councilman position in the western region once he graduated. He'd told Devora all the wonders of the exceptional teachers, delicious food, and exquisite living facilities of the academy. Devora couldn't wait to go.

What would Tristan do if I didn't attend Vlacklear?

The absurd thought surprised Devora and she almost laughed outright. But a warning niggled at the back of her thoughts, and she still wondered where Tristan's loyalties lay.

When she first started meeting Tristan, Sir Jacques, the tax collector, warned her about him. Sir Jacques explained that he heard rumors from other citizens about a "strapping young man from Vlacklear" wooing all the ladies in Grenly. Though, when Sir Jacques described the accuser to look exactly like Tristan, Devora brushed the warning off as nothing more than the knight's jealousy. Mama said Sir Jacques fancied her, but Devora wanted nothing to do with the knight. Regardless, Devora needed to make sure Tristan was hers before she told him about her curse.

Letting out a small cough, Devora laid her hands on Tristan's broad shoulders. "Tristan, what would you do if I didn't go to Vlacklear? Would we still be together?"

The moments ticked by slowly, agonizing her heart as she waited for an answer. Lifting her chin, she stared at him with anticipation. As the silence lengthened, Devora frowned.

Tristan gave her a confused look, then chuckled deeply. "Honeybee, you're going to get in." He cupped her hips with his strong hands. "I know you can categorize for Vlacklear perfectly." He gave her a winning smile, displaying his perfectly white teeth.

Devora pursed her lips. He evaded her question and didn't answer how she expected. Or wanted.

"If I wasn't confident in your abilities, would I give you this?" He bent down on one knee.

Devora gasped as Tristan pulled out a shining silver ring with an emerald secured to the top. Inside, a delicately carved inscription read *refined through fire*. It was the jeweler, Master Riggs', brand he burned into every piece he crafted.

Before Devora could react, Tristan grabbed her hand and slid the ring on her finger. A cool tingle danced across her skin from the cold metal.

"Marry me," Tristan whispered, squeezing her hands. "And know we'll be together."

Devora's mouth hung agape as she blinked at the shining gem. After a moment, she finally answered. "Yes, of course."

Should I tell him about my curse?

But before Devora could utter another word, Tristan bounced up and kissed her cheek. "It's settled then." He tilted his head to the sky and frowned. "My love, I apologize, but I do have an academy appointment to attend." He quickly released her from his grasp. The midday breeze cooled where his warm hands just held her.

Devora stood frozen as Tristan leaned forward and kissed her forehead before motioning to the vine. "It'd be my honor to assist you over the wall, my lady." He gave a mock bow.

Shaking the shock from her limbs, Devora strode toward the wall and grabbed the vine as Tristan placed his hands under her foot. Bouncing on her toes, Devora jumped from Tristan's palms, clinging to the thick tendril as she scurried up the wall.

"I'll do my best to be at your Categorization Call tonight, and then we'll be on our way to Vlacklear," he whispered then blew her a kiss.

Devora nodded, still starstruck, as Tristan sauntered along the edge of the wall. After a few steps, he climbed up and over a different section.

Devora studied the shimmering emerald on her finger. It was beautiful, but something about the rushed proposal didn't sit right with her. She shuffled her body and shimmied down the other side of the wall trying to suppress the gnawing doubt at the back of her mind.

Hurrying back to her house, Devora curled her long ebony braid around her hand, the emerald ring winking at her in the afternoon sun. While the ring was lovely, she always expected to feel happier at the thought of marriage.

So why do I feel nothing but unease?

Devora slowed her steps, her mind racing through what just happened. Though they had quick meetings in the past, her time spent with Tristan seemed to be getting shorter. And, although he proposed, he evaded her question about Vlacklear. Plus, he said he would *try* to be at her call tonight. Not that he'd definitely be there.

Shouldn't my future husband support me on one of the most important days of my life?

Devora played with the purple sash on her chest as doubt crept into her thoughts. She had also wanted to tell Tristan Papa may be coming in tonight. Tristan had put off meeting the governor of Grenly for a while and Devora wasn't sure why. Tristan was tall, handsome, and intelligent. The perfect man for someone of Devora's status. Papa would certainly approve, especially since they were engaged now.

Stopping in her tracks, Devora spun around. She had to know Tristan's true feelings. She was sure she was being silly, and everything was fine between them, but she needed reassurance.

Devora quickly padded back toward the wall by the jeweler, deciding she would start there to locate Tristan.

But as she hurried past the back of the bakery, just before the jeweler's, a familiar, deep laugh swiveled through the air. Devora stopped, her foot mid-air as her lips parted.

Standing where she had just stood was another woman wrapped in Tristan's arms.

Chapter Two

Grenly, Southern Region, Tenton

Devora waited for tears to build in her eyes and tumble down her cheeks, but they never came. Instead, she felt cold fury.

"How dare you?" She glowered at the cooing couple.

Tristan and the woman in the canary yellow dress spun toward her with frightened eyes.

Devora thought her heart would break, but the only thing that shattered was her pride. She hated to admit it, but the woman was beautiful. Long, shining cinnamon hair—where Tristan's fingers were currently tangled—rolled down her back. Devora gritted her teeth. It wasn't insufferable like her own knotted ebony mane. And the woman's skin. It was creamy and smooth like milk. A contrast to Devora's own skin, tanned by Grenly's relentless sun.

Devora swallowed the bitterness in her throat. This woman was not from the southern region of Grenly, but from the north, near Vlacklear. Devora curled her fingers into a fist, her fresh engagement ring biting into her flesh.

Tristan reluctantly released the woman, "Honeybee."

"You lying scoundrel!" Devora shot at him, her cheeks hot from anger and the embarrassment of being a fool. "Never show your face here again."

Ripping the ring from her finger, she launched it at Tristan, nailing him in the eye. Tristan cried out while the girl gasped and cowered away from Devora like she was a monster.

Boiling with rage, Devora fled from the couple and ran home.

How dare Tristan string me along like I was a commoner?

She was Lady Devora Medee, Governor Cusha Medee's daughter. She was worth more than any flighty female from the academy.

As Devora barreled along the street—lost in her own thoughts— someone rammed into her chest. Devora landed on the ground with a thud. A girl around Devora's age blinked up dazedly from the dirt as fresh produce rolled from the girl's basket.

Glaring at the girl, Devora noticed the tattered dress and smudges on the girl's dark skin.

Why is someone from Lower Grenly here, in Upper Grenly?

Devora glanced down at her own pristine turquoise dress. Gasping, she ran her fingers along a thick smudge of smashed berries, staining the silk fabric. It was her favorite dress, and it was ruined.

"Look what you've done!" she accused, her fury from the encounter with Tristan pouring onto the girl. "Get out of here! Go back to where you belong."

The girl bit her quivering lip, quickly gathered up the dusty fruit, and scurried away.

Devora didn't bother watching the girl as she stomped back home and burst into her house. Thankfully the servants were still on their lunch break.

Rage fumed in Devora's chest as she raced into her room. *How could I have been so naive? Of course, Tristan would only want to marry me because of my status. If he were engaged to the daughter of a governor, his path to become a councilman would be easy.*

Panting, she threw herself on her thin mattress. She was still expecting a full waterfall of tears to erupt from her eyes, but when they didn't come, Devora sat up with a huff.

So, maybe she had an inkling that Tristan wasn't honorable. Maybe she had heard about his previous fickle relationships but didn't want to admit it.

Devora grabbed a round teal pillow with golden tassels and smashed it on her face. Sucking in a deep breath, she screamed with all her might into the velvet fabric until her lungs ached. Her perfect future began to shatter.

Placing the pillow on her stomach, Devora stared up at the white canopy hanging over her bed. Sir Jacques warned her about Tristan. But, because the tax collector was only three years her senior, Devora only thought he was trying to win her affections. Now she saw that he was only trying to help.

Grunting, Devora knew she purposefully ignored the warning because she liked Tristan's biceps.

Scrubbing her hands over her face, Devora groaned. So, Tristan wouldn't work out like she thought. But Vlacklear still would. She would still be able to attend and become the next governor of Grenly. Her Categorization Call was this evening. She should practice her stones one more time to be sure and ignore her irritation and hurt toward Tristan.

But as she relaxed into her bed, the weight of the morning took a toll on her body and mind until the heaviness of sleep fully consumed her.

Nothing appeared in the abyss where Devora stood. No sound echoed through the void. No movement. Only darkness. Panic coiled in her throat.

Why am I having a vision? The awful dung tea is supposed to keep my Seeing powers suppressed.

Devora frowned as she searched the endless night. She knew she couldn't stop a vision once it started.

After walking a few steps, an oppressive heat pulsated into her feet. Jumping, Devora quickly grabbed her foot and inspected it. No burns. She never felt the elements in a vision. Why was she experiencing them now?

The heat intensified with each step, as if her foot would burn off entirely. Every few feet Devora paused and lifted her foot, expecting it to be covered in blisters or charred. But the bronze skin and five toes remained intact.

As she placed her foot down once more, a bright light exploded below. Devora lifted her arms to shield her eyes.

When the light dimmed, she peered down. Cautiously, she pressed her palm to test the strength of the invisible wall keeping her from entering the scene below. It seemed solid enough. Lowering herself to her hands and knees, Devora looked through the clear surface.

White light coated vast, blinding sand. A hard breeze cut by. Sand seared her skin—sharp and biting. But she focused again on the miles of desert below.

The only desert this large was the natural barrier between Tenton and Kadesh, the Edo desert. Devora pursed her lips. Well, it was the barrier until the king of Kadesh, King Redore IV, attacked eastern Tenton twenty years ago.

Devora's eyes narrowed as she studied the sand, waiting for something to happen. By the pain in her knees, it seemed as if she had been crouching in the darkness for an eternity.

Maybe this wasn't a vision at all, but only a strange dream.

As she tried to surrender herself to deeper sleep, Devora noticed a line of small black dots coming from the east. Suddenly, the invisible wall that had kept her above the vision vanished. Shrieking, Devora plummeted to the sand below. As the grains blazed hot all over her, she jumped to her feet and frantically brushed them off. Her confusion rose. She had only ever seen her visions play out, never had she been a part of one.

The sand whipped ferociously around Devora as her body jolted forward, pushed by a demanding, unseen force. She sucked in a breath, her peripheral vision blurring as she sped across the airy desert toward the black dots. The only image she could make out as she flew was a tall palm tree.

As she drew nearer, the dots changed. Devora's heart palpitated with terror. The dots transformed into terrifying creatures, gnashing their spiked teeth. Iron armor covered their grotesque, hairy bodies. Their throaty howls rang between her ears, stiffening her muscles and chilling her core.

Devora tried to back away from the army of iron-armored beasts before the scene around her shook with vigor. The ground beneath her broke open and she screamed as it sucked her in.

A loud knock sounded at her door. Devora bolted up from her pillows, sweat beading at her brow. A faint knock pounded again, this time on the front door. The pitter-patter of servants' footsteps echoed throughout the usually quiet house.

Lifting her hand, Devora wiped the sweat away when realization hit her like a boulder. The king's Categorizer. Her Categorization Call. It was time.

Lunging from her bed, Devora hunted for her stones. The knock rapped gently on her door again.

"Coming!" she gasped, trying to swallow the nerves exploding through her body.

Why am I so nervous?

"Devora?" Papa's deep, soothing voice asked as he popped his head around the door. Strands of white speckled his cropped ebony hair as he carried in a tray with a clay cup and a pink package.

"Papa!" she cried, running to embrace him. "You're here!"

Papa placed the tray on her bedside table before he wrapped her up in his large arms, squeezing her tight. Peace blanketed her frantic heart. Mama's elegant voice drifted from the front foyer, welcoming the king's Categorizer and his guards into their home.

Devora reached out and snatched the pink package, knowing it was her favorite rose-scented soap. Papa always bought her some when he returned from his journeys to the capital city, Juro.

As she unwrapped the delicate parcel, Papa asked, "I said I would come to your Categorization Call, did I not?" Beneath the thick black mustache, a smile tugged at his lips before it fell. "Did you drink your tea?"

Devora's fingers paused on the thin pink paper. She opened her mouth to reply when her father pointed to her vanity. Frantic, she rushed to the mirror.

"Oh no," Devora cried, staring back at the two bright violet eyes. The dung tea was supposed to cage her prophetic powers and erase the purple eyes of a Seer. "No, no, this can't be happening. Not today. Not now." She ran her hands over her hair, now frizzy from her impromptu nap.

"Shh, it's all right," Papa said, walking to the table beside her bed where he placed the tray. "Here." He handed her the cup of dung tea.

Devora snatched the cup and gulped it down, not caring about its putrid smell or taste. Wiping her mouth with the back of her hand, she stared at the mirror, her pulse returning to normal as the violet Seer eyes faded into a natural caramel brown. Devora breathed a sigh of relief before acknowledging the rotten tea taste sitting on her tongue. Rushing to the pot of spearmint growing by her window, she promptly tore off a leaf and crunched it between her teeth. The sweet mint banished the dung tea from her mouth. She flopped on her bed, relieved.

"I remembered when you had your final exams last harvest season, and your powers broke through." Papa smiled, joining her on the bed. "So, I had a feeling they might resurface today because of the stress of your call. Thankfully, Madge made another batch without question." He nudged her shoulder. "You'll do wonderfully, Devora. Just remember who you are."

Swallowing, Devora took another shaky breath then stood tall. Undoing her messy braid, she combed her long hair out and plaited it again.

Facing her father, Devora straightened her shoulders and held her chin high. "Well?"

Papa stood and adjusted the sash on her chest. "Beautiful, as always."

Another knock sounded at the door before Mama stepped in. Though Devora inherited her mother's taller frame, she wished she had Mama's silky straight hair and beautifully thin figure. Maybe then Tristan would've stayed. She shoved those thoughts aside.

Mama wrung her delicate fingers, worry clouding her round brown eyes as she hurried to Devora.

"Are you ready, my dove?" She smoothed the frizz that was already popping up on Devora's head. "The king's Categorizer is set up and waiting. I've been asking Tunri to guide your categorizations."

Devora wanted to retort that Tunri's guidance had done nothing for her. But she stayed quiet. "Thank you, Mama."

If Mama wants to rely on Tunri, that's her choice. But I will rely on myself.

Taking a deep breath, Devora strode through her bedroom door with her parents following behind.

This was it. Even though Tristan was a flop, she would still attend Vlacklear and eventually become the next great governor of Grenly. Everything she had planned, everything she had worked for, was finally falling into place.

A small ornate golden table stood before the Categorizer as he sat in the front foyer of the governor's mansion. Intricate carvings of birds and flowers spiraled down each of its four legs. The white stone walls of the home surrounded the Categorizer, making his tanned, weathered skin and forest green tunic stand out even more. Unruly gray hair curled from his head, matching the long beard cascading from his narrow chin. Beady black eyes blinked at Devora from behind thick, round glasses.

Though the Categorizer looked frail and timid, the two guards flanking his sides did not. One was Sir Jacques, the monthly tax collector for Grenly. When Devora would give the young knight their taxes, Sir Jacques always tried to cheer Devora up with news of the outside world. Unfortunately, Mama had misinterpreted their conversations and sought to arrange a marriage between him and Devora. Thankfully, Papa squashed the idea before it was set.

But something was different about Sir Jacques today. The playful, gentle, soft demeanor the knight usually held was gone, replaced with a hardness Devora had never seen from him. With his average height and sandy blond hair, Sir Jacques was usually all smiles and encouragement. Now, his hazel eyes burned into the back wall, refusing to even look at her.

Something was off. Even on official duties, Sir Jacques still acknowledged her presence. Her skin bristled at the dismissal, but she let her annoyance pass as she studied the other knight.

At least thirty summers, the knight was a stout, muscular man with layers of swirls and spirals inked onto his hands and shaved head. His skin was creamy white, but his eyes were black as night as he glowered at Devora.

Devora met his glare with her own as she continued toward the king's Categorizer. If the short knight thought he could intimidate her, he was wrong.

"Ah, Lady Devora," the Categorizer said with a gentle smile. "I've heard great things about you." He brought out a dark, wooden box and set it on the table. Carefully, the old man lifted the lid, revealing five shining stones.

Devora's eyes widened, remembering that each student had to use the Categorizer's stones, not their own. In the past, there had been participants who tried to manipulate the stones to benefit their color pattern. In order to rid the regions of cheating, King Atol ruled that each participant in the call must use the king's Categorizer's stones or be sentenced to death.

"They're beautiful," she breathed, gawking at the shimmering stones.

The Categorizer chuckled. "Yes." He plucked the stones out of the box and placed them before Devora. He then pulled out a small, golden needle, ready to prick Devora's finger and place a drop of her blood on each stone. "I know this won't take very long. But before we begin—" he waved to Sir Jacques.

Clearing his throat, Sir Jacques interjected, "Before you begin, King Atol requires each participant to read this."

Devora glanced up at Sir Jacques, annoyed. *Now he's going to talk?*

The knight handed the rolled parchment to Devora.

"What's this?" Papa asked, his sturdy height hovering over Devora's shoulder. "I didn't hear of any news from the king."

"A decree from His Majesty," the tattooed knight replied in a gravelly voice. "We were given it before riding here."

"Sir Conan is correct," Sir Jacques agreed, his square shoulders slumping. "It was just finalized earlier this week." He cast a hesitant glance at Devora, as if apologizing.

A feeling of dread immediately twisted Devora's stomach as she grasped the paper. The last time the king made a proclamation, she should have died.

Fingers trembling, she untied the scarlet ribbon. It was as if time had slowed as she unrolled the parchment and read the decree.

BY THE KING OF TENTON

A PROCLAMATION

On the Categorization Call in the Kingdom of Tenton, year 335

The war with Kadesh has left Tenton with no other options. His Majesty, King Atol of Juro, has hereby altered this year's categories for the Categorization Call. By his power under the Kingdom of Tenton, if any participant in the Call does not comply with these new categories, they will be forced to spend the rest of their days in His Majesty's dungeon, where they will be sentenced to death.

Given at Royal Council at Maldove Palace, the Forty-Seventh Day of the Summer Season, in the Twentieth Year of the King's Reign

Tunri save the King.

BY THE KING OF TENTON
A PROCLAMATION
ON THE CATEGORIZATION CALL IN THE KINGDOM OF TENTON, YEAR 335

THE WAR WITH KADESH HAS LEFT TENTON WITH NO OTHER OPTIONS. HIS MAJESTY, KING ATOL OF JURO, HAS HEREBY ALTERED THIS YEAR'S CATEGORIES FOR THE CATEGORIZATION CALL. BY HIS POWER UNDER THE KINGDOM OF TENTON, IF ANY PARTICIPANT IN THE CALL DOES NOT COMPLY WITH THESE NEW CATEGORIES, THEY WILL BE FORCED TO SPEND THE REST OF THEIR DAYS IN HIS MAJESTY'S DUNGEON, WHERE THEY WILL BE SENTENCED TO DEATH.

GIVEN AT ROYAL COUNCIL AT MALDOVE PALACE, THE FORTY-SEVENTH DAY OF THE SUMMER SEASON, IN THE TWENTIETH YEAR OF THE KING'S REIGN

TUNRI SAVE THE KING.

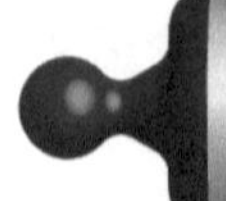

Devora's eyes ran over the parchment again and again, not believing what she was reading. Her heart pounded against her ribcage, as her fingers unrolled the rest of the

paper and the new categorization patterns the king had assigned appeared.

Holding her breath, she started at the top and worked her way down. It seemed that most of the categories were the same. Teachers were still red, green, yellow, purple, blue. Bakers were still purple, blue, red, yellow, green. Devora's shoulders relaxed a little as she read the same color patterns for artists, blacksmiths, and tradesmen as well. But as she made her way to the bottom of the list, she wanted to throw up.

"No," she whispered. Her head whipped up to Sir Jacques, whose eyes were downcast. "There has to be a mistake."

"Devora," Mama said, gently holding her shoulders as she leaned over. "What is it? What does it say?"

Devora kept her eyes focused on Sir Jacques, as if this were somehow his fault. She mechanically held up the paper to her mother, who snatched it out of her hands. She knew Papa would read it as well. Silence weighed heavily in the foyer as the governor cursed, and the first lady gasped. The crinkle of parchment broke the thick tension as the decree floated to the marble floor.

"Sir Jacques, is this true?" Papa demanded, his voice rising with rage. "Has the king really changed the categories starting *today*?"

Sir Jacques glanced up; his gaze heavy as he nodded. He turned to Devora. "I'm so sorry, Lady Devora."

Devora stared at her fingers, cursing her own blood. Some people's blood could pattern the stones a hundred different ways. But not hers. Her blood would only categorize for Vlacklear. She always thought it was a sign that her destiny for greatness was sealed.

"This is an outrage!" Papa slammed his fist against the white wall. "King Atol has had opportunities to change the color patterns in the past, but he has always abstained. Why change them now?"

As Sir Jacques tried to explain the king's reasoning behind the change, every cell in Devora's body numbed. A summer breeze danced through the open windows and guided the decree to her feet. The new categories mocked her arrogance at only being able to practice one category for the past sixteen years of her life.

Devora glared down at the page, wishing she could burn a hole in it. The decree annotated her worst fear. The category for Vlacklear had been switched by one pebble. When the stones reacted to her blood and she categorized them, they would no longer represent becoming a scholar. Instead of Vlacklear, she would be heading to the Fortress.

Nausea churned her stomach, threatening to climb up her throat.

How could this happen now?

She could only categorize for Vlacklear, which was now the color pattern for the military academy at the Fortress. She wouldn't become a scholar, but a scrag in His Majesty's Army. All she knew about wars and fighting were what she learned from her war tactic books and reading the weekly battlefront updates.

"The king can't make last-minute decrees," Papa boomed, slamming his thick fist on the golden table. The Categorizer yelped as the shining stones clattered to the ground. "He's already taken the young men of our regions. Now he wants to kill our daughters, too?"

"Cusha," Mama gasped, trying to calm the governor down.

"He can, and he has, sir," Sir Conan sneered, wrapping his fingers around the hilt of his sword. "I would be careful with your next words. Even a governor can be tried for treason."

Fear struck Devora's heart. She had never seen Papa react in such a way. He was always so calm and poised. Regardless, she couldn't allow anything to happen to Papa. Grenly needed him. And this guard looked ready to arrest anyone who defied him.

"It's all right, Papa," Devora said in a weak voice. "I'll categorize."

"Devora," her parents replied simultaneously, rushing to her sides.

"I'm fine," she responded through clenched teeth, forbidding her tears from falling. She would not be weak.

Sir Jacques quietly collected the Categorizer's stones and placed them on the table.

With a shaky hand, Master Chita pricked Devora's pointer finger and squeezed one drop of blood on each stone. The stones glistened as they absorbed her blood, allowing her to control which way they moved.

"Whenever you're ready, my lady." Master Chita folded his hands on top of the gilded table.

Swallowing her fear, Devora glowered at the stones winking back at her. She had been planning for this since she was a child, and in one day, her entire future shattered.

Squeezing her eyes shut, Devora waved her hand over the stones, knowing how they would stack. The five colorful stones stacked exactly as they should have for Vlacklear Academy. The cairn disassembled and she categorized four more times, each the same as the first. A cry came from her mother's mouth as her father cursed.

Suddenly, the ripping of fabric sliced through the air and Devora realized her purple sash had been torn from her chest.

"In His Majesty's Army, we're all the same," Sir Conan informed her, the silky sash clenched in his meaty fingers. "We train the same, eat the same, and dress the same." The knight balled up the sash and threw it on the floor. "You won't be needing this any longer, Medee," he added, his voice dripping with disdain as he said her name.

"Sir!" Sir Jacques cried in horror as Devora's jaw hung open in shock. "That is uncalled for. Whether in the military or not, Lady Medee is still of noble birth."

Devora stared at the crumpled purple fabric beneath Sir Conan's boot, her throat dry. She knew she wouldn't have her noble rank or her parents to help her any longer. From now on, she only had herself.

Chapter Three

"I will not allow this," Papa roared.

Before anyone could stop him, the governor reared back and swung his thick fist into Sir Conan's face. Bone cracked beneath the governor's large hand as the knight fell to the ground.

"Oh, Tunri!" the Categorizer gasped, jumping up from his chair. He swept the stones into the box before rushing out of the house.

"Governor Medee," Sir Jacques cried, wrapping his lean arms around the governor's wide chest. "Control yourself. Assaulting a knight is a felony by His Majesty's law."

"I don't care about His Majesty's laws," Papa growled, stomping toward Sir Conan. Sir Jacques dug his heels into the floor, but the governor barreled on.

Devora's pulse raced as her father marched toward the knight, who was wiping his bloody nose and lip.

Assaulting a knight is a felony? When did that happen? Is everything a felony these days? What is wrong with the king?

Devora sprinted past Papa and stood between him and Sir Conan. Not that the disrespectful knight deserved her defense, but she couldn't let Papa be sent to prison. What about Mama? What about Grenly?

"Papa, please." Devora held out her arms to stop him. "I'll go to the Fortress, and I'll succeed." She swallowed the tears threatening to escape. Weakness was not allowed. Especially now. "I'll be the best soldier Tenton has ever seen."

Sir Conan scoffed behind her, and Devora wanted to slap him in the face.

Papa growled but stopped his pursuit. With a sigh of relief, Sir Jacques released the governor and faced Sir Conan.

"Sir Conan, need I remind you of your place?" Sir Jacques panted as he gently moved Devora out of the way. "Lady Devora will become not just a soldier but an officer in His Majesty's Army. She will not be one of *your* scrags, but Captain Blake's. You are not allowed to touch her."

Sir Conan glared at Sir Jacques as he stood. Blood dripped from the stout knight's swelling nose and mouth, staining the sleek, white floor.

"She is a lady no more," Sir Conan seethed. The knight took two steps forward and leaned toward her. The horrid stench of body odor wafted from his armor. "Welcome to His Majesty's Army, Medee."

"Leave this house. Immediately," Papa commanded, stepping between Sir Jacques and Sir Conan. "I will be reporting your actions to King Atol and Warden Hazor at once."

Sir Conan clucked his tongue, shaking his shaved head. "Jacques was right. The punishment for assaulting a knight is a felony. I'm going to have to arrest you, governor."

The knight yanked iron manacles from his belt and clamped them around the governor's wrists.

"No!" Devora and her mother cried out, but Sir Jacques grabbed their arms.

"Don't," he whispered harshly. "You'll make it worse."

"I'm all right, my loves," Papa replied, straightening his broad shoulders like the regal leader he was. "I will accept the consequences of my actions." Lifting his chin, the governor strode past Sir Conan to the guards waiting outside.

"First Lady," Sir Conan said sardonically with a bow. "You are hereby placed under house arrest until Governor Medee has had his trial with the king."

Mama glared down her thin nose at the knight, just like Papa had, but she didn't argue.

"Let's go, Governor." Sir Conan pulled on Papa's manacles and Papa followed without another word.

"Come, Lady Devora," Sir Jacques said quietly, loosening his grip on her arm. "It's time."

Devora's heart cried out, but she kept her face composed. Sir Jacques allowed her and Mama one final hug before he led her out of her home and onto the deserted street. The shops and streets were always bare when the Categorization Call happened each year. Everyone was at home, preparing for the king's Categorizer to come and start their grand futures.

But not her.

Sir Jacques silently led Devora to a series of carriages that waited at the edge of Upper Grenly. Crooked wooden boards on wheels comprised the transportation, leaving gaping holes between the panels. Nails protruded from the slats around the smudged carriage window. Devora scrunched her nose at the haphazard construction. Not even a peasant would ride in such a thing.

"*This* is what I'm traveling in?"

I've fallen so far, so quickly.

These carriages were nothing compared to Papa's lavish mahogany one. Devora already missed the plump velvet lining.

"I'm afraid so," Sir Jacques murmured as other individuals gathered around them.

The young faces of the others who had completed their categorizations were a mixture of shock, nausea, and anger as they approached the terrible carriages.

Devora watched the other noble-born children her age gather around. Their futures were ruined as well. Her eyes scanned over the group of disheveled faces. They all seemed so defeated.

Devora wrapped her arms around her stomach. She wanted to give up right now. But she wouldn't. She promised Papa she would succeed at the Fortress, and she intended to.

The gait of cautious feet sounded behind her and Devora glanced over her shoulder. Sir Jacques stood with his shoulders drooped as if he were trying to hold the entire world on them. Shadows rimmed his usually youthful hazel eyes as he held out his hand. Shock replaced Devora's controlled face as she looked upon the torn purple sash in Sir Jacques' gloved fingers.

Sir Jacques cleared his throat and turned away as Devora took the sash from his hand. She ran the tattered silk fibers through her fingers. This was all she had left of who she was.

"My apologies, Lady Devora," Sir Jacques whispered while assessing the others. "All knights of the Fortress are forbidden from handling those participating in the Categorization Call. Sir Conan's actions were dishonorable and will be reported to Warden Hazor upon our return to the Fortress." He peered down at her, his gaze softening. "I'm so sorry, my lady."

Turning away, Sir Jacques strode to help the guards with another participant that was screaming threats against the knights of the Fortress.

Devora stared at the fabric, surprised at Sir Jacques' kindness. She was no longer nobility, yet he still respected her. Maybe everything would turn out.

"So, the Lady Devora is being sent to the Fortress like the rest of us," a gruff voice asked. "Not so high and mighty now, are you?"

Devora composed her face into one of authority as she faced her accuser. Niche, the large son of the tailor, bore down on her. Greasy black hair splayed across his slick forehead while his sunken brown eyes accentuated his bulbous nose. He crossed his arms in front of his flabby chest as he shot a wad of spit inches from her gemmed sandals. Devora glared at him as she had Sir Conan. She wouldn't begin a fight with anyone. But if they provoked her, she would have no problem defending her honor.

"I never said I was better than anyone," she countered, even though she knew she was.

Devora winced at the thought. *Not anymore.*

Just last week, when she was desperate to get out of the house, she accompanied Mama to Lower Grenly. Devora remembered decking herself out with the latest fashions and jewels, strutting around Lower Grenly like Princess Haden herself. But now, that was all gone.

A weight settled in her stomach, making her queasy. While Papa and Mama helped the people in Lower Grenly, Devora only flaunted her wealth and position.

"You tell her, Niche," a small boy, barely to Devora's shoulder, added. "She always looked down on the rest of us."

As soon as Devora shifted her glower to him, the scrawny boy cowered behind the bully.

Niche stalked closer and snatched the sash out of her hands. "If you didn't think you were better than us, then why were you always wearing this like you were the queen?" He waved the purple sash in her face, trying to taunt her into grabbing it.

"Toss it here, Niche!" Another greasy boy called before Niche balled the sash and threw it to him.

"Stop that," Devora commanded, trying to stay calm. "Give it back."

The boys laughed and threw the sash back and forth as if they all hadn't just been sentenced to their deaths. Everyone knew the soldiers from the Fortress never returned home.

Devora didn't think that these hooligans were capable of categorizing for Vlacklear. Typically, only those of noble-birth, *noble-blood*, categorized for Vlacklear. So why were they going to the Fortress with her?

"Jacques, ready the recruits!" Sir Conan stomped by, not bothering to stop the boys as he passed.

He paused momentarily and Devora noticed that the knight didn't even have the decency to clean the dried blood on his nose and mouth from Papa's right hook. Devora forced her lip not to curl in disgust as Sir Conan marched to the front of the caravan, not sparing her a second glance.

Fury rattled in her chest. *After humiliating me and arresting my father, he has the audacity to ignore me? Who does he think he is?*

Devora's thoughts froze, her anger dissipating. He was one of Warden Hazor's guards, a knight of the Fortress. While she was nothing more than a scrag in His Majesty's Army, trained to follow orders and not question. By the king's new law, she was no better than the criminals in the prison she was going to.

Devora bit her tongue, balling her hands into fists, hating what Tunri had allowed.

"All right, all right, that's enough," Sir Jacques called, waving his hands in the air. His shaggy blond hair bounced as he made the motion.

The boys barely even glanced at him.

"What are you going to do, tax collector?" Niche laughed. "Bet you can't even wield your sword."

In mere seconds, Sir Jacques unsheathed his sword, wrapped his toned arm around Niche's chest, and held the blade against his throat. The big boy blanched, his throat bobbing as the sword rested against his skin.

"One more comment from you and I'll make sure you're personally escorted to the Behemoth's cell."

Gasps collected among the group of new soldiers, and they backed away from Sir Jacques. They all knew the stories of the Behemoth in the Fortress' basement. It was rumored that Warden Hazor had captured the beast himself and fed it disobedient criminals.

Devora shuddered, remembering the first time she heard the story as a little girl. She couldn't sleep for weeks after.

"Now," Sir Jacques said, his voice as sharp as a blade. "You are soldiers in His Majesty's Army. You will do as your superiors say *without question*. Do you understand?"

Devora fiddled with her fraying sash, not knowing how to react. By the whispers and rustling around her, it seemed the others felt the same way. Sir Jacques had only been collecting taxes in Grenly for a few years, but they all knew him. That was probably why he was helping with the Categorization Call. He was always smiling and kind. Now he was an entirely new person.

"Do you understand?" he barked, and the group straightened.

"Yes, sir," they answered, except for one girl who started crying.

Sir Jacques released Niche and shoved him to the ground. The large boy quickly scrambled away and rejoined his gang. Clearing his throat, Sir Jacques marched to the front of the carriages and unrolled a large scroll that had been secured to his belt.

"Welcome young recruits," Sir Jacques started, his voice flat. "You have all been selected for the highest honor to serve your kingdom." The knight glanced up at the group of frightened faces. Clearing his throat, he continued, "Upon your arrival at the Fortress, you will be assigned two uniforms. You are responsible for making sure that your uniforms are clean for each day's trainings. You will also be assigned a cell—er—room. Once we reach the Fortress, your training will begin immediately."

Sir Jacques rolled up the scroll and motioned to the carriages. "It's a three-day journey to the capital city of Juro. Inside the carriages, you will find accommodations to suit you for the change in climate as well as rations for the next few days."

"And," the knight added. "Don't fantasize about desertion. You will be met with a quick but painful end."

The group was silent except for the girl who had been crying before. At the mention of death, her sobs grew even louder.

Devora glanced over and recognized the girl she had knocked over earlier. Smudges still covered the girl's arms as she buried her face in her hands and cried. Devora's heart stirred. Just a few hours ago, she had treated this girl like dung. Now they were equals.

Sir Jacques strode to the girl and placed a gentle hand on her shoulder before whispering something in her ear. The girl nodded quickly and hurried into the carriage.

The knight soon separated the other recruits into the waiting carriages. Thankfully, Niche and his followers were all assigned to one carriage.

As the boys and girls shuffled into their wooden cages, Devora was able to see the kingdom's seal painted on the side door: interlocking circles with each color of the stones as the borders. The colors, of course, were in the order of Vlacklear Academy: blue, yellow, green, red, and purple. On either side of the circles, the horns of an elk were painted, protruding from a gilded crown, symbolizing Tenton's strength and endurance as a great nation.

Devora narrowed her eyes at the seal, having seen it many times on her father's papers and in her history textbooks. She used to believe the color order was a sure sign she was destined for Vlacklear and her noble blood would take her there. Now the seal was a taunt, mocking her of the future stolen from her.

"Are you ready, Lady Devora?" Sir Jacques asked, holding open the door to the last carriage.

Devora took a step back. "Sir Jacques, where did you learn to move that fast? I thought..." she began, but clamped her mouth shut. All her thoughts had been wrong lately.

"That a kind man can't be a deadly one?" Sir Jacques smirked, but it didn't reach his eyes. "Although I enjoy helping others, my training with Captain Blake has proven useful many times."

"Captain Blake?" she questioned, the name tickling her thoughts.

Sir Jacques helped her into the carriage. Inside was the crying girl from before. "Captain Blake is Warden Hazor's second in command," Sir Jacques explained, handing Devora the filthy purple sash. "He is the best warrior and soldier I know."

"Oh," Devora replied, not knowing what else to say as she sat on the hard bench seat.

Taking the sash, Devora winced as pieces of the splintered wood poked through her dress, biting into her legs.

This is going to be a horrible journey.

"The Fortress is a hard and nasty place, Devora," Sir Jacques continued, lowering his voice as he leaned into the carriage. His shaggy blond hair fell into his eyes. "I'll help you when I can, but you'll have to learn to defend yourself."

Devora wrapped her thick braid around her hand as Sir Jacques closed the door to the carriage. With a yell from the driver, the carriage took off, bouncing along the stone path, away from her home.

Devora stayed silent as the lush, verdant landscape of Grenly rolled by her cracked window. *Is Tunri punishing me because of my arrogance? Maybe I should have visited Lower Grenly with Mama more. And said my prayers more. Anything would be better than where I'm headed.*

Or, is He mad that I see His "gift" as a curse and don't use it?

Devora ran her finger along the edge of the window and immediately flinched as a splinter jammed beside her nail. Tunri had to know that if she used her curse, the king would kill her, just like he did to all the other Seers sixteen years ago. How was she going to keep her curse concealed in the Fortress after the dung tea wore off?

As Devora tried to dig the splinter out, the girl in front of her spoke.

"I know you," she sniffed, wiping the tears from her cheeks.

Devora's regret resurfaced as she studied the girl from Lower Grenly. Dark ringlets sprung from her head, revealing her thin oval face and tear-stained cheeks. Her skin was the shade of cocoa, much darker than Devora's. Her watery, swollen eyes blinked slowly, exhausted from all the tears.

"Yes," Devora said, holding back a wince.

Mama and Papa would've never scolded someone from Lower Grenly. But as much as Devora knew she should apologize, the words fell flat on her lips.

The girl nodded, running her hands over the tan thread-bare dress she wore. "I'm Ida. You saved my sister from being killed when we were younger. Do you remember?"

Relief washed over Devora when she realized she didn't have to apologize. *She doesn't remember me from outside the bakery earlier.*

"I was near the gate to Upper Grenly," Ida began, "and heard you yelling about a viper, so I went to check on Jil, my sister, to make sure she was all right. When I got to our garden behind our house, I caught sight of the viper, only a few feet away from her." Ida closed her eyes, as if trying to hold back more tears before shaking her head. "She was only three then. My mom had left her for just a moment while she grabbed another basket. It was the scariest day of our lives."

Devora stared down at her torn sash, remembering the day like it was yesterday. It was her first vision. She remembered being so frightened of the viper in her vision, she went running into the streets.

"I'm glad my screaming paid off," Devora muttered, trying to tie up the tears in her sash.

Ida studied her for a moment, then giggled. She quickly covered her mouth as if she weren't allowed to laugh anymore. "I know prophetic visions are forbidden, but I'm glad you have them," she whispered.

Devora reared back, the blood draining from her face as she stared at Ida.

How does she know?

Since the day of the viper vision, Mama called a special healer to come and assess Devora's curse. That was how the dung tea entered Devora's life and was forced down her throat every few weeks since she was a child.

Devora's mind raced as she bit her nails. *I should have asked Sir Jacques to grab me herbs for the dung tea. Or I should've grabbed them myself before I left home. Now, in just a few weeks, everyone will know I'm a Seer, and I'll be taken to the king and killed.*

Ida's smile vanished as she took in Devora's tense state. "Oh, I'm sorry. I was just guessing. How else would you have known something like that would happen?" Ida gave a sad sigh before bringing her knees to her chest and staring out the window. "I suppose there really aren't any more Seers. Either way, I'm grateful for what you did."

Devora quickly turned away, not understanding the warmth wrapping around her heart at Ida's words. Ida *admired* the Seer's curse? More importantly, she was thanking Devora. Why would she do that? Especially after Devora made it known how much she despised Lower Grenly.

Devora kept her thoughts to herself as she faced the dirty window. She hated her visions; she hated this curse. Without it, she could've traveled from Grenly and met someone better than Tristan. Maybe she could've avoided the Categorization Call altogether. If Devora could throw her curse back at Tunri, she would. It had brought her nothing but misery.

Chapter Four

The Edo desert, Kadesh

"Is there a reason we're moving to the middle of Edo, Jarrick?" Erza placed both hands on her wide hips. She refused to move until her husband gave her a different answer than the one he had been claiming.

Erza had been perfectly happy until a few days ago when her husband decided to pack up all their things and move them to the blistering desert. They had a beautiful home filled with everything her heart desired back in Renta. So why leave?

"My dear," Jarrick said, throwing Erza's beautiful azure rug over the smelly camel's back as it knelt in the dirt. "You know we were instructed by General Sage to move farther south."

Erza hated the heat and humidity Edo brought, especially during the summer season. She tightened her headdress around her cinnamon-brown face and shot another glare at Jarrick.

How she hated General Sage. If the general said, "Jump!" Jarrick would be the first to harm himself in trying to jump the highest.

Or move the farthest, Erza thought grimly as she crossed her arms over her chest and leaned to one side.

"Farther south means into the blazing heat where there's no water, food, or civilization anywhere." She gestured to the vast dunes awaiting them.

Jarrick sighed before shuffling over and grabbing his wife's hands. "The general told us to move, so we must. We are in his good graces now." Jarrick reached up and stroked her cheek. "I don't want that to change."

Erza ripped her hands out of her husband's and spun away. She never wanted to be in General Sage's good graces. He was a monster. A murderer. She would never forgive him for what he had done.

Erza stomped away and climbed onto the camel's back. Before Jarrick could join her, she slapped the camel on the rump, and it stood to its full height.

Jarrick hung his head, his tan headdress sweeping his broad shoulders before he craned his neck to look at her. He brought his thick, bronzed hand up to his eyes, shielding them from the scorching sun.

Pity stung her heart, but Erza knew Jarrick would do anything for the general.

"That barbarian of a man killed our only son," Erza spat. "You should remember that before bowing so readily to his requests."

With a click of her tongue, Erza nudged the camel's side before it started through the sand, leaving Jarrick to trudge behind.

Chapter Five

Northern Region, Tenton

The journey to the capital city of Juro was the worst experience of Devora's life. Every time she moved, she caught a splinter, bashed her knees, or fell onto Ida. And every few feet, the carriage creaked as if it were about to burst.

"Most high honor indeed," Devora muttered, remembering the words Sir Jacques had read while she clung to the sides of the rickety carriage.

Devora reached to adjust her sash, only to find it wasn't draped across her chest as it usually was. Dropping her hands to the wrinkled bundle in her lap, she ran her fingers along the torn fabric. She empathized with the sash. She, too, was soiled, ripped, and fraying at the edges.

Her chest tightened as her mind ran over the events of the previous day. Tristan, the Categorization Call, the Fortress. Devora leaned her head against the splintered frame of the window. Though she was doing her best to keep it together, she could feel her anxiety building, begging to unleash. And if that happened, her secret would be revealed. Though the king had claimed only to observe the Seers sixteen years ago, none of them were ever seen again. Everyone knew the king had killed them all, but no one knew why. If her secret were revealed, Devora knew death would instantly follow. Closing her eyes, Devora prayed her powers would wait to resurface until she wasn't with Ida or anyone else.

Devora shifted her gaze to the sleeping girl, her remorse returning. Ida had probably planned on attending Vlacklear, as well. Someone from Lower Grenly attending Vlacklear was rare, but it happened occasionally. It would have been a great honor for her family. Once she graduated, Ida could have helped her parents and siblings out of their impoverished state.

Devora gritted her teeth, the words of the king's ridiculous decree burning in her thoughts. The king's law had affected Ida and her family too. How many of the others would be affected by his insanity? And why would he allow women in the army when he hadn't for twenty years?

Devora's mind then ran over Ida's conclusion that she was a Seer. Would Warden Hazor, the leader of the Fortress, know? If he discovered her power, he would kill her on the spot. Devora threaded her sash through her fingers. Somehow, she would have to make sure no one found out.

The carriage swayed back and forth before jerking hard to the right. Devora's arm slammed into a nail protruding from the wall. Wincing, she rubbed the tender spot as the carriage came to a sudden halt, throwing her to the floor. Ida rolled on top of her and both girls squealed.

"What's going on?" Ida scrambled to stand. Disheveled onyx curls sprung around her weary face.

"I don't know," Devora grunted.

"Stay in the carriages!" Sir Conan bellowed from outside.

Devora opened the door and gasped before slamming it shut. A giant sprinted toward them, full force. Paralyzed by the sight of the enormous man, Devora didn't know what to do. Should they try to flee?

"Stay put, recruits," Sir Jacques yelled down the line of the carriages. "Ready yourselves," he then called to the other guards. "Remember their powers."

Snapping out of her panic, Devora quickly cleaned the smudged window with the sleeve of her dress to get a better look. The giant barreling toward them was at least four carriages tall. Devora staggered back as the ground rumbled.

A flash of bright red leg hair streaked across the window as the giant sped by, screaming a language Devora didn't know.

Ida clamped her hands around Devora's arm. "Brace yourself!" Ida cried. "He's going to shift the soil."

"What?"

The ground quaked beneath the carriage. In a matter of seconds, the soil elevated into a plateau, lifting their carriage higher and higher in the sky. The girls screamed when a freckled face with blazing green eyes glared at them through the window.

Devora gasped and clutched the wooden bench. She'd always heard giants could manipulate the earth, but she never thought she'd experience it. Not many were seen in Tenton since Kadesh had bribed the giants with gold and jewels in exchange for their loyalty to King Redore IV.

"Attack!" Sir Conan yelled.

The plateau grew beneath their carriage as the battle cries of the Fortress' guards ricocheted through the air. The knights descended upon the giant, but they were no match. With a flick of his fingers, the giant easily formed three boulders out of the dirt and squashed nearly a dozen guards.

Pulse racing, Devora tore her eyes away from the motionless bodies. How many had the giant killed? How many were left to protect her and the others? She had never seen the point of praying to Tunri before, but now seemed like a good time to start.

Please don't let me die here. The cry came unbidden, rushing her thoughts to Tunri, though she'd never seen the value of praying to Him before.

The giant commanded more boulders to stop Sir Jacques and Sir Conan, but they dodged the flying rocks.

A large, hairy hand reached toward them, and Ida burrowed into Devora's side. Grasping the wooden carriage off the plateau, the giant yanked off the door. Devora held onto Ida tight as a large green eyeball scanned over them.

"*Das inka krastal?*" the giant's crackly voice boomed.

"'Where are the jewels?'" Ida translated between sobs.

Devora cast a baffled look at the trembling girl as her mind raced for a solution. How would Papa handle this situation? He was always confident and strong, never showing any weakness. What would he do?

Finding her courage, Devora knew Papa would try to reason with the giant and calm him down.

After she pried Ida off her arm, Devora lifted her chin. "There are no jewels here, sir." Being polite never hurt.

"*I-ishta no k-krastal, pardon,*" Ida said, her voice shaking.

Frowning, the giant shook the carriage with vigor, jumbling the girls inside. Ida shrieked, tears streaming down her cheeks. Devora tried to crouch into a ball to protect herself from being tossed around, but it was no use. She was sure she'd find splinters and bruises everywhere.

"*Das inka krastal?*" the giant bellowed again.

Ida screamed, but Devora had enough. Her voice *would* be heard.

Once the carriage stopped shaking, Devora squared her shoulders and braced herself against the doorframe. She never gave in to bullies before and she definitely wouldn't now. The crashing and clanging of the guards trying to force the giant to release them sounded so far away. She thought she heard Sir Jacques shout something, but she couldn't make it out.

"Listen here," she scolded, causing the giant to lift the carriage to his eye. Devora's stomach lurched at the quick movement. Once it settled, she continued, "I already told you. We don't have any jewels. We're traveling to the Fortress as new recruits in His Majesty's Army. Unless you'd like to enlist, I demand you put us down."

She waited for Ida to translate, but the giant had understood enough.

His large face paled. "*De Fortress?*" he asked and threw the carriage down.

Devora and Ida screamed as the poorly made carriage shattered around them. Thankfully, the soil the giant collected cushioned their fall, but Devora felt as if she had fractured her ankle.

The earth quaked again, and Devora glanced up to see the giant race into the setting sun.

"After him!" Sir Conan cried to the few soldiers left. The knight freed his horse from the carriage reins and took off into the horizon.

Two followed Sir Conan while the other five stayed with Sir Jacques.

"Lady Devora," Sir Jacques panted, offering her his hand. "Miss Ida." He offered the crying girl his other one. "Are you two unharmed?"

Taking Sir Jacques' hand, Devora slowly stood, wincing from the pain in her ankle. "I think so."

Her hands burned from shards of wood and glass buried in them. Small drops of blood dribbled down her wrists as she wiggled her fingers. Cringing, Devora tried to move but found more pieces of wood piercing other sensitive places.

Those aren't going to be fun to pluck out.

Ida mumbled some words between sniffles, but she stood as well.

"You two will join one of the other carriages," Sir Jacques informed. "We still have two days left."

Devora's head snapped up. *Two days? How are we going to survive the next two days if we were already attacked by a giant? What other horrible things will happen?*

Running her hands over her dirt-covered dress, smearing the fine fabric with blood, Devora decided not to argue as she hobbled to the nearest carriage. Luckily, it was empty inside, so she assumed this was where Sir Conan or some of the other soldiers sat when they weren't riding their steeds.

With a sad smile, Sir Jacques provided ointment and bandages for their wounds. The knight closed the door to their carriage and ordered the others to continue. Thankfully, no other knights or new recruits joined them, so Ida and Devora were alone. In a matter of moments, the caravan rolled steadily along as if nothing had happened.

Devora and Ida sat in silence while they bandaged and treated their injuries. It wasn't until later in the evening that Ida finally spoke.

"I've never seen a giant before," Ida confessed, staring at her bandaged fingers before nibbling on a piece of dried meat.

They had both been successful in plucking out most of the shards of wood, but Devora was sure more would appear later.

After rubbing more ointment on her calf and ankle, Devora wrapped them in a bandage and responded, "Me neither. I thought all the giants fled to Kadesh."

Leaning back, Devora recalled the history lessons she learned with her tutor. At the start of the twenty-year war with Kadesh, Tenton had been victorious. But as the battles continued, Kadesh gained the upper hand due to their recruitment of the giants in Tenton. Because of their ability to manipulate earth, King Atol wanted to imprison the giants for "observation." But everyone knew the king would slaughter them all. Just like he had done with the

Seers. So, all giants who had been in Tenton had fled to the enemy, seeking the promises of gold, land, and freedom.

Devora studied the small girl before her, remembering how Ida easily translated the giant's foreign language. "How did you know what he was saying?"

A tiny smile came to Ida's plump lips as she tried to comb her dark ringlets with her fingers. "I intended to study linguistics at Vlacklear." She tapped her ear. "I have a very 'tuned ear,' as my mother would say." Ida's smile brightened then dulled. "Most people think giants are a disgrace and abomination to our kingdom because of their power."

Devora focused on her feet, refusing to look at Ida. *Am I a disgrace because of my power? Am I the same as that awful giant?* Discomfort squirmed in her middle at the thought. She'd never had these thoughts of doubt before and hated how they made her feel worthless.

"But I don't think so," Ida continued, interrupting Devora's thoughts. Devora's chest lightened, hope filling her heart once again. "I think that Tunri made us all different for a reason, and if the king saw things that way, maybe the giants would've stayed and fought for Tenton."

Ida grinned and Devora realized the girl was talking about more than giants. Devora gave a hesitant smile back. She wasn't sure why Ida was being kind—especially since Devora had been cruel to her—but even so, Devora couldn't trust her. Anyone could turn her in to the king.

Their conversation soon died down, and when nightfall came, Ida dozed off quickly. Thankfully, the rest of their journey had been uneventful, but Sir Conan and the other guards hadn't returned. Devora wondered what had happened to the rude knight. Maybe the giant had squashed him.

Ida snored softly, filling their carriage with the sound of sleep. But Devora wouldn't allow herself to drift off. At least not for too long. Rubbing the exhaustion from her eyes, Devora straightened. She hadn't had a vision since right before her categorization. The dung tea Papa had given her should hold for a little longer. Hopefully she could find something else to hide her curse. Devora didn't want to think about what would happen if she couldn't. She tugged lightly on her braid, not wanting to tempt fate by falling asleep.

Devora threaded her ripped sash through her fingers, remembering the iron-armored beasts with pointed teeth coming for Tenton. How long did they have until Kadesh attacked?

Sleep pulled her lids closed and Devora allowed herself to rest for a few minutes before pinching her thigh. Stifling a yelp, her eyes shot open. When she fell into a deep sleep, she sometimes fell into a vision. And she couldn't let that happen.

Often times her visions would cause wild reactions. She'd beat and punch at anything within her grasp. While she alone in her room, her only victims were a few pillows. But in this tight space, Devora couldn't risk harming Ida. The poor girl had already been through enough.

To keep herself awake, Devora recalled the events from the past two days. Tristan's betrayal, the Categorization Call, the king's decree, and the giant's attack. She shook her head, still trying to wrap her mind around it all. She had been so sure of her future, so confident of her path, and now it was all gone. Tristan, Vlacklear, her family, everything—gone .

The carriage bounded across the bumpy road as dawn broke through the dark night. It was the final day of the journey, and Devora hadn't slept more than a few scattered moments. Though her eyes were heavy, and she was sure she looked worse than death, she was proud she hadn't succumbed to the lure of sleep.

Once the rickety carriage came to a halt, the door was wrenched open. A frigid breeze slipped around the girls, causing Devora to wrap her arms around her stomach and Ida to squeak before jolting up. This biting weather was a far cry from Grenly's lush tropical forests and mild temperatures.

"W-where are we?" Ida asked, teeth chattering as she rubbed her bare arms.

"This is the last stop we'll make before we arrive at the Fortress," Sir Jacques said as the weary faces of the other new recruits stepped out of the carriages.

"We're just outside of Juro," he continued, "The Fortress is on the outskirts. As new recruits, once you enter, you will not leave until setting out for battle." His eyes dimmed as he studied the young recruits staring back at him. They had all filed out of the carriages and were huddled against each other, trying to find warmth against the bitter northern wind.

Devora tightened her grasp around herself before she remembered Sir Jacques had said there was clothing for their journey north. Peering back in the carriage, she found two large black cloaks. She handed one to Ida, who took it quickly and wrapped it around her shivering shoulders.

Devora secured the oversized wool cloak around her frigid form, welcoming its warmth. The new recruits wandered around the desolate landscape of the northern region. Bleak, brown land stretched out before them.

Devora shuddered and pulled the large cloak tighter. *This place is awful. It's cold, miserable, and ugly.*

Devora scanned the horizon. Where were the flowers? The plants? There wasn't a tree in sight. No thick, vibrant emerald leaves for shade. No roses from Mama's garden to sniff. She craned her neck to the gloomy clouds. Even the sky was gray. Devora scrunched her nose. She wished she'd never laid eyes on the fruitless north.

Taking a few steps to stretch out her legs, Devora noticed the jagged outline of the closest city, Juro. She straightened her stance to get a better view. If she looked hard enough, she could see the cubic shape of the Fortress beyond it.

"Are you all right, Lady Devora?" Sir Jacques appeared at her side. The harsh shadows under his lower eyelids were darker than before, as if he hadn't slept in the last three days either.

Wiping the desire for rest from her eyes, she gave him a curt nod. "I'm well, thank you Sir Jacques. And you don't have to call me lady." The memory of Sir Conan ripping her sash came into her thoughts and Devora clenched her jaw. "As your comrade made painfully clear, I no longer hold that position."

Sir Jacques gave her a strange look. "It may not be your title, but it's your nature." The knight stared up at the gray clouds rolling by. "But I suppose we will have to see if he's right."

Devora turned to reply but found Sir Jacques striding away. Furrowing her brow, she headed back into the carriage. The next time she exited, she would be at the Fortress.

Chapter Six

The Fortress, Northern Region, Tenton

Blaring trumpets bounced against the wooden walls of the carriage as it rolled along the cobblestone streets of Juro, the capital city. Carefully sliding across the bench, Devora peeked out the window. Gray stone buildings lined the streets, each one almost identical to the next.

Devora curled her lip in disgust. *This is the shining capital of Tenton?*

But what caught her eye were the people. They weren't bronzed and golden from the sun like the recruits from Grenly, but pale and sickly, shuffling with downcast faces. Devora tilted her head as she studied them, reminded of the girl entwined in Tristan's grasp. She shook the memory from her head. Tristan was no longer a part of her life. She wouldn't waste her thoughts on him.

The shaky carriage hit every crack and hole in the street before leaving the city and entering the barren country-side. Within a few moments, the wheels stopped. The carriage rocked as Sir Jacques and another guard descended from the front. Devora and Ida shared a glance before the door swung open.

Sir Jacques stood outside, donning his helmet, shield, and sword for the first time. Devora's eyes widened at his stern brow and harsh gaze. Though she had seen Sir Jacques frequently in his armor, now that he was completely armed, intimidation radiated from him.

"You'll be given your uniforms and assigned your room upon entry of the Fortress." Sir Jacques' voice echoed through the chamber of his helmet before he moved out of the way, offering Devora his hand.

Taking his cool, armored fingers, Devora stepped out of the carriage and instantly craned her neck up. Built on a mound of snowy rocks stood a huge stone building, its top disappearing into the thick gray clouds. Dark and unwavering, the chiseled stone formed sharp corners and smooth walls as each level stacked on the next.

Terror rattled in her chest as she joined the rest of the recruits waiting for their miserable futures. As she huddled with her cowering comrades, her eyes never wavered from the stone prison. This dank, horrendous building would be her new home.

A shudder ran down her spine as an icy wind blew past, freezing her exposed cheeks. Her opinion of the northern region grew worse by the minute.

Pulling her cloak tighter, Devora scanned the majestic building in the distance. It was an exact opposite of the Fortress. Pure white stones layered on one another to create a vast castle. Cylindrical towers stood perfectly spaced along the perimeter. The beautiful building beamed with excellence and opulence. Was it Maldove Palace?

"That would be Vlacklear Academy, Lady Devora," Sir Jacques said, answering her unspoken question. He removed his helmet and gave her a sympathetic smile.

Devora tightened her grip on the cloak, her heart crumbling. "It's so close," she whispered. Her dream of becoming the next governor of Grenly within her reach, but she could never touch it. And Tristan would be right next door, seducing more girls than he could handle.

Devora straightened. *Tristan is in the past.*

"Yes," Sir Jacques replied with a nod. "It seems that the creators of Vlacklear wanted their students to be reminded of where they could end up if they disobeyed."

"What?" She gave the knight a look of disbelief. Her parents had never spoken of such things when reminiscing about Vlacklear.

"Grenly was protected from a lot of horrors of the world because of your father. The rest of Tenton is not as pleasant as you may think," Sir Jacques explained before turning to the others. "Step in line, everyone." The recruits stared at him, their faces white with terror. "Forgive me, Lady Devora," he whispered. "But I must use you as an example." Sir Jacques sighed before he grabbing Devora's arm from beneath her cloak and dragging her toward the front entrance. "Let's go!" he shouted.

Devora released a small cry as his frigid armor bit into her flesh.

Sir Jacques bent low as they neared the solid iron doors at the base of the Fortress. "I mustn't show affection or weakness. The warden will not take kindly to you if he knows of our friendship."

Hope buzzed in her chest at the notion. A secret friend was better than no friend at all.

"Move out of the way, scrags!"

Devora's body tensed as she recognized Sir Conan's arrogant bellow. Apparently, he hadn't been squished.

The young recruits shuffled out of the way, allowing the knight to pass with a thick metal chain in his hands. The ground quaked beneath their feet as Devora traced the silver links with her eyes before she gasped. Attached to the end of the chain was the giant that attacked them. Thick metallic gauntlets secured his wrists while a large piece of fabric gagged his mouth. The giant lurched forward, muffled noises coming from his covered lips. Anger flared in the giant's green eyes as he stomped along the cold ground.

Sir Conan held the chain tight as other guards surrounded him, attaching more chains around the giant's ankles and neck. Though Devora feared the enormous man, something in her heart ached, seeing him bound like he was some kind of beast.

The heavy iron gates creaked open, pulling the recruits' attention away from the flailing giant to the entrance of the Fortress.

A rush of humidity mixed with the stench of bad hygiene swept over Devora. Try as she might, she couldn't hold back a cough.

Sir Conan snorted, puffing out his chest in an attempt to look fierce. But he only looked like a small dwarf compared to the restrained giant behind him. "Nobles are so weak.

You better get used to that scent, Medee. That's the smell of home now."

Devora wanted to gag but swallowed it down. An eerie feeling crept over her skin as a sturdy man exited the Fortress and approached the shivering group.

Almost a foot taller than her, the man peered down at the recruits with piercing black eyes. White, slicked hair waved back from his scalp, never moving as the fierce wind roared around him. A matching trimmed mustache adorned his upper lip.

Anticipation clung to the frigid air as the mustached man patiently strode down the line of frightened faces, hands behind his back, tightening the fabric of his dark shirt and leather jerkin.

When he reached Sir Conan, he stopped and peered beyond the knight. The giant growled, yanking on the chains binding him. The man narrowed his eyes and addressed Sir Conan.

"A giant?" his deep voice asked, vibrating with command and authority.

Sir Conan crossed a balled fist over his chest and bowed before straightening. "Yes, sir. He attacked our company as we left Grenly. Luckily, I was able lure him away from the scrags and capture him."

Sir Conan yanked on the main chain. The giant reared back. If it weren't for the other soldiers' support, Sir Conan would have been tossed across the lake to Vlacklear.

"Actu—" Devora started but felt Sir Jacques grip tighten around her wrist, warning her to stay silent.

Huffing, Devora blew a stray hair out of her face and glowered at Sir Conan. He hadn't lured the giant away. The giant fled after *she* told him about the Fortress.

With a grunt, the mustached man continued down the line, boots clacking against the stone ground.

As the man approached the new recruits, Sir Jacques pulled Devora closer. The mustached man stopped in front of her. His dark eyes were an abyss as they analyzed her.

Straightening her shoulders, Devora stared back at him. His black eyes narrowed before a slight smirk came to his stern lips.

"Governor Cusha Medee's only child," the mustached man stated nonchalantly. "It's been some time since we've had nobility within our walls. What are your thoughts, Jacques?"

Devora blinked. *How does this man know Papa?*

"I'm not sure what you mean, sir," Sir Jacques answered stoically.

But, even with the frigid wind, Devora could see the thin sheen of sweat accumulating on the knight's forehead.

Why is Sir Jacques nervous?

The mustached man studied Devora. "I don't deal kindly with nobles. Because of people like you, this war has gone on for far too long." The blood fled from Devora's face as the mustached man turned to the knights restraining the giant. "Tell me, should we allow this girl to atone for the sins of her class?" He whipped out a dagger from his sleeve and held it at Devora's throat.

"What?" Devora cried, unable to stop herself. "But I haven't done anything!"

Sure, she hadn't helped the people in Lower Grenly and didn't say her prayers, but did that mean she deserved to be murdered on the steps of the Fortress?

"Silence," the mustached man replied coolly. The tip of the blade nicked her throat, and Devora clamped her lips shut.

This man had to be someone important to know her father. A horrible thought crossed her mind. *Does he know about my curse? Is he trying to finish me off quickly?*

"We could take care of that right now," Sir Conan chimed in. "There's a gallows in the back. Quick, clean, done." The knight brushed his hands against one another, like ending Devora's life was nothing more than another duty to complete.

Devora's eyes widened, but with the knife at her throat, she was too terrified to defend herself.

Sir Jacques squeezed her arm and cut in. "Sir, I don't believe it's necessary to give Lady Devora the punishment of other nobles, much less take her life. She has come willingly to fight in His Majesty's Army." He never once looked at her but kept his grip firm on her arm.

Devora was comforted by his defense, but what would that mean for him?

The man's gaze darted between Devora and Sir Jacques. He stroked his white mustache and Devora could see the wheels in his head churning.

"Is that so? Are you willing to take her place, Jacques?"

Devora's pulse raced, her heart pounding as if it would burst out of her chest. But she kept her eyes trained on the man, not willing to let him see her fear. Papa had already been arrested for defending her. She wouldn't allow Sir Jacques to be taken too.

Sir Jacques took a shaky breath. "If you wish me to, sir, I will."

"No," Devora interceded, knowing she would probably make things worse. "Please. Sir Jacques has done nothing wrong."

Sir Jacques sucked in a breath as the mustached man's animalistic gaze focused on her. Devora refused to cower even though she felt like a small mouse in the paw of a tiger.

"I don't think anyone needs to be killed today, Warden," a crisp voice intervened.

Fear spiked Devora's heart. *The mustached man is Warden Hazor?*

She wanted to slap herself for not realizing it sooner. When other members of the King's Council visited Papa, she had overheard terrible stories of how Warden Hazor tortured the criminals of the Fortress with barbaric contests. No wonder the giant had run when she mentioned where they were going.

Warden Hazor tilted his head then retracted his dagger. He spun around, blocking Devora's view of who was speaking. "And why is that, Blake?"

"For one, Jacques can't lie," the voice replied coolly. "You've seen him play Kings with the other guards. His left eye always starts twitching when he has a good hand and lies about it. That's why he's lost so much coin."

The other knights still holding the giant and surrounding the new recruits all chuckled. Sir Jacques' face turned a bright shade of cranberry as he swallowed, trying to muster a smile.

"Second," the voice continued, "although nobles are fickle, arrogant idiots, I believe this one will be a valuable asset to us. She's young and moldable. If we train her correctly, we can use her to our advantage within the court."

Devora's lips parted in shock at the man's frankness before fury took over. If she weren't trying to stay alive, she would have had a lot to say about this man's comments of her being so easily influenced.

Warden Hazor glanced over his shoulder, his eyes gleaming with mischief as he studied Devora. "All right, Blake. We'll let her live. For now."

Sir Jacques' grip on her arm relaxed. Devora pulled away slowly, allowing the blood to return to her veins.

Devora watched Warden Hazor stalk to the middle of the open iron gate. His gaze scanned the recruits, as if memorizing every little detail about them. They were eyes that didn't miss anything. Devora shivered. How was she going to keep her curse a secret now?

"I'm going to owe him so much for that," Sir Jacques muttered under his breath before turning to Devora. "Lady Devora, while I appreciate you standing up for me, please don't do it again. If the captain hadn't stepped in, we'd both be dead."

Devora frowned. She already hated the topsy-turvy justice system of the Fortress.

"I'm Warden Hazor," the warden declared from his position in front of the Fortress' iron gate. "I command every aspect of this tower. I know everything that happens within its walls. If you step out of line the slightest bit, I will know, and you will be punished."

The group of recruits stiffened as the warden continued, "General Teague of His Majesty's Army has granted me the authority to train troops for the front lines. I, in turn, have given some of that authority to my second in command, Captain Blake. He will oversee your training. He is the best, and I won't tolerate failure from him or any of you."

With another chilling glance, Warden Hazor marched back into the stone prison. The recruits focused on the struggling giant trying to break free, but Devora's gaze stayed glued on the cropped chestnut hair and flawless sun-kissed skin of the warden's second in command. A twinge of anger burbled in her chest as she tried to keep her jaw from dropping. The man standing in front of the Fortress was none other than Tristan.

Medee

Chapter Seven

The Fortress, Northern Region, Tenton

Devora scrutinized the officer from across the Fortress' entrance. He wasn't Tristan. This man was at least four summers her senior and was much taller and leaner than Tristan.

She pursed her lips. *Definitely not as muscular.*

Captain Blake's sharp, square jaw clenched tight as his calculating gray eyes assessed her. This had to be Tristan's older brother.

The captain kept his steely gaze on her until Devora looked away, not wanting anything to do with Tristan or his brother.

"Take that creature to Level Five," he commanded, flicking his hand toward the still riling giant. "Lock him up in the large cells until the warden decides what to do with him."

The giant screamed more muffled words. The soldiers binding him yanked his chains and dragged him into the Fortress.

"All right, Blake. No need to sound so mighty in front of the scrags." Sir Conan snorted as he picked at his soil-ridden nails. "We all know who you are."

Captain Blake's eyes flashed before he took two steps toward Sir Conan, towering over the short, bulky knight.

"Do I need to remind you of your place, Conan?"

Goosebumps covered Devora's skin at the captain's low, threatening voice, and she tightened her cloak around her shoulders. Tristan's tone had always been smooth and silky. Why was his brother's so cold?

Sir Conan puffed out his chest before Captain Blake reared back and punched him in the jaw. Devora jumped in surprise. With a yelp, Sir Conan stumbled back as his tooth went flying, landing in front of Devora's feet. Gasps and squeals came from several of the girls among the recruits.

Sir Conan worked his jaw, placing a hand on it before he spit a bloody wad on the ground. "Apologies. It won't happen again," the knight growled. "Sir."

"Make sure that it doesn't." Captain Blake lifted his square chin before he strode steadily toward the group of frightened girls.

"Follow me," he commanded without sparing them another glance. His sturdy steps clacked along the stone ground as he marched through the iron gate.

"Let's go," Sir Jacques called, following behind the captain.

The boys quickly filed into line, but the huddle of girls hadn't moved, staying crunched behind Devora. She didn't know why they had chosen to hide behind her, but they couldn't stay out in this freezing weather for much longer.

Squaring her shoulders, Devora held out her hands to the girls behind her. "Come on," she said, keeping her eyes trained on the broad shoulders of Captain Blake. "We go together."

Icy fingers latched onto Devora's arms as the group shuffled toward the menacing iron gate. Silence choked the new recruits as they entered the Fortress. Gasps and cries escaped the quivering group as the iron gates clanged shut behind them.

Captain Blake stood as tall as the jungle trees in Grenly as he waited for the group in the dimly lit hallway. Holding his hands behind his back, he pinned his hard gaze on Devora again.

"Males, you will follow Jacques." Captain Blake thankfully moved his penetrating stare from Devora as he pointed to Sir Jacques. "He will show you to your cells."

The boys stood rigid at the mention of staying in prison cells. Devora resisted the urge to shudder. *Living in prison cells?* At least Sir Jacques tried to sugarcoat things to make living at the Fortress sound better.

As soon as the boys and Sir Jacques were gone, Captain Blake took three steps forward, his shined ebony boots catching the light of the torches lining the walls.

Nails dug into Devora's arms, and she peeked over her shoulder to find the number of girls had grown.

Are we the first women to enter the Fortress and His Majesty's Army?

"Devora Medee, daughter of the Governor and First Lady of Grenly," Captain Blake commented, pulling her attention from the girls. His stern lips twitched as if he knew she was his brother's latest fling.

"Yes?" Devora asked defiantly. She met the captain's gaze, unwilling to let her weakness show.

Does he know about Tristan's proposal? Is that why he thinks I'm "moldable? The thought stoked a fire of fury in her chest.

Though she was thankful he saved her life, Devora would not be as influenced by the captain's tactics as he thought. She would use her own mind to become the best soldier and save Papa. She had to.

Captain Blake smirked then leaned toward her. Cedar, smoke, and steel wafted from his crisp uniform.

"Defiance will not stop your inevitable fate."

Ice coated Devora's veins as her throat tightened. *Does he know about my curse? How could he know?*

She thought that Ida's guess was just a fluke. But now that Captain Blake had said something as well, was her curse seeping out of her in a different way?

Devora took a steady breath and waited, remembering how Papa coached her to keep a straight face when someone questioned her about anything controversial. She kept her gaze steady on the captain's gray eyes, noticing the flecks of gold and brown in them. If they weren't owned by a man trying to scare her out of her skin, she would've thought they were beautiful.

"Only I decide my fate," she replied, locking her knees to keep them from shaking.

Captain Blake quirked a brow then addressed the girls still cowering behind her. "I do not tolerate crying, weeping, or whimpering. Follow me. We'll begin in the basement." He didn't wait for them to respond before continuing down the hallway and making a sharp right around a corner.

Ida clawed at Devora's left forearm, white fingertips clinging with fear. Wincing, Devora turned and met the girl's terrified caramel eyes. The wicked northern wind had tossed Ida's tight black curls, leaving them a mess on her head. Devora reached over and gave Ida's hand a quick pat, trying to offer some comfort.

"Come on," Devora said, encouraging the group while she gathered her own courage. "We'll be okay."

After rounding the corner, the girls were greeted by a long arching hallway made of dark stone, identical to the exterior. Flaming torches lined the walls every few feet. Their shadows danced wildly as the girls shuffled by. Though the light tried to break through, darkness was king.

Blood, sweat, and grime poisoned the air. Devora held her breath as long as she could. She couldn't believe Warden Hazor approved of soldiers living in such a stench. How she wished for her rose soap and bathhouse. She hadn't realized how blessed she was until now—when everything was gone.

Captain Blake continued down the corridor, silent, as the girls tried to follow. Devora only knew which way to go because of the echo of his boots against the eerie silence.

As they hurried past another corner, a large arched cell formed along the side of the wall. A series of growls rolled from the three slots carved at the top of the giant iron door. The girls gasped and clumped a bit closer. Another girl with chin-length hair and squared bangs squeezed Devora's hand so tight, the feeling in her fingers disappeared.

Captain Blake stopped at the iron door. Another low, guttural growl seeped through, shooting fear into Devora's veins.

Help me, a voice whispered in her thoughts.

The hairs on the back of her neck rose and she took a step back. *What's in that cell? And why is it talking to me?*

"The basement is the lowest level of the Fortress. In here lies the Behemoth, the fiercest creature known to Tenton," Captain Blake explained matter-of-factly. "If you do not adhere to Fortress regulation, you will be locked in with this monster and die." He assessed the girls, his face stoic and unreadable.

Devora sucked in a breath. Captain Blake spoke of such terrible things so absentmindedly. She recalled how the captain punched Sir Conan in the face for back-talking. How could the captain and Tristan be related? Captain Blake was completely barbaric.

After a few moments of silence, Captain Blake asked, "Are there any questions?"

"Is this where we're staying?"

The captain locked onto her, sending another chill across her skin. "No. We have several more levels to go before we get to your cells." He turned and continued down the hall.

Devora quickened her pace to catch up with the captain. The other girls stayed bunched behind her, their shadows lengthening against the flickering torches.

Captain Blake sped around several more corners before steadily marching up a flight of spiraled stairs.

A countless number of cells lined each wall, only a few inches of stone separating one from the other. These cells were different than the Behemoth's. They were smaller and comprised of iron bars instead of a sheet of metal. The bars allowed Devora to easily see the desperate and hungry faces of the inmates staring back at them.

Captain Blake continued through the prison hall without a care in the world.

"I don't like this," Ida whispered, tears pricking her eyes. She scooched closer to Devora.

"Me either," Devora whispered, watching Captain Blake march through the hall. "But we don't have a choice."

The captain strode strongly, ignoring the curses and jeers the inmates threw at him. It was as if he were a stone wall. Nothing fazed his hard demeanor. He stopped near the end and spun around, waiting.

Swallowing her fear, Devora grasped her cloak around her neck and hurried toward the captain.

"Look at those pretty eyes," a raspy voice called out as she passed by. Devora jutted away from the outstretched hand. "I'd like to take a closer look. Why don't you come here?"

"Forget the eyes, look at everything else," a lecherous voice added from the other side.

Devora tried to avoid his grasp, but another inmate grabbed her cloak and pulled it through the bars. Panicking, her fingers flew to the knot over her throat, scrambling to undo it before she felt grimy hands grab at her body.

"That's enough!" Captain Blake yelled. He wrapped his long, toned arm around Devora's waist and grabbed the fabric. Devora's stomach flipped as she watched the captain wrench the cloak away from the filthy inmate's grasp then shove him through the iron bars.

The man stumbled back before landing on his back side, sputtering a series of colorful curses.

Captain Blake handed Devora her cloak, his glower more intense in the light of the torches outside of each cell. "Your reflexes are weak," he stated, releasing her from his tight grasp. "We'll fix that. Let's continue."

The other inmates grumbled as the girls strode past their cells, but none of them gave the group any more problems.

Devora studied the back of the captain, still feeling the warmth of his arm where he had hauled her away from the prisoner. She hated that he called her weak. She never allowed herself to be mentally weak. That's why she studied Tenton's martial law and read the weekly battlefront update. But she hated more that he was right. She *was* weak. In the end, Captain Blake freed her from the grabby inmates. She was useless.

Once the group reached the end of the hall, Captain Blake explained, "Level Five houses the Fortress' most dangerous and ruthless inmates—all of them have committed at least one murder. If you do not adhere to regulations, you will be sent here and will most likely die."

Or worse, Devora thought as she wiped the feeling of the hands from her hips and arms. The captain was brutally honest.

Captain Blake stood like a statue at the top of the stairs before leading them through the next hall of cells. While no one tried to assault them, threats, curses, insinuations, and promises suffocated the air around them.

Devora did her best to ignore the prisoners' comments by watching Captain Blake. Once again, he marched through the corridor, shoulders back, head high, every insult and curse bouncing off him. If she hadn't already decided to dislike the man, Devora would've admired his strength.

As the girls survived another level, a few of them stepped to the front of the line, finding their confidence and bravery. Devora was thankful to not be the only one guiding the pack.

"Level Four houses Tenton's traitors. If you do not adhere to regulations, you will be sent here and will probably die."

Devora cocked her head. Did the punishment for disobedience depend on the specific crime? If someone minorly disobeyed, were they sent to a lesser level than if they committed a greater offense against the warden? Or did every punishment just end in death regardless?

"Does every punishment end in death?" Luckily, her voice came out as a whisper and Captain Blake hadn't heard. But the girls around her cracked a few strained smiles.

Devora shook her head. The justice system in the Fortress was strange and didn't make sense. But after witnessing Warden Hazor try to kill her without cause and Captain Blake almost break Sir Conan's jaw for talking out of turn, she decided to keep her thoughts to herself.

The girls found that Level Three was the same as the others. But, this time, when Devora's leg was grabbed, she whipped it around and kicked the inmate in the face, annoyed at having already endured two levels of prisoners.

Captain Blake spun around at the prisoner's cry, his brows rising as he glanced from Devora to the prisoner clutching his nose. "Better, but still weak."

Devora huffed, pushing a stray strand of hair out of her eyes. She wasn't trying to impress him. She was trying to defend herself.

Why does he keep commenting on my awful fighting skills?

Of course, she didn't fight well. She wasn't meant to be a soldier. She was meant to be a scholar.

Once they fled up the next spiral of stairs, the girls discovered the previous level of the Fortress housed thieves. Captain Blake waited for them at the next entrance.

As she came closer, Devora noticed an arched solid metal door bolted by three iron bars. Fear crept up her spine. Didn't Level Five house the worst inmates?

But as Captain Blake slid the iron pegs out and opened the door, only silence answered.

The captain steadily strode through, beckoning the girls to follow. Once over the threshold, Devora looked around and frowned. These cells were empty.

Chapter Eight

Captain Blake marched to the middle of the long hall then faced the group.

"This is the first war in history where the kingdom has taken citizens below eighteen summers to fight. Unfortunately, it no longer matters whether you're a woman, a giant, or a combination of them." His stern angular features softened slightly.

Devora shared a quick glance with Ida. *Does he feel sorry for us?*

"You'll be housed here," Captain Blake gestured to the empty iron-barred cells. The hard lines of his face caught in the flickering torch light. "You're the first to arrive from the surrounding regions. More may join you in time. For Warden Hazor to keep order, males and females, regardless of region, breed, or gift, will be kept separate except for at mealtimes and training rituals."

Devora furrowed her brow. *Gift? Are there others like me here?*

Captain Blake strode to the adjacent wall, the clicking of his boots echoing against the vacant cells before he reached a lever protruding from the stone. He pulled it down, and the cell doors swung open simultaneously.

"Your uniforms are on your beds. Make sure you're dressed by dawn. Tardiness will not be tolerated. Your training begins tomorrow." Captain Blake turned and marched down the hallway, leaving the girls speechless and utterly confused.

"We have to stay here?" a girl with golden ringlets squeaked once the captain was gone.

"Scared of a little dirt?" another girl, rotund with shoulder-length red hair, chuckled.

Devora quirked a brow at the girl. *Where was that confidence a few moments ago?*

"He's terrifying," Ida whispered with a shudder. She gestured to where Captain Blake had just stood.

Devora studied the iron door the captain exited. "Yes," she agreed, though something about the frightening captain intrigued her.

"I don't know. I thought he was nice to look at." A tall, thin girl leaning against the dingy wall stepped out into the shivering crowd. She was one of the few that had joined Devora at the front of the group. Black braids wrapped down her stick-thin back, her sharp eyes gazed dreamily in the direction Captain Blake went.

Devora scrunched her nose, annoyed. Captain Blake was the rudest man she had ever met. Not to mention the scariest. How could anyone possibly think he was attractive?

"We're in a prison, preparing for war, and you're thinking about men?" a girl who was the exact same height and weight as the braided girl asked. She pulled out an abacus and shifted the metal beads to the right. "By my calculations, most of the men here will be ugly with bad hygiene. Honestly, Hestia, get your head out of the clouds. They probably wouldn't like you anyway."

Devora studied the two girls, noting their jade-colored robes weren't the only thing identical about them. They were twins.

As more girls went to inspect the open cells, Devora ran a hand over her long, tousled braid as she took in the hallway. The iron cells continued past her vision. There were far more cells than the girls present, so at least they could each have their own space, and she wouldn't have to worry about bunking with any other prisoner. But Captain Blake did say there may be more females coming. Devora's heart sank. More women like her, condemned to prison without reason.

Devora crossed her arms over her chest. *Why would King Atol want this? Why would Tunri want this?*

A wave of exhaustion rolled over her. "I think I'm going to lie down for a bit," Devora announced to the group as she padded to the open cell on the right.

Surprisingly, the cell wasn't as filthy as she imagined. Maybe Warden Hazor did care about his troops.

Two wooden beds hugged the opposite walls. Crisp white blankets adorned each bunk, and a matching pillow laid on top. Devora pursed her lips at the absence of multiple pillows, or color, but the bedding looked comfortable enough. At the edge of each bed lay two sets of identical uniforms. Devora sighed at the mud-colored fabric. She missed her colorful dresses already.

As she started toward the bed, the twins and Ida rushed into her cell, startling Devora.

"It's our first night here," Hestia began, flicking the ends of her braids with slender fingers. "If it's all right with you we'd…"

"We'd like to stay together," Ida finished with a smile, clasping her hands in front. "Just until we're all comfortable."

The other twin with the abacus scoffed and rolled her eyes. "I'm not staying in here with Grenly dung."

Devora straightened her stance at the remark. "Are you referring to me?"

The twin ignored Devora and focused on counting her beads.

"Reese," Hestia hissed before giving Devora an apologetic look. "Just ignore her. So, can we stay?"

Devora ran her gaze over the girls. While Ida's skin was a rich umber, the twins' skin was golden as the sun in Grenly. And while Devora had always thought she was tall, the twins stood a head taller than her. Although the three girls were different, they all stared at her with the same expectation.

"Why do you want to stay with me?" Devora asked, flinching at the harshness of her tone. Up until this point, everyone else hated her because she was a noble. Reese disliked her, but why did Ida and Hestia insist on befriending her?

"You stood up for that knight, Sir Jacques," Ida said, a blush coming to her cheeks as she twisted her fingers.

Hestia nodded, but Reese scoffed as her fingers moved over her abacus. "Warden Hazor should have killed you without question. I don't know why he didn't."

"Reese!" Hestia scolded, snatching the abacus out of her sister's hands, and chucking it out of the cell. Reese squealed and raced after it. Hestia scrubbed her forehead and faced Devora. "Reese is a bit difficult with new people. Please don't pay her any mind."

Devora quirked a brow but said nothing.

"I'm thankful Warden Hazor didn't kill you," Hestia continued. "And I hope you'll allow us—" she paused, "Well, at least me, to stay. Just one night."

Devora sucked in a breath. After not sleeping for three days, she really just wanted to rest.

What will happen if I have a vision while these girls are here?

Although she had just taken the dung tea a few days ago, it would wear off in two and a half weeks. The only question was when.

Just as she was about to say no, something twisted in her chest. It surprised her that the girls didn't condemn her for her noble rank. Even when she first met Ida in the carriage, the girl from Lower Grenly had been kind.

After Devora took another look at the pleading faces of Hestia and Ida, she scratched her cheek and replied, "I guess it would be okay."

The girls cheered and began rearranging the two beds in the cell to make one giant bed in the middle. They quickly sprawled out on the thin mattresses and began chatting.

"Who would've thought the king would make such a crazy decree?" Hestia asked as she hiked up her robe and crisscrossed her long legs.

"Shush, Hestia," Reese chided, from the doorway. "There's bound to be—" she clanked three beads together—"At least twenty spies within the Fortress walls." Reese moved more of the beads around. "Maybe more."

"They can't do much worse to us than they've already done," Hestia sighed, slumping back on the bed. "And Father just let us go."

"He didn't have a choice," Reese bit out. "Father needed the coin, and the king provided. We were just part of the bargain."

"What are you doing here?" Devora asked, remembering the girl's vile comment. "I thought you didn't want to stay with Grenly dung."

Reese pursed her lips and looked away. "I don't want to stay in a cell alone," she murmured under her breath.

"You can stay here," Devora replied, crossing her hands over her chest. "But I require an apology."

Reese curled her upper lip and turned away. "I refuse."

"Come on, Reese," Hestia encouraged, hugging a pillow to her chest.

Reese clacked the beads on the abacus, screwing her lips tight. "Fine. I'm sorry."

Hestia reached out and squeezed her sister's hand before placing the pillow on her face. "This is terrible. How am I going to survive with all the ugly, smelly men?"

"I'm sure we'll be okay," Ida encouraged with a soft smile. She sat on the cot and brought her knees to her chest. "Right, Devora?"

The three of them faced Devora, and Devora froze. They were looking to her for direction and affirmation. She would've expected this after she had trained at Vlacklear, but not in the middle of a prison cell.

Why did they pick me?

She had never cared about others, and frankly, she only wanted to focus on getting out of here and to Vlacklear, where she belonged. But once again, her chest squeezed, and she couldn't dampen the mood.

"Yes," Devora agreed, flipping her braid over her shoulder. "I think, if we stay together, we'll be okay."

The girls immediately relaxed at her words. Devora was shocked by how powerful a simple word of encouragement could be.

With a wave of her hand, Ida beckoned Devora over. Devora hesitated then decided to join them. The bed groaned as she sat down but held her weight fine. Glancing up, Devora noticed the metal water basin with a pitcher in the front corner of the cell. Beside that sat a small, black chamber pot. She scrunched her nose. She definitely wished she were back home.

As Hestia braided Ida's wild curls, Devora curled up on the cot, too exhausted to think of anything but sleep. She heard one of the girls murmur something, but Devora's eyes had already closed. Cradling the hard pillow, she welcomed her long-awaited slumber.

Darkness cocooned her like a warm blanket, shielding her from the horrors of the Fortress. Devora enjoyed the sweet, desolate silence of the black void but knew it wouldn't last.

No one had screamed at her violet eyes. The dung tea was still holding strong. But exhaustion and stress pushed against the boundaries she set in her mind, trying to get in. She could fight the visions when she was awake, but now, she was too tired.

Oppressive heat radiated under her feet, causing her to jump up in surprise. Furrowing her brows, Devora thought back to the last prophecy. It had started the same way. Never had she experienced the same vision twice.

A harsh breeze cut against her face as the white light blinded her. She shielded her eyes before she was sucked into the prophecy.

The events of the vision unfolded faster than the first time. She sped across the desert toward the black dots. Once again, the only image Devora grasped clearly was a singular palm tree.

Why the repetition? There was nothing new to see.

Terrifying creatures with snarling pointed teeth and iron armor growled and snapped their jowls. Then Devora was thrust upward. The creatures stampeded over the place where she'd stood. Riders in bronze sat upon their backs, baring the Kadeshian seal of interlocking golden circles behind a golden sparrow.

Turning, Devora watched the horrific scene play out in front of her. Tenton's army raced toward the Kadeshians and their iron-armored beasts. But they were no match for the creatures. The bodies of Tenton's soldiers laid sprawled across the sand, staining its cloud-white granules crimson with their blood. Devora's eyes widened, trying to take in every detail. Based on the latest reports of the battlefront she had read a week ago, this battle hadn't happened yet.

Just then, the bloody battle stopped and faded to black. Devora expected to wake up, to make better sense of it. But the prophecy wasn't finished.

Within seconds, she stood outside the Fortress. Her body flew through the building, higher than she had been in her physical state, and stopped at a stone door bearing Tenton's seal. Before she could think, Devora passed through the doorway.

Inside, a circular wooden table sat with chairs around it. Seated in the chairs were various people dressed in finery. Devora identified some of them as members of the King's Council, but others were foreign to her. She found herself sitting among them.

With stern faces, they simultaneously turned to her with expectation and suspicion.

What would the King's Council want from me?

Devora jolted up with a gasp, sweat matting her filthy hair to her face. The others had fallen asleep around her, curled against one another like a litter of kittens. Still groggy from her vision, Devora squinted through the dark to see another body soundly asleep on the edge of the beds. She stifled a gasp as she took in the cropped corn-colored hair and deep snoring.

Why is there a man in my cell?

Captain Blake had said male and females had to be kept separate. Devora would've jumped up if Hestia wasn't lying on top of her legs.

Shifting her weight, Devora tightened the blanket around her, exhaustion layering over her. Maybe this was all a part of a dream.

The man's breath, if he was really there, stayed steady as he slept. He wouldn't be waking up anytime soon.

Wiping the sweat from her brow, Devora slowly laid back down and stared at the stone ceiling thinking about the vision. One of the faces of the King's Council stood out. It was *his* face. The face that she had seen by her side was none other than Captain Blake's.

Chapter Nine

Level Two, The Fortress

An ear-piercing squawk sent Devora flying out of bed and onto the floor with a thump. Chest heaving, she placed a hand on her forehead. The squawking sounded again, and Devora craned her neck up. A black crow perched on a metal rung in the upper corner of the cell. Bald spots covered its scrawny body, and every time it cawed, its singed wings shook.

Devora rubbed her eyes. Everything hadn't been a dream. She was really living in a nightmare. When she glanced up at the bird again, she noticed the cell door had been shut. Fear struck her still. She remembered leaving it open. A rustling behind her alerted every one of her senses as she recalled the new cellmate that had come in the night.

As she turned to the group of sleeping girls, her jaw dropped. The person that had joined them in the night wasn't a man, but a girl with blazing yellow hair shaved close to her scalp. Last night, Devora had only seen the back of the girl's head, it was dark, and she was still half asleep. She let out a breath of relief, thankful she had been mistaken.

As Devora stared at the girl, the girl's round eyes shot open before she launched out of the bed. Devora jerked back at the girl's calf-length black pants and billowing white shirt. Women never wore pants in Grenly, especially not women of nobility. Her tan hands grabbed at the strands of her short hair as her chocolate eyes darted around the cell. She looked about the same age as Devora and the others. If the Categorization Calls in all of Tenton were the same as Grenly, then this girl had to be at least sixteen.

"No, it all really happened," the girl whispered, her head whipping around until her frantic eyes landed on Devora. She flinched then narrowed her gaze. "Who are you?"

Before Devora could answer, the group of girls started to stir.

"Reese, I can't feel my arm," Ida whined.

"Five more minutes, Mama," Reese replied, drooling on Ida's shoulder.

"No, no. You have to wake her like this," Hestia said, jumping up then diving back onto the bed. Reese and Ida flew into the air, landing on the cold stone floor.

"What are you doing?" Reese gasped, accusation in her eyes. A strand of ebony hair stuck to the corner of her mouth before she looked around. "Where is it?" she cried, flinging off blankets. "Did that Grenly girl take it?"

Reese frantically searched through the sheets until she found her abacus and cradled it in her arms like a baby.

Devora cleared her throat. "I have no use for your little toys. And we have another...*recruit*." Crossing her arms over her chest, she kept her face calm. "Now, who are you?"

The new girl looked at Devora. "I'm Nadia Lapith and I'm from—" she stopped then stared at the giant bed. An excited smile spread across her lips. "What a brilliant idea! I never thought of making two beds into one. Just a moment." She took a small notebook from her pocket. Pulling a piece of charcoal from behind her ear, the girl licked the tip and scrawled on the parchment. "Yes. It definitely provides more space and comfort." After a few more scratches on the parchment, she snapped the book shut. "What was I saying?"

Devora eyed the strange girl. "Your name?"

The blonde girl shoved the notebook back in her pocket and slumped on the bed. "Right. Nadia Lapith."

"I'm Devora. Why are you in this cell? There are other empty ones."

Nadia's eyes shot up, their rich chocolate color more pronounced than before. She scratched her cheek. "Yes, I saw those. But I'm used to bunking with several others, so the thought of being alone was...not ideal."

Hestia and Ida nodded in understanding.

Devora pinched her lips. At this rate, His Majesty's entire army would be bunking with her.

"Did you categorize for Vlacklear, too?" Devora asked.

Nadia nodded. "There were rumors the law had changed, and that those categorizing for Vlacklear would be sent to the Fortress. But it was never confirmed." Nadia twirled the piece of charcoal between her fingers, covering her sun-kissed skin in soot.

"Wait," Hestia said, hugging a pillow to her chest, her almond eyes wide. "You didn't know about the king's decree?"

Nadia's gaze hardened as she balled her hand into a fist. "Since the king ravaged Yekel, he hasn't sent many messengers."

Devora undid her messy braid, her chest weighing with grief. Her mind flitted back to her readings from *Tenton: A Condensed History*. When Tenton first started losing the war with Kadesh, King Atol ordered troops to invade Yekel, a southeastern city known to hold people who have been blessed by Tunri with the ability to invent tools and contraptions. The king desired weapons of torture, so he captured the top Tinkers. But, being a peaceful people, the Tinkers refused. For punishment, King Atol sent soldiers to Yekel and burned their citadel to the ground.

"Oh no," Ida said, taking Nadia's charcoaled hand in her own. "You've gone through so much already."

Nadia nodded, patting Ida's hands before pulling away. She ran a hand through her short hair. "Once I categorized for Vlacklear, I felt a prick on my neck, and everything went black. The next thing I knew, I was shivering outside of the Fortress."

"Why would they waste drugging on people from Yekel?" Reese sneered. The clanking of her metal beads followed. "Everyone knows the Tinkers are dead and gone."

Devora's lips parted in shock, her fingers tangled in her hair as Ida and Hestia gasped.

"Reese!" Hestia cried. "Watch what you say."

"I refuse to believe that," Nadia replied calmly, but pain lingered in her eyes.

Reese snorted and went back to her calculations.

Devora eyed the bitter twin, but she knew Reese was probably right. Although the city of Yekel was taken by Kadesh, the countryside around the city was still under Tenton's control. *Was the king so desperate for soldiers that he drugged citizens and carted them off?*

The kingdom had been careful with what information leaked to the public. Even Papa, who held a position on the King's Council, knew very little of the actual events at the front lines.

The beasts from her vision came to her thoughts again, and Devora shuddered. If the war wasn't bad already, it would be. She had to tell someone about the coming forces, but who? And how? Who could she tell who would believe her and not take her to the king? She'd barely spoken a word to Warden Hazor, and he wanted to kill her.

The room stayed silent save for the still-cawing crow.

Nadia glowered at the bird. "*Pahga*, won't that bird be quiet?"

Taking a device from a pocket on the side of her pants, Nadia closed one eye and pointed it at the bird before her thumb pulled back on a small lever. A minuscule orb jutted out of the device, smacking the bird in the chest. A painful cry exited its beak as it retreated from the cell.

Devora jumped.

"I'm not sure that was a good idea," Ida cried, concern for the bird swimming in her eyes.

"Barbaric Yekelians," Reese muttered.

A smirk lined Nadia's pink lips. Shrugging, she loaded another ball into her device and shot it at Reese's arm.

"Ow!" she cried, her abacus clanging to the ground. She glared daggers at Nadia as she rubbed her arm. "What was that for?"

Nadia lifted a shoulder. "Where I'm from, if you say nasty things, you get reprimanded."

Reese glowered at Nadia before swiping her abacus off the ground and stomping out of the cell. Hestia didn't try to stop her.

Once she was gone, Devora finally said, "I'm so sorry about what happened to you and the others from Yekel. We were attacked by a giant on our way here."

Ida nodded fervently.

"That sounds a lot more exciting," Nadia snorted as she strode toward the water basin. Her shoulders were relaxed, her gait confident as she poured a small amount of water in her hands and ran it through her spiked hair, slicking it back.

"And why are you apologizing?" Nadia asked, pulling her leather notebook out again. "It's not your fault we're all here."

"I—" Devora began but was instantly enraptured with what the girl was doing.

Nadia stalked toward the space in front of bed and crouched down. Running her fingers along the wooden frame, she took out her stick of charcoal and notebook and started muttering to herself.

"If I take the rod and bend it in a curved form, I should be able to puncture the stone at its stress points, making it stick without an adhesive." Nadia's thin brows furrowed as she placed the piece of charcoal behind her ear. Her eyes scanned the scribbles on the page again before snapping the book shut. "Yes, I'm positive it'll work."

Ida gave Devora a worried look as they watched Nadia reach beneath one of the bunks and yank out a large, metal rod. Setting one end on the ground, she placed both feet on the other end and pressed down, slowly bending the rod into an arch.

Once finished, Nadia inspected the wall to Devora's left. "Now, I just need to find the correct places."

Devora, Ida, and Hestia watched curiously as Nadia ran her fingers along the intersections of stones.

Taking out the charcoal again, she made two marks on the gray wall before returning the writing tool behind her ear. With a grunt, Nadia slammed the two ends into the two marks.

"What are you doing?" Devora cried, jumping from the bed. Who knew what the punishment for vandalism was?

"You'll see." Nadia smirked, ripping the blanket off Hestia and hoisting it over the curved metal rod protruding from the wall.

Nadia grabbed the chamber pot and water basin and placed them behind the curtain. Stepping inside, she pulled the blanket all the way around until she couldn't be seen.

After a few moments, she poked her blonde head out and said, "Getting a little privacy."

Hestia giggled and clapped her hands. "I want one in my cell!" She turned to Devora. "If Nadia makes us a privacy space, we'll happily leave your cell."

"I would like one in my cell, as well," Ida added quietly. "If you can."

"I'd be happy to put one in all your cells-er-rooms?" Nadia scratched her head.

"Yay!" Hestia bounced on her toes before grabbing Reese and Nadia's arms and tugging them toward the cell across the hall.

Devora watched Hestia drag Nadia out of the cell and couldn't help a small smile. She wished she could find the same joy in such a dismal time.

"Thank you for letting us stay with you," Ida said, pulling Devora's attention back to her. "And for being so strong."

Devora startled at the comment. She had felt nothing but weak and helpless since this all began.

"I'm just trying to make it through, one day at a time." Devora gestured to the cell. "You're more than welcomed to stay, if you'd like."

Ida smiled, lighting her whole face. "Thank you, Devora, but I think I'm ready to accept this new future."

The guilt Devora felt at treating Ida so horribly resurfaced. She didn't want to treat people the way Reese did.

"Ida, before you go," Devora started, extending a hand to the petite girl. Ida stopped and faced her. Devora fumbled with the hem of her sleeve. She was never good with apologies because she'd never thought she was in the wrong. Until now. "I just want to apologize for how I treated you the day of the Categorization Call. It was uncalled for." A lightness filled Devora's heart, almost as if a giant had been sitting on her chest and suddenly stood.

A smile crept across Ida's pink lips. "Thank you, Devora. I appreciate your apology. Though it wasn't necessary." She reached out and squeezed Devora's hands before exiting the cell.

Now that things were a little quieter, Devora examined the curtain and rod, impressed with Nadia. *Is Nadia one of the last Tinkers from Yekel? How could the king waste another amazing mind intended for Vlacklear?*

As she ran her fingers across the white sheet, Devora noticed the pile of crumpled clothes at the foot of her bed. Dread filled her stomach as she remembered what Captain Blake had said about their training starting today.

They needed to be dressed and ready before dawn.

But what time of day is it?

Devora spun around, searching for any sign of the sun. There were no windows anywhere, just the flickering torches outside of each cell. She didn't even know if it was still the middle of the night. The flapping of wings pulled her attention back to the corner of the cell where the loud crow had returned to his iron-bar perch. He shook his singed feathers and squawked again.

"That didn't take as long as I thought," Nadia said, brushing her hands against one another. She placed her hands on her wide hips and glanced around the cell. "Most of the other cells are taken. Since I don't like being alone, could we be roomies?"

Devora took in the sincerity in Nadia's eyes. Though Devora wasn't sure if sharing a cell with anyone would be a good idea, her gut told her Nadia was not an enemy. Before Devora could say anything further, the crow squawked, and Nadia spun around.

"He's back." She frowned and pulled out her small device.

"No, wait." Devora held up her hands. "I think he's our clock."

Nadia readied her device, closing one eye to aim at the crow. "What?"

"Captain Blake said that training would begin tomorrow—or today—and that we needed to be dressed before dawn for breakfast. I think that crow is here to tell us it's time to start the day."

The crow cawed and fluffed its wings, as if agreeing with Devora.

Nadia narrowed her eyes at the bird but put her device away. "That makes sense."

Devora nodded and rifled through the crumpled uniform on her bed. A wrinkled white tunic and mud-colored pants tumbled from her grasp. She held them up with disbelief.

How am I supposed to wear these?

Rubbing the coarse fabric between her fingers, Devora frowned. This would definitely mar her flawless skin.

What am I going to do without my lotions and perfumes?

"A uniform, huh?" Nadia strode over and grabbed her own pile, holding up an identical set. "Looks like we're twins like those two." She motioned to Reese and Hestia bickering across the hall.

Devora said nothing but continued to inspect the pants. They were awful. No sheen or shine, jewels or colors. Just two pieces of fabric slapped together. One could hardly call them clothes.

"What's wrong?" Nadia asked, examining her own bundle.

"I've only worn dresses."

Pants were for workers and laymen. Definitely not for ladies of her status. Devora had chests and trunks of beautiful, soft dresses at home. Her heart squeezed.

Will I ever return home again?

Just the thought of Mama under house arrest reignited Devora's hatred of Sir Conan.

And what about Papa? Has he had his trial with the king?

"I see." Nadia's brows rose to the top of her narrow forehead. She took out her small notebook, scratched a few lines, then returned it to her pocket. "Well, you can't train in a dress, can you?"

Devora glanced down at her once beautiful, now destroyed, turquoise dress. Sadly, Nadia was right. Even when she was merely walking in Grenly, Devora's dresses tangled beneath her steps. She glanced back up to see Nadia's back facing her.

"Go ahead and put them on." The girl waved her hand behind her head. "The first time is a bit strange. I'll spare you an audience."

Devora wasn't sure why Nadia was being kind, but she was thankful for her new roommate's respect.

Assessing the strange pants once more, Devora slowly placed one leg in. The fabric scratched against her smooth skin, reminding her of the harsh woolen cloak from the carriage. It felt strange on her legs, but she preceded with the other. She pulled the pants up around her waist and they immediately fell to her ankles. Yelping, Devora wrenched them back up.

The sizing was completely off. They would probably fit a giant.

"Try using a belt." Nadia snickered. "Tie something around your waist. It'll keep them up."

Devora raised the pants again and spotted her tattered purple sash. Waddling to the bed, she snatched the sash up and tied it around her waist. Hesitantly, she let go and smiled when the pants stayed in place. At least she had a little color on her outfit now.

Devora quickly removed the rest of her dress and yanked the white shirt of her uniform over her head. The fabric was thin, allowing the chill of the prison to overtake her. Thankfully, she still had her undergarments, but goose-bumps lined her skin. Chattering, Devora tucked the shirt into the pants and folded her arms over her stomach, trying to warm herself from the cool air.

"Finished," Devora said, alerting Nadia she could turn around.

"How did you change so fast?" Devora asked, impressed.

"Practice," Nadia explained, striding to the giant bed. She started hauling the first bed away from the other.

After a few moments of watching her work, Devora realized she should probably offer to help.

"Let me help you," she said, crouching beside Nadia. She cupped her hand under the bed and pulled. The bed was heavier than she thought. Either that, or she was just weak.

How did Hestia and Ida do this by themselves?

With a few more tugs, they secured Nadia's bed back on the side of the wall.

"I just had a brilliant idea for a machine that can move heavy objects." And before Devora could get a word in, Nadia was mumbling away into her notebook.

As Devora stood by the side of the bed, her gaze landed on a pair of black leather boots. Pulling them out, she placed her foot in the worn boot, hating the thick, stretchy fabric. It was not her silk slippers. She noticed the straps around the sides for tightening and tied the boots with a secured knot before standing. Taking a few steps, Devora decided the boots and pants weren't that bad.

"Nice boots," Nadia commented.

Devora snapped her head up to see that the girl had finished her muttering and was strapping on her own boots. Nadia sashayed around the cell and Devora couldn't help but giggle.

"What do you think?" Nadia motioned to herself.

"Hmm." Devora placed her hand on her chin and circled her roommate, assessing her uniform then taking in her own. "It's very brown."

"It's better than my old clothes," Nadia snorted before placing her charcoal, notebook, and the small weapon, in her pants pocket. She made it just in time, too, because once she finished, the door leading to the stairwell opened.

Chapter Ten

Level Two, The Fortress

As Devora and Nadia exited their cell, a yelp sounded from across the hall.

"Ow, ow, ow," Reese groaned as she fled from the cell. "You're hurting me."

"If you would stop griping, I'd be done by now," Hestia said, holding a strip of fabric in her hands. "Now stop complaining and come back here. I haven't finished your braids."

Growling, Reese held her head as Hestia twisted the last stray strands a few more times and tied them off with the fabric.

"Ouch!" Reese cried.

"Oh, stop," Hestia said, smacking her sister's shoulder. "You've done nothing but complain and be rude since we got here."

"I don't see why I need to fix my hair," Reese replied, snapping the abacus beads back and forth. "My calculations conclude that looking pretty won't make me a better soldier."

Hestia rolled her eyes. "Maybe it'll make you a nicer person."

Reese scoffed and turned away, the chinking of her abacus following.

"They look lovely, Reese," Ida added, stroking her own two braids.

A rotund girl with chin-length blonde hair came toward them and sneered. "There's a war going on. Why are you wasting time on hair?"

"My point exactly," Reese agreed.

Hestia scoffed and flicked her hand at the blonde. "Maybe if we all had short, boring hair like you, we could train without fixing it." She ran her thin fingers through her long ebony braids. "Some of us have been blessed with beautiful hair that shouldn't have to suffer these terrible conditions."

The other girls that had joined them snickered, and the rotund girl humphed before stalking away.

"I think you look great," Nadia grinned. She ran a hand through her short bright waves. "I wish I could have those braids."

"I can do tiny braids," Hestia squealed.

As Nadia and Hestia discussed hairstyles, Devora surveyed the other girls in their uniforms. They had been creative on how to fix the large sizes to fit their smaller frames. Ida folded the fabric on her arms to the right length, while Reese and Hestia had tied off the extra fabric with pieces of string. Where they found the string, Devora had no idea.

"You would think they would have some sense not to give everyone the same sized uniform," Hestia commented, tugging at the extra fabric she tucked into her pants. Though she was taller than any of the other girls, the shirt was still enormous. "Does the warden really suspect all women are the same size?"

"It is a bit uncomfortable," Ida added, pulling at her baggy pants.

"At least we all look terrible together!" Nadia said with a grin. She snaked an arm around Devora's and Reese's necks. "Right, girls?"

Devora smiled and heard a few more giggles from behind. Turning, she saw more than a handful of young women had joined the floor that night. Unfortunately, it seemed that all of Tenton's regions were represented.

A throat cleared, and all the girls spun around to face Sir Jacques. A white tunic with tan pants and black boots dressed his slender form. His shaggy blond hair had been combed away from his amused hazel eyes.

"Good morning, ladies," the knight said, bowing deeply. When he straightened, he donned the kind smile he always wore while collecting taxes in Grenly.

"Sir Jacques?" Devora questioned with a frown. "I thought Captain Blake was escorting us to breakfast."

The knight quirked a brow. "I'm sorry to disappoint you, my lady. But Captain Blake had some urgent matters to attend to. Fortunately, he'll be at your training session later today."

The girls behind her giggled, and Devora's cheeks warmed. She hadn't *wanted* Captain Blake to be the one escorting them.

"Please file into line and follow me," Sir Jacques said. "We're already late."

Sir Jacques led them through the iron door at the end of the hall, up another set of stairs, and into the dining facility. As soon as she strode through the door and smelled burnt bread and sweat, Devora knew breakfast was going to be troublesome.

A large, arched room stretched before them. Poorly made wooden tables with benches on either side stood next to one another. As Devora peered closer, she noticed slivers of wood poking out from the benches. With a wince, Devora thought back to the carriage ride and immediately dreaded having to sit on the wooden bench.

At the far corner of the room sat a large iron pot atop a spitting fire. Behind it stood an intimidating brute of a man with spiked black hair. Circles of ink decorated his thick arms as he grasped a long metal ladle. The man grumbled loudly for the next person to come as he stuck the ladle into the pot. The heavy scent of salt and dough billowed through the dining hall. Though it wasn't an alluring aroma, Devora's stomach growled.

Footsteps clacked off the stone walls as a lengthy line of inmates—*soldiers*—held out stone bowls in retrieval of whatever was in the pot. Devora's stomach growled again, and Nadia chuckled.

"Hungry, Dev?" she asked, giving Devora a playful jab in the side. "I know I am."

A few of the other girls murmured their agreement with Nadia. Devora smiled wearily, remembering that she hadn't eaten a full meal since the morning before the Categorization Call. She didn't care what was in the pot. She was starving.

Yet, as they followed Sir Jacques, the weight of the soldiers' stares sent uneasy chills over her body.

If Sir Jacques noticed the men's leering eyes, he said nothing but continued to lead the hesitant group toward the end of the serving line. The knight directed them around the far perimeter of the room, where a small, squared table held stacks of stone bowls.

Reaching out, Devora quickly grabbed a bowl and returned to her place, avoiding the gaze of the inmates. Out of the corner of her eye, the tower of bowls shrank as each girl followed her lead.

"Your pot or no grub," the man with the ladle grumbled. His thick fingers extended toward her.

Devora jumped, not realizing she had reached the front of the line so soon. She tried not to stare, but it was impossible not to. Thick and thin lines of black ink coated the cook's bulging arms. The patterns were immaculate and beautifully painted. She had heard of those who branded their skin but, other than Sir Conan's hands, had never seen it up close.

"I ain't interested in your gawking, young miss," he snapped. Devora jolted at his baritone voice. He motioned down to her stone bowl. "Your pot or move along."

"Oh, yes, sorry." Devora fumbled and brought the bowl to his ladle.

The man huffed as he scooped a hefty slob of white goop into her bowl. While it didn't look horrible, it wasn't enticing. She peered up at the man, who was already shooing her along.

Sighing, Devora said, "Thank you, sir." She turned toward the wooden tables.

Half of the soldiers stared at her while the other half stared at a table in the far-right corner. Relief flooded her as she saw Nadia's bright blonde hair indicating where the rest of the girls had gone while she dawdled.

But her relief soon vanished when she noticed the leering pairs of eyes staring back at her. Others, with their shoulders slumped, kept their heads down and eyes focused on their mush. Just as before, an array of skin tones and sizes flooded the large hall.

Devora wanted to cry out to Tunri to save her from this terrible place, to take her away and imprison her anywhere but here. But she couldn't pray. Tunri wouldn't listen. He hadn't listened when she asked Him to take back His terrible curse. Why would He listen now?

Taking a breath, Devora kept her gaze fixed on the table of girls. She would survive the Fortress with or without Tunri's help.

Just like when the others walked through the dining hall, not even a whisper permeated the room as Devora strode gracefully to the back table. No prisoner touched her, nor did they look away. She caught the eye of a few of the young men from Grenly, but it was nothing more than a quick glance. Niche and the others obediently ate their morning gruel with no tricks or jokes. Their hair had been cropped close to their heads in the same style.

"You made it," Hestia tipped her head to Devora as she slid onto the bench.

Devora sighed with relief, thankful to turn her back on the stares as she sat in across from Hestia and Reese. The angry twin kept her gaze focused on her morning mush, refusing to look Devora in the eye.

Eventually, the prisoners returned to their own meals. The growls and grumbles of murmured conversations soon filled the dining facility, relaxing Devora's tense muscles.

"What *is* this?" Hestia asked, bringing the bowl up to her face and sniffing. She wrinkled her small nose. "It doesn't smell like anything."

"It doesn't taste like anything either," Nadia added as she scooped a bit into a small bowl-shaped object with a handle.

It looked like a spoon, but there was something different about it. Devora watched as the small device carried the food until Nadia popped it into her mouth. Nadia made a disgusted face, then reluctantly swallowed. She squeezed her eyes shut and stuck out her tongue.

"Nadia," Devora said, intrigued. "Is that a spoon?"

Nadia held up the spoon between her round eyes, making them crossed. "This is a *ligula*. Perfect for all kinds of soups, stews, and prison mush. It's like a spoon, but better." Nadia pressed a small button at the bottom of the spoon, and a knife whipped out from the other end.

Devora jerked back in surprise. That's the second weapon she had seen on Nadia.

Nadia has to be a Tinker, but why does she have so many weapons?

"I would like one of those," Ida commented quietly, wringing her fingers in her lap. "I'd feel much safer with it."

"Here." Nadia produced another *ligula* and held it out to Ida with a wink. "I always keep a few, just in case."

Ida nodded in thanks and took the small object in her hand before pressing the button. The knife whipped out, and Ida sat a little taller as a confident smile stretched across her plump lips.

"Just in case of what?" Reese narrowed her gaze at Nadia.

Nadia shrugged and scooped another spoonful of mush onto the *ligula*. "You never know what's going to happen."

After forcing herself to swallow, Nadia offered a ligula to Devora.

"It seems like you're on everyone's bad list, so you may want one, too."

Devora wanted to tell Nadia the soldiers hated her more because she was supposed to be dead. If her being a noble wasn't bad enough, she was a Seer, as well. She had to find a way to collect the herbs for the dung tea. Though she took an extra dose before her Categorization Call, with all the anxiety she endured, she had no idea how fast it would wear off.

"By my calculations, there's an eighty-six point two percent chance you'll need it," Reese offered with a smug grin before Hestia elbowed her in the side. Reese jerked away.

Dread slithered down Devora's back at the statistic and she quickly took the *ligula*. "Thank you, Nadia."

Devora studied the strange object before dipping it into the mush. The metal spoon sunk into the thick white grains before she yanked it out. With a grimace, she brought the mush to her mouth and swallowed. Though the substance tasted like nothing, it ceased the rumbling in her stomach.

After they finished their breakfast, Sir Jacques and Sir Conan stood at the entrance of the dining hall. An immediate silence descended, and all eyes turned to the warden's knights. Sir Conan's right cheek was swollen and when he opened his mouth, a giant gap showed from where he had lost his tooth.

Captain Blake has a serious swing, Devora thought as she and the others faced the knights.

"Training hour is upon us," Sir Jacques announced, his face as hard as stone as he scanned the crowd of prisoners. Devora shrank back at his intimidating stance, wishing she had taken more time to know the knight when he was away from the Fortress. "Those of you new to the Fortress, follow me. The rest will follow Sir Conan to the training grounds."

"Let's go, scrags!" Sir Conan roared, trying to cover the slight whistle his words had due to the missing tooth.

Devora winced at Conan's gravelly voice, but the other prisoners seemed unfazed. Leaving their bowls on the table, they rose and followed Sir Conan through the doorway, heads down–defeated.

The group of new recruits, now lieutenants, obeyed in silence and stood before the knight. Sir Jacques paused, as if unsure he should speak.

"Young recruits," the knight began. "Although, I suppose you are all officers now. I hope you enjoyed your meal. Please follow me." As the group shuffled behind the knight, Sir Jacques spoke again. "I know this is not what any of you desire," he commented softly to the group of boys and girls. "But know that if you are being sent to war, we will make sure you are the best soldiers in Tenton before you go."

The rest of the group's eyes went wide, shocked by Sir Jacques' sympathy and encouragement. But Sir Jacques quickly straightened and turned before marching down the corridor.

Devora's heart warmed at the kindness of the knight. She hated that he had to put on a hard exterior so that Warden Hazor wouldn't harm those he cared for.

But how had Sir Jacques ended up in the Fortress in the first place?

As she followed the knight, Devora realized she didn't know anything about him.

Sir Jacques took the group down the hall and up another set of stairs before they entered yet another stone corridor. Thirty paces from the stairs stood a set of dark wooden doors, waiting to be opened. Sir Jacques marched forward and pulled the metal handles. As soon as the hinges creaked, the scent of dust, sweat, and blood filled the hall.

Devora wrinkled her nose, unfamiliar to the different odors, but quickly realized they shouldn't be combined.

Hestia covered her nose and mouth with her hands. "Ugh, that smells terrible."

"Like those lowly people in Grenly and Yekel," Reese agreed with a nod.

Devora swiveled around. "If you have something to say, then say it."

Reese suddenly yelped and jumped in the air, rubbing her backside.

Nadia stepped out from behind her with a chuckle. "My new invention works! I just needed the right rat to test it on."

Reese whispered curses under her breath but said no more as a series of grunts and groans escaped from the doors.

"I'm not sure about this," Ida whispered, twisting her fingers.

Sir Jacques propped open the doors and motioned the lieutenants into another room.

Devora's brows lifted as she took in the large indoor arena. It was twice the size of the dining hall. A series of weapons and obstacles were splayed around a circular sand-ridden floor. At the far end, a large iron door sat snug between the stone. Glancing up, Devora saw many of the soldiers seated on rows above the sanded area.

Was this room meant for spectators before it was for training? She felt the blood drain from her face, remembering the rumors of Warden Hazor hosting contests in the Fortress.

A man dressed in dark pants and matching black tunic rose from the stands and marched down the stairs. Devora's eyes locked on him and immediately recognized Captain Blake. His stance was different than the others. While most of the soldiers, and even some of the guards, slumped their shoulders and kept their eyes downcast, Captain Blake kept his head high and his eyes forward, strong and confident.

A sharp cry shifted her focus to two men dueling with wooden swords at the far end of the arena. One had struck the foot of the other, causing blood to dribble out onto the sand.

The mush from breakfast churned in Devora's stomach as Ida gave a small squeak. Taking a steadying breath, Devora willed the gruel down. She would have to endure more than the sight of a minor cut if she wanted to survive battle.

"This is going to be fun," Nadia deadpanned.

Devora glanced over at her roommate to see that the jovial quirkiness in her eyes had dimmed.

"This is the Theater of the Fortress," Sir Jacques explained. "It's where you will learn the different skills of combat from hand to hand—" he motioned to two prisoners fighting without any weapons at the far side of the arena— "to self-defense." The knight pointed to two other prisoners fighting, but this time a knight coached them on how to fight. "And close-range dueling." Sir Jacques finished by gesturing to the duel a few feet from them.

Panic welled in Devora's chest as she took in the Theater. *How am I going to survive this?*

The first time she ever used physical violence was when she kicked the prisoner yesterday. She had no idea how to fight or use a weapon. Gripping the sash around her waist, Devora shook the worry from her mind. No, she would learn. She would become the best and save Papa. There was no other option.

The familiar clacking of boots rippled down the stone stairs until the sand muffled their sound. Devora turned and her heart lurched.

"Ah, Captain Blake," Sir Jacques said with a hint of admiration. "Ready to train your new officers?"

Chapter Eleven

Captain Blake clasped his hands behind his back as he paced before the group. His gray eyes analyzed each of them, assessing their potential and capability.

He then pulled a piece of folded parchment from his pocket and handed it to the knight. "Please complete this by the end of the day."

Sir Jacques took the parchment and opened it, his thin brows shooting up before his head jerked to the captain. Whispers tittered among the new lieutenants as Devora studied the silent discussion between the knight and the captain.

Refolding the parchment, Sir Jacques placed a fist over his chest and bowed. "Yes, sir."

As Sir Jacques marched out of the Theater, Devora felt Captain Blake's scrutinizing stare burn into her. She turned her head and matched his gaze, unwilling to let him see that he intimidated her.

The captain's lips twitched in an almost smile before he addressed the officers.

"Line up," he commanded.

The whispers and comments ceased as the new lieutenants scrambled to stand next to one another, doing their best not to appear frightened.

Devora wedged herself between Nadia and Ida, remembering how Captain Blake punched Sir Conan for speaking out of turn. Though she disliked the captain, he had earned her grudging respect.

Captain Blake stalked to the other end of the line. He kept his strong square jaw firm as he studied the blanched faces. Devora peeked around Nadia, watching the confident gait of the captain's long legs. His stride was the exact opposite of Tristan's. While Tristan was all swagger and play, this man was straight lines and order.

"During my Categorization Call, I categorized my stones exactly how I intended to," the captain explained. "Not just three times, like some of you," he glanced to the lieutenants at one end of the line. "But all five times."

A few gasps sounded, but not from Devora. If a participant categorized for any duty all five times, they were completely prepared to accept that position. She had categorized perfectly for Vlacklear Academy all five times. Indignation burbled in Devora's heart. If the king hadn't switched the categorization color orders, she would be able to boast like Captain Blake, as well.

"Do you know what that means?" the captain asked coolly.

No one answered.

The captain started toward Devora's end of the line, and her chest squeezed. "That means that I'm fully capable of my position and can do whatever I desire. No one will question my judgment or decisions."

Nadia tensed and Ida sucked in a breath. But Devora bristled. *Is he threatening us?*

The perfectly shined tips of the captain's ebony boots stopped before her. Devora lifted her gaze and met his scrutinizing stare without fear. He said nothing as he scanned her uniform. Yet his eyes flashed at seeing the purple sash keeping her pants from falling.

"The governor's daughter," he mused. "We meet again."

Devora wasn't sure whether he was mocking her or not. But when she glared into the captain's stormy eyes, she decided to keep quiet. Though, for reasons she couldn't explain, her stomach tied in knots as his hard gaze searched hers.

"Captain," Sir Conan called from the stands.

Captain Blake released an irritated breath and spun around. "Speaking out of turn again, Conan? Need I remind you of what happened last time?"

Sir Conan clenched his jaw and gave a contrived salute. "Permission to speak, sir."

A bemused grin stretched across the captain's face. "Granted."

The knight pointed to Devora's purple sash. "It seems that one of your lieutenants is out of uniform." His words came out lisped. "You know we have a strict code regarding uniforms at the Fortress." Mock reluctance covered Sir Conan's face as he shrugged. "I don't want to have to report this violation to Warden Hazor. Though I do believe it will go under disobedience."

Devora placed her hand on the sash. "You can't have it," she blurted.

She wouldn't allow Sir Conan to take it again. But as she contemplated her words, ice trickled down her spine. What level of the Fortress would she be sent to for disobedience?

Surely not the Behemoth's cell.

The captain's shoulders tensed, but his face stayed composed. Waving his hand, he said, "I'll allow it. Get back to training your soldiers, Conan. They need more assistance than my lieutenants."

With one last glare at Devora, Sir Conan returned to yelling at his soldiers.

Captain Blake suddenly spun to Devora, "I expect you to comply with Fortress and army uniform regulations tomorrow. If you don't, you will be subject to punishment. I will not spare you a second time."

Devora's pulse thundered between her ears. She wanted to tell him she didn't want his protection. She didn't need it. But she knew that was false and nodded. The heat of embarrassment crept up her neck as Captain Blake marched back down the line.

"Tenton has been losing against Kadesh for many years," he explained, returning to the center of the line. "The leadership in our military is dwindling. This is the reason you were brought here. Tenton needs more officers and King Atol has chosen to go to extreme lengths to find them."

Devora clenched her fists. How could the captain be so forward with his words? Papa had always been so careful when speaking with or about King Atol. It was known throughout the kingdom that King Atol didn't like to know all the details of war or what was happening on the front-lines. According to a Grenly gossip column, the king was happy with his frivolous, fickle life and didn't want anything obstructing it. One slip up, and the king could sentence anyone to the dungeon for speaking of it.

Devora's shoulders sagged. But that didn't matter anymore because Papa was already in the king's dungeon, and it was all her fault.

Tears pricked Devora's eyes, but she swallowed them down. She couldn't cry. Especially not here when she was already viewed as weak.

"Though you all lack the basic qualities of an average soldier," the captain continued, "I will make you into the best officers you can be before going to battle."

Nadia leaned over and whispered in Devora's ear. "Did he just tell us we're screwed?"

"Sounds that way," Devora whispered back, gripping the ends of her purple sash. Tunri wouldn't have sent her here just to be slaughter on the battlefield, would He? Did He care at all?

Captain Blake then pulled out a different piece of parchment from his belt. Untying the black ribbon around it, he unrolled the thick paper.

"In addition to your daily training," he began. "You will each be given a job to complete in the evening hours. Honor, integrity, and courage are formed through hard work, and you *will* work harder under my command than you ever have." His eyes roamed over them as if waiting for one of them to object. "I will not accept apathetic degenerates."

A fire of fury burst through Devora's chest. *Who does this man think he is? How dare he talk to us like we're so beneath him?*

Devora opened her mouth but stopped. She *was* beneath him. Glancing down, she stared at the ripped purple sash around her waist. It didn't mean anything anymore. She was no longer Lady Devora Medee, daughter of Governor Cusha Medee of Grenly. She was Lieutenant Medee, a scrag in His Majesty's Army. A nobody.

"You cannot switch tasks with another recruit," Captain Blake continued. "Once your task is assigned, it's yours until we head to battle." He focused back on the parchment and started reading.

"Marcus Winnow, laundry duty," the captain barked.

A small, chubby boy with cropped crimson hair jumped at the call. He quickly put a fist to his chest. "Yes, sir."

"Ida Shabawn, sanitation."

Ida sucked in a sharp breath and bit her lip. Devora could see the tears building in the girl's round eyes, but they didn't fall. Instead, Ida met the captain's gaze and bowed the same as Winnow.

Captain Blake continued to call out the names until he finally got to Devora. "Devora Medee, stables."

Devora bunched her brow. *What stables?*

She hadn't seen any horses or other creatures inside or outside the Fortress—unless she counted the prisoners. Her mind flashed to the memory of the Behemoth in the lowest level of the Fortress. *That couldn't be the stables, could it?*

Chewing on her bottom lip, Devora hesitated. She had seen how Captain Blake reacted to Sir Conan talking out of turn. But how was she meant to complete her job if it didn't exist?

Gathering her courage, Devora cleared her throat. "I haven't seen any stables."

The captain stopped reading off the parchment and glanced up. The rest of the line shrunk back, leaving her to face Captain Blake alone.

Lowering the parchment, Captain Blake focused all his attention on her. "Tell me, Medee, were you brought all the way through the Fortress when you first arrived? Or have you already forgotten the personal tour?"

Devora blanched at the condescending tone before irritation swirled in her stomach. She knew she shouldn't respond. She should bow and cower away like she'd seen the others do. But she couldn't accept the captain talking to her like she was a fool. Flicking her braid over her shoulder, Devora lifted her chin.

"Yes, I remember it quite well. There were no stables or animals here other than that creature in the basement."

The soldiers training in the Theater stopped and watched the pair.

Captain Blake rolled the parchment and stuck it back in his belt before taking four strong strides to stand in front of her. He was so close she could smell his musky scent of iron and wood. It wasn't sweet, like Tristan, but still made Devora's pulse race. Or maybe that was the apprehension crawling in her stomach.

Now that he loomed over her, Devora hadn't realized how tall the captain was. At more than a foot taller than her, he easily towered over her frame.

"I'm only going to say this once," he said, his voice low. "I will be addressed as Captain Blake or Sir, and you will not speak out of turn again. Do I make myself clear?"

The threat in his voice vibrated through her spine down to her toes. Devora swallowed, lowering her gaze. She had never been spoken to that way, and it frightened her. The last thing she wanted was to be punished.

"Yes, sir," she ground out through clenched teeth. Keeping her gaze on the sand, she didn't look up until the strong clank of Captain Blake's boots walked away.

"The stables are through Level Five and the basement. I advise you to be quick about your job, Medee. We wouldn't want any accidents to happen," the captain said.

Devora locked her jaw to stay silent.

Once Captain Blake finished assigning the lieutenants their tasks, he addressed the group again. "As Jacques informed you before, there are three combat techniques we teach our soldiers and officers: hand-to-hand combat, weaponized combat, and self-defense. By the end of your six-week training here, you will have mastered them all."

Devora's throat tightened. *Six weeks?*

That was no time at all. Six weeks and she would be battling Kadeshians and their terrifying iron-armored creatures.

A thumping sounded from the hallway, followed by the chink of chains dragging against the stone. The ground quaked beneath the lieutenants' feet, and they all held on to one another for support. Suddenly, the door to the Theater burst open, revealing the giant who attacked Devora's caravan.

Six guards held the chains wrapping around the large man: one for each leg and two for each arm. Devora studied the rusted links, noticing the extra thick cuffs made of a shined stone around the giant's wrists.

Back in Grenly, Devora had many beautiful rings and jewels that Papa bought for her birthday each year. Tristan's engagement ring flashed in her mind, but she shoved it away.

Yet out of all the jewelry she had, she'd never seen stone like the manacles binding the giant. *Are they for stopping his earth manipulation power?*

"Captain Blake, sir," one of the armored knights with flaming red hair said as he marched up to the captain.

He bowed deeply and Devora bit her tongue. *So, that's the subservient attitude the captain wants.*

It was going to be a lot harder to comply than she thought.

"Babshee, as you requested," the knight said.

"Thank you, Sir Tocha." The captain gave the giant a once over before facing the lieutenants. "This is Babshee the Horrid. He's a Kadeshian deserter that Sir Conan and his men captured in the eastern region."

Devora bit her tongue harder. A metallic taste swirled in her mouth as she swallowed her rebuttal. Sir Conan could have all the glory if he really needed it. Even though his victory was because of her.

"*Ishrah!*" Babshee spat at the captain. "If your king hadn't started this bloody war, there would be no need for deserters! So many of my people are gone because of your foolish king!"

Devora blinked in surprise and nudged Ida. "Has he always known our language?"

Ida shrugged and whispered, "Giants come from all over Tenton and Kadesh. He could easily know many languages."

Captain Blake turned to Sir Tocha, his face void of emotion. "Restrain him."

Sir Tocha tugged the chain and a zapping sound buzzed from Babshee's wrists. Yellow sparks jutted off the stone cuffs and the giant howled, slamming to his knees. The ground trembled again, and Devora grabbed Nadia's shoulder to steady her stance.

Captain Blake nodded to the knight. "In order for me to decide where to begin our training, I need to know how much combat experience you have."

Panic coiled around Devora's throat. She had absolutely no combat experience whatsoever. Ever since she received her categorization stones, she had been training her *mind* for Vlacklear, not her muscles. Devora looked down at her thin, lanky arms. This wasn't going to be good.

"You will have three minutes to show me everything you can do regarding fighting," the captain continued, pulling out a blank piece of parchment and a rod of charcoal. "It doesn't have to be pretty, but hopefully effective." He scribbled something down. "Your opponent will be Babshee. He will stay chained to avoid fatalities."

The young lieutenants released a collective gasp as the knights holding Babshee extended the giant's chains. Babshee growled but complied and stomped to the dark brown mat in the center of the Theater. The rest of the soldiers that had been training filed out of the Theater and relocated to the seats above.

Devora wanted to throw up. *Fighting against a giant?*

Even with Babshee chained, he could easily squash her. She glanced from the captain to the mat. *What is this crazy man thinking? How could any of us have a chance against a giant?*

Mind reeling, Devora suddenly realized that Captain Blake was trying to familiarize them with the enemy. Because most giants fled to Kadesh, none of the lieutenants had ever seen one. By having them face Babshee first thing, the remaining combat trainings wouldn't seem as difficult.

Very strategic, Captain, she thought.

But as soon as the compliment floated through her mind, she wanted to take it back because right then, Captain Blake glanced up from his parchment with a conniving smirk.

"Because of your noble status, Medee, you're first."

Chapter Twelve

The Theater, The Fortress

"What?" Devora exclaimed, her feet plastered to the ground. "You can't be serious."

When she still attended lessons with her peers, Devora always had the best marks in her class. That never helped her with making friends, but she was always the first one to turn in her assignments and receive the best rewards for them. But now she didn't want to be first. She'd give anything to be last.

"Did I ask for your opinion?" the captain barked. "Move!"

Devora squealed and rushed to the mat. Her heels barely grazed the edge as she stood as far away from Babshee as possible.

Cackles rained upon her. Devora glanced toward the stands, her eyes meeting the mocking gaze of Sir Conan. His thin lips twisted into a wicked grin.

Before Devora could dwell on the cynical knight, Captain Blake's voice boomed through the Theater. "Begin!"

"Come here, *ya nadai*!" Babshee lunged forward.

Devora didn't have time to scream before the giant grabbed her waist and tossed her onto the thin leather mat.

Bright splotches of light burst in her vision as pain pierced her back. Her head smacked against the hard floor, teeth jamming shut. Devora was too stunned to even cry out. Gasping for air, she held back tears, blinking slowly until they disappeared.

"Come on, *nadai*. Are ya goin' ta fight back?" Babshee sneered through his red beard. Droplets of spittle rained on her face and hands.

Devora didn't respond, too focused on trying to regain the feeling in her limbs to stand.

"Enough with the name-calling, Babshee," Blake called, his voice back to its cool commanding tenor. "Get-up, Medee. If you were in battle, you'd be dead."

"I'd rather be dead," Devora muttered, but made her way to stand, her muscles screaming in protest.

"Again," Blake commanded, scratching his observations on the parchment.

Babshee went for her again. Only this time, a chilled sensation fluttered behind Devora's eyes. A vision of the giant grabbing her arms flashed through her mind a split second before Babshee moved. Devora quickly dodged the giant's sweaty palms and sprinted between his hairy legs to escape.

"Aye, where'd ya go?" The giant twisted around his shoulder.

Another vision of Babshee reaching around his waist with his left hand and grabbing Devora's legs appeared in her thoughts. As the giant made for her feet, Devora leaped over his hand, retreating to the other side of the mat.

Panting, Devora wiped the sweat matting her brow. She hadn't been moving that much. It must be the rapid use of her Seeing ability that was exhausting her. Never had she been able to summon her visions on command. If she wasn't prompting them, who was?

Is this Tunri's doing? Why is Tunri helping me now? He never has before.

Devora dodged the next round of Babshee's attacks, all while feeling Captain Blake's judgmental gaze trail her.

The Theater had grown silent as the other soldiers watched the fight. Nothing but the sound of Devora's scuffling feet and Babshee's curses echoed against the hard stone walls.

"Ah, I see what's going on here," the giant cackled, a cruel grin spreading across his large mouth. "*Ya se fisi.*"

Devora's heart jumped to her throat. *Has he discovered my secret? Have my eyes turned purple?* She had no way of checking without raising suspicion.

Before she could blink, Babshee ripped the chains out of the knights' grasps. He wrenched the iron shackles off his ankles and then the shining stone manacles off his wrists. A powerful aura billowed from the giant and Devora's blood went cold.

Wriggling his fingers, Babshee faced the stones of the outer wall of the training arena. Instantly they trembled. "If *ya fisi* gets to use her powers, then so do I."

"Get those irons back on him, now!" Captain Blake shouted, throwing down his parchment.

Everything around Devora slowed as the captain sprint-ed toward her. The knights clamored to gain control over Babshee, but it was too late. A pile of stones, taller than her head, spun toward Devora, flying too fast for her to dodge. Though everyone had the power to manipulate the small pebbles for the Categorization Call, only giants could command rocks and boulders as they pleased. In only a moment, Babshee's powers had pinned her to the side of the Theater. Gray stones covered her hands and feet, squeezing her bones together.

Devora struggled against the cold rocks but couldn't break free. She waited for Babshee to finish her off, but the giant had other plans. Lifting his hands, Babshee slammed his fists on the ground. A large snap reverberated off the circular walls as a crack zigzagged across the Theater's floor. The soldiers in the stands scrambled in every direc-tion, fleeing from the crazed giant.

Babshee raised his hands again and Devora knew the Theater couldn't take another blow without causing se-vere damage. As the giant brought his arms down, Captain Blake lunged forward and clapped a shining stone manacle around one of the giant's wrists. Babshee's powerful aura immediately dissipated from the air, allowing the captain to secure the other manacle in place. As if on command, the stones holding her captive plummeted to the ground and Devora fell with them. Pain ricocheted through her knees as she crashed and skidded onto the hard floor.

Slowly, Devora sat up and rubbed her wrists, knees throbbing. *Did anyone hear what Babshee said?* Though she didn't speak the giant's language, she was confident a "fisi" meant Seer. She prayed everyone in the Theater had been too caught up in the giant's attack to listen to his words.

Captain Blake's shoulders heaved as he locked the stone manacles and chains around Babshee's wrists.

"Take him to his cell," he demanded.

Babshee didn't fight when the knights pulled him away. Instead, his head and his shoulders shuddered, almost as if he were crying. Though Devora was frightened of the giant, the scene tugged at her heart. The manacles around his wrists had taken away his power. She glanced down at her own hands. Though she didn't want her Sight, it had always been a part of her.

"Medee," Captain Blake called, his tone gentler than before.

Devora froze and cautiously met the captain's gaze. Stopping before her, the captain extended his hand. Devora jerked back to defend from the strike before realizing he was offering to help her stand. When she faced him again, regret raced across his angular features before it disappeared.

Reaching out, Devora grabbed his calloused palm and stood. Her hand was so small and smooth compared to his. Flutters erupted in her stomach, and she quickly released the captain's hand.

"Good work," he said, gruffly. "I didn't know the governor's daughter could anticipate attacks so well."

Me either, she wanted to reply, but decided to stay quiet. She had already aroused enough suspicion.

Devora had never processed her visions so fast. Though she was exhausted, and her muscles were on fire, it was exhilarating. Maybe Tunri hadn't forgotten her after all.

But her excitement at her new discovery was trampled as soon as Captain Blake spoke again.

"Your defense was mediocre at best. I expect you to improve." He stalked toward the other lieutenants who were scattered around the Theater. "Line up!"

Too tired to be offended, Devora hobbled to where the other lieutenants stood. Pain singed her limbs with every movement. All she wanted to do was lie down.

"Though Medee did well, she has spoken out of turn several times," the captain began. "Because of this, you will all assist in cleaning up the giant's mess. Then, starting today and every day after, you will give me seventy laps around the Theater after one hundred sets of core exercises."

The lieutenants stood shocked before grumbling and shooting nasty glares toward Devora.

"Sorry," Devora whispered under her breath, twisting her sash in her hands.

"I'll find a new opponent for the rest of you to test your skills against," Captain Blake continued. "You will start your jobs this evening. I will see you tomorrow." He gave them all a once over before directing a group of knights with cement and stone to repair the Theater floor.

"Medee," Captain Blake said, keeping his face trained forward as he stopped in front of her. "Go to the infirmary. Lapith will escort you. Once you receive treatment, I want you both back here with the others. Understood?"

"Yes, sir." Devora nodded, keeping her focus on her scuffed boots.

As soon as the captain was gone, Hestia, Ida and Nadia gathered around her. Reese hung behind but stayed close enough to eavesdrop.

"Are you okay?" Ida asked with wide eyes, grasping Devora's hands.

Devora nodded. "Just tired."

"You were amazing," Nadia exclaimed. "I jotted down all your moves." She patted her pants pocket where her notebook made its home.

"That guy is insane!" Hestia said, throwing her hands in the air.

Ida nodded in agreement, studying the blue bruises forming on Devora's wrists. "But why would he put new soldiers against a giant?"

Reese fidgeted with the abacus. "By my calculations, you should've been beaten to a pulp, Devora."

"Reese," Hestia groaned, dragging her hands down her face.

"I'm glad your calculations were wrong, Reese." Devora smirked, cradling her tender wrist. "But I think the captain wanted us to take the war seriously."

The girls blinked in surprise.

"You understand that barbarian?" Hestia blurted.

Devora's heart thudded against her rib cage as she explained, "Past Tentonian commanders have used similar tactics. When their soldiers face the real enemy, they won't panic." She paused, remembering her readings from *Tentonian War Tactics.* "In battle, we'll probably have to face giants. Captain Blake wanted to shock us initially so that our other training doesn't seem as intense."

"Unfortunately, that does make sense." Reese tapped the abacus on her narrow chin. The metal beads chinked back and forth. "I'm just glad you're the one he chose to get beat up."

Devora rolled her eyes, too tired to reply.

The rest of the girls and the other new recruits joined the clean-up crew that was repairing the crack in the floor.

Nadia offered Devora her arm, "Come on. Let's get you to the infirmary."

Devora's shoulders relaxed as Nadia helped her limp down the hall. They soon reached the infirmary where the medic gave her a pain-reducing balm and wrapped her bruised ribs.

As Nadia sat with her, she commented, "You know, not everyone faces a giant and lives to talk about it. I think people will be super impressed with you now." She gave a sparkling grin. "Maybe you'll start to get fans."

Devora laughed, realizing Nadia was right. Amazingly, she was still alive. Maybe, Tunri really was there and finally wanted to help.

The dinner gruel sat like a rock in her stomach as Devora limped toward the stairwell to Level Five. Her bandaged fingers ached as she gripped the *ligula,* its knifed end pointed out. If she had to venture to Level Five alone, she wasn't going to be completely defenseless.

The doughy scent of the dining hall fled the air as she hurried as best she could, ready to complete her job. She didn't want to spend any more time in the lower levels than was necessary.

Groans and whispers seeped from the cells as Devora passed. With every noise she jumped and scrambled away from the sounds. Finally, she reached Level Five. The large iron door was closed shut except for three spaces carved into the top. As she reached for the metal handle, a familiar voice paused her hand.

"You're never so cruel to your soldiers, especially new lieutenants. What was that today in the Theater with Lady Devora?" Sir Jacques' voice questioned.

Swallowing, Devora pressed her ear to the cool metal door. *Who was Sir Jacques talking to?* She had never heard the knight so riled up before.

"I can't allow nobility to be treated any differently than the other soldiers," Captain Blake replied.

"You made her go first, knowing she would be defense-less," Jacques scolded. "She could've died, Matthias. All of your new recruits could've died fighting Babshee. Is that what you wanted?"

Devora's heart warmed. Though she'd never had romantic feelings for Sir Jacques, she was thankful *someone* defended her. Captain Blake certainly had an issue with her, and it was good he was being challenged for his decisions.

She realized Sir Jacques hadn't called Captain Blake by his title like everyone else, but by his first name. *Matthias.*

Devora hated that she liked how masculine and heroic the name sounded.

Are Sir Jacques and Captain Blake friends?

"That would've been...regrettable," the captain answered.

Devora reared back and glared at the door. *That's it? Her dying would be 'regrettable?' Or was he referring to all of his recruits dying being 'regrettable?'*

But Captain Blake wasn't done. "Your chivalry will get the better of you, Jacques," he scolded. "These recruits, including the women, are meant to be soldiers, and I'm meant to train them to be the best. Though I don't agree with females on the frontline, I don't want them to lose their lives because I was too soft." The captain's words flew at Sir Jacques before the knight could reply. "Do you have feelings for Lady Devora, Jacques? Is that why you care for her so much?"

Devora's breath hitched as her name and title rolled from the captain's lips. His tone wasn't condescending as before, but there was a genuine desire to know the answer.

"Matthias," Sir Jacques groaned, and Devora wished she could see what was happening between the two men. "We've been over this. She only has eyes for that criminal brother of yours. Plus, I could never be with anyone else after what happened to Helene."

Devora bit her lip, heat blossoming in her cheeks. *How dare Sir Jacques gossip about me? And to Captain Blake of all people.*

"Did you ever warn her about him?" Captain Blake inquired.

There was no response from Sir Jacques, so Devora assumed the knight nodded. She remembered his warning when she first started seeing Tristan.

If only I had listened.

"And she still went to see him?" the captain asked, his voice laced with disbelief.

Silence sounded, and Devora knew Sir Jacques nodded again.

Devora's heart sank. *Is that another reason why Captain Blake dislikes me? Because I was a fool?*

She stared down at her ratty boots, her feet and ankles bandaged beneath the worn leather. She *was* a fool. She had seen through Tristan's charade long before he had found another woman, but she willingly ignored it. Devora shook her head, disgusted with herself.

"That still doesn't explain why you singled her out," Sir Jacques countered, bringing Devora's focus back to the conversation. The silence between the two men stretched for so long, she thought they had left the hall.

"You wouldn't understand," Captain Blake finally answered, his voice low, defeated.

"We both fought through the Fortress ranks," Sir Jacques said. "Plus, we've been friends since before that. What wouldn't I understand?"

Pulse pounding, Devora smashed her ear against the biting metal. *Sir Jacques and Captain Blake had been in the Fortress? Did that mean they were both criminals? Or was it only a job?*

"It's not polite to eavesdrop," a deep baritone voice said from behind.

Devora leaped in the air, screaming before plastering her back against the iron door. Pointing the sharp end of the *ligula* out, her eyes traveled up the man hovering over her. Her throat constricted as she took in his massive height and long, lanky limbs. He wasn't as tall as a giant, but he may as well have been.

Bending his neck to look down at her, the man's charcoal locks flattened as he cocked his head to the side. Thick iron shackles hung around his thin, white wrists, matching the ones around his ankles. He clasped a bowl of white mush from dinner in his long fingers. But what really set Devora back were his onyx eyes, piercing straight into her own.

"Lady Devora?" Sir Jacques asked before the door whipped open.

Devora didn't have enough time to react before she fell straight on her rump. Pain smacked her backside as her face grew hot.

"Ow," she said, squeezing her eyes shut. She couldn't bear to meet the eyes staring down at her.

"Are you all right?" Sir Jacques asked.

When Devora opened her eyes, she saw a tanned hand reaching down to her. Without thinking, she gripped the calloused palm and stood.

"Thank yo—" she began before she saw that it was Captain Blake who had helped her.

She quickly pulled her hand away and dusted off her oversized pants. Flipping her braid over her shoulder, she looked the other way.

A twinge of guilt pricked her heart. Captain Blake was only trying to help, and he was right that she had been a fool about Tristan. But she was a fool no longer. Helping or not, the captain still set Babshee on her, and that was unforgivable.

Out of the corner of her eye, Devora saw Captain Blake's hand curl into a fist before he placed it by his side.

"One Shot," Sir Jacques said, bringing their attention back to the tall, thin man in the doorway. "Why aren't you in your cell?"

The man ducked further to fit through the doorway before stretching to his full height. Devora took a step back, her back brushing into Captain Blake's hard chest.

When did he move behind me?

She shuffled away then focused back on the prisoner. He had to be *at least* part giant.

"I wanted seconds," One Shot stated simply, striding past Sir Jacques. "Good evening." He nodded at Devora then continued to the farthest cell on the right of Level Five.

Devora followed the prisoner's slow, easy steps. *That man is a murderer?*

"How did he get out?" Captain Blake questioned, watching the lean man open his cell door and shuffle inside.

Sir Jacques shrugged, lifting his arms up while making a confused face. Devora giggled, missing the knight's animated side.

"Lady Devora," Sir Jacques bowed before grabbing Devora's hand and kissing it. "It's so good to see you unharmed after today's events."

Shock froze Devora's thoughts as she shook her head and gently pulled her hand away. "There's no need for that, Sir Jacques. I'm a prisoner here, just like everyone else." She motioned to the cells around her and couldn't help noticing Captain Blake flinch at her words. "But thank you. I'm thankful that Tunri decided to protect me today." Devora blinked, surprised that she actually *was* thankful for Tunri giving her foresight against Babshee.

"You're not a prisoner, Medee," Captain Blake clipped, straightening his stance. "You're a soldier, training to be an officer. It may not seem like an honorable position in your eyes, but it is to those of us who've had to work for it." Devora's lips parted as the captain glowered at Sir Jacques. "Make sure One Shot's cell is secured and he can't escape again," he growled through clenched teeth.

"Yes, sir!" Sir Jacques snapped his heels together and placed his fist over his chest. A wry grin danced upon his lips as they watched the captain stomp away.

Chapter Thirteen

Level Five, The Fortress

"What was *that*, Sir Jacques?" Devora asked, her skin tingling from where the knight kissed her hand.

Sir Jacques had just said he didn't have feelings for her, and then he *kissed her hand* in front of Captain Blake.

Sir Jacques ran a hand through his sandy blond hair before chuckling. "Ah, yes, I apologize. I was trying to prove a point to Matt-er-Captain Blake and unfortunately had to use you as an example." He bowed his head then gave her a gentle smile. "Forgive me?"

"Of course," Devora replied, enjoying seeing the Sir Jacques she befriended.

Sir Jacques' playful grin vanished. "I truly am sorry about what happened this morning, Lady Devora. If I could have stopped it, I would have."

"It's not your fault." Devora peered down at her palms. Thick healing ointment blobbed around the bandages covering her hands. Thankfully they weren't too injured, but her back was almost entirely blue from bruises. "I'm happy that Captain Blake stepped in when he did."

Though she didn't want to admit it, it was true. If Captain Blake hadn't stopped Babshee, the giant would've probably killed her and everyone else in the Theater. Of course, it was Captain Blake's fault in the first place that she and the others were in that situation at all.

Devora shook her head. "I'm also thankful that you're here."

Sir Jacques returned her smile and offered her his arm before the two strode through Level Five.

The murderers weren't as lively and vicious as her first trip here and Devora was thankful for that. Though the cells were quiet, she still gripped Sir Jacques' arm tightly. How silly she probably looked in her military training uniform as the knight escorted her through the hall. It wasn't as if they were going to a ball, and she was in one of her lavish dresses. Yet she clung to his arm all the same.

"If you squeeze any tighter, I'll lose my arm," Sir Jacques laughed.

She quickly unlatched her nails from the knight's lean bicep. "I'm sorry."

"I was the same way when I first got here," he chuckled before leading her toward the stairwell to the lowest level of the Fortress.

"Sir Jacques, why are you here?" Devora asked before rephrasing the question. "I mean, how did you get here?"

They stepped down a few stairs toward the basement before he answered.

"I decided I wanted a different path in life from the one I was given."

Devora quirked a brow, ready to probe further until she reached the final step and saw the giant iron doorway.

Fear danced through her heart. *The Behemoth. Will I have to care for the creature in the basement?*

"Devora," Sir Jacques said, placing his hand over her own. "What's wrong?"

Devora eyed the door, and a guttural growl rumbled from within the cell. A shudder ran down her spine. "That's the monster. The Behemoth."

Sir Jacques shifted his gaze from her to the door. "Yes, but it's subdued right now." He patted her hand. "It won't hurt you. Come, I'll show you where the stables are."

Devora quickened her steps as they crossed in front of the Behemoth's cell, dragging Sir Jacques with her. She wanted to leave the basement as soon as possible. Yet, as the two of them rounded the corner, a gentle whisper swirled from the Behemoth's cell bars.

Help me.

Whipping her head around, Devora's long braid wrapped around her neck as she stared at the monstrous door.

Is the Behemoth talking to me? Again?

She waited a few moments, blinking at the large door before Sir Jacques called out to her.

"Lady Devora? Are you all right?"

Swallowing, Devora raced away from the monster, wanting nothing to do with it.

As soon as Devora reached the knight, Sir Jacques placed two metal buckets at her feet. He then plucked a giant metal hook with a leather handle from the wall and dipped it into a metal icebox. After he fished around, he pulled out a bleeding piece of raw meat.

Devora staggered back, her stomach churning at the bloody piece. She covered her nose and mouth with her hands so she wouldn't vomit.

"What is that?" she managed to say, gagging before covering her nose and mouth again.

"Part of your job," Sir Jacques said with a wince as he slapped the piece of meat in the bucket.

Devora kept her nose covered and held her breath as she peered inside the box. Thick slabs of raw meat—oozing blood— piled on top of one another. She almost retched the white gruel from dinner.

"Hunting is one of Warden Hazor's favorite hobbies. It's actually how he found the Behemoth." Sir Jacques flung slabs of meat into the metal buckets. "Your job is at the stables. That means you get to take care of Warden Hazor's hunting wolves."

"What?" Devora squeaked as Sir Jacques finished layering the meat.

While the people of Grenly had to deal with vipers and tigers, Devora would take them any day to dealing with wolves. From her lessons in *Tenton: The Northern Region*, she remembered reading how vicious the northern pack animals could be.

Sir Jacques cleaned the hook with a rag before grabbing a torch from the wall and setting the fabric on fire.

"Why are you doing that?" Devora cried, jerking away from the flaming cloth. It only took a few moments for the fire to burn the rag to ash.

"Fire purifies," Sir Jacques explained as he stomped out the glowing embers. "Animal meat can carry a number of diseases. The intense heat kills them." He then held the hook above the flame until the metal glowed red.

Devora stared at the shining metal, remembering when she and Papa had visited the jeweler in Grenly, Master Riggs. Papa would always buy Devora a new piece of jewelry for her birthday during the early spring season. However, when they went earlier this year, Master Riggs was busy creating a crown for Queen Leza. The jeweler explained that the queen personally sought him to create a diadem for her to wear at Princess Haden's eighteenth birthday ball.

As Master Riggs had showed them the silver he was melting for the crown, Devora expected it to be shining and beautiful. But instead, there was a thick black sludge coating the top.

"Silver must be refined and purified before it can be beautiful," Master Riggs said when she curled her lip at the filthy metal. "The heat from the fire will draw out the impurities."

Because Master Riggs had been occupied with the queen's request, Devora never received a piece of jewelry for her birthday. Tristan's engagement ring resurfaced in her thoughts, and Devora shooed it away, thinking of the silver vat instead. *Refined through fire*, was the inscription Master Riggs chiseled into all his pieces so his customers would know their jewelry had been purified of all impurities.

The memory nudged Devora's heart and she thought of how she had treated Ida and all the others in Lower Grenly. *Do I need to be purified?*

The metal hook clanged softly against the stone as Sir Jacques hung it back on the wall, and Devora refocused on her job.

"I'll carry this one, but that one is all yours." He took one bucket, leaving Devora to carry the other one.

Bile rose in her throat, but she shoved it down. Holding her breath, Devora grabbed the thin metal handle with both hands and followed Sir Jacques down the corridor to another door. Once she stood by his side again, the knight grabbed a key from his belt and unlocked the door. Devora gasped as the cool evening breeze slapped her face. She hadn't realized how much she craved the outside air, even if it was brittle.

Devora stepped out into the frigid night, the chill racing straight through the thin fabric of her uniform. Goose-bumps rose on her flesh, but she welcomed the cleansing air.

Barren land stretched out in all directions until it was disrupted by the magnificent castle in the distance—Vlacklear Academy. The beautiful white building stood not even a half day's ride away. The future she craved, that she trained so hard for, was right before her and she couldn't reach it.

Devora paused, her mind churning with a new possibility. Maybe she could make a run for it. She didn't want to harm Sir Jacques, but if she swung the heavy bucket exactly right, it could possibly knock him out, and she could flee this terrible place. Her heart twisted at the thought. How horrible for her to think of harming Sir Jacques just to get out of the Fortress. He had been nothing but kind and offered to give his life for her when the warden asked. Plus, even if she did succeed in escaping, where would she go?

"Lady Devora," Sir Jacques called.

Devora banished plans of escape from her mind. With a sigh, she shuffled over to find the knight standing in front of a wooden shack thirty paces away from the Fortress. Placing the bucket down, Devora found her gaze wandering back to Vlacklear's shimmering castle.

The knight followed her line of sight and his shoulders fell. "The wolves will sense your fear and attack you if you try to run. Many prisoners have tried and died. The warden likes to set his wolves free when an inmate tries to escape." Sir Jacques's face turned red. "Not that you're an inmate. You're an officer." He saluted her with a smirk.

Devora knew he was trying to lighten the heavy tension, but after seeing Vlacklear and hearing that the wolves would happily eat her, she was in no mood to laugh.

Sir Jacques licked his lips before facing the shack. One hand gripped the wooden handle of the door, while the other held the metal bucket. "Now, you need to be quick when doing this."

Before she could respond, Sir Jacques wrenched open the slatted door, tossed the contents of one bucket in, then the other, and slammed it shut. He latched the lock with intense speed and leaned his back against the doorway, breathing a sigh of relief.

Barks and growls bled through the panels as the wolves devoured their meal. The gruel rose in Devora's stomach again, and this time she couldn't keep it down. Turning away from Sir Jacques, she vomited her dinner on the ground.

"Lady Devora!" Sir Jacques cried, running to her side. He gently lifted her braid so it wouldn't get in the way.

Devora kept her face down. How disgusting and rude of her to vomit in Sir Jacques' presence. He already knew of her foolishness with Tristan. What would he think of her now?

A perfectly white handkerchief entered her vision. She glanced up to see Sir Jacques' brows furrowed with concern as she straightened.

"Thank you," Devora mumbled, taking the handkerchief. She coughed a few times into the soft cloth before wiping her mouth. "I'm not sure if you want this back."

The knight laughed. "You can keep it. I have others."

Sir Jacques escorted her back inside the Fortress where he showed her how to wash and purify the metal meat buckets.

"The wolves don't need to be fed every day, so you can come down here every few days and it will be fine," he explained as they took the stairs to Level Two.

"Have you cared for the wolves all this time?" Devora inquired.

Sir Jacques shrugged, his easy demeanor back in place. "On and off. The other knights and I would rotate responsibilities when we weren't away from the Fortress. Sometimes I would take my time returning from collecting taxes in Grenly, so I wouldn't have to clean the cells." Sir Jacques sighed, and Devora laughed. "But now that Blake has his job system, a lot of our other duties are being taken by the new lieutenants." He peered over at her with a grin. "Which we're not *too* upset about."

A small smile crept across Devora's lips as they reached her cell. Nadia sat on the floor with various items sprawled around her in a semicircle. Hestia and Ida sat opposite of her, poking and prodding the different tools and weapons. Reese sat on the bed with her back turned, trying to ignore them. But every once in a while, she would peek over her shoulder. Strangely, Devora's heart swelled at seeing them. If she had fled the Fortress, she would've left them all behind.

"What's this?" Ida asked, holding two needles attached by a wire up to her eyes.

"That's one of my favorites." Nadia grasped one needle in her hand and flicked her wrist. The other needle soared through the air before wrapping around the bars of the cell door. Sir Jacques jerked away as the needle came within an inch of his leg.

"Whoa," Hestia said, not acknowledging Sir Jacques' and Devora's presence. "Charles would love that."

"Charles?" Reese asked, giving her sister a skeptical look over her shoulder. "Are you fraternizing with the lower class again?" But Hestia had already returned her attention to a metal sling.

"It can also be used to pierce an enemy," Nadia continued. "One end can puncture through the skin, and then you can reel it back and impale again." She tugged on the string, and the needle released, retracting to the foot-length size it was before. Nadia's eyes suddenly got wide. "Although, if I change one side to be a handle and the other the be a thicker needle, it could do more damage." She handed the weapon back to Ida and excitedly whipped out her notebook and charcoal stick. Her murmurs soon filled the cell as Ida blanched.

"I'm not sure that's the right fit for me," Ida confessed quietly, pushing the weapon away. Her fingers found the long sleeves of her tunic, and she started fidgeting.

"Technically, you're not supposed to have any of this," Sir Jacques informed as he and Devora stepped into the cell.

Hestia squealed and dove under the bed while Reese pretended to focus on her abacus. Ida blushed upon noticing Sir Jacques, lowering her eyes to her lap. Nadia kept scribbling, consumed by her ideas.

At their reactions, the knight laughed heartily. "Not to worry, ladies. We'll keep this our little secret." He winked at Ida, and she blushed even harder.

Sir Jacques faced Devora. "Tonight is the last night I can help you, Lady Devora." A hint of regret filled his voice as he ran a hand through his shaggy blond hair. "I'm thankful Captain Blake didn't mind you eavesdropping, but if it were Conan or another knight, he would've accused you of espionage. Unfortunately, to keep you safe, I must keep my distance."

Disappointment sat like a rock in Devora's stomach, but she nodded. "I understand."

Sir Jacques placed a hand on her shoulder, his hazel eyes stern. "You're strong like your parents. I know you'll get through this."

He focused back on the different weapons and tools Nadia had sprawled out and crouched down. Rubbing his pointed chin, Sir Jacques reached out and grabbed the needles Ida had pushed away.

"I think this is the perfect fit for you," Sir Jacques said, giving Ida a wide grin. He gestured to her arm. "May I?"

Ida peered up through her long lashes and nodded. Sir Jacques wrapped the weapon around her small wrist and carefully tucked the needles between the wires, transforming it into a thin bracelet.

"There." Sir Jacques' hands lingered on Ida's skin a bit longer than necessary. "It's the perfect place to conceal a weapon like that."

"Thank you," Ida whispered, running her fingers along the wire bracelet.

Devora watched Nadia and Hestia share a look before Sir Jacques stood.

"Well, good night, ladies." He cast another glance at Ida before leaving the cell.

"Sir Jacques, wait," Devora called, jogging to catch up with him. The knight glanced over his shoulder. "Have you heard any news of Papa? Are he and Mama safe?"

Her heart thrummed as she waited for his reply.

Turmoil swirled in Sir Jacques' gaze. "I'll see what I can find out," he replied quietly before bidding her goodnight once more.

When Devora returned to the cell, Nadia glanced up from her work on the metal device in her hands. "So, is there anything I should know about with you and Sir Jacques?" She waggled her blonde brows.

Devora snorted and shook her head.

"He's kind of pale," Reese commented, rolling a wooden wheel between her fingers. "And skinny."

"Maybe he's Ida's lover," Hestia snickered.

They all turned to the timid girl sitting cross-legged on the ground. Her fingers hadn't left the wire around her wrist since Sir Jacques had placed it there. "I think he's nice," she said finally.

"And gorgeous!" Hestia added, pulling back the leather of the sling and snapping it. "Captain Blake is nice to look at, but after today, I wish Sir Jacques would train us."

Reese rolled her eyes while Nadia laughed.

"Why don't you talk to Sir Jacques more, Ida?" Nadia probed.

"Oh, I don't think we'd be right for each other," Ida replied and stood abruptly. "I'm very tired from today. I think I'll go to sleep." As she headed toward the door, she reached out and grasped Devora's hand. "I'm glad you're doing better after everything today. Hopefully tomorrow will be better."

"Thank you, Ida," Devora replied.

"Are you sure you don't like Sir Jacques, Devora?" Hestia asked once Ida left.

Devora laughed. "No, he's just a friend. He was teaching me how to do my job at the stables."

"I hope it's better than laundry," Hestia groaned, wrinkling her nose. "Washing uniforms takes forever."

"Maybe if you didn't flirt all the time, you'd get your job done sooner," Reese sneered.

"I have kitchen duty," Nadia piped in, holding up her raw palms.

As the girls chatted about their evening jobs, Devora stepped around the different weapons scattering the floor to get to her bed. Her limbs ached from this morning and all she wanted to do was lie down.

But as she reached her bunk, she saw a perfectly square pile of cloth. A crisply folded piece of parchment sat on top. "What's this?"

Nadia jumped up from the floor and dusted off her pants before collecting her devices. "Dunno. It was here when I came back from the kitchen earlier."

Curiosity ignited a series of questions in Devora's mind as she unfolded the parchment and read the capitalized writing.

THESE SHOULD FIT BETTER. -M

"M?" Hestia read over her shoulder. "Who's 'M'?" The tall girl gasped, bringing her thin fingers to her mouth. "Have you met a guy?"

Reese snorted and clanked her metal beads. "She has a ninety-seven point six percent chance of meeting a guy, Hestia. But I don't know why anyone would want Grenly dung."

Hestia ignored her sister and hovered over Devora. "Did you meet him during mealtimes? In the infirmary? During training? While we were cleaning up the Theater?"

Devora raised her brows.

"What?" Hestia placed her hands on her hips. "If we're going to die soon, I'm going to have fun before I go."

"Well, that's certainly depressing," Nadia commented as she scribbled in her notebook.

Hestia shrugged then pointed to the cloth. "Well? What is it?"

Devora didn't respond as a jolt of excitement surged in her stomach. Taking a quick breath, she unfolded the fabric to find a new pair of pants with a black leather belt.

"Pants?" Hestia frowned, cocking her head to the side. "Not what I would call romantic." She chuckled then pushed Devora behind the privacy curtain. "Well, try them on."

Devora slid her oversized pants off to put on the new ones. The fabric was amazingly smooth and felt far better against her skin than her first pair. She placed the black belt around her waist and tightened it until it was comfortable. When she stepped out of the curtain, the girls squealed.

"They fit amazing!" Hestia said, throwing her hands in the air.

"How did this "M" know your size?" Nadia asked, stroking her chin as she scrutinized the pants.

Devora ran her hands along the smooth fabric when a thought shot through her mind, and she froze.

M. No, it couldn't be. M as in Matthias? As in Captain Blake? Why would Captain Blake give me pants?

Devora tucked her white tunic into the pants, remembering how Captain Blake had let her uniform violation pass. If she were in violation again, Sir Conan would definitely report her to Warden Hazor. Who knew what terrible punishment the warden would give her after he already tried to kill her?

Devora swallowed. Captain Blake didn't want her to be punished. It seemed that in his own strange way, he was trying to protect her. But why?

"Well, whoever this 'M' is, they seemed to have taken quite a good look at you because those pants fit great." Hestia lifted her brows and Devora blushed, not wanting to think about Captain Blake assessing her legs.

Chapter Fourteen

Devora smashed her flat pillow over her ears as the crow squawked too early the next morning. The shrill cawing rattled her bones, forcing her awake.

With a curse, Nadia sprang out of bed and shot it with another ball from her contraption. The crow flew away for a time then returned while the girls readied themselves for another day of training.

"We should name him," Nadia said as they hurried to breakfast. Reese, Hestia, and Ida had joined them and were chatting amongst themselves. "Maybe Bernard or...oh, I know!" Her plump lips spread into a mischievous grin as she snapped her fingers. "It *has* to be Sir Blakesalot! Then I could throw rocks at our horrible captain every morning." She clapped with delight. "What do you think?"

Devora snorted, trying to stifle her laugh. Captain Blake would be furious if he discovered they named their singed alarm bird after him.

As they stepped up the stairs to the dining hall, Devora's hand grazed against the black leather belt. *Why would the stern, judgmental captain give me a gift?*

The thought had been spinning through her mind since last night and she still couldn't figure it out.

"It would be funny..." Devora started before Nadia interrupted.

"Sir Blakesalot it is!" Nadia cried before pulling a wooden object from her pocket. She immediately began sharpening it with the knife of the *ligula*. How Nadia could whittle and walk, Devora had no idea.

"Are you making another weapon?" Devora questioned, staring at the sharp piece of wood.

"We are in a prison." Nadia motioned around them as they entered the dining hall. "And everyone looks like they want to kill each other. So, weapons are a good idea."

The other prisoners ignored them as they walked to breakfast. Relief washed over Devora as she filed into line for their morning mush.

"You had those before you came here," Devora countered, taking a stone bowl from the pile.

Nadia snorted, stuffing the new device in her pants pocket before grabbing her own bowl. "You need weapons from where I'm from."

"I'm so sorry, Nadia," Devora said.

Nadia shook her head as if brushing off her sorrow. "Don't be. My friend, Rae, kept us safe from the Kadeshian troops plundering our city. That's why my hair is short, and I love pants." She grinned, patting her hip. "Rae disguised us as men so the soldiers would leave us alone." Her smile fell. "Unfortunately, her fate was worse than mine."

Ida, peeked around Reese and clutched Nadia's arm. "What happened to her?"

Nadia held her bowl out to receive the morning gruel, adverting her eyes. "The last I saw her, she offered herself to General Yada, to serve him in any way. She diverted the soldiers' attention away from us, she gave herself up." Nadia nodded in thanks to the burly man serving out the mush. Surprisingly, he gave her a nod back.

As the girls strode to the table, Nadia continued, "I don't know what happened to her. I don't even know if she's alive. General Yada may have placed her in the Temple as a priestess or he may have killed her, but I would have no way of knowing." Nadia stared into her bowl. "Rae is the strongest person I know, so if anyone could survive Kadesh's siege of Yekel, it's her.

Devora gripped her fingers around the bowl, the rough surface burning into her flesh. She hated what this war had done to the people of Tenton—torn from their families and citadels like Yekel destroyed. So many tragedies and lives lost.

"I'm sorry, Nadia." Tears well in Ida's eyes

Nadia patted Ida's hand. "Thank you, Ida. She would have loved you all."

Devora stared at the hardening gruel. *General Yada. Is he the one leading the iron-armored beasts coming for Tenton?* Her visions had yet to tell her that information.

"You lyin' cheater!" A raspy voice shouted from the table behind them.

Devora twisted her head to see a middle-aged man with speckled brown hair throw a handful of cards with enough force they bounced and scattered on the table.

"You said you had a solid hand, and you didn't! I know you didn't!" The man reached into his pocket and shoved a handful of copper coins on the table. The coins clinked and clanged against one another as the man cursed.

"Calm yourself, Enesh." Captain Blake's voice layered in cool threats. "You don't want to spend another night with the Behemoth, do you? You are one of the few that has survived."

The middle-aged man blanched and bowed. "No, sir. Forgive my outburst. It won't happen again."

Captain Blake nodded. "Unless you wish to lose again, you're dismissed."

Enesh scampered away from the table, leaving Captain Blake to count his winnings.

"What was that all about?" Hestia asked, her mouth full of mush.

Devora turned to Hestia to see a frizzy blond boy sitting quite close to her.

"They're playing Kings." Reese pulled out her abacus and moved three beads on the top bar to the right. "It's a card game the knights and officers play with the inmates or soldiers. The probabilities continuously change. It's quite fascinating to watch."

"When have you watched anyone play a card game?" Hestia asked, eyeing her twin.

Reese shrugged and slid another bead to the right as she chewed her mush.

"Who will challenge the captain next?" a stout man with a scraggly beard and missing teeth asked.

Devora scanned the dining facility. No one was jumping at the chance to play against the captain. *Is he that good?*

"I would like to request a specific individual to challenge me," Captain Blake announced. He pushed his stacks of coins to the side before fanning the cards between his long fingers. After shuffling them, he reached into his pocket and pulled out a piece of parchment and a small bundle wrapped in tan fabric and twine. "I have here a note and a gift for our very own Lieutenant Medee from Governor Cusha Medee, her father."

Devora's stomach jumped to her throat. *A note from Papa? Had Sir Jacques found out something?* Devora's mind reeled. *But what is Captain Blake doing with the note?*

"If you would like either of these things," the captain explained, nonchalantly. "You must beat me at a game of Kings."

The confusion fled from Devora's mind, irritation taking its place. How dare Captain Blake goad her into playing his silly game? That note belonged to her, she shouldn't have to win it. The prisoners surrounding Captain Blake stared at Devora, waiting for her to decide.

"Captain Blake is undefeated," Reese explained in a low voice. She flicked the abacus beads back and forth quickly. Her dark eyes studied the orbs. "By my calculations, you have a ten-point six percent chance of winning. The odds are against you."

Devora noticed how Hestia didn't scold Reese for her probability prediction this time.

"Be careful, Devora," Ida whispered.

Closing her eyes, Devora took a breath. She had to get that note. Captain Blake may be undefeated, but Devora never cowered from a challenge.

Devora narrowed her eyes at the captain and pushed up from the table. "Thank you for your probability, Reese, but I'm going to win."

Nadia hooted when Devora stood. The other lieutenants applauded as she squared her shoulders and marched to the adjacent table. A smug smirk played across Captain Blake's thin lips.

"Please explain the rules," Devora said evenly, sitting across from him. Her pulse roared between her ears, even though she fixed the captain with the most coldhearted stare. "Sir."

Captain Blake almost laughed as he shuffled the deck again. "This deck consists of kings, queens, generals, soldiers, and laymen. Each player receives seven cards." He placed seven cards in front of Devora and seven in front of himself. "During each turn, a player picks up a card and places down another, trying to create a solid hand. A solid hand is one king, one queen, two generals, and three soldiers. You must keep seven cards in your hand at all times, or you will be immediately disqualified."

Devora picked up her cards, trying to hide them from the curious eyes around her. Two kings, four soldiers, and a general stared back at her. Masking her face to show nothing, she glanced back up to find the captain watching her carefully.

"When you have a solid hand," the captain continued. "You declare 'Kings,' and you're the winner. However, at any time, you can declare 'Kings.' If your opponent challenges your declaration and you don't have a solid hand, they win. If your opponent challenges and you do have a solid hand, you win. Any questions?" His calculating gray eyes stared back at her from behind his fan of cards.

Devora met his gaze head-on. She had been playing card games with Mama since she was old enough to walk. A standard Tentonian deck held forty-five cards consisting of four kings, four queens, three generals, sixteen soldiers, and twenty laymen. The kings, queens, and soldiers shouldn't be hard to gain, but the two generals would be tricky. She peered down at her hand. She already had one general, but she would have to find another one before Captain Blake. And, although the rules were easy enough, Devora knew that the captain would try something to trip her up.

"No, sir," she replied.

"Let's begin." Captain Blake picked up the first card from the deck in the middle and placed it face up.

For the next ten minutes, Devora barely blinked as she examined the deck and the cards in her hands. She assumed Captain Blake would call 'Kings' early on in the game to humiliate her, but judging by the minute narrowing of his gaze, it seemed the game wasn't playing out how he anticipated.

Painted portraits of King Atol and Queen Leza stared up at Devora as she studied her hand. She had acquired the queen within the first few moments of the game. The only card she needed to win was another general.

The dining hall was silent as the two faced one another. Devora focused on her cards, trying to ignore the heavy breathing of a soldier seated too close to her. While she wanted to tell him to give her some space, she couldn't break her concentration. Since the game started, she had been keeping track of the cards that had been placed face-up. It was a trick Mama taught her long ago. If Devora had been tracking them correctly, within six more turns, she would have the general.

Four turns passed. Devora glanced up.

Is that a sheen of sweat across Captain Blake's forehead?

She placed down a card and picked up another. It was the captain's turn. Once his turn finished, a general should be sitting there, waiting for Devora to take.

Captain Blake's steely gaze scanned over his hand before he straightened from his hunched position. Something devious played in his eyes. "You've done well, Medee. First you evade the giant's attacks during training, and now this. I'd be lying if I said I wasn't impressed."

Devora quirked a brow. *Is he trying to distract me? It won't work.*

"Thank you, sir. I know you judge others by a high standard, so your compliments hold weight." She rearranged her cards. Once he played his next card, she would win.

A baffled look crossed Captain Blake's face before he quickly covered it. "Yes, I hold others to the same standard as I hold myself. Though some have come close, none have reached where I am." Cocking his head to the side, he continued, "I thought you would, but unfortunately, this game is finished. I call Kings."

The crowd gasped and Devora's heart shattered. She was only one turn away from smashing the captain's arrogance back in his face. Her head throbbed from focusing on tracking the cards, and she was fairly certain she hadn't blinked in the last ten minutes. Pain pulsed behind her eyes. She couldn't have lost. She needed Papa's note.

Mind spinning, Devora thought back to how Tunri had helped her against Babshee. Maybe He would help her again.

Suddenly, as if Tunri plastered them in her mind, Devora remembered the rules of the game. The captain could be bluffing. But did she want to take the chance? The note from Papa laid between Captain Blake's forearms resting on the table. Devora recognized the large, rushed writing on the front. It was a chance she had to take.

She thought through it again and was fairly confident the captain was bluffing. Even if he wasn't, Devora swore to herself she'd find a way to get Papa's note.

"An interesting declaration, sir," Devora answered finally, her heart pounding against her rib cage. She licked her lips. "I call your bluff."

The prisoners gasped again and focused on Captain Blake.

"What grounds do you have to challenge my word?" he asked, leveling a threatening glare at her.

A chill wrapped around her. *Is this why the other prisoners gave in? Were they scared the captain would punish them?*

Devora lifted her chin. She didn't care about the punishment she would face; she *would* get that note.

"I've been keeping track of the cards played since we started. It's not possible for you to have gained a solid hand during this round." Her words sounded smooth and confident, but Devora's pulse raged as heat crept up her neck. She kept her fingers clamped around her cards, preventing them from trembling. "In fact, I would have called Kings and won on my next turn."

"Is that so?" Captain Blake asked, fiddling with the note on the table.

She nodded. "The next card is the one I need." Feeling confident, she placed her extra soldier down and held the general card from the deck up to Captain Blake's face. "I've won, captain," she said, splaying the rest of her cards in front of her.

The crowd gathered around to see if Devora's statement was true before erupting into cheers. As Captain Blake analyzed her, his face went white, his eyes wide.

Clearing his throat, he slid the note across the table. "You need to leave," he growled under his breath. "Now."

Confused, Devora began to ask why when the crowd quieted into curses and gasps. The prisoners who were once cheering for her now looked at her with contempt and shock. As she turned, the other lieutenants scrambled away, fear lacing their features.

"Dev," Nadia said, her eyes wide.

Hestia and Reese had their hands cupped over their mouths, their eyes wide with fright.

"Devora," Ida said softly, touching Devora's arm. Devora glanced up into Ida's warm brown eyes. "Your eyes, they're violet."

Chapter Fifteen

The Edo Desert, Kadesh

The clanging of the metal stakes pierced Erza's skull. She hated the desert almost as much as she hated General Sage. Jarrick banged the stake into the ground again before tying the flailing fabric of their tent around it. Erza gritted her teeth. Grains of sand rubbed against her tongue as she handed her husband another stake.

She loved Jarrick more than anything, but he was easily persuaded by the highest buyer. Jarrick had been creating weapons and armor for Kadesh's army for years. And while Erza had enjoyed the benefits of her husband's labor, she didn't like how General Sage controlled Jarrick. The general would ask for weapons on short notice, and Jarrick would spend every hour of the day and night creating them. Regular weapons of swords and shields were bad enough, but when the general ordered Jarrick to make custom armor for his hideous fanged beasts, Erza knew the man was crazy.

"One more, my love, and we're finished." Jarrick glanced up at her with a soft grin.

Erza's heart melted. General Sage constantly took advantage of Jarrick's talent and skill. How much more could the general ask of them? Jarrick put everything into his work. If General Sage requested anything else, Erza feared what would happen to her husband.

A burning rage swept through her chest as she stared out into the distance, picturing the arrogant general in his lavish home while she was burning in the desert. No, she would not allow Jarrick to work himself into the ground. General Sage had already taken her son. She would not allow him to take her husband, too.

Chapter Sixteen

Devora jumped up from the table. Lifting her hand, she shielded her purple eyes from the gawking crowd. The prisoners around her now held weapons, ready to slay her like the king had wanted to years ago. Her pulse roared.

Why is this happening now? I just took the tea two weeks ago. Why is it fading early?

She scanned the dining hall. She needed to escape, but how? There were people everywhere. Taking a breath, Devora spun toward the exit. She would have to barrel through. But when she took the first step, a fire erupted in her body. Her nerves became engulfed in flames before everything went black.

Devora placed a hand on her forehead then realized she was in a vision. Her head whipped around. This was the worst possible time.

Before panic could set in, her body jerked forward, landing outside of the Fortress. The end of her last vision repeated as she soared through the building, higher and higher until she stood outside the stone door bearing Tenton's seal. In a blink, she was through the threshold and seated around the circular wooden table.

The people at the table assessed her before shifting their gaze to the person beside her. Devora turned to her left. Captain Blake's shoulders tensed, his eyes cold as he glowered at everyone in the room. Instead of his everyday training gear, a stunning suit of armor fit perfectly across the captain's chest. Devora felt herself blush. Now was not the time to be gawking at the captain. She needed to focus.

Turning her attention to the table of people, she noticed that one of them was Warden Hazor. With his white hair perfectly combed, he, too, sat in shining armor.

"Welcome and congratulations, Lady Medee. You have succeeded in winning Regulus Protecti. What is your request for pardon?"

Before Devora could respond, the vision pulled away from her until the sound of beating claws vibrated between her ears. Blazing heat seared her flesh as the claws almost trampled her. She ran, only taking a moment to look back. A scream erupted from her throat when an iron-armored beast barreled toward her, its grotesque yellow teeth gnashing with each stride.

Devora quickened her pace, but she was too slow, and the beast plowed over her.

"No!" Devora shot up with a scream, sweat pouring down her temples.

Her chest heaved as she gasped for air. A strong, firm hand rested on her arm to steady her. Panicked, she jerked away, only to see Captain Blake seated next to her.

"Where am I?" Devora demanded, placing a hand over her racing heart.

She took in the sterilized space and crisp white bed beneath her. A series of other beds lined the walls, each filled with a body.

The blood drained from Devora's face as she noticed the man in the cot next to her. Purple boils oozed over his entire body. Sweat dripped from his exposed skin; sheets clung to his limbs. He shivered uncontrollably, teeth chattering.

"You're in the infirmary," Captain Blake answered, curling his hand into a fist as he placed it on his knee. His mouth drew into a tight line as he followed her gaze. "He's a victim of gumberry poisoning. Terrible stuff, but extremely effective. One drop in your blood and your body goes into shock. The chills and the boils are the final stage."

"Who would use such a thing?" Devora gaped, turning back to the captain.

"General Sage. He's one of Kadesh's three generals. Though Generals Yada and Beta are equally ruthless, Sage is the most bloodthirsty."

A shudder rippled over Devora's body as Captain Blake handed her a cup of water. Devora took it and downed the whole thing, not realizing how thirsty she was until the captain poured her another glass.

"Thank you."

The captain nodded. "I wasn't sure if you'd be all right after you fainted in the dining hall."

Devora blinked at him. It had been years since she had been overcome by a vision so forcefully.

When she was a child and just beginning to understand her prophetic gift, Devora had a vision that a terrible woman with long dark hair was coming to kill her. She'd passed out in the middle of the street while visiting the shops with Mama and woke up screaming. It took her parents weeks to convince Devora that she was safe, and no one was coming after her. But Devora never forgot the sleek black hair and outstretched hand holding a knife, ready to strike.

At the thought of the memory, Devora gasped as the earlier events resurfaced in her thoughts: the game of Kings, her victory, Captain Blake warning her to leave, and Ida telling her about her eyes.

Lurching away from Captain Blake, Devora shielded her eyes with her hands. "Please don't kill me," she whispered. She hated how weak and pathetic she sounded. "I need to save my father."

"Why would I kill you?"

Cautiously, she peered over at the captain. His face was still composed and stern as it always was. But he wasn't looking at her with contempt or horror, like those in the dining hall. Instead, Devora witnessed a deep sorrow lingering behind the usually hard eyes.

Captain Blake held out Papa's note in one hand and a silver ring with a shining opal in the other. "What I'd like to know is why the Governor of Grenly would send his daughter this?" He pinched the ring between his thumb and pointer finger.

Ignoring the ring, Devora snatched the note and scanned its contents. Papa was alive. For now. But he was still locked in the king's dungeon until his hearing. Tears pricked Devora's eyes. This was all her fault. If she had categorized for anything other than Vlacklear, she wouldn't be in the Fortress and Papa wouldn't be imprisoned. Clearing her throat, Devora reached the end of the note:

I didn't have the chance to give you your categorization gift. The king and queen recommended this stone themselves, so I thought it would be suitable for you.

She sucked in a breath. After everything, Papa still believed she was meant for Vlacklear.

"It's a gift for my categorization," Devora explained. "But it doesn't really matter since I'm here and not at Vlacklear."

Still wary of Captain Blake staring at her violet eyes, Devora hesitantly lifted her gaze. Dark shadows rimmed the captain's eyes, and a deep frown marred his lips.

How long have I been in the infirmary? How long has he been here with me?

Captain Blake fisted the ring in his palm. "Do you know what this is?"

"A ring?" Devora deadpanned, remembering the ring Tristan had given her. She didn't want any more rings for a long time.

The captain ignored her remark and continued, "This ring has an imperial opal in it. It's extremely rare. Usually, only royalty can obtain it."

"Papa said the king and queen recommended it." Devora handed Captain Blake the note.

He read it quickly and Devora studied him to catch his reaction. But nothing happened besides a brief narrowing of his eyes.

Captain Blake leaned closer, lowering his voice. An earthy blend of cedar and steel wafted from his brown training uniform. "Devora, imperial opals suppress anointed power. If a gift bearer wears imperial opal for too long, their power will fade, and the gift bearer will die. Why would your father give this to you?"

Devora's jaw unhinged, and she stared at the ring. She had never heard of an imperial opal. But now that she saw it up close, it was the same material as Babshee's shackles. If what Captain Blake said was true, she had no idea why Papa had given it to her.

"You can't wear this," he said with finality, tucking it into his pocket. "I honestly thought you would lose Kings and I could dispose of it. Was your father trying to help you hide your abilities? If so, there are other ways that won't end your life."

"I-I don't know." Devora squeezed her eyes shut and pressed her palms to her temples. Her head ached from the vision and the overwhelming information. It felt as if a weight hung around her neck, pulling her head to the floor. "Wouldn't you want me to wear it to be rid of me?" she mumbled.

Captain Blake was silent for a long while before he asked, "What was your vision about?" Devora opened her eyes and gave the captain a side-long glance. "Your eyes went completely white before you passed out," he continued. "I've seen it before."

The pain from her head instantly fled. "You've seen it before? When?"

The captain blinked. "Tell me your vision."

Devora scrunched the crisp sheets between her fingers, knowing she had to tell someone about what was coming. Captain Blake was Warden Hazor's second in command. If he could deliver the message of Kadesh's attack, maybe she would finally be free of the terrible visions.

Taking a steadying breath, she explained, "Kadesh is planning to attack again through the Edo desert before heading to the capital. I don't know when, but my visions are getting closer together and repeating the same scene. They've never done that before. I think Tunri is trying to send a warning." She tucked a few strands of hair behind her ear.

"They're not just coming with giants this time. I don't know where they found them, but the Kadeshians now have iron-armored beasts capable of destroying Tenton's army. I wanted to tell Warden Hazor when I first got here, but..." She trailed off, knowing that the captain remembered he was the one who had saved her from the warden's hand.

When she glanced up, Captain Blake's eyes were darting between hers and she could almost see his thoughts whirling as he processed the information.

"And that was your vision? The one you just had?"

Devora focused on the wrinkles she made in the white sheet. She still didn't understand what contest Warden Hazor was talking about. *Should I ask Captain Blake about it?*

Before she could breathe a word, the captain clipped, "If you don't want to be murdered the second you leave the infirmary, I suggest you tell me everything you know."

Devora pinched her lips shut, unsure of whether to trust the captain or not.

The captain's shoulders drooped ever so slightly. "I won't make you confide in me, but if you want to see your parents again, you're going to have to trust me."

She twisted the sheets around her palms. "We were taking an audience in front of Warden Hazor. I had just won some competition," Devora mumbled, waving her hand in the air.

"So, you already know about it."

She glanced up to find Captain Blake crossing his arms over his chest as he eased into the wooden chair.

Devora shook her head. "I have no idea what it is."

With a heavy sigh, the captain explained, "As soon as you passed out, the prisoners were ready to cut your throat. Luckily, your friends shielded you until I could get through. Warden Hazor is having a meeting with King Atol and the other members of the council to decide your fate."

Devora blanched. "What?"

Captain Blake shifted uncomfortably in his chair. "Many council members wanted to throw you on the gallows immediately, but someone gave King Atol the idea to have a contest to test your abilities." The captain pinched the bridge of his nose. "If you succeed, they want to use your abilities to win against Kadesh."

"But it doesn't work that way," Devora exclaimed. "I can't control what I see."

Her stomach twisted, threatening to push her breakfast up her throat. She quickly covered her mouth, not wanting to vomit in front of Captain Blake like she had with Sir Jacques.

Squeezing her eyes shut, Devora steadied her breaths, realizing her fate. "If I don't die, then I'll become a puppet for the king."

The captain's voice was so quiet, it was almost a whisper. "I'm afraid so."

Chapter Seventeen

The Infirmary, The Fortress

"Help me," Devora blurted before she could stop herself. "Give me special training. Sir Jacques said you were the best soldier in Tenton." Devora blinked away the tears threatening to spill. Of all times, now was the worst to show weakness. But she needed more help. Tunri was helping with the extra visions, but she wasn't physically strong enough to win against other soldiers.

Devora bowed her head. "Please, sir. Give me a fighting chance. My father has been imprisoned by the king and I need to help him. Once he's free, maybe he can convince King Atol to leave me be. That can only happen if you help me win. I can't do this on my own."

The silence stretched for what seemed like hours until Captain Blake replied, "If we're going to work together, you can't question me. And you can't ever ask about or wear this—" he held out the opal ring.

Hope lighted her chest and she raised her head. "You'll help me?"

The captain gave a curt nod before gesturing to the ring. She studied it. *Did Papa know it would drain my power?* Surely, he wouldn't have sent it if he knew the risks.

Devora held her hands up. "You can have it."

Captain Blake tucked the ring back into his pocket. "Your name has already been recorded as a participant in the tournament." He straightened his white tunic. "Did your vision include General Sage? Was he the one leading the beasts?"

Devora shook her head.

The captain's lips thinned. "Inform me of any additional information you receive. I'll do my best to convince the warden, but without any proof, it'll be near impossible." He ran a hand over his thick, chestnut hair.

It was the first time Devora had ever seen the captain distraught.

"Meet me in the Theater after you finish your work at the stables. Then we'll begin. It also wouldn't be a bad idea to carry a few weapons on you from now on."

"Should I try to cover my eyes?" Devora asked, gesturing to her face.

Captain Blake shook his head. "Your secret is out, Medee. You might as well accept it." As he started to exit, he paused. Slowly, he glanced over his shoulder. "Did you use your gift to win Kings?"

Devora frowned. "No, of course not. I'm not a cheater. And I told you, I can't control what I see."

With a smirk, the captain turned and marched out of the infirmary.

Devora watched his broad shoulders leave. Though the captain infuriated and scared her at times, she was thankful he agreed to help her. If there was any truth in Tristan's stories and Sir Jacques' opinions, she knew that Captain Blake was one of Tenton's fiercest warriors. With his training and enough practice, she might win whatever tournament the king made and, hopefully, save Papa.

After another night and day in the infirmary, Devora returned to her cell. As soon as she arrived, Nadia, Ida, Reese, and Hestia showered her with care and questions.

"I was so surprised," Hestia exclaimed, inches away from Devora's face. "You know, your eyes are a beautiful shade of violet."

"Like lilacs in bloom," Ida agreed, giving Devora a soft smile.

"They're a bit unnerving," Reese mumbled.

"Reese!" Hestia scolded, slapping her sister in the shoulder.

"It's okay. I agree." Devora said, placing her hands up. She twisted her braid around her palm. "Before I came here, I would drink a special dung tea to suppress the purple color."

Nadia choked. "You drank poop?"

"No!" Devora cried and the girls all laughed, easing the tension. "No, it was a tea that looked and tasted like dung. So that's what I called it."

Nadia leaned back on her bunk and began whittling a new piece of wood. "I don't know, Dev. If it looks like poop and smells like poop..." she trailed off, causing Hestia and Ida to burst into a fit of giggles. Reese tried to hide her smile as she fiddled with her abacus.

Though she was hesitant at first, Devora told them everything about her gift and the dung tea. They laughed again at her name for the awful herbal blend and soon changed the subject to her victory over Captain Blake.

While Hestia styled her hair in intricate braids, Devora listened to her friend's chittering conversation as she tried to keep her anxiety about her fate contained.

"Soldiers!" A voice rang out from the back of the dining hall at dinner the next evening. Devora cringed as she recognized its gravelly arrogance. "Today is a very special day," Sir Conan continued as he stood on one of the tables to be seen.

The prisoners glanced at the stout knight then ignored him and continued their conversations. Chatter filled the dining hall once more until Sir Conan stormed down the table and kicked the stone bowls out of the prisoners' hands. They cursed and glared at him. Sir Conan growled back then held his hands out to the now silent dining hall.

"As I was saying, today is a special day. Warden Hazor has been granted permission by our great King Atol to issue a tournament. All soldiers are eligible to participate in Reg-ulus Protecti: a tournament to find the next Defender of Tenton. Whoever perseveres through all three rounds will win an audience with Warden Hazor, receive one pardon of their choosing, and gain the ability to assist the king in controlling Tenton's armies."

Shouts immediately erupted from the prisoners as they stood on the tables and argued with one another.

"I helped in the siege of Yekel," a stocky man with three teeth and no hair shouted. "You young scrags have no experience like I do."

"Step aside, old man," another said, flexing his bulging muscles as he shoved the older man aside. "Tenton wouldn't want a dried-up old prune as their defender."

The man growled and swung his right hook into the muscular man's cheek. In a matter of moments, a full-out brawl exploded in the dining hall.

"How awful," Ida whispered, shaking her head, her tight curls springing.

"How barbaric is more accurate," Reese added, watching the fight. She swept the abacus beads to the left. "The bald man has a sixty-six point three percent chance of winning."

In two more swings, the bald man had punched out his opponent.

Hestia shuddered. "You're scary, Reese. You know that, right?"

"Only one person has defied my probabilities," Reese narrowed her eyes at Devora. Tilting her nose up, she added, "I have to say I am impressed that you won Kings."

Is she actually giving me a compliment? Devora thought as another fight spilled over onto their table, causing the girls to scramble away from the grunting men.

Taking advantage of the fight, Devora slipped out of the dining hall. She didn't want to be late to her first training session with Captain Blake. Grabbing her *ligula*, she headed for the stables. Upon noticing the murderous glint in many of the prisoners' eyes, she remembered the captain's advice about carrying a weapon. She would have to remember to ask Nadia about more weapons later. Now that she knew Papa was still alive, Devora wouldn't go down without a fight.

As she strode through Level Five, Devora peered into the farthest cell on the left. She paused, studying the tall figure lying on the bunk. His long legs stretched past the bed's end.

"Is there something I can help you with?" he asked, keeping his eyes fixed on the ceiling.

Devora tensed. She didn't plan on speaking with the criminal, she was simply curious about him since he had caught her eavesdropping on Sir Jacques and Captain Blake.

"I—er—," she started, but figured she should ask what she'd been wanting to know. "Is your name really One Shot?"

The tall man sat up slowly, folding his thin legs in front of him. His stringy ebony hair splayed across his forehead before he flicked it away. While Devora expected the man to have wrinkles that matched the age in his eyes, there were none to be seen. He was barely a few summers older than herself. "That's what they call me."

"Why?"

"I murdered four men in one shot," he replied casually before laying back down on the cot.

Fear tingled down Devora's spine as she took a step back. "Oh, well, thank you, One Shot," she breathed. Not wanting to offend the hardened criminal, she backed away slowly. "I hope we can talk again soon."

"Before you go," One Shot said, lifting a hand in the air. "If that giant causes you any more trouble, remember to shoot between the eyes."

"Uh, thanks." Devora nodded and dashed away to the lowest level of the Fortress.

A shiver ran through her as she made her way past the large metal door holding the Behemoth. Pausing, she waited for any voices, but none came.

Did I imagine the voice before?

After another moment of silence, she shook her head and continued to the icebox down the hall.

Grabbing the metal hook from the wall, Devora held her breath and tried not to look inside the cold container as she filled the two buckets with raw meat for the wolves. After the buckets were full, she grabbed a torch from the wall and held the hook in the fire until it glowed red. The roaring flames transfixed her mind as memories of Master Riggs' silver vat entered her thoughts again.

Devora huffed and blinked the thought away. *How much refining do I have to go through? Do I have that many impurities?*

Devora remembered her opinions about the people of Lower Grenly.

She shook her head, disappointed at her past self. Ida was from Lower Grenly and she had been nothing but kind to Devora since they'd met. And now, even after she knew about her curse, Ida still was her friend. If they hadn't been sent to the Fortress together, Devora would've never befriended Ida because of her own arrogance.

Swaying back and forth, Devora trudged to the door, trying to balance with the large pails while blowing a strand of hair out of her face. With a huff, she placed the buckets down and held the metal door handle.

She had always heard that members of the king's court spent their time throwing parties and eating delicious treats while their people were dying on the battlefront. But had she been any different? While she enjoyed rose-scented baths and secret dates with Tristan, the people of Lower Grenly were working hard, trying not to starve.

Twisting her wrist, Devora opened the metal door. The crisp night sent pleasant chills against her warm skin as she grabbed the buckets and headed to the wooden shack.

She did exactly what Sir Jacques had shown her, and though the wolves snarled and growled as they ate their meal, triumph flooded her veins. She completed the task on her own *and* without vomiting. A smile raced across her lips as she leaned against the wooden door, breathing in the frigid night. Maybe Tunri had sent her here as punishment. But maybe, she could also learn from it. He had sent her the vision that she would be victorious in the contest. And He had helped her endure the fight with Babshee. Maybe she would survive after all.

A series of whimpers escaped the wooden hut and Devora paused. It didn't sound like the usual growls the wolves made.

Devora faced the door. She should just leave. She was already late to her lesson with Captain Blake. But something prompted her to check on the wolves.

Biting her lip, Devora gripped the splintered door handle.

"Please don't let me get eaten," she prayed aloud as she cracked the door open.

She expected the wolves to jump out and attack her. When they didn't, Devora cautiously poked her head inside. There among bales of hay and blankets curled two wolves: a plump female wolf and a male wolf snug beside her. Only, upon further inspection, Devora realized the female wolf's stomach was pregnant.

A soft smile glided across her lips as she watched the male wolf lay his head on his mate. Even a barbaric, ruthless creature had compassion.

Quietly closing the door, Devora hurried back to the Fortress.

After washing and returning the buckets to their spot next to the icebox, Devora took the steps two at a time. The wolves and her life contemplations had taken longer than she intended them to.

"You're late," Captain Blake commented as soon as she rushed into the Theater.

"I know. I apologize." Devora heaved as a loose strand of hair fell between her eyes. She bowed before placing the strand back in her braid. "One of the warden's wolves is pregnant. Someone should call a doctor to make sure she's well."

Once she straightened, she sucked in a breath, taking in the bare, chiseled back and dark training slacks facing her. Her chest squeezed. *How can I concentrate when he looks like that?*

"I will relay that information to the warden," he replied, keeping his toned back to her. "If you don't want to be killed in the first round of Regulus Protecti, I suggest you do your job efficiently, so we have more time to train." He turned around, scanning her appearance with scrutinizing eyes as he wrapped his hands with thick strips of cloth. "I've seen the other prisoners who are entering the contest. Most have been in the Fortress for many years. They will not hesitate to cut your throat."

Devora took a step back. *Can I really face such dishonorable men and win?*

For a split second, she wanted to argue that she would be victorious against such barbarians. But Captain Blake was doing her a favor by training her after hours. "I know," she said, finding the humble words not as hard to say as she anticipated. Bowing her head, she added, "I appreciate your help. Please forgive my tardiness. It won't happen again."

After a moment, she slowly stood to find that Captain Blake had stopped wrapping his hands. His gaze wasn't as cold as it usually was, but surprised. Before she could react, he tossed a ball of dark fabric at her.

"Wrap your hands tight enough so that they're secure, but you can still move your fingers."

Devora held the ball and started to wrap her left hand with the coarse black fabric. She checked the captain's hands to see if it was right. But as she started wrapping her other hand, the fabric kept slipping from her grasp.

After her third failed attempt, she growled. If she couldn't complete this simple task, how was she going to win Regulus Protecti?

"Do you need help?" the captain asked.

"No," she snapped, fumbling with the fabric again before it tumbled out of her hands. Frustration balled in her chest. Now she was making a fool out of herself.

Before Devora could retrieve the fabric, strong, lean fingers entered her view. Her eyes darted up to see Captain Blake holding the ball.

He carefully took her hand and wrapped the rough fabric snugly around her palm and fingers. Her breath hitched as his calloused fingers brushed against her skin.

Once Captain Blake secured the strip, he gave a firm nod and strode to the other end of the room. Devora studied the perfect wrapping, her skin tingling from where his warm hands had held hers. She balled her fingers into a fist. She couldn't allow herself to have feelings for Tristan's brother. Captain Blake was doing her a kindness by helping her train. A teacher and student, that's all they were.

"We're going to review what we did in training," the captain explained, placing an hourglass on the stone ledge wrapping around the sandy floor. He flipped it so the sand trickled into the empty bottom. "And then we're going to learn something new."

After an hour, the golden sand finally fell to the bottom of the hourglass, announcing Devora could take a break.

Sweat dripped from her brow as she leaned against the cool wall. Her arms felt like they were on fire from all the training, but she was improving.

After Captain Blake reviewed that morning's material of hand-to-hand combat, Devora tried to block, dodge, and return his punches. Unfortunately, she didn't fare so well in the beginning and received a large bruise on her cheek after the first punch he threw. After that, the captain held back his full power until she was ready. If her cheek hadn't been throbbing with pain, she would've noticed the remorseful look adorning Captain Blake's face after punching her square in the jaw.

But that one punch was enough incentive because Devora quickly learned how to execute all three strategies to save her skin. Literally.

"Good," Captain Blake commented as he retreated to the far end of the Theater. He returned with a bucket of water and a smooth gray stone.

He handed her the ladle to drink from first. Devora gulped the water down hungrily, enjoying how it felt dripping from her chin to her neck. She couldn't wait to cleanse her skin of all the sweat and grime. She glanced over at Captain Blake's amused face.

"What?" she asked, daintily wiping her mouth with the hem of her shirtsleeve before lifting her chin.

A small smirk came to his thin lips. "I've never seen a lady drink in such a way."

Heat flared in her cheeks, and she turned away. He was right. But she wasn't a lady anymore.

"Devora, I'm joking," he said, relaxing as he crossed his hands over his bare chest and leaned against the wall.

Her stomach twisted, hearing her name from his lips. She needed to control that response. "Here." He handed her a stone. "For your bruise. It'll help with the swelling."

The smooth oval stone was freezing cold and felt amazing against her hot, sweaty body. She carefully placed it on her tender cheek and sighed with relief. The chilled stone immediately cooled the radiating heat from her injury. Devora closed her eyes, relishing the slick surface. When she opened them again, Captain Blake was staring at her.

She blinked and lowered the stone. "What have I done wrong now?"

"Nothing." He straightened before marching to the mat Babshee had flung Devora on during her first time in the Theater. "We're going to learn another fighting technique called *hemna*. It's a fierce fighting style and I think it will help you at least advance through the first round. After that, we'll need a miracle."

Devora bit her tongue, knowing he was right. However, she did notice the captain's use of "we" instead of "you".

"*Hemna* is all about subduing your opponent in as few strikes as possible," Captain Blake explained. "By focusing your strength on specific areas of the body, you can stun your opponent's muscles, giving you enough time to attack. Some soldiers look down upon the technique, but it will save your life if done properly."

Devora studied the captain, running her eyes along his sun-kissed skin. She had thought it was flawless, but now that she saw it up close, white lines of scars covered his arms and back. *How does Captain Blake know this technique?*

Taking in a deep breath, Devora sent a prayer of protection to Tunri before nodding. "I'm ready."

Chapter Eighteen

Level Two, The Fortress

Devora's muscles screamed in protest as she forced them to run their daily laps. She had trained with Captain Blake every evening that week and it was catching up to her. Thankfully, once she warmed up, the muscle toning exercises weren't as bad.

Encouraged by her progress, Devora completed the next set of exercises when Captain Blake arrived.

A white tunic and brown pants, the same as the other soldiers, wrapped around his form. But with Captain Blake's toned limbs, Devora found herself enjoying the uniform on him more than anyone else.

Stop that, she chided herself, forcing her eyes away.

"Today, you will learn how to fight with a weapon." The captain pulled a wooden sword from a bucket next to him. "A mech is the standard issued weapon His Majesty provides for each soldier. While it looks pathetic, it can do severe harm if used correctly." The sword looked like one jab would snap it in two. It was practically an oversized needle.

Nadia snorted and covered her mouth, trying to suppress her laughter at the Captain Blake's frankness. Biting her lip, Devora tried to do the same. Hestia didn't hide her giggle and gained a glare from the captain.

"This is, of course, a training version of the mech," the captain continued, "Once you learn how to wield this, you will be given a real one."

Captain Blake's gaze roved over his lieutenants until they landed on Devora. A smile ticked at the corner of his lips as he grasped the wooden sword. "Now, for a demonstration." Whipping around, the captain stalked to the other end of the Theater where Sir Conan just entered with his troops.

Reese towered over Ida's small frame and leaned toward Devora. "What's he doing?" she asked.

Devora paused. "I'm not sure."

Rearing back, the captain jabbed Sir Conan in the back. The knight jerked forward, bringing a hand to his lower back with a curse. The group of new lieutenants snorted, trying to suppress their giggles. Spinning around, Sir Conan sent a fiery glare toward Captain Blake.

"Some of us have work to do, Captain," he growled.

"Sir Conan," Captain Blake boomed, his eyes lit with competition and mischief. "It's been too long since we battled formally. With Jacques off collecting taxes, I know no other knight that will not be immediately defeated by my superior skill. Join me in a duel." He held his arm out, as if inviting the entire Theater to witness their battle.

Devora grinned. This was the first time she'd seen Captain Blake genuinely smile. It was full and bright, filled with joy and laughter. It transformed his stern face into something warm and comforting.

Sir Conan didn't need to be asked twice. Muttering more curses under his breath, the knight barreled toward the bucket of wooden swords. He wrenched the closest one out before swiping at Captain Blake. The captain easily avoided the swing, returning with another jab in Sir Conan's ribs. Jerking away, Sir Conan growled before his stance melted into a predator. He shot a wad of spit to the floor and stalked around the captain with murder in his eyes.

Something in the air shifted and Devora's smile vanished. While Captain Blake had meant for the duel to be comical, Sir Conan didn't look like he was in the mood for games. Anxiety tightened her chest. She knew the captain was skilled, but she didn't trust Sir Conan to play fair.

Anticipation lingered over the recruits. The Theater quieted as the two men circled one another. The previous mischief from Captain Blake vanished as he homed in on Sir Conan. Sir Conan then muttered something under his breath, causing the captain's shoulders to tighten.

Captain Blake was lightning quick as he attacked, his jabs fierce and efficient. If Devora blinked, she would've missed them. In a matter of moments, the captain had Sir Conan pinned to the wall.

Captain Blake's shoulders tensed as he gripped Sir Conan's thick neck, the knight's face turning white before red blotches appeared on his greasy skin. The captain's long fingers tightened around the knight's throat further. Eyes bulging, Sir Conan begged for mercy. Captain Blake quickly released him, and Sir Conan landed with a thud, gasping for air. Throwing his wooden mech to the ground, the captain stomped toward the young officers. They straightened and tried not to look him in the eye.

Devora sucked in a breath, terror lodged in her throat. *What did Sir Conan say to make him so angry?*

"Familiarize yourselves with the mech until I return," Captain Blake barked before storming out of the Theater.

"Well, that was exciting," Hestia said, nudging the frizzy blond boy who seemed to always be around her now. He nodded in agreement though he looked shaken from the entire episode.

"Captain Blake scares me," Ida whispered, running her fingers along her wire bracelet before she and Reese paired up.

"Why's he so mad?" Nadia jutted her chin toward the exit of the Theater. She then picked out two wooden mechs and handed one to Devora. "He picked the fight, didn't he?"

"I don't know." Devora took the sword, shaking her head. She focused on the door Captain Blake had stomped through. "I think he meant for it to be for fun, but Sir Conan didn't share the sentiment."

Devora's gaze drifted to Sir Conan, who was escorted out of the Theater by one of his soldiers before another knight took over instructing his troops. Based on the angry red marks around his neck, Devora assumed Sir Conan was heading to the infirmary.

An hour passed and Captain Blake hadn't returned, so Devora's group played around with the swords until Sir Jacques came and taught them the basic steps to wield the mech in combat. The lieutenants perked up at Sir Jacques' gentle yet informative instruction. After their lesson, Devora caught her friend before he left.

"Sir Jacques, how are you?"

She had been wondering about the knight since the evening she overheard his and Captain Blake's conversation. He'd been scarce in the Fortress and Devora was curious as to who Helene was.

Sir Jacques sighed as he collected the wooden swords in the bucket. "I don't know where he went."

Devora let out a nervous laugh, twirling the end of her braid between her fingers. "I don't know what you're talking about."

Sir Jacques turned around. Running a hand through his shaggy blond hair, he leaned down and whispered, "I know Captain Blake is helping you train. I don't know what happened today, but I know Blake left the Fortress. I don't know when he'll be back."

Devora stepped back, fear wrapping around her heart. "What?"

"I'm sorry, Lady Devora." Sir Jacques shook his head, bowed, then exited the Theater.

Devora's thoughts swirled, hundreds of questions forming in her mind. But she couldn't answer any of them over the heavy disappointment laying over her heart.

How am I going to train for the tournament now? Round One is only a week away.

Without Captain Blake's training, she would be killed the second she stepped inside the arena.

Which is exactly what Warden Hazor wanted.

Her disappointment hardened and chilled to a cold rage. Had Captain Blake given her false hope by training her, only to allow her to be slaughtered?

Devora gritted her teeth and left the Theater before any of her friends could catch her, hating that she had trusted Captain Blake.

Almost a week passed and there was no sign of Captain Blake. Sir Jacques took over teaching their group the skills of combat. He was a great teacher, kind and instructive, unlike the captain. All the girls loved Sir Jacques and vied for his attention during training sessions. But though she hated to admit it, Devora missed the cold stares and forward thoughts of Captain Blake.

Nadia took over Devora's training in the evenings. How her roommate had known that Devora was entering the tournament and why she wanted to help her learn *hemna* was unclear. How *Nadia* knew *hemna* was also unclear. But after three days of her roommate's heavy training, Devora was beginning to understand the kicks, punches, probes, and blocks of the intense fighting style.

Running a hand over her bicep, Devora smirked at the toned muscle hardening beneath her skin. It was encouraging to see the results of all the training she'd done.

Once the captain returns, I can show him... She stopped her thoughts. She had caught herself thinking about Captain Blake too many times in the past week. He'd left and didn't have the decency to tell her why.

"Are you done admiring yourself?" Nadia questioned with a snort and Devora glanced up from her arm. "Or can we continue?"

Devora chuckled and wiped the sweat from her brow before readying her stance. Nadia had been teaching her a shoulder jab combined with a roundhouse kick. Though she'd fallen flat on her rump the first hundred times, Devora was finally starting to complete the move.

Closing her eyes, she sucked in a deep breath then released it, focusing her gaze on Nadia's palms. In one fluid move, she jabbed toward Nadia's right shoulder, brought her left knee tight to her chest, twisted her body, and extended her leg with as much power as she could muster. A loud smack vibrated throughout the empty Theater. Devora jumped back and lifted her arms, shielding herself like Nadia had taught her.

"*Pahga*!" Nadia cursed as she shook out her hands.

Devora peeked over her defense, watching Nadia blow on her bright red palms then rub her shoulder. Devora strode over to her friend, offering one of the cool, smooth stones. "You okay?"

Nadia took the stone and clasped it between her palms. "Ah. That's better." She turned to Devora with a wide grin. "That was awesome, Dev. Keep kicking like that and you'll be saved in no time." The smooth stone slipped from Nadia's hand, slamming onto her toes. "Pahga!"

Nadia held her foot as Devora crouched down and retrieved the stone. She handed it back to her roommate before asking, "'Pahga', what does that mean?"

Since arriving at the Fortress, Devora had heard a range of colorful curses used by the inmates. Some she'd heard in the streets of Grenly, others were brand new and left her shocked when she discovered their meanings. But Nadia's favorite expression was one she hadn't heard from anyone beside her friend.

Nadia clamped her hands around the slick stone again. "You don't know the Queen of Heaven, the goddess, Pahga?"

Devora furrowed her brows. *Goddess?* She had never heard of any other deities besides Tunri.

Nadia scoffed and lowered herself to the ground, placing the stone in one hand while reaching for the charcoal stick behind her ear with the other. "Well, it's probably better that you haven't." She twirled the charcoal between her fingers, leaving lines of black across her tan skin. "Pahga has brought me nothing but pain. That's why I curse her name."

Devora pushed a few stray hairs off her forehead and joined Nadia on the sandy ground. "What has Pahga done to you?"

Nadia's gaze darkened. "When I was young, I brought an offering of my family's wealth every week to Pahga's temple in exchange for protection. And what did she do?" Nadia stopped her twirling and flung the stone in her hand against the hard wall, where it shattered.

Devora winced.

"First, she allowed our own soldiers to invade our land and steal our top inventors, taking more than half of our village with them, including both of my parents. Then, she allowed those Kadeshian brutes to finish off the rest of us." Nadia growled, fisting the charcoal in her palms.

Devora sucked in a breath, unsure of how to respond. But Nadia's raw anger struck her heart. *Is that how I sounded when I spoke of Tunri? Filled with anger and contempt at what He'd done to me?*

As Nadia took out her notebook and started scribbling with a scowl, Devora's mind raced back to a story Mama once told her. When Mama was the age to categorize, she desperately wanted to become the king's royal gardener. She practiced the categorization for the position every day until it was time for her Categorization Call. But when the day came, Mama said it was as if Tunri categorized the stones Himself. They didn't stack for the position of royal gardener. They stacked for Vlacklear.

Devora remembered how Mama said she was heartbroken, then angry at Tunri. She didn't want to be trapped with snooty intellectuals. She wanted to be free with the flowers and herbs. But Mama followed Tunri's guidance and told Devora if she had never attended Vlacklear, she would have never met Papa and eventually had Devora. Mama said though Vlacklear wasn't her original plan, it had been a better one, bringing her more joy and happiness than she ever would've gained as the royal gardener. Papa, of course, made sure Mama had the finest garden, filled with any flower or plant she desired.

Devora blinked, focusing back on Nadia. *Could my situation possibly be like Mama's?*

The answer to why Devora was sent to the Fortress was right in front of her this entire time. Even though the king switched the categorization colors, Tunri still guided her here. And, although she didn't enjoy her Sight, Tunri's visions had always been true. He had never failed her before, would he fail her now? Or would he come through like He always had?

"I don't know anything about Pahga or any other deities for that matter," Devora said, leaning against the Theater's wall. "But I do know of one God that is true to what He says."

Nadia glanced up from her notebook, eyebrows raised.

Seating herself next to Nadia, Devora brought her knees to her chin. "Since I received my categorization stones, I wanted to go to Vlacklear. While others could create different color combinations, I could only stack Vlacklear's color category, knowing that was where I was meant to go."

Nadia placed her charcoal and notebook down and fully faced Devora.

"But the day of my Categorization Call, the categories changed. Instead of achieving my dream, I was sent here,"—Devora gestured to the domed ceiling of the empty Theater— "literally to prison."

Nadia smirked.

Seeing her relax, Devora eased into her story. "I hated Tunri for bringing me here. Why hadn't He given me what I wanted?"

Nadia nodded, her eyes swimming with understanding and empathy.

Devora ran her finger through the sand, drawing circles. "What I didn't realize was what *I* wanted wasn't the best for me. Would I achieve at Vlacklear? Yes. Would I be the top of my class? Probably."

Nadia laughed. "Confident, aren't we?"

Devora grinned. "But where would I be after that? Would I have any friends, or would I be drowning in my own studies, caring too much about my future to even look at another person?"

She studied her blistered hands and chipped nails. They had once been so smooth from never having to lift a finger. "I would never know how rewarding it felt to learn how to defend myself. Or what it was like to have friends and laugh at nonsense." Devora thought of Ida's kindness, Reese's intelligence, Hestia's laughter, and Nadia's creativity. Their friendship filled a void she hadn't realized had been gaping inside her. Devora had grown used to having them around and didn't want to remember her life without them.

"Though I still dislike the Fortress, I'm beginning to be thankful that Tunri sent me here."

It was true. If Devora had been caught with her curse back in Grenly, the people would've killed her on the spot. In a twisted way, the Regulus Protecti tournament may be the very thing that saved her life.

Though, the coming battle still worried her. In just a few weeks she would be at the frontlines, battling Kadesh. Maybe—hopefully—Tunri had bigger plans for her than to send her out to the battlefield to die.

"If Tunri hadn't sent me here," Devora continued, trying to dismiss her dismal thoughts about war. "I would've never met you or have learned how to kick your butt."

Nadia's head shot up, her eyes watering before she burst out laughing. "I guess I have Tunri to thank for all the bruises on my arms then, huh?"

She held up her forearms to show the blue smudges forming from all Devora's ill-aimed kicks and punches.

Wincing, Devora gave Nadia a sheepish grin. "I apologize for those injuries, but I meant what I said. I'm thankful Tunri sent me here if it was only to gain your and the others' friendship."

"Aw, Dev." Nadia wrapped an arm around Devora's neck. "I don't know this Tunri, or if I want to know another god, but, if He's real, I'm thankful He brought us here, too."

Chapter Nineteen

The Theater, The Fortress

Dipping her hands in the washbasin, Devora smoothed the murky water over her hair to tame the frizz. Today was the first round of Regulus Protecti. Everything she'd learned flashed through her mind as she waited for Nadia to finish getting dressed.

Devora stretched her arms above her head. Her muscles ached, but she was surprised to discover excitement, not fear, making her nerves jittery.

Will I be able to pull this off?

Reese kept reminding her that the odds were greatly stacked against her. But if Tunri had sent the vision of her meeting with Warden Hazor and the other officials, Devora had to have earned an audience with them somehow. Her vision gave her hope.

Devora glanced at the purple fabric peeking out from her pillow. Padding to her bed, she pulled out the wrinkled silk sash. Had she worn beautiful clothes like this every day not so long ago? It felt like an eternity—a dream, too amazing to be real.

Thoughts of Mama and Papa churned in her mind. *Where are they now? Are they okay?* Though she had continuously inquired about her parents when running into Sir Jacques, she still hadn't heard anything since the note. What had happened to them? And what had happened to Captain Blake? She hadn't seen him since he stormed out of the Theater a week ago.

The captain's face invaded her thoughts. His strong jaw, furrowed brow, and stormy eyes that seemed to hold more sorrow than they let on. But Devora pushed the image away. There had been no word from the captain. He left her alone—without a teacher, without guidance, without a hope.

I was a fool again.

Smoothing the sash between her palms, Devora laid it over her shoulder and across her chest before tying it at her waist. Though she was no longer nobility, she would represent her family. When she won Regulus Protecti, honor would reign on the Medee name once again.

"You ready to kick some convict butt?" Nadia asked, jumping out from behind the privacy curtain. She punched her fists in front of her as she jogged in place, her short blonde hair flopping into her eyes.

Devora laughed. "I sure hope so."

Her other friends couldn't believe Devora entered the tournament. Devora had to quickly make up an excuse that the king personally recommended her for it. A few of the other new recruits had entered, as well, though they'd been advised against it, seeing how they were all new to combat.

So, Devora's lie wasn't completely unbelievable. She didn't want her friends to be involved with any conflict because she was a Seer.

"I'm glad I'm not you," Nadia confessed, slicking her hair back with the murky water from their basin. "Being stuck in a pit with a bunch of ruthless, smelly brutes?" She flicked the droplets from her fingers. "No, thank you."

"You could easily win," Devora replied, giving Sir Blakesalot a wad of dried-up mush she saved for him the other day. The bird cawed before pecking at the hard treat. After a flap of his singed feathers, he chowed down.

Nadia's eyes flashed. "I only know how to fight because I had to survive. I don't want to fight any more than I have to."

Devora guided Sir Blakesalot to his bar on the top corner of the cell. "I'm sorry. Before you told me, I had no idea the encampments were so terrible."

Nadia opened her mouth to respond when Ida appeared outside their cell.

"Are you sure about this, Devora?" Ida clasped her hands in front of her. "It seems extremely dangerous to participate in this...competition. Even with the king's blessing."

Devora tried to muster up a smile as she and Nadia exited their cell. "I'm sure I'll be fine. Plus, there are other new recruits too."

Reese eyed Devora's sash before holding out her abacus. "By my calculations, your probability of winning is twenty-two point three percent."

"Reese," Hestia hissed, elbowing her twin in the rib. Reese rubbed the spot and gave Devora an apologetic look.

"Don't listen to her, Devora. Crush them into the dirt." Hestia ground her fist into her palm and growled.

Devora chuckled nervously, tugging at her sash. "Well, that's a higher probability than yesterday. I only had a fifteen percent chance then." But she knew Reese was right. Without Tunri's help, she was a goner.

Nadia gave her a quick hug. "Be careful," she whispered.

The others joined in, hugging and encouraging Devora before she marched to the Theater.

Devora's heart thundered as she stood before the double doors. Every person in the Fortress was required to attend the three rounds of Regulus Protecti. Plus, she had heard rumors that the king and queen, along with other noble families, were invited to attend as well. Devora's heart clenched, thinking about all the people she once aligned herself with. While she was fighting for her life, they were merely seeking entertainment.

Devora glanced down at her scuffed boots and torn sash. *If I was among them, as a noble, would I enjoy this entertainment as well?*

Placing her hand on the metal door, Devora bowed her head and for the first time, she fully surrendered her plans to Tunri. *Tunri, if this is your way, help me make it through this. Alive.*

The metal door creaked on rusted hinges as she pushed it open. Squaring her shoulders, Devora entered the Theater. The seats surrounding the center were packed with the fine silks and frills of nobility, their bodies squished together as the guards tried to shove more in the stands. The variety of bright colors overwhelmed Devora as she took in royal families from all over Tenton. The fear she hadn't felt before slid around her, squeezing her lungs until it was hard to breathe.

Cold sweat dripped down her neck as she slowly strode to the edge of the Theater where the other competitors stood. All the practice equipment had been put away, leaving the sandy center of the arena bare. Peeking down the line of competitors, Devora recognized the tall, dark head of One Shot. Fear paralyzed her limbs. How could she defeat the man who had killed four men in one shot? Devora's eyes further drifted to Babshee and she lost all hope completely.

"Why hasn't someone killed you yet?" Sir Conan growled behind her.

Devora spun around, assessing the simple gray Fortress uniform the knight was wearing, identical to her own and all the other competitors. *Is he competing too?*

Upon seeing her violet eyes, Sir Conan flinched but quickly covered it by rearing back and spitting on the ground, only inches from her feet.

Devora curled her toes in her boots, forcing herself to not to break her gaze from the stout knight's glower. Although Sir Conan was no longer wearing his armor, he still had a few inches of height on her and ten times the muscle. Devora wanted to shrink away. She didn't *want* to be here. She hated the Fortress. But she was still alive and refused to die at the hands of Sir Conan or anyone else. Grabbing the end of her sash, Devora lifted her chin.

"I was requested to compete," she declared. "By King Atol, himself."

"Even if the king did request you—which is likely the only reason you're still alive—every competitor needs a sponsor to vouch for their skills and intent." Sir Conan scanned her body, stopping at her sash. His eyes blazed. "That's not Fortress attire." He barreled toward her, his arm outstretched, ready to destroy her sash like he had at her Categorization Call.

Devora planted a foot behind her, ready to attack Sir Conan when a warm, strong hand grasped her shoulder.

"Sir Conan, I'll ask you only once not to touch my competitor," Captain Blake commanded.

Devora's heart almost exploded at the sound of the captain's chilling voice. Her stomach twisted in so many knots, she might be sick. She scolded her treacherous heart for leaping for joy at the presence of the steely-eyed captain.

Sir Conan lifted his hands in mock surrender as he backed away with a conniving smirk.

"Let's go, Medee," the captain said, and Devora matched his strides.

As soon as they were out of earshot, Captain Blake leaned down, his warm breath tickling her ear. "Sorry I'm late."

Devora's stomach clenched, and she swallowed before answering, "I'm just glad you're here."

She could've sworn she saw the captain grin, but when she looked again, his hardened jaw was locked in place.

"Where were you?" she asked. But when she looked up for a reply, he merely shook his head as if he couldn't answer. Or didn't want to.

They continued until they were at the opposite wall of the Theater. Devora glanced up, trying to find her friends among the sea of nobility in the stands, waiting for her failure. She cringed at the clinking of gold coins as the wealthy gambled for their favorite competitor.

Devora frowned. *How can they choose already? The tournament hasn't begun.*

Captain Blake cleared his throat and faced her. Uncertainty danced across his face. "Medee. Devora. There's something I need to tell you."

Her pulse thumped between her ears. "What is it?"

"It's your—"

Warden Hazor's deep voice boomed from the top of the Theater. "Competitors, today is the day you may redeem yourself for your past crimes."

The warden peered down at the group of forty prisoners, including Devora. His white hair shone like a halo against the bright torches lighting the arena. "Sponsors, now is your time to exit the circle."

Captain Blake's strong hands gripped her shoulders. Warmth flowed through the thin fabric of her uniform. Though the captain's lips formed a line, his eyes were bright with worry.

"Remember what Nadia taught you. Deflect and dodge as much as you can. Engage at the last possible moment." He squeezed her shoulders. "I know you can do this."

With that, he released his grip and marched toward the stands.

Devora's heart raced as she watched him leave. *How did he know about Nadia? Was he the one who asked her to train me?*

The other sponsors exited the Theater, leaving her alone with thirty-nine blood-thirsty prisoners, eyeing her like she was their next meal.

"Competitors, you will have thirty minutes to subdue as many opponents as you can with your bare hands. When the bell chimes, those that are left standing will move on to Round Two. Those that have fallen will gain three more years to their sentence and duty as a soldier."

The warden flipped the hourglass, and a bell rang, echoing throughout the Theater. In an instant, every ferocious prisoner rushed at one another.

Three more years at the Fortress? Her throat tightened as she gasped for air, panic encroaching upon her. *How am I going to survive this?*

Growls and snarls bounded through the Theater as Devora pressed herself against the smooth wall. Everything Nadia had taught her vanished.

A bulky, tall man slammed another man's head into the wall, knocking him unconscious. Another new recruit jumped on the back of a middle-aged man with graying hair and bit his ear until it bled.

Trying to tear her eyes away, Devora scrambled away from a trio of men equally bashing one another. Maybe she had seen her vision wrong and Tunri hadn't claimed her victorious. Her thoughts started to spiral down when they hooked onto something Captain Blake said.

I know you can do this.

The vision of her seated across from Warden Hazor reentered her thoughts. Tunri knew she could do this too. The vat of boiling silver appeared in her mind's eye. The training and tournament were just another step in refining her to become who she was truly meant to be. Not some silly girl who only cared about herself, but a warrior, ready to fight and defend what was right.

"Devora!" Nadia cried above the crowd, waving her hands in the air.

Devora snapped her head toward her friends. Ida's hands clasped to her chest, her lips moving as if praying. Hestia jumped up and down, cheering while Reese smacked her abacus beads back and forth, looking like she was going to be sick. Devora focused on Nadia, who was pointing to her chest. It took a moment for her to realize that Nadia was referencing her sash. Devora gripped the purple silk, finding the confidence she needed.

She wouldn't cower. She would fight. And she would win.

Chapter Twenty

The Theater, The Fortress

The prisoners dove after one another, punching, kicking, and biting to subdue their opponents. It wasn't anything close to formal fighting. In fact, it looked like a giant pile of animals, vying for the spot of alpha. The crowd roared as the competitors tackled one another, cheering at the top of their lungs.

Devora dodged a body that smacked against the wall. A sickening crack came from the man before he slid to the ground, motionless. She stifled her gasp as she wove through the sweaty, swaying competitors.

"Engage at the last possible moment," she whispered to herself, ducking between the legs of Babshee, who had almost broken her in half the first day. She definitely didn't want to engage with him.

Babshee reached down and grabbed a petite man with long black hair. Laughing wildly, the giant spun the man around by his ponytail and slammed him on the ground. The crowd gasped, then cheered.

Sickened by the nobles' love for violence and bloodshed, Devora swerved through the growling competitors. "Dodge and deflect as much as you can."

"Come here, Seer! Let's see if those cursed eyes will save you now," a short man with bulging biceps and an eye patch yelled, lunging at her.

Devora yelped and darted out of the way. She lifted her hands to defend herself when a long leg shot out and tripped the short man who pursued her. The man's face planted into the ground, a large foot smashing his head into the sand.

Panting, Devora glanced up to see One Shot.

He gave her a nod. "Careful."

Devora stared at One Shot as he hoisted the short man up and launched him at the wall. Devora's eyes widened as the man crashed into the stone then fell to the ground with a thud. His legs twitched before his eyes rolled back.

One Shot gave her another polite nod then disappeared back into the chaos as Devora gripped her sash and looked around. At least half of the competitors were already unconscious. Bodies laid sprawled upon the sandy ground of the Theater. How much time had passed?

Swallowing, Devora sped to the other side of the Theater. She didn't want to get caught standing still for too long. Glancing wildly up at the hourglass, she found the golden grains of sand were more than halfway to the bottom. Relief blossomed in her chest. She was almost there. Only a few more moments of avoiding these monsters.

But her hope soon vanished when heavy steps clomped behind her. Before she could run, a strong hand grabbed her thick braid and yanked it back. Crying out, Devora brought her hands to her head. She tried to free her hair from her opponent's grasp, but they wouldn't relent.

"I told you, you shouldn't be here," Sir Conan breathed against her ear. "There's only one place a Seer belongs, and that's in a grave."

Nausea boiled in Devora's stomach as rotting fish and bad hygiene fumed off the knight. She scrunched her nose. *Has he ever taken a bath?*

"You reek," she spat, trying to free her braid from his grasp, but it was no use. He twisted her beautiful hair around his dirt-covered hands, pulling Devora closer until his putrid stench surrounded her.

"But you smell so good," he whispered, and Devora wanted to crawl out of her skin.

"Let go of me," she growled before rearing her head back and slamming it into Sir Conan's face.

A crack erupted from his nose, but Devora didn't waste any time. As soon as she heard the break, she spun around and jabbed Sir Conan in the throat. When the knight choked and grabbed his neck, she took advantage of the opportunity. Bringing her leg up, Devora performed a roundhouse kick flawlessly as her boot dug into Sir Conan's stomach. For a moment, the knight stood still, and Devora feared she was no stronger than when she first entered the Fortress. But when he released a gust of air and doubled over, Devora knew she could escape. Sprinting past the knight, she kicked him in the rear, and he toppled over with a grunt.

Tying her braid into a knot as she leaped over more unconscious bodies, she risked a glance up. The last few grains tumbled into the bottom of the hourglass and her shoulders relaxed.

"Time!" Warden Hazor called.

Devora placed a hand against the wall, her chest heaving. *Thank Tunri. I made it.*

"You," Sir Conan growled, spitting blood and saliva on the ground through the gap in his teeth from Captain Blake's punch.

Her heart dropped as the brutish guard stomped toward her, clutching his stomach. A horrible blue bruise had already formed on Sir Conan's now crooked nose.

"How dare you attack me." The knight revealed a small blade hidden in the sleeve of his uniform. "Prophets and nobles are filth. And you're both."

Devora pressed herself against the wall, panic paralyzing her limbs. He wouldn't kill her in front of everyone would he? There were too many witnesses.

Remember where you are, Dev, she scolded herself. She was a Seer. They wanted to kill her anyway. Sir Conan was just speeding up the process.

Unlike Devora, these men had actually committed crimes and would do anything to get out of the Fortress. But Sir Conan was a knight. One of the warden's guards. Was he a part of Warden Hazor's plan to kill her?

Suddenly drawn to Sir Conan's attack, the crowd gasped as the knight reared back and jabbed the knife at her heart. Shouts of cheating echoed through the Theater as Devora jerked to the right at the last moment. The knife lodged itself in a crack in the wall. Cursing, Sir Conan gripped it with both hands, trying to free his weapon.

"I believe the warden said 'Time,'" Captain Blake's cool voice said.

Devora spun around to find the captain hovering over them from the stands. His face was composed, but his gaze could cut iron. The captain held out a long, thin blade. With his arm extended, Captain Blake could easily slice Sir Conan's throat in one swipe.

With a loud grunt, Sir Conan wrenched his dagger out of the wall, stumbling back a few steps. He righted himself, fixing Captain Blake with a toothy grin. Then he flipped the knife around and used the tip to clean his yellow teeth.

Devora scoffed. He was going to stab her with a knife he used to clean his nasty mouth? At least have some decency and kill her with a clean weapon.

"I should slice your throat for cheating," the captain threatened, probing the blade under Sir Conan's chin.

Sir Conan took a step back. "I don't see why you care so much about her, Blake." The knight tucked the weapon back in his sleeve. "This one's done for, and you know it."

Devora wanted to correct Sir Conan and inform him that Tunri had shown her winning this competition, but her focus was on Captain Blake. His hardened demeanor broke for a moment, and it was enough for her to see fear flash across his eyes.

"All right, Conan." Warden Hazor appeared next to the captain. Though both men were the same height, Warden Hazor's wide shoulders and thick muscles made the captain look like a child. "Somehow Medee made it through Round One, and we have to respect that."

Sir Conan spat again, glaring at Devora before exiting the Theater.

"Forgive my competitor," the warden said in a smooth voice, but Devora heard the sarcasm riling beneath the apology. "He has a bad temper."

"I didn't think you would pick a competitor, sir," Captain Blake replied, sheathing his blade. "It's unlike you to pick a favorite, especially one that doesn't follow your rules."

Warden Hazor let out a hearty laugh. "Blake, the king may be running Tenton into the ground, but the Fortress is my domain. I will do what I wish."

Captain Blake's lips thinned, but he bowed anyway, and Devora knew Sir Conan would get away with whatever he wanted, so long as the warden approved of him.

As if hearing her thoughts, Warden Hazor focused his dark eyes on her. "Lady Devora Medee. I was wondering what would become of you when you entered my prison. Who would've thought Cusha was hiding such a prize in Grenly." Warden Hazor stroked his groomed white mustache as he scanned her, stopping at her sash. The smirk returned, but his eyes were stone. "We haven't cut ties with the family, I see."

Devora gripped her sash. She wouldn't allow the warden to take it from her. She needed the strength of her parents to make it through the next two rounds.

Warden Hazor analyzed her again then faced the captain. He clapped the captain on the shoulder. "You were right, Blake. Maybe our little Seer will prove useful to us after all. I'm glad you talked me out of killing her."

Devora tightened her fingers around the sash, wanting to lash out at the warden. But after a quick look from the captain, she bit her tongue.

"I am, as well, sir," Captain Blake replied.

Warden Hazor's eyes narrowed before he started toward the stairs. After a few steps, he stopped and peered over his shoulder. "And Blake? See that your competitor does more than run away like a frightened child. Our audience would like more action, and I want to enjoy this competition."

"Understood, sir," Captain Blake said without hesitation. He bowed again, not standing upright until the warden exited the Theater.

The Theater had cleared out of all spectators and competitors. Now the medics from the infirmary started collecting the last of the unconscious competitors. Once the final body was lifted between two hefty medics, they trudged out of the Theater, leaving Captain Blake and Devora completely alone. The iron door clicked shut, echoing through the barren space.

As soon as the door closed, Captain Blake reeled to Devora, eyes flaming. "What were you thinking wearing that?" The captain hurled the question at her, pointing to her sash. "You already have a target on your back. Do you *want* to be killed?"

Devora's lips parted at the outburst before she clenched her jaw shut. How silly of her to think he would congratulate her. She *had* survived the first round. Barely, but still.

Devora raised her chin. "I know I'm not nobility anymore, but I won't forget my family. I will bring honor back to the Medee name."

"Not by getting killed," he shot back.

"I clearly didn't get killed," she snapped, motioning to herself as her face heated with anger.

Why is he being so cruel?

"You need to be smarter, more careful," he said, jumping down from the stands. He landed perfectly on both feet and rushed to the middle. "Let me show you a different move. This one is quicker and will help you escape faster." Captain Blake pulled out one of the wooden poles the soldiers trained on.

Devora held back her groan. She wanted nothing more than to take a bath and sleep.

But as she watched the captain pound the wooden pole, she began to realize he wasn't training for her benefit, but his own. Sweat beaded at his brow as he reared back and attacked it from different angles, grunting as he damaged the wood.

As he continued, Devora noticed a thin chain wrapped around the captain's neck, hidden beneath his tunic. When he lowered his stance to jab at a different angle, the chain popped out, revealing the imperial opal ring Devora's father had sent.

Devora sat a little straighter and peered at the gem. She thought he had gotten rid of it. *Why is he wearing it?*

As she watched the captain, Devora thought about Mama and Papa. Were they okay? Had Mama been able to leave the house? When would they be together again?

Lost in her thoughts, Devora didn't know how much time had passed since Captain Blake started unleashing his wrath on the pole. Exhausted, Devora seated herself on the ground. Pulling her knees to her chest, she wrapped her arms around them and waited.

As Devora rested her chin on her knees, she watched the captain perform strike after strike. Each move seamlessly flowed into the next. There were no mistakes, no interruptions. It was beautiful.

Captain Blake's shoulders heaved as he finally slowed down. He stared at the wooden pole as if seeing something or someone else in its place.

"Are you all right?" Devora called from her spot on the ground.

The captain flinched, his head whipping to her with wide eyes. He had forgotten she was there.

Maybe she should have left, but she couldn't bring herself to leave Captain Blake so distraught. Clearing his throat, the captain ran a hand over his mussed chestnut hair and straightened his shirt. A dark blue tunic and pants wrapped around his lean, muscular frame. Devora had seen Papa dressed in the same formal wear when he met with King Atol. *Did Captain Blake meet with the king? Or did he dress up for the tournament?*

Captain Blake wiped the sweat from his brow before striding toward her. Silently, he sat on the ground next to her, his warm shoulder brushing against hers as he crisscrossed his legs.

"You did well," Captain Blake finally said, keeping his eyes glued to the wooden pole in the center of the Theater. "If you evade Conan, I think you have a chance."

Devora wanted to laugh. If her abilities hadn't been exposed, she would've never been in this position. She would've never asked for Captain Blake's help. But, strangely enough, she was thankful for both.

"Thank you," she replied quietly, rubbing her fingers along her still throbbing skull. "I don't know why he hates me so much." She studied the thin fibers of her pants. "Well, I do. But he hated me before anyone knew I was a Seer."

Captain Blake leaned his head against the wall and closed his eyes. "Conan was arrested for theft. He was courting a noble girl just to steal her jewels and was caught. It seems he hasn't gotten over it."

Devora stuck out her tongue. "Ugh, I can't believe any woman would want to court him." Captain Blake chuckled, and Devora found herself loving the sound. "Anyway," she continued, "I appreciate your help. But you don't need to help me anymore. I know you have many responsibilities."

She didn't want to feel the heavy void if he had to leave again. He was a high-ranking officer, after all. It was better to call off their agreement now so he could be free, and she didn't have the hope that something more would happen.

Devora caught the captain's look of surprise in her periphery.

His brows arched in confusion. "I don't think so. You don't know how to wield a mech properly. I don't want you going into the weapons round without knowing that. If any round is going to be nasty, it'll be Round Two." He brushed the sand off his shiny boots. "Lucky for you, I'm not only an expert at hand-to-hand combat, but at weapons combat, as well." He gave her a small smile.

"Sir Jacques taught us while you were away," Devora replied. "I can figure out the rest on my own." She worked up a smile, but knew it fell flat. She drew lines in the sand with her finger as she confessed, "I don't want the warden to punish you because of me."

She was silly to have even thought of asking for Captain Blake's help. Did she really think anything would come of it? She was just as foolish as she had been with Tristan. She shouldn't have allowed herself to get so close.

Devora straightened her legs and started to stand.

"I don't care what the warden thinks," Captain Blake said, his shoulders lifting as he took a breath. "And I understand what you're going through."

Devora faced him so he wouldn't miss one fleck of her violet eyes. "You know what it's like to be taken from everything you know and love and thrown into prison?"

He leaned his head against the wall, meeting her gaze head on. His features softened into a somber expression. "Yes, actually, I do."

She slowly sat back down, waiting for him to explain.

The captain pushed out a breath, rubbing the back of his neck. "You're not going to like it."

She crisscrossed her legs. "Try me."

"Tristan has always been a troublemaker," Captain Blake began, and Devora's heart plummeted. Tristan was the last person she wanted to talk about.

The captain kept his gaze focused on the empty stands of the Theater. "When we were kids, it was little things like stealing an extra cocoa cake from the bakery or swiping vanilla cane from the fields. But as we got older, he got into deeper trouble than he could handle."

"What happened?"

Pinching the bridge of his nose, the captain squeezed his eyes shut. "Tristan has a gambling problem. One that my father and I could barely keep up with. My father owns a vineyard in Ballear, so we didn't have much."

Devora nodded, remembering her studies on the four regions of Tenton. The western village of Ballear was more rural than the other surrounding cities. From what Papa said, it was a peaceful area, but not many citizens traveled there. Earning income was hard for the people in the western region. The majority of their wages came from agriculture, but with the war, most of their produce went to the soldiers. Additionally, the king didn't compensate the farmers well, if he compensated them at all.

Devora studied Captain Blake, trying to picture him pruning vines and squashing grapes instead of training officers and soldiers. The thought warmed her heart.

"With me being in my second year at Vlacklear, money was extremely tight. Books, uniforms, it's all extremely expensive."

Devora flinched. "*You* went to Vlacklear Academy? But you said you categorized for the..." she stopped.

He had said he categorized five times, but he had never said for what. Devora shook her head. She had assumed he had categorized for the military academy that was now held at the Fortress.

Sneaky wordplay, Captain.

"Ah, you figured it out." He smirked, tapping the toe of her boot. "I was wondering if you'd catch it. I started at Vlacklear and yes, I still categorized for it five times, perfectly."

Devora lifted her brows. *Just like me.*

Captain Blake's lips flattened. "The gang Tristan gambled with demanded he pay up or they would kill him. Instead,

Tristan took matters into his own hands and killed their leader first."

Devora choked. "What?"

The captain bowed his head, clamping his hands into fists. "They were going to send him here, as a prisoner. I knew my brother would be killed within a few days. And after our mother was taken by the kingdom, it would destroy my father for Tristan to be gone too. So, I contacted Warden Hazor and made a deal. Tristan and I could switch places. I would take his place in the Fortress, as a prisoner, while he would take mine at Vlacklear. If he followed the rules and graduated on time, he would be pardoned."

Devora's mind flashed to Tristan kissing the creamy-skinned girl by the wall outside her home. He had said he was on break when he met Devora, but Grenly was a long way from Juro *and* Vlacklear.

She turned to Captain Blake but couldn't bear the thought of telling him. His shoulders sagged, his head bowed. Her heart squeezed. He looked so defeated, nothing like the strong, confident man she had gotten to know over the past few weeks.

"So, you came here?" Devora questioned with disbelief. "For a crime you didn't commit?"

He rubbed his eyes. "Yes. I befriended Jacques, who had just started working here, and we worked our way through the ranks of the Fortress until Warden Hazor saw us fit to become his guards. Vlacklear contacted the warden and told him my brother had dropped out of school, so they wanted me to fill his spot." His voice was nonchalant, as if he had removed every emotion from his heart regarding Tristan.

Devora's heart fell to the pit of her stomach. *Dropped out?* Anger swirled in her chest.

"How dare he?" she exclaimed, jumping up. Devora paced in front of Captain Blake, shaking her fist in the air. "After everything you sacrificed, and he dropped out? What a terrible person! I can't believe I even—"

The captain's gray eyes twinkled as he chuckled. "You even what? Please continue."

Devora opened her lips before closing them. She crossed her arms over her chest. "It doesn't matter. It's definitely not happening now."

Captain Blake stood, his tall body leaning over hers. Devora held her breath. Wood, dust, and sweat never smelled so good. "That's good to hear."

Her heart raced, her stomach flipping before she turned away. She couldn't get close. She wouldn't be fooled again.

"I'm sorry about Tristan," she said quietly, threading her braid between her fingers. "That must have been hard."

The captain took a step away from her and she immediately felt the distance. "It's in the past. But—" he continued, "what's not in the past is Round Two of Regulus Protecti."

Devora blinked, still comprehending the quick change from the captain's tender side to his militant one.

"Did you really think you could get rid of me that easily?" He stood tall and shook his head. "Get some rest tonight, Medee. Tomorrow starts your weapons training." A devious glint came to his steel-gray eyes along with a smirk. "We'll give the warden a show to remember."

Chapter Twenty-One

Level Two, The Fortress

Devora ran back to her cell, ready to grab her other clean uniform, so she could finally take a bath. She couldn't wait to cleanse herself of all the sweat, grime, and Sir Conan's awful stench. A shiver ran through her as she remembered how close the knight had gotten. And he had touched her hair with his soiled hands. *Who knew where those nasty claws had been?*

As she flew through the halls, Devora noticed more prisoners nodded her way or acknowledged her with awe instead of contempt.

Is it because I prevailed through Round One?

Not wanting to dwell on the thought, she burst into the cell to find Nadia seated on her bed, murmuring to herself while scribbling in her notebook.

"Hey!" Nadia said, hiding something behind her back as she bounced up from her bed. "You did great out there."

"Thank you. I wouldn't have made it without your help."

Nadia bowed. "Of course. I'm not happy about Sir Conan, though. It was low of him to use your hair against you."

"I agree," Devora replied, running her hand down her braid. "But Warden Hazor didn't give any other rules."

"True. That's why we have to be smart and find a loophole." Nadia held out her hands, a wide grin splitting her oval face. "Surprise!"

Devora's eyes widened as she gazed upon a delicate silver hairpin, perfectly balanced on Nadia's charcoal-covered palms. A trio of pink pearls adorned one end while the other was sharpened to a deadly point.

"I thought this would help hold back your long hair, so there aren't any more repeats of what happened today." She pushed the gift toward Devora.

"Nadia," Devora breathed as she reached out and gently grasped the pin. It was as light as a feather; she was scared it would break. "It's beautiful. Where did you get the materials?"

Nadia shrugged. "Kitchen duty has its benefits. Gerard knows a lot of people."

Devora quirked a brow. "Gerard?" Her mind raced back to the angry man with the tattoos and soup ladle. "The tattooed man that serves gruel?"

"He's pretty pleasant once you get past all his growling," Nadia chuckled. "Oh, one thing you should know about your hairpin: not only is it a stunning work of art, but if wielded properly, you can disarm and subdue your opponent with a single prick."

A laugh erupted from Devora's mouth. "Of course, it can." She leaned over and hugged Nadia. "Thank you for this. It means more than you know."

"Well, go on!" Nadia waved her hand at Devora's braid. "Let's see if my design worked."

Grabbing her braid, Devora twisted it into a bun and wove the pin throughout her thick ebony strands. She dropped her hands to her sides and gently shook her head. Everything stayed in place.

Nadia pumped her fist in the air before circling Devora.

"It could probably be better if I elongated the pin; that way, you have more material to weave through this wild mane."

Devora scoffed, but Nadia was already off scratching new ideas in her notebook, muttering to herself.

"You're back!" Hestia cried, flinging her arms around Devora. "We were so worried."

Ida came behind and hugged Devora as well.

Reese cleared her throat. "I've redone my calculations, and it seems your probability has increased exponentially."

Devora laughed. "Thank you, Reese."

"Are you hurt in any way?" Ida asked, gently touching Devora's arm. "What Sir Conan did was awful."

"My head is a little sore, but other than that, I'm okay," Devora answered, scratching her scalp.

"That dirty scoundrel," Hestia sneered, balling her hand into a fist. "If I see him again, I'll punch him right in the jaw."

"Hestia," Reese sighed, shaking her head. "You'll see him at training again tomorrow, and we both know you won't do anything."

Hestia paused and tapped her narrow chin. "Well, I'll send him a nasty glare."

Sir Blakesalot crowed twice, knowing that if he squawked a third time, a rock would be thrown at his head. Nadia and Devora got up and dressed for another day of combat training. There were only two weeks left before they were to be sent to the frontlines. Devora's anxiety was rising by the day. How could time pass so quickly? Two weeks before war, two weeks before the tournament ended, two weeks to find out whether she was going to live or die.

Sucking in a breath, Devora undid her messy braid. She couldn't think about that. Tunri had guided her here and, so far, she had been okay. She had even made it through the first round of Regulus Protecti.

Papa would be proud. Devora sent a prayer, hoping her parents were still alive.

Once her wild strands were tame, Devora plaited her hair again, and the long braid smacked against her back. As she turned to fix her sheets, Nadia's hairpin shone in the corner of her eye.

Devora leaned down and picked up the delicate piece from inside her pillow. She had wrapped it in her tattered sash and hidden it away like her other treasures. Taking her long braid, Devora spun it in a spiral at the nape of her neck before weaving the hairpin through. The pin was so thin, she thought her hair might break it, but when she lowered her hands, the intricate knot stayed.

"Looking good," Nadia said with a wink. "Maybe Mister Pants will make another appearance."

Devora snorted in response before the two girls joined the others and went to breakfast, enduring another helping of white mush. A trio of prisoners passed by them and waved to Devora as they entered the dining hall.

"Making more friends, are we?" Nadia chuckled.

"I'm just glad they don't want to kill me anymore," Devora confessed as she grabbed her bowl. Taking their bowls of gruel, Devora and Nadia sat at their table with the others.

"Is there any variety here?" Devora asked, narrowing her eyes at the glob in front of her.

"I'm not sure if I'd want to know what it was," Ida said, frowning at the mush.

"Unfortunately, no," Nadia replied, stabbing her food with a wooden stake she had carved. The piece of wood cemented in the center. Nadia wrenched it out, leaving a hole where the weapon had been.

"It's not that bad, guys," Hestia piped in, scooping a heaping pile of mush into her mouth.

Nadia laughed. "Even though I work in the kitchen and know how the gruel is made, I still think they're poisoning us."

"If that were true, Tenton wouldn't have any soldiers left to fight," Captain Blake interrupted.

Devora jumped at his voice. Hestia squeaked, her mush falling from her mouth as Ida cowered and scooted closer to Nadia and Reese.

Glancing over her shoulder, Devora saw the captain dressed in the ugly white and brown training uniform the rest of them had to wear. Though she hated the boring uniform on herself, it stretched perfectly over the captain's toned, lean body.

Biting her lip, Devora tried to subdue the thought.

"Medee." Captain Blake peered down at her.

Her eyes shot up to his. The hardened gray steel was back, assessing her abilities and finding her weaknesses.

She stood and placed a fist over her chest before bowing. "Sir."

"Warden Hazor has given permission for competitors of the tournament to train with their sponsors during their scheduled group trainings. You will join me for weapons training while Sir Jacques teaches the rest of the officers." Without waiting to hear her reply, he spun around and marched out of the dining hall.

Devora watched him exit before turning back to the others. Hestia and Ida shared a look before giggling.

"What?" Devora asked.

"Nothing, nothing," Hestia squeaked, smiling widely.

Reese stayed focused on her abacus, but a sly grin stretched across her small lips.

Devora turned to Nadia, who shrugged. "Better catch up to the cap, Dev."

Nodding, Devora grabbed her *ligula* and started toward the Theater.

When she arrived at the entrance, she found Captain Blake standing by another iron door adjacent to the Theater. As she studied the door, her eyes caught several other doors lining the walls next to the Theater entrance.

The captain pulled a key on an iron ring from his pocket and unlocked the first door. The iron door swung inward, revealing a dark room. "These rooms used to be where they would torture prisoners of war for information," Captain Blake explained as he strode into the space, lighting the torches adorning the walls. The flames illuminated the long rectangular area. It was barren save for a pile of wood in the far-left corner. "Since the war began twenty years ago and the military was moved to the Fortress, these rooms were converted into training rooms for individual combat sessions."

"I see," Devora replied, not stepping further into the room.

How many people have been tortured in this room? How many people killed?

Goosebumps rose on her arms as she stayed planted in the threshold.

"Devora, no one has been killed in here," Captain Blake deadpanned as if hearing her thoughts. He pulled out two wooden mechs and handed her one. "If you want to surprise your opponents, the only way is to practice privately. Which is why I chose for us to practice here."

Nodding, she grasped her hand around the wooden training sword. "Have you told Warden Hazor about my vision?"

The captain sighed. "Warden Hazor is not a religious man. Any vision or gift from Tunri or any other god means nothing to him. The only way to save Tenton is by proving your worth. Win the tournament, and I guarantee he will listen to anything you say."

"Is that why he listens to you?" Devora probed. "You've already proven yourself?" Captain Blake stayed silent. "What did you have to do?"

He shifted on his feet, uncomfortable with the new topic of conversation. Clearing his throat, the captain said, "We don't have time to reminisce. Though you did well in Round One, Round Two will be a completely different game. First things first"—he held up the mech— "I need to make sure you know how to wield this properly."

Devora frowned at his dismissal of her question. *What is he hiding?*

"The mech has been used in Tenton for centuries. It's the best close contact tool to destroy Kadesh's forces," Captain Blake began. "Learning the bow and arrow or more complicated weapons takes time, which is something we don't have."

The iron-armored monsters and their gnashing teeth echoed in Devora's ears until Captain Blake's voice broke through.

"It's an irregular blade, but it's the best for a large numbers of soldiers." He held the sword in one hand and swiped it through the air. "While it functions properly in my dominant hand"—he tossed the weapon to his other hand and jabbed the air— "it works just as well in my weak hand. The mech was formed to allow our soldiers to learn to fight with either hand to increase our success."

Devora gripped the wooden sword in her right hand, then moved it to her left, feeling the hilt slide easily into both palms.

Captain Blake stood next to her. "Another interesting detail is that the mech can be held with both hands simultaneously."

He took her hands, placing one on top of the other before curling his long fingers around hers. His strong hands cocooned hers in warmth as he adjusted her grip until it was in the correct position. Devora's breath hitched when she felt his shoulder rub against hers.

"There," the captain said, completely unfazed by their closeness. "That's how you properly hold your weapon with both hands for combat. Memorize it now because you'll need it for the competition and battle."

Devora studied her hands, committing to memory the way her fingers curled around the handle while pushing thoughts of Captain Blake out of her mind. Time was short. She needed to focus.

"Good. Now, on to some attacks."

Captain Blake went into long, specific details about the various attacks one could make with the sword. He demonstrated each one, explaining where to place her feet, shoulders, and hands with every move. Surprisingly, Devora found it fascinating. She loved learning that the way she held her wrist or placed her foot made all the difference when facing an opponent.

She was even more impressed with how much Captain Blake knew. He had to have known a lot, considering he went to Vlacklear. But his intellect went beyond book knowledge. There was experience behind his words, and that made his lesson more interesting than the one Sir Jacques had given about the mech.

After Captain Blake demonstrated a few techniques, he allowed Devora to try them on her own. She was clumsy with the sword at first, but after a few rounds, she began to understand.

"Excellent," Captain Blake commented, rewarding her with a smile as she successfully disarmed him. "I know you're a fast learner, but I'm still impressed by how quickly you've applied everything." He then frowned. "I don't know why the king changed the categorizations. You should be at Vlacklear." He coughed, then amended, "As all the new lieutenants should be."

Devora lowered her sword, shocked by his compliment. "That was my plan. I could only stack the category for Vlacklear, thinking it was my path." She peered down at her scuffed-up boots and smiled. "But Tunri knew better. I'm not sure how I would've turned out if I'd gone to Vlacklear. I'd probably still be hiding my gift."

She glanced up at him, surprised at herself for calling her abilities a gift and not a curse. The captain's encouragement had rubbed off on her.

"But, as much as I hated coming here," Devora continued, "I've finally accepted who I am. If I'm to die in the tournament or on the battlefield, I'm thankful I'll die as this version of me."

A pained looked swiped across Captain Blake's face and he turned away from her. He placed a hand on his neck, rubbing the thin chain that held her ring beneath his tunic. "Devora, I need you to know—"

A loud rap sounded from the metal door, and Devora jolted at the harsh echo. Captain Blake growled then stomped to the door.

Yanking it open, he boomed, "What is it?"

"Matthias," Sir Jacques' voice came barely above a whisper. "Your presence has been requested. Again."

Devora watched Captain Blake's shoulders tense then fall. He rubbed his eyes and Devora saw the defeat in his stance.

Who requested Captain Blake? And for what?

"I'm sorry," Sir Jacques' voice came out pained. "I tried to offer my services, but he only wants you."

"No, Jacques, I wouldn't want you to have to take my place," the captain replied. "You have no debt. You're free, my friend."

Is he talking about the debt Tristan ran up? Is Captain Blake still paying for his brother's gambling problem?

Devora gave a gentle cough to remind the captain she was still standing there, listening to every word. Captain Blake opened the door wider so Devora could see Sir Jacques standing in the threshold, holding a piece of parchment.

"Jacques, I hate to throw this on you, but can you help Medee with her mech training? I don't want her to lose Round Two on my account."

Sir Jacques' gaze darted to Devora before returning to the captain. He saluted. "Of course, sir."

Captain Blake smirked. "No need for formalities, Jacques. Lady Devora knows a good amount about us already."

Sir Jacques stammered. "What?" He whipped to Captain Blake. "What did you—"

"Just enough," the captain interjected before turning to Devora. "I'm sorry, Devora. I hope you'll forgive me one day."

His eyes filled with regret and longing as he looked her once over before marching through the door.

Chapter Twenty-Two

Level Five, The Fortress

After several sleepless nights worrying about Mama, Papa, and Captain Blake, and then an excruciatingly long lesson on the history of the mech by Sir Jacques, Devora was ready to release her restless energy by exercising in the Theater. Round Two of the tournament was tomorrow, and she needed to practice what she had learned. Though she hated training at first, it had become therapy to slam her fists and feet into the wooden poles.

Once Sir Jacques finally finished explaining the ideal grip to hold the mech, he dismissed the class and Devora bolted out of the Theater. She wanted to hurry and feed the wolves so she could get back and practice the bladed hands technique Nadia demonstrated the night before.

Sprinting through Level Five, Devora waved to One Shot as she headed to the basement below. She and the prisoner hadn't exchanged many words since Round One, but after he saved Devora from the rabid prisoners, Devora considered him an acquaintance.

Devora shook her head as she hooked and piled the raw meat into the buckets.

Friends with a murderer? What would Mama and Papa say?

The thought felt like a stone in her stomach. After reading the note from Papa, Devora hadn't heard any other news about her parents. She asked Sir Jacques about them, but he said he hadn't heard anything, good or bad. Devora's heart wrenched at the thought of Papa being imprisoned for defending her. She sent a prayer to Tunri, hoping both her parents were safe and they would all be reunited soon.

Lifting the two pails, Devora easily strode to the door. She really was getting stronger, and she enjoyed the pull of her muscles beneath her skin. As she lowered the buckets and unlocked the metal door, the evening wind pierced her cheeks. The air had grown more frigid since she first arrived at the Fortress four weeks ago.

Has it only been a month?

So much had happened in such a short amount of time. She'd made friends, was successfully learning *hemna*, and had even gotten the prisoners to stop growling at her because of her Seeing abilities.

She smirked. *I'd call that a victory.*

Devora's worn leather boots squashed through the wet slush on the ground as she headed toward the wooden shack. It looked as if it had rained earlier. Not that she would know what the weather was like. The Fortress had no windows to the outside. The only time she was able to breathe the fresh air was while feeding the wolves. She wondered if it would ever snow. Papa had told her of the white crystals cascading from the clouds in the north. They sounded beautiful.

As her foot slid through a muddy patch, Devora grunted. Could something that sounded so beautiful come to the Fortress?

Her eyes roamed the horizon until they landed on Vlacklear. Its cloud-white towers gleamed in the moonlight as each window flickered with a warm orange glow. Devora sighed and tore her eyes away. Hopefully, Tunri knew what He was doing.

Stepping up to the wooden shed, Devora prepared to check on the pregnant wolf when a raspy voice called out to her.

"They said you would be here."

Devora dropped the bucket and spun around, ready to defend herself. Nadia had given her another weapon, a cylinder of wood the length of her hand with a sharpened sickle on the end. Devora whipped it out of her pocket and pointed it at an old woman.

"Settle down, girl," the old woman wheezed, shuffling from around the corner of the basement doorway. "I'm not here to hurt you. I'm here to help you."

"What do you want?" Devora asked, tracking the wrinkly hag's every move.

Thinning gray hair wisped across the hag's sagging face as the bitter wind rolled by. A thick black cloak draped over her hunched shoulders and head as she wobbled toward Devora, leaning on a crooked cane.

"I know you have a desire to attend Vlacklear, and I'm here to give you that future."

Devora eyed the old woman. There was something about the hag that reminded Devora of the black-haired woman with the knife from her first vision as a child. Could the woman from her first vision and the woman before her be the same?

Yet this haggard woman said she could help Devora get to Vlacklear. Her life-long dream. Could she really attend the academy and leave the Fortress behind? Could she quit playing soldier and become the scholar she truly was? Was this Tunri's way of rewarding her obedience?

Her thoughts paused. But even if she could leave the Fortress, she still had her Sight. Would they kill her at Vlacklear because she was a Seer?

Straightening her stance, Devora placed the small sickle in her pocket and replied, "I appreciate the offer. But regardless of me being at the Fortress or Vlacklear, I'm still a Seer." She pointed to her violet eyes. "I don't think Vlacklear would accept me with my gift."

The hag gave a throaty chuckle before producing a small vial filled with a metallic-colored liquid. "Drink this, my dear, and Vlacklear will accept you, no matter what."

Devora perked up, ignoring the wolves' whines behind her. "Really?" She started toward the woman's outstretched hand. The liquid shimmered as Devora grabbed it and rolled it between her fingers.

"What do you want in exchange?" she asked, still skeptical.

The hag laughed again and patted Devora's hand. Chills raced down Devora's spine, sending her senses on alert. "My payment will come in time."

Devora stared at the woman then focused on the vial. When she glanced back up, the old hag was gone.

Searching around the wooden hut, Devora tried to ignore the bad aura surrounding the vial. The wolves barked wildly, and Devora jerked, remembering her job. After calming her pulse, she cautiously opened the door with the bucket held in front. The male wolf growled but allowed her to enter. Based on the extra blankets and hay, Captain Blake was good on his word and told the warden about the pregnant wolf. The female wolf lay on her side, her eyes closed. Her swollen belly moved up and down with each of her breaths. Devora felt discomfort for the wolf and prayed her pups would be delivered soon. After piling the meat on the ground, Devora scurried out of the hut and ran to the Fortress, making sure to lock the door behind her.

The wolves had momentarily calmed her from the eerie old hag, but her unease returned swiftly.

Who was that woman? Devora laid the vial on her palm. Its thick metallic liquid winked back at her. *And why did she want to help me get to Vlacklear?*

Shaking out her chills, Devora tucked the small bottle in her pocket and sterilized the meat buckets before racing down the hall. She wanted to get out of the basement as quickly as possible.

But as she approached the great iron door of the Behemoth's cell, a soft voice called out to her.

Help me.

Devora froze, her muscles tensing as the voice spoke to her again.

Help me.

Slowly, she faced the Behemoth's cell. The iron door ran from floor to ceiling with multiple locks sealing it shut. What kind of monster was the Behemoth for it to be so securely caged? Was it as terrifying as the iron-armored creatures from Kadesh? Or worse?

Fear crept along Devora's skin, and she forgot all about the old woman as she stared at the door.

Ever since arriving at the Fortress, she had been fearful of the monster. When she would feed the wolves, Devora sprinted past the Behemoth's cage, holding her breath as she went. Now that she stopped and studied the front of the cell, she saw a smaller, human-sized door carved into the lower-left corner.

There had to be a reason why the Behemoth was at the Fortress. This was a prison that housed Tenton's most dangerous criminals, so the Behemoth had to be dangerous to that caliber. And who was she to question the warden's choices in imprisoning creatures?

But a powerful aura from behind the door tugged at her, and Devora couldn't resist. It wasn't dark and heavy like the old hag's, but feathery and light, like bright clouds on a summer day.

Her heart thrashed in her chest, blood rushing between her ears as she trudged to the door, each step feeling heavier than the last. Swallowing her fear, Devora placed her hand on the cold, metal handle and pressed the latch, wondering if it would open.

"There she is," a nasally voice cried.

Gasping, Devora spun around to see three men rushing toward her. Though they varied in skin tone and height, their eyes gleamed with the same hatred. Quickly patting her pockets, Devora pulled the small sickle out, hoping it would be enough to save her. She had thought the prisoners were beginning to accept her, but not all were as easily won, it seemed.

A stocky man with a long blond beard launched at her, swinging his thick arm toward her jaw. "You should've died long ago. We're here to right that mistake."

Devora quickly shifted in defense as she recollected everything she'd learned. Ducking, she dodged the left hook and returned a solid jab to the man's stomach. With a wheeze, he bent over and coughed. Devora sliced the man's cheek with the sharp sickle then shoved him away. But the other two men appeared behind him, wielding identical knives.

Devora prayed Tunri would give her the speed to dodge their strikes.

The taller of the two jabbed at her shoulder. Spinning, Devora barely missed the blade.

"Grab that!" one of the man snarled.

The sickle was ripped from Devora's grip. She flailed to grab it but cried out as a stabbing pain tore through her bicep. A knife, covered in her own blood, protruded from her arm.

Panicked, Devora flung her arms out, scratching the tall man across the face before elbowing him in the chin. Biting back the pain in her arm, she wrenched the blade out and hurled it at the second man. He lunged out of the way, knocking into the bearded man she kicked before.

Devora's head spun as blood poured from her arm, staining the sleeve of her white tunic. She had to find something to wrap the wound before it was too late. A rush of steps headed toward her again. Readying her stance, Devora watched as the three men froze, their faces whiter than the mealtime gruel. Their gazes darted behind her before they screamed and fled.

Panting, Devora faced the iron door of the Behemoth's cell to see a large violet eye staring back at her. Terror clawed at her throat as she screamed and raced down the hall. She was so frightened she didn't see the puddles of water she had trekked in from outside. With her next step, her boot slid across the slick surface, flipping her legs beneath her before her head slammed to the stone ground. Her vision blurred then went black entirely.

"Welcome and congratulations, Lady Medee," Warden Hazor said. "You have succeeded in winning Regulus Protecti. What is your request for pardon?"

Devora blinked, reaching up to press the knot on her head before remembering the wound on her arm. She was bleeding out in the basement of the Fortress. She needed to get out of this vision and save herself or else she would bleed out on the dirty floor.

Lifting her gaze, Devora studied the stern faces surrounding her and froze. It was the same vision that kept repeating and building on itself. Forgetting her injuries, Devora twisted her head to survey the room. Had she seen King Atol and Queen Leza?

Devora opened her mouth then closed it again, not knowing what to say. Could she ask for a pardon for Papa? The idea sparked like wildfire, and she hurried to add it to the vision, but those words weren't the ones that rushed through her lips.

"I have not committed a crime to pardon, but I would like to pardon another," Devora responded, the words tumbling out of her mouth before she could stop them. Captain Blake tensed in her periphery. "I would like to pardon One Shot of his crimes."

Those around the table gasped and Devora almost gasped herself. One Shot? Why would I use my pardon on One Shot?

But Warden Hazor stared at her stoically before he nodded. "Very well."

Why did Tunri want to pardon One Shot? *Devora thought before the vision spiraled into another scene.*

The table and people disappeared, all except Captain Blake. But instead of beside her, he was now behind her. His strong, armored arms wrapped around her waist as they rode atop a large animal. Devora's stomach clenched as Captain Blake tightened his hold on her, but it soon disappeared as she peered out and saw two giant white antlers lining her vision.

What are we riding on?

The balmy air returned, whipping around her face as the creature galloped through the desert sand surrounding them. Devora held on tight, praying not to fall off when the vision spun again.

"Let me go!" a female voice commanded.

Devora hid behind a barrel. Captain Blake and the creature were gone.

Peeking from around the wine-scented wood, Devora stifled her cry. Bound in thick ropes and chains was the daughter of King Atol and Queen Leza, Princess Haden. Her chin-length, blonde hair stuck to her cheeks as a soldier tied a piece of soiled fabric around her head, preventing her from speaking. Terror shone in the princess's green eyes at the man gagging her.

Devora could only see the man's back, but the broad shoulders covered in bronze armor told her enough. This man was a soldier from Kadesh.

"No need to struggle, Princess," the man chided, his voice deep and hoarse. "We won't hurt you—yet." A cackle erupted from him before he spun around.

Black cropped hair and caramel skin were common for Kadeshians, and this man had both. But what made him stand out was the jagged pink scar slashed horizontally across his eyes.

"What are you doing here?" the man shouted at Devora and she jumped.

Am I actually where Princess Haden is being held?

Devora scrambled to escape but found herself stuck between more barrels and the edge of the tent. The man with the scar came closer, unsheathing a curved blade. He raised it to strike before the vision went black.

Devora sat up with a gasp, droplets of sweat streaming down her temples.

"Tunri, what are you showing me?" she whispered into the dank air surrounding her.

Heaving for air, Devora tried to move her arm and cried out. She stared at the puddle of red lying beneath her blood-stained tunic. As she grappled at the wall to stand, her vision blurred. She needed to get to the infirmary fast. Leaning her uninjured shoulder against the stone wall, Devora slumped forward while placing pressure on her wound. As the hallway grew longer with each step, her strength waned.

Will anyone come to the basement?

After a few more staggered steps, she arrived at the stairwell only to trip on the first stair. Grunting, Devora crashed onto the stone steps. Tears spilled down her cheeks. What was the point of her trying so hard to train when she was going to die in the basement of the Fortress?

"Devora?" the familiar commanding voice bounced down the winding stairwell. "What are you doing down here?" The clacking of boots flew down the stairs.

Stifling her sobs, Devora twisted her neck to see Captain Blake.

Chapter Twenty-Three

"What are *you* doing here?" Devora asked weakly. Five days had passed since he left her in the training room with Sir Jacques. She suddenly felt cold and shivered. "Sir."

"What happened?" Captain Blake growled, glowering at the blood seeping between her fingertips. Hurriedly, he yanked a knife from his boot and cut off a long strip off his tunic before wrapping it tightly around Devora's arm.

Gritting her teeth, Devora bit her tongue, trying not to scream. Though her arm was on fire, her heart leaped for joy at the sight of him. He came back.

Without waiting for her to reply, Captain Blake hoisted her into his arms and carried her up the stairs. His heart thumped rapidly against her ear, and she cuddled closer, enjoying being so near to him.

Once the captain made it to the top of the stairs, Devora expected him to command her to walk. But he didn't. Instead, he carried her up the next four levels of the Fortress to the infirmary. Heavy breaths escaped Captain Blake's lips, but he never stopped. Though her head jostled against the ring around his neck, she tried not to move. Some of the prisoners wanted her dead. Why was Captain Blake trying so hard to keep her alive?

Suddenly, Captain Blake's steps slowed before he kicked open the doors to the infirmary. Parchments flew to the ground as the medics bolted up in surprise. As soon as they saw Devora's bloodied arm, they rushed to prepare a space for her.

"Make sure Medee is treated immediately," the captain barked as he laid her down on a spare bed.

"O-of course, sir," a medic with auburn hair stuttered and dashed around the room for supplies.

Devora stared at the white curtains and sheets surrounding her, head spinning.

Why am I here again? Her eyes felt so heavy. She just wanted to rest.

"Devora." Captain Blake placed a warm hand on her cheek. "Tell me what happened."

She blinked at the captain, darkness creeping at the corners of her vision. "Captain Blake, you came back. I'm so glad you're back," she breathed.

"There were strict orders from Warden Hazor that competitors were not to be harmed outside of the tournament," Captain Blake said, the threat of violence lurking beneath his words.

"Apologies, sir," a weak voice replied. "None of my men were in the basement when she was attacked. I interrogated them all."

Silence hung in the air before the captain spoke again. "I see. Thank you for your diligence, Tocha. I'll question the others soon."

Devora's eyes shifted beneath her lids. Her arm felt like a thousand stones were heaped upon it. Cracking her eyes open, she slid her gaze around the room. She was in the infirmary. Which was a very bad thing, considering Round Two was only a few hours away.

Turning her head, Devora expected to see the soldier poisoned with gumberry, but other than a soldier with a broken leg, she was the only one there.

"You're awake," Captain Blake said, striding to the side of her bed. Lines of worry creased his eyes as he analyzed her. He started to reach out to her but paused and placed his hand back at his side. "What happened?"

Wincing, she sat up in the bed, her hand brushing against the vial from the old hag in her pocket. *So it hadn't been a dream.*

She then noticed the thick white bandages covering almost the entirety of her arm. Though the pain was dull, the wound throbbed.

"I apologize, Captain," she croaked, her throat dry. "I was hurrying to complete my evening job when I was attacked by three men," Devora started before remembering the vision she had right after that.

Should I tell him about it?

Glancing down at her wound, Devora sighed. Someone needed to know about the princess. "Also, Princess Haden has been captured...or she will be." As she lifted her gaze, she found Captain Blake hanging on her every word. "Thank you for your kindness, sir. You didn't have to save me, but I'm glad you did."

Rubbing his eyes, Captain Blake slumped into the chair beside her bed. As he scrubbed his face, Devora peered down at the captain's ebony boots. They were shined to perfection. If she had been a little closer, she probably could've seen her reflection. Her eyes slowly drifted up, assessing Captain Blake's pressed dark blue pants and matching dark blue tunic. He was wearing his formal wear again.

She sucked in a breath. "What did the king want?" she asked before she could stop herself. "Sir."

Captain Blake gave her a weary look, swatting his hand in the air. "You can drop the 'sir'. It's too painful for me to hear it."

Devora averted her gaze, clamping her lips shut.

The captain sat back with a sigh. "I only intended to be gone for a day. I—," he started but stopped himself. He took a breath. "I apologize for leaving you to train with Jacques and Nadia after I agreed to train you. If I would've known this would happen—" he motioned to her injury— "I would've sent someone to the king in my stead. I didn't know you needed to be protected."

Indignation rose in her throat at his exasperated tone. She wasn't a child that needed his protection.

Lifting her chin, she began, "I'm not fighting to win a pardon, Captain; I'm fighting for my life. Luckily, Nadia has helped me learn more *hemna*, and you did ask Sir Jacques to help me learn the mech. But now with this—" she pointed to the bandage—"I don't stand a chance. I fended them off as best as I could." Her voice wavered at the end. Sorrow tugged at her thoughts, pulling her deeper and deeper into defeat.

"That's not true. An experienced soldier knows how to use their weaknesses as strengths."

Devora rolled her eyes. "If you haven't noticed, I'm not an experienced soldier. I'm not like you."

Captain Blake chuckled. "I saw the men who attacked you. For not having any experience, you put up a good fight. It seems your best is good enough to save your life."

Devora couldn't help but smile at the compliment.

Relaxing his hard exterior, the captain brushed an imaginary fuzz off his shoulder. "I'm glad Nadia actually listened to me."

Devora quirked a brow. "You asked Nadia to help?"

Captain Blake nodded, then ran his hand through his cropped chestnut hair. The shadows beneath his eyes became more prominent as he leaned forward.

"With what Lapith—Nadia—has taught you already, I know you'll be fine for Round Two in a few hours. Why else do you think I left you in her care?"

Although Devora's heart warmed at the thought, she shook her head. "I'm not so sure if I'll be fine, but I don't really have a choice."

After a long stretch of silence, the captain asked, "How are you feeling?"

Devora placed a hand on her wound. While it still throbbed, she was thankful it was bandaged and cleaned. "I'm okay."

She faced the captain, waiting for his reply. It had been five days since she'd seen him. Five days since the king had requested his presence. Five days since he'd left her. Again.

Gathering her courage, she asked, "Why do you keep leaving?"

Captain Blake immediately stiffened, and he turned away from her. "There are certain obligations I've agreed to. I must see them fulfilled whenever I am called."

"What kind of obligations?"

"Obligations I can't discuss with lower-ranking officers," he clipped, shutting down the conversation. He stood and straightened his blue tunic. "The medic says you can return to your cell whenever you feel ready. One of the other knights will escort you there."

Before Devora could utter another word, Captain Blake left the infirmary.

Another guard escorted Devora to her cell where her friends were waiting.

"We heard you were attacked!" Hestia exclaimed, flinging her arms around Devora. "Are you okay?"

"Careful, Hestia," Reese scolded. "Her arm is injured. Don't you see the bandages?"

"Thank you," Devora said to the knight. He bowed and retreated before Devora faced her friends. "I'm okay. It's sore, but it won't have to be cut off or anything."

Ida gasped at the statement before Nadia sprang from her bed.

"If you need a new arm, I can make one that holds all sorts of weapons, so no one will ever attack you again!"

Devora burst out laughing, enjoying not thinking about old hags, basement monsters, or brooding captains.

As the girls settled into their conversations, Devora noticed a pristine pink package sitting on her bed.

"Nadia," Devora said above the chatter. "What's this?"

Nadia glanced up, black charcoal staining her face from where she had rubbed her nose. "Your secret admirer left another gift." She nodded at the crisply wrapped rectangle. "Reese said she saw someone come by our cell about an hour ago while I was finishing work in the kitchen, but she couldn't tell who it was other than that it was a knight."

Reese swiped her abacus beads. She had been more pleasant toward Devora ever since she had won the game of Kings against Captain Blake. "I'm seventy-two point eight percent positive it was a knight."

"Oh," Devora replied, hating that she hoped the parcel was from the captain.

"Well, don't just stare at it." Hestia gestured at the pink package. "Open it. I want to see if it's our mysterious 'M' again."

"Ah yes, Mister Pants," Nadia said, furrowing her brows at her notebook. "I wonder what he left this time."

"Go ahead, Devora," Ida encouraged, sitting next to Nadia. "Open it."

Holding her breath, Devora reached for the small box. The crisp paper glided across her fingertips the same way it always had when Papa brought her gifts from his journeys north. She peeled back the rose-tinted parchment and lifted the white lid. The alluring aroma of roses wafted from the box, wrapping her in her favorite scent of home. Inside lay two beautifully carved roses of Devora's favorite soap.

"First pants, now soap?" Reese snorted, eyeing the soap.

Nadia barked out a laugh, leaning her back against the wall. "Who taught this guy how to win a lady's heart?"

"I haven't smelled something so lovely in such a long time," Ida sighed, admiring the beautiful packaging.

"I wish someone would buy me pants and soap," Hestia sighed, falling onto Devora's bed. She elegantly placed a hand over her heart, her dark braids sprawled around her.

Devora cupped the soap in her hands, bringing it to her chest. Whoever left this gift knew her heart. It was more than beautiful; it was personal. It was the best gift her father had gotten her. Every time she saw the pink package waiting on her bed at home, she knew he had returned home safely.

Is this gift a clue that Papa is okay? But how did it get here?

Ida giggled at Hestia's dramatics before asking, "Is there a note, Devora? Maybe you can figure out who sent the gift."

Devora searched for a piece of parchment, praying to see the same squared letters as the first note. But after a thorough search, there was no note to be found. The only person who knew her family well enough to give her something so kind and personal was Sir Jacques.

Did Sir Jacques sign the first note with 'M' to throw her off?

Devora held the delicate rose soap in her palm as her hopes plummeted.

"No note," she sighed, placing the soap back in the box. "But I'm thankful for whoever gave it to me. Tunri knows I need a bath."

Chapter Twenty-Four

The Theater, The Fortress

"I think you're going to do great," Sir Jacques encouraged after the three hours of sleep Devora had before Round Two. She wasn't sure why the knight had come to collect her instead of Captain Blake, but she was too exhausted and too sore to question anything.

Her arm still ached every time she moved it, so she also wasn't sure how she was going to succeed in Round Two. Devora squeezed the wrinkled purple sash across her chest. The thought of losing and having to stay at the Fortress to be a soldier for another five years made her stomach churn.

"Thank you, Sir Jacques. I appreciate all your help while Captain Blake was away."

Sir Jacques gave her a side-long glance before nodding, keeping his lips tight. After a moment, Devora asked, "Sir Jacques, why is Captain Blake so moody?"

The knight stopped; his lips parted before he barked out a loud laugh. A group of soldiers gave him a strange look as they passed by.

"Forgive me, Lady Devora." Jacques wiped a tear from his eye. "Captain Blake has a lot of demands from people of authority."

"Like the king?"

Sir Jacques blanched, his laughter dissolving. "I don't know specifics, but I know Blake always has a lot on his mind." The knight relaxed as they continued walking. "Although, ever since I've known him, he's always been moody." He gave Devora a wink.

After a few more strides in silence, Devora and Sir Jacques stood outside the Theater's entrance. Roars of laughter and cheers pounded against the metal door. It sounded as if the crowd had doubled since the last fight. Devora's stomach squeezed.

"Here we are." Sir Jacques turned to her. His sandy blond hair was pushed back, revealing a thin sheen of sweat glinting off his forehead. Taking a breath, Sir Jacques lowered his voice, "Lady Devora, I was instructed not to tell you this, but I will disobey orders this once."

Devora cocked her head. "What are you talking about?"

Sir Jacques looked both ways before grabbing her uninjured arm and tugging her around the corner, away from the Theater.

Leaning down, the knight whispered, "There is information I must tell you, but it's private." He glanced over her head, waiting for a group of nobility to shuffle by.

Devora leaned forward, her pulse rising. "What is it? Is it about my parents?"

Sir Jacques pulled her farther from the Theater, as if others were eavesdropping. "I've received word that your father had his trial with the king."

Devora's heart dropped to her feet.

Papa just had his trial? But it's been weeks since he was arrested.

While she was training and flirting with Captain Blake, Papa had been imprisoned in the king's dungeon.

"The Governor and First Lady were charged for treason and sentenced to death."

"What?" Devora exclaimed, clutching Sir Jacques' wrist. She winced at the pain shooting down her arm at the sudden movement. "All for defending me? That can't be true! We must go to the king and do something." She started to move when Sir Jacques grabbed her shoulders.

"Devora, listen to me," he hissed, causing her to freeze. Sir Jacques never lashed out. "We're not sure if the knowledge of your abilities was the real reason behind the harsh punishment." Sir Jacques paused, waiting for more people to hurry by. "By the time the information of their sentence was passed to the Fortress, we thought it was already too late. We weren't sure if that was done on purpose or not."

The morning gruel threatened to rise up her throat, and Devora placed a hand on her stomach. Was it her Seeing abilities that had caused her loved ones more harm than good? She should just take the tincture from the old hag and be done with her curse altogether, just to be sure.

"However," Sir Jacques continued, igniting hope in her heart. "*Someone* came to their aid and spoke as a witness to support their actions. *Someone* who is very convincing and good with words. And because of this convincing, high-ranking, *someone* your parents are safe."

Devora's mind moved faster than the wolves eating dinner. The first time Captain Blake had left, it was because of something Sir Conan had said. The captain was furious and stormed out of training. The next time he left was because Sir Jacques had given him a summons from King Atol.

Devora brought a hand to her mouth, realizing Captain Blake had left because he wanted to save her parents. And he succeeded. The brooding man who hardly smiled convinced the king not to kill Papa and Mama. Devora's knees weakened. She wanted to cry.

How can I ever repay him?

Tears welled in her eyes, and she braced herself against the wall, stunned at the conclusion. "Why would he do that?"

She thought back to the pink box. It came almost immediately after Captain Blake returned.

Did Papa tell Captain Blake to give it to me? Assuring me that he and Mama were okay?

Sir Jacques wrapped an arm around Devora's waist, trying to hold her steady. "Lady Devora? Are you all right?" He cursed. "If I knew that this would be your reaction, I wouldn't have disobeyed Matthias' request."

Just then, Captain Blake rounded the corner. He stopped, his eyes darting between Devora and Sir Jacques' embrace before his demeanor hardened further.

"Medee, Jacques."

Devora's head whipped to the captain, her heart soaring. She scrambled away from Sir Jacques, the knight doing the same.

"Matthias? You're back already?" A frown marred his lips. "That was a long list. What happened?"

The captain leveled a steely gaze at Sir Jacques. "Not every name needed to be erased. The king saw that my reasoning was sound." Sir Jacques' shoulders relaxed with relief as Captain Blake shifted his attention to Devora. "I came to see if my competitor was prepared for today's events. I wouldn't want her head to be distracted by anything else."

"Of course," Sir Jacques bowed then straightened under Captain Blake's glower. The knight turned to Devora. "Good luck, my lady." He caught Devora's eye and shifted his own gaze to the captain, giving a slight nod before marching past her.

"Medee," Captain Blake's crisp voice broke through her thoughts. "You need to focus on today's round. They're pairing up competitors at random, but I received a tip that the pairings will be rigged."

Devora didn't listen to a word Captain Blake said as she stared at him. His brows were furrowed as he clasped his hands behind his back. He looked so militant and unwavering. But beneath his hard exterior was something beautiful. He saved her parents from the king's wrath. Before she could stop herself, she wrapped her arms around his lean waist and hugged him. Tears rolled down her cheeks as she buried her face in his chest.

The captain's words immediately stopped, his body stiff as stone as she tightened her embrace. The aroma of sand, wood shavings, and steel wrapped around her nose as she laid her cheek against his toned chest.

"Thank you," she whispered. "I don't know how I can repay you, but thank you."

A gentle hand wrapped around her waist, holding her close. It felt...nice.

"That's not necessary," he replied softly.

After a moment, Captain Blake cleared his throat and Devora jumped away from him, furiously wiping the tears from her cheeks.

"I'm so sorry," she blurted, avoiding his gaze. "That was completely out of line." She glanced over her shoulder. Round Two would be starting soon. "I need to go."

Devora turned back to him, expecting the hard glare to be scrutinizing her weak crying, but it wasn't there. In its place was the sorrowful, guilt-driven eyes of a young man, pleading for help.

She took a step closer. "Captain, what's wrong?"

Before he could reply, a voice boomed from the Theater. "All competitors to the Theater for Round Two!"

Captain Blake straightened and smoothed out his tunic, locking away any emotion he felt. "That's you, Medee. Make me proud." He quickly strode past her and into the Theater.

Sucking in a quick breath, Devora jogged behind him.

As she stepped through the threshold, the roar of the crowd smacked her out of her haze. The words Captain Blake said returned to her mind: *They're pairing up competitors at random, but I received a tip that the pairings are rigged.*

Devora's stomach tied into a knot. She should have paid more attention to the captain rather than snuggling into his warm chest. He looked so broken. What happened?

As her gaze floated along the spectators, it stopped on a familiar face. Joy exploded in her chest.

"Papa," she breathed, unable to stop her grin.

Papa was alive and well, sitting with the other members of the King's Council. Devora noticed he was dressed in his official uniform. The dark blue jerkin and pants were pressed crisply. Though Governor Medee looked a bit thinner than before, there were no physical ailments that Devora could see.

As she tried to catch Papa's eye, her thoughts stalled. *Does Papa know I'm fighting for my life?*

She thought back to the imperial opal ring that Papa sent. Captain Blake said that if she wore it for too long, it would kill her. But why would Papa send her something like that?

As soon as Warden Hazor approached the top of the Theater, the cheers died down. He stretched out his hands to the crowd of nobility.

"For Round Two of Regulus Protecti, each competitor will be allowed one mech to use against their opponent. There are six competitors left. Three will fight against three. The last three standing will move on to the final round. You are meant to disarm your opponent only." A sly grin came to the warden's face as he peered down at the competitors, his gaze lingering on Devora. "By any means necessary."

The crowd cheered again, and the warden returned to his seat. At his right sat Captain Blake, leaning all the way forward, his dark eyes glued on her. By the way he cupped his hands over his mouth, Devora would've thought he was worried.

Squaring her shoulders, Devora took the wooden mech handed to her. Captain Blake didn't need to be worried. Tunri was with her, and she would win.

Devora searched the crowd and found her friends. Nadia gave a thumbs up and a grin while Reese and Ida were holding hand-made signs that scrawled out her name. Hestia had somehow procured a horn and was blaring it loudly.

Devora smiled and touched the three pearls extending from the pin in her hair. She then adjusted the purple sash across her chest. She was thankful to have the strength of her family and friends with her.

"Time for the pairings," Warden Hazor roared, and the crowd silenced once more.

A rotund knight handed a scroll wrapped in a scarlet ribbon to the warden. Grabbing the parchment, Warden Hazor dismissed the guard and untied the scroll. Slowly, he read off the pairings. Sir Conan was called first. His pairing was a tall thin man, looking half the knight's weight.

Of course, Devora mused.

Captain Blake said the pairings were rigged, and it was obvious. There was no way the gaunt man could beat Sir Conan. He was as thin as parchment and would blow away if Sir Conan sneezed.

Devora thrummed one hand against her thigh as the other gripped the mech. *Who will I be paired with?*

In the corner of her eye, she saw that One Shot and Babshee had made it through to this round, as well.

Please Tunri, not either of them. Please, please, please, no.

Babshee was paired with One Shot and Devora feared for her friend until she remembered he had given her advice about how to defeat the giant.

When her name was finally announced, Devora peered down the line to see she had been paired with a man named Jin Hadeed. He was about her height, but that's where their similarities ended. Black ink swirled across his cloud-white skin, down his neck and arms. His short chestnut hair stood tall on his head as he turned and grinned at her. Devora jerked back as his menacing smile revealed black, decaying teeth. Once she won this competition, she would have to speak to the warden about the prisoners' hygiene.

"To make things more interesting," Warden Hazor continued as he rolled up the parchment. "I decided to heighten the stakes of Regulus Protecti."

The crowd "ooh'd" and "ah'd" as the stout guard and five more returned to the center of the Theater where they began laying thick ropes on the ground. The circular space was soon divided into three sections, each section like a thick slice of cocoa cake.

A wicked grin split the warden's face. "Each pair must stay in their indicated section. If you step into another area of the floor, you will be immediately disqualified, receive three lashings, and five additional years onto your sentence."

Gasps broke among the crowd, followed by the clinking of coins.

A cold sweat broke out across Devora's forehead. *Three lashings and five years at the Fortress?*

Trying to calm her panic, Devora stood on the wider end of the section, closer to the wall of the Theater. Tunri had told her she would win. She just had to have faith that He was right.

With her new resolve, Devora stared at the man swaying in front of her.

"This will be fun," Jin Hadeed hissed through rotting teeth. He continued moving back and forth on the balls of his feet.

Devora gripped her mech with both hands, keeping her eyes glued on her opponent.

"Round Two begins now!" the warden bellowed. A bell rang and Jin Hadeed threw his mech across the arena, barely missing One Shot's head. The assassin's focus didn't waver from the giant.

"I dislike His Majesty's weapons," Jin Hadeed said, pulling a small blade from his pocket. He ran his thumb across the blunt edge of the blade, causing three more knives to fan off the first.

Devora's hands became clammy as she tightened her grip on the mech, injustice flaring in her heart.

"That's against the rules," she declared, pointing her sword at the prisoner.

Jin Hadeed sneered and stalked forward, still swaying. Devora moved away, not realizing what he was doing until she was at the smaller end of their section. One wrong move and she would stumble into another area, disqualifying her from the competition and sentencing her to more years in prison.

"Rules are meant to be broken," the prisoner chuckled, and he flung the first knife at her ankle.

Devora darted to the left, but pain ricocheted down her arm from last night's injury and she stopped too soon. The knife sailed into her ankle, piercing the flesh beneath her boot. Gasping, she peered down at the protruding knife.

Devora yanked out the blade, feeling warm blood dribble through her toes. She threw the knife down and growled. Now she had a wounded ankle and an injured arm.

"Why tell me I would win when I'm clearly losing, Tunri," Devora grumbled under her breath.

Scowling at Jin Hadeed, a cool aura flittered behind Devora's eyes. When she blinked, she found the prisoner rearing back to launch another knife at her. Devora ducked then glanced up to see Jin Hadeed staring at her, brows furrowed in confusion. He still held the three blades.

Realization swirled in her thoughts. Tunri was giving her foresight of her opponents moves again, just like He had with Babshee. Tunri hadn't forgotten her.

"Thank you," she breathed then focused on her opponent.

"Are we going to stand here and look pretty, or are we going to fight?" Devora leveled her sword at Jin Hadeed.

The prisoner snarled before whipping a blade at her forehead, just as she had seen. This time Devora spun to the right, intercepting the knife with the blade of her mech. Her muscles screamed with the movement, but Jin Hadeed's knife whooshed into a different section.

Jin growled and threw another blade. Another vision soared into her mind and Devora dodged to the right again, intercepting the weapon. The knife ricocheted off Babshee's calf. Grunting, the giant spat at Jin Hadeed for ruining his attack against One Shot. The wad soared through the air and completely doused Jin.

The crowd roared with laughter as Jin wiped the saliva off his body. He cursed at the giant but didn't move any closer.

Devora focused on Jin, trying to ignore her throbbing muscles. If she could convince him to throw his other weapons, he would be defenseless, and she could strike.

"You only have two knives left." She nodded to the blades in his hand. "And you have no mech. If you throw those at me, does that mean you forfeit, and I win?"

Jin Hadeed yelled, fisting a knife in each hand as he lunged at her.

Adrenaline rushed through Devora's veins as she waited to see the attack beforehand.

But none came.

Instead of the cool sensation from before, a rush of heat jabbed behind her eyes, and something snapped. Devora cried out as one of the knives sliced her cheek. Jerking back, she slapped Jin Hadeed's head with the flat of her blade and retreated to the wider edge of the section.

Placing a hand on her temple, Devora blinked furiously before staring at her opponent. A swirling ball of gray light bobbed against his chest, right over his heart. Devora leaned forward and narrowed her eyes at the light.

What is that?

"Have you seen the future where I kill you?" Jin Hadeed cried, coming after her again.

Devora heard her name in the crowd but couldn't spare a glance. Pushing her focus away from the swirling gray light, her weeks of training returned to her muscles. Bending her knees, Devora spun around and kicked her opponent in the chest. Jin Hadeed folded forward, dropping his blades. Pain exploded in Devora's ankle, but she kicked the knives out of their section, away from Jin Hadeed.

"Filthy Seer," Jin Hadeed croaked. "You were born cursed, and you will die cursed."

Growling, Devora raced forward and punched Jin in the chin, sending him flying into the section with Sir Conan and his opponent. Jin Hadeed knocked into Sir Conan's opponent, forcing them both into a different section.

"Jin Hadeed and Ben Adade are disqualified," Warden Hazor called.

Sections of the crowd cheered while others shook their fists at the disqualified contestants, no doubt upset at losing their bets. Jin Hadeed and Sir Conan's opponent, Ben Adade, jumped up and began fighting one another. The crowd instantly became distracted by the new brawl and cheered.

Sir Conan snarled at Devora, "Bloody Seer. I had him right where I wanted him." He raised his mech toward her. "Watch your back. When your watchdog isn't around, you're mine."

Panic tightened her chest. *Watchdog? Is he referring to Captain Blake?*

Sweat matted Devora's brow as she stared at the glowing blue swirl on Sir Conan's chest. What did it mean?

Shaking her head, she blinked, seeing a variety of blue, yellow, and gray swirls adorning each person's chest in the Theater. Devora pushed her palms against her temples. Her head was on fire, her eyes ready to explode. What was happening to her?

Tunri, she pleaded. *Please help.*

Squeezing her lids as tight as she could, Devora opened them again to find the swirling lights gone. She breathed a sigh of relief. Whatever had happened was over.

The bell sounded. Round Two was finished.

Chapter Twenty-Five

Devora hobbled to where she kicked Jin Hadeed's blades. Wincing, she crouched down and grasped one in each hand before facing Warden Hazor. She expected booing and threats. Yet, as she thrust both blades into the air, cheers erupted from the crowd. With a wide grin, Devora turned in a circle, making sure to find Papa to show him that she would become the best warrior. Papa stood with the others, cheering loudly. Devora couldn't remember the last time she'd seen him so excited.

Completing her circle, Devora ended at Warden Hazor. She crossed one arm over her chest and gave him a deep bow, wanting to make sure he enjoyed his show.

The warden's studied her then gave a nod of approval. Devora shifted her gaze to Captain Blake, who was standing and clapping with an impressed grin.

Once the cheering died down, Devora, Sir Conan, and One Shot were escorted to their own training rooms to rest without any distractions. She couldn't believe One Shot defeated Babshee. Though she was thankful she wouldn't have to face the giant in Round Three, unease rippled in her stomach about having to fight with Sir Conan and One Shot.

Devora sat on the cold ground of her training room and leaned against the wall. Closing her eyes, she took in a few deep breaths. While she enjoyed the break from the roaring crowd and not being sentenced to more years in the Fortress, she couldn't forget the colored swirls she had seen.

What were they?

It was as if her Sight had driven into each person, allowing her to see what was inside their soul. But what did the different colors mean? Devora rubbed her eyes, not knowing if she had the energy to figure it out.

The door to her training room squeaked. Devora's eyes shot open, and she instinctually jumped up. Bending her knees, she outstretched her arms, ready to defend herself. She didn't think anyone was allowed to visit her. Yet as the long legs and torso of Captain Blake stepped through the doorway, she relaxed, the ache in her wounds returning. He carried a pail of water and a circular package wrapped in cerulean parchment. The same shade of cerulean as the swirl of light on his chest. Devora frowned, narrowing her eyes at the light.

Does blue mean sorrow?

"I see you're not resting as you should be," the captain commented, taking in her defensive stance as he closed the door behind him.

Devora lowered her hands, feeling the awkward tension pull between them. Embarrassment heated her cheeks as she recalled the embrace they shared earlier. And how much she enjoyed it. She tried to look away, but the blue light glowing on Captain Blake's chest pulsed brightly, keeping her focus on him.

After a few moments of silence, Captain Blake said, "I wanted to apologize for all the times I left so suddenly." He stood as still as stone in front of the closed door. As if she would attack him if he took a step closer. "And for my remarks. Jacques says I need to learn tact when addressing others." He sighed. "I hoped this would help you forgive me."

The captain placed the bucket on the ground and took two long strides forward, holding out the blue package. The scent of sugar and chocolate danced through the air. Devora's mouth watered as she leaned in. Her stomach growled and she quickly clamped her hands over it.

"Please." He pushed the package closer, and Devora couldn't resist.

"Well," she said with a grin, swiping the package out of his hand. "I guess I can accept your apology."

Sitting back on the ground, she carefully unfolded the crisp blue paper. Wafts of sweetness tickled her nose. Devora licked her lips when a moist slice cocoa cake came into view. It felt like it had been years since she enjoyed the succulent treat.

"How did you know I loved cocoa cake?" she asked, slowly unfolding the rest of the crisp paper.

White powdery sugar coated the dark chocolate cake. Devora licked her lips again. She didn't want to eat it all in one bite, but she could easily stuff the whole cake in her mouth.

Devora ripped off a piece and laid it on her tongue. The rich chocolate melted in her mouth, enveloping her senses in sugary delight.

She closed her eyes to relish the sensation. "Mmmm."

"So, what happened out there?"

Devora peeked at the captain. The cerulean swirl on his chest tightened as if anticipating her answer.

She swallowed the delicious treat then offered him some. "What do you mean?"

Captain Blake lowered himself next to her before tearing off a piece of cocoa cake. Pinching it between his fingers, he explained, "You had Hadeed in your hands, and then you froze. It was as if you were having a vision, but you didn't pass out."

Devora studied the powdered sugar coating the cake. "I'm not sure what happened but it felt as if something inside me snapped." She peered down to see a swirl of violet light on her own chest. "I can see something now that I couldn't before."

"What is it?" Captain Blake asked, finally popping the chocolate piece into his mouth.

Devora turned to him and focused on the blue swirl. It seemed heavy, full of sorrow. But what was it?

"There's a swirl of light, right there," she said, reaching out.

As she laid her hand on Captain Blake's chest, a vision, or something like it, immediately shot into her mind.

A comforting warm breeze danced through the afternoon air. A rich sunset on the horizon. Lines of vines bearing succulent grapes, ripe for harvest. A boy with chestnut hair, no more than twelve, laughing as he threw grapes at a younger boy with the same coloring. The bubbly laugh of a middle-aged woman with the same hair and bright violet eyes.

Devora gasped and retracted her hand. Captain Blake's mother was a Seer. With the same violet eyes as Devora, she had to be. That's why he knew so much about visions.

"What did you just do?" The captain stared at her, his eyes wide. He leaned back, jaw tight and a vein pulsing in his neck.

Fear spiked her nerves and she leaned away from him. "I-I'm sorry." Devora cradled her hand to her chest, fixated on the captain's swirl. It was fuzzy around the edges. She had disturbed it and it was angry.

What did I see? It was as if she had touched the captain's very soul. *Has Tunri given me soulsight?* There wasn't much to study on Seers, seeing as how King Atol destroyed all information about them. But she remembered overhearing Mama speaking to Madge, their head servant, about something similar when Devora first showed signs of her gift.

Captain Blake placed a hand over his heart, covering the agitated swirl.

"I'm sorry," Devora whispered again, blinking back the tears building in her eyes. "I didn't know that would happen."

The captain peered over her, and she thought she saw a tear trickle down his cheek. But when she blinked, it was gone.

Captain Blake stood. "Make sure you rest," he said stiffly and exited the training room.

As soon as he left, Devora buried her face in her hands. Chocolate crumbs littered the dirt from where they had enjoyed the cocoa cake together.

Why did I reach out and touch the light?

Frustrated, she flicked the crumbs across the ground. Based on Captain Blake's reaction, she had unveiled a private memory.

A few moments after Captain Blake left, Devora was escorted from the training room to the infirmary. Hands of the other soldiers patted her on the back or gently punched her in the arm in congratulations. After several punches, she preferred the pats on the back. Devora tried to engage the soulsight again but couldn't.

Maybe it was a onetime thing.

The medic shoved the crowd out of the infirmary before ushering her to a bed. He quickly gave her a tincture for the pain and began cleaning the wound on her ankle. The minty tincture slid down Devora's throat, numbing the throbbing in her arm and foot.

After the medic wrapped her ankle, Devora exited the infirmary and took a roundabout way back to her cell. By the time she arrived, her ankle was on fire, but it was worth it to avoid the demanding crowds of soldiers and prisoners wanting to speak with her.

With a grunt, she heaved her leg on her bunk and laid down, allowing her body to relax into the cot. In the quiet of her cell, she could finally think.

What happened with Captain Blake? Had I seen his memories?

She had known there had to be a reason why he knew so much about Seers, but she never expected his mother to be one.

Chapter Twenty-Six

Level Two, The Fortress

Devora closed her eyes, wondering when she would see Papa again, then drifted off into a deep sleep. The vision of Princess Haden's capture returned, and Devora awoke with a gasp. She pushed loose strands of hair from her forehead, her fingers brushing the vial from the old hag. Groggy, she pulled the vial from her pocket. At one point, she thought about discarding it. If there were a tincture that could vanquish her Seeing abilities, her parents would've found it by now. But after her ability had strengthened and Captain Blake pulled away from her, Devora wasn't sure if she wanted the responsibility of being a Seer anymore.

"You're here!" Nadia beamed as she strode into their cell. "We were wondering when you would come back!"

Devora hid the vial back in her pocket then propped her arms behind her. Carefully, she moved into a sitting position. A towering pile of parchments and various weapons lay in Nadia's arms. Hestia, Reese, and Ida came behind her with more.

"We were so worried!" Ida cried, dropping the items in her hand and rushing to give Devora a hug. "I couldn't imagine you getting those lashes and being sentenced to five more years here!" Ida softly sobbed on Devora's shoulder.

Hestia nodded, joining Ida in squashing Devora in a tight embrace.

Devora winced but welcomed the closeness.

"I had no idea you were that skilled with a mech," Reese commented, absentmindedly staring at her abacus. "If I would've known, my probability for your success would've been much higher."

"That means she's glad you're okay," Hestia whispered in Devora's ear before bouncing up and collecting the items she had thrown on the ground.

Devora smiled at Reese's sentiment then leaned forward. Eye patches, parchments, knives, and a variety of other odd items littered the cell floor. "What is all this?"

"From your fans!" Hestia cried, dumping the items at the base of Devora's cot. After searching through them, she picked up a wooden peg. "I think this is some guy's leg he wants you to sign."

"Ew." Devora curled her lip then laughed. She never thought *she* would gain favor among the prisoners. Especially after those men attacked her in the basement and Sir Conan's threat.

"You know," Nadia said, snatching the leg from Hestia. "With the right modifications, this leg could be deadly."

She rotated between her hands, scrutinizing the splintered wood.

Ida snorted, then giggled before she and Reese started organizing Devora's fan mail.

"So," Hestia said, flopping on Devora's bed. Her dark almond eyes glittered with mischief. "I heard a rumor that you've been visiting a special someone on your way to your nightly job."

Devora blinked. "What? From who?"

"Hestia, leave her be," Reese scolded as she smoothed out a crinkled sock. "She just had the fight of her life. She doesn't want to gossip right now."

Hestia stuck out her tongue. "You're just mad your probabilities were wrong again."

Reese turned her nose up at the comment.

"I haven't been—" Devora started then stopped. She reared back in realization. "Are you talking about One Shot?" Groaning, Devora shook her head.

"One Shot?" Hestia gasped, bringing her hands to her parted lips. "The assassin from Level Five? He's your secret lover?"

"No!" Devora exclaimed, heat rising up her neck.

"How do *you* know who he is, Hestia?" Reese glared at her twin.

Hestia shrugged. "Charles knows people."

Reese rolled her eyes. "Charles only has a fifteen-point eight percent chance of knowing more people here than we do."

"I met One Shot once or twice when I had to clean out his cell," Ida piped in, lining up a group of knife handles, also needing signatures. "He was very polite."

"Hmmm," Nadia said, stroking an invisible beard on her chin as she waggled her brows. "Do you think he's your secret 'M'?"

"Oh no, Dev, you can't!" Hestia cried, placing her hands over her heart. "What about Captain Blake? I can see him challenging One Shot to a duel for your heart and losing." Hestia feigned fainting on the bed. "A tragic love affair."

"Don't be so dramatic," Reese deadpanned.

"It would make a great story, though," Ida said with a soft grin.

Hestia popped up and bowed her head. "Thank you, Ida."

Devora's heart flipped at the mention of the captain. She needed to find him and explain what happened earlier in the training room.

"Don't worry, Hestia. I don't think it was One Shot who sent me the gifts," Devora answered.

Nadia slumped onto her bed and pulled out her notebook. "Too bad. An assassin boyfriend may not be a bad thing."

"And there's nothing going on between Captain Blake and me." Devora laughed nervously as she scooched to the edge of the bed. Her skin was crawling with sweat and sand from Round Two, and she wanted to do nothing else until she bathed.

"Sure, there isn't," Hestia replied with a grin. The other girls laughed. Even Reese couldn't stop a smirk.

"There's not," Devora claimed and gathered her soap and clean uniform from the corner of her bunk. She slowly stood, trying not to put pressure on her ankle. Though Captain Blake confused her, she found herself missing his company when he wasn't around. She needed to talk to him.

The girls all giggled again and Devora gave up on trying to convince them about her and the captain.

Tilting her head to the side, Devora sniffed her shoulder and reared back. She definitely needed a bath before finding Captain Blake.

Once she had taken enough weapons to protect herself and satisfy her friends that she would be perfectly safe walking alone, Devora headed to the baths. As she came to the first stairwell, a group of soldiers chatted about how they wanted her name tattooed on their arms. Devora slowly crept away from the stairs, deciding to take a different route.

Who knew that taking out Jin Hadeed would give me such fame?

Later, as she lathered her hair with the rose soap, Devora thought about the final round of Regulus Protecti. What would be waiting for her? The competitors had already battled hand to hand and with weapons. What other terrible exercise could Warden Hazor think of? Would they have to battle *him*?

Devora grabbed the bucket and splashed the lukewarm water over her head, then squeezed the excess out. Whatever it was, she couldn't fret for long because Round Three of the competition had been scheduled for tomorrow morning.

Devora wiped the water out of her eyes. A few weeks ago, she would've never thought she would be in the final round of Regulus Protecti with Sir Conan and One Shot. As she wrapped a towel around herself, Devora frowned.

While she was happy for One Shot, she couldn't say the same about the knight.

After drying herself off and getting dressed, Devora wrung her hair out and twisted it into a knot before securing it with Nadia's pin.

And what happened to Papa? Would he attend Round Three? Would Warden Hazor allow her to talk to him? Devora shook her head, not knowing the answer to any of those questions.

There was also still the matter of the swirling lights. Why had it suddenly awakened during the tournament and not earlier? The idea of seeing someone's soul was fascinating yet terrifying.

Devora headed down the hall, her boots softly padding against the stone floor. Though she didn't have time to find the answers to all her questions, whatever awaited her, she would be ready.

During dinner, Devora signed too many pieces of parchments and an eye patch. Reese ordered Devora's fans into a single line that wrapped around the table. After Devora's hand cramped up, Nadia and Hestia made sure no one else bothered her so she could eat in peace.

"Are you all right?" Ida asked, sliding beside her.

Devora gave a tired smiled and shook out her wrist. "Yes. I'm just a bit overwhelmed." Although the popularity was nice, she wouldn't mind having some alone time.

Ida stirred her *ligula* in her mush. "That's understandable. But at least everyone has accepted you and your gift."

Devora nodded, realizing Ida was right. The prisoners and nobles no longer looked at her like she carried a plague. Although the Fortress was feeling more normal, her dream of Vlacklear still lingered in her mind, and she thought of the vial of shining liquid from the old hag.

"Drink this and Vlacklear will accept you, no matter what." Isn't that what the old hag said?

Once the crowd died down, Devora slipped out of the dining hall and escaped to the Theater. She took in a deep breath, relishing the silence surrounding her. The benches were empty and the torches dim. For some reason, the room that held so much violence gave her peace.

Devora slowly strode to the center of the Theater, her limping footsteps silent along the sandy floor. Though the medic's tincture had taken away most of the ache in her arm, sharp pain still zapped up her foot every few steps.

A few training posts had been mounted into the ground. Devora placed her hand on one, her fingers grazing the splintered wood. She had come so far in just a few weeks. Looking back, she could hardly recognize the girl who'd entered the Fortress.

Reaching into her pocket, Devora pulled out the hag's metallic tincture. A sheen appeared on the liquid as she tilted it in her hand. It reminded her of imperial opal.

Would it be so bad to leave the Fortress behind and chase my dreams head on?

She wasn't sure what the liquid would do, but, right now, it sounded better than having to face Sir Conan or One Shot in Round Three of Regulus Protecti tomorrow.

Devora popped the cork and a salty aroma spiraled from the small vial. Maybe she could only take half of it, just to see if anything happened. As Devora brought the vial to her lips, a voice called from the doorway.

"If you're going to poison yourself, I suggest you do it somewhere more private."

Devora dropped the vial and spun around to find Captain Blake wrapping his hands, preparing to train. Her stomach twisted at his presence.

"I wasn't poisoning myself," she replied hastily.

The captain's face stayed impassive.

Glancing down, Devora jumped back as the metallic tincture ate away at the sand, creating a large hole to the stone underneath. A few droplets landed on her bandaged ankle and easily disintegrated the fabric.

Gasping, Devora clawed at the bandage. She tore off the piece and threw it on the ground.

"I didn't know," she whispered, defeat weighing her shoulders.

Sinking to the ground, Devora didn't care that she was in the middle of the Theater. As she brought her knees to her chest, she hid her face between them. She couldn't bear the weight of Captain Blake's scrutiny as she cried.

"When the war with Kadesh began," the captain started, his footsteps coming closer, "King Atol rounded up all the Seers for observation. Including my mother." Devora peeked over her arm and watched as he tightened the fabric on his hands, his face a mask of calm. "Which meant he murdered them all."

Devora sucked in a breath as the woman with the chestnut curls and bright violet eyes resurfaced in her thoughts. "That's why you tried to warn me when the dung tea wore off."

The captain furrowed his brow. "Dung tea?"

Heat blossomed in her cheeks, and she looked away. "It's an herbal tea I had to take to suppress my power. It smelled and tasted like cow dung."

A smile tugged at the corner of the captain's lips before he faced the wooden poles. "I couldn't see another person with my mother's gift be killed. That's why I convinced the warden not to kill you *and* came up with the tournament to train you. If I could train you to be the best, you'd live."

Devora's pulse elevated. "But you stopped Warden Hazor from killing me when I first came. You didn't know I was a Seer then."

Captain Blake turned, his calculating eyes analyzing her. Devora lifted her head, her body keenly aware of his stare.

When she gave up that he was going to explain, the captain asked, "Are you going to tell me what that was?" He gestured to the empty vial on the ground.

"It was a false hope," Devora answered, thankful she hadn't drunk the tincture. She knew it was too good to be true. How could a vial get her into Vlacklear? She'd been too easily swayed by the hag's manipulative words.

"You should be careful of what people give you," Captain Blake said, rubbing his hand across his forehead. "Devora, if you want to take your life, all of this"—he motioned to the Theater— "will have been for nothing. Don't you realize you'd be giving them what they want?"

She pinched her lips shut, unsure of what to say.

Captain Blake stared out into the stands. "Seers are powerful, and that's why the monarchy fears them. They know too much. But if that power is used to right wrongs, isn't it worth using?"

Devora placed her chin on her knees. *Could I really use my abilities to help people?*

She remembered Ida's story—how her vision of the viper saved Ida's little sister. Peace coursed through her veins as she roved over the revelation. Captain Blake was right. If she had the power to bring justice to the world, she should.

Captain Blake sighed and seated himself next to her before glancing at her haphazardly bandaged ankle. A thin oval of blood seeped through the white bandages, covering the burn marks from where the tincture had eaten through the outer material.

The captain leaned forward. "Who wrapped this?" He carefully probed the bandages on her leg.

Devora's breath hitched. Warmth flowed through the thin cloth securing her leg. "The medic in the infirmary."

"He did a terrible job." Captain Blake took the towel he was holding and began ripping it into pieces.

"What are you doing?" she gasped.

He glanced up at her. "The wound won't heal properly if it isn't wrapped correctly. The medic did a lousy job." A smirk played across his lips. "Don't worry, the material is clean."

Shuffling closer to her, Captain Blake gently placed her foot on his lap and unwound the bloodied fabric. Pleasant chills danced across her skin, her body relaxing as the captain cleaned the blood around her wound.

"I saw my father in the stands," she said as she watched him bandage her foot. "Do you know where he is now?"

The captain shook his head. "I'm sorry, Devora, but he should be on his way back to Grenly. The king said he would lift the house arrest as long as your father didn't attack any more of his guards." Captain Blake paused. "Though, Conan is infuriating so I can understand your father's reason for hitting him."

Relief flooded her veins. Papa and Mama were safe, and it was all thanks to Captain Blake.

Devora laughed at the captain's comment. "It was a good punch."

"I wish I could've seen it," he replied with a grin. His face then turned somber as he rewrapped her ankle. "I want to apologize for being so hard on you since the beginning. It was unfair of me to expect so much of someone who had no combat training."

Devora studied the captain as he worked diligently on securing her ankle.

"I hated your criticism," she replied. "It infuriated me because it reminded me that I wasn't good enough. Even when I got better, it still wasn't enough. I always had something to work on." Devora extended her fingers through the sand covering the ground. "I could never meet your expectations."

Captain Blake opened his mouth to reply, but Devora gently placed her hand over his.

"But now, I appreciate your criticism because it makes me work harder. It makes me want to become something better than I could ever dream of being. Without your criticism, I wouldn't have made it this far."

Captain Blake stared at her, lips parted, hands paused on her foot.

Satisfaction rolled off Devora as she removed her hand and she giggled. For once, the captain was speechless.

After a moment, Captain Blake recovered with a smirk. "So, you're saying the only reason you made it this far was because of me?" A mischievous glint twinkled in his stormy eyes as he secured the final wrapping over her ankle. He pushed up from the ground and offered her a hand.

Devora snorted and took it before playfully pushing him in the chest. "The only reason I made it this far was because *I* was trying to prove you wrong."

A low laugh escaped the captain's lips as he looked down at where her hand had grazed his chest. "I'm glad you did." But when he raised his head, the laughter was gone. "And I hope you can continue to succeed because Round Three will be impossible."

Chapter Twenty-Seven

Devora was up and dressed before Sir Blakesalot cawed. In fact, the black bird was still curled upon itself, sleeping soundly. Gathering her hair in a knot, she wove the pin through the thick strands and crept out of the cell, careful not to wake the bird or Nadia.

Her footsteps were silent as she slowly padded down the long corridor. All the other girls were still asleep, but Devora couldn't rest. Captain Blake said Round Three would be impossible. She asked what was waiting for her, but the captain only shook his head. He then explained that Warden Hazor was keeping the competition for Round Three a secret. No one knew the stakes. But Captain Blake said he had worked for the warden long enough to know it wasn't something good.

Not only had the mystery of the final round kept her from sleep, but she kept having the same vision of Princess Haden being captured. Devora squeezed her tattered purple sash lining her chest. She knew that if she ran to Warden Hazor with the information—if she could even reach him—he would laugh in her face and then probably try to kill her. Even after her success in both rounds, he still looked like he wanted to murder her.

Devora wrapped her arms around her stomach.

Did Warden Hazor send the old hag to give me the vial? Did he send the men to attack me?

She felt as if the warden would stop at nothing until she was dead. If Tunri wasn't protecting her, Devora's life would've been taken weeks ago. Why did the warden hate her so much? He seemed to generally dislike everyone, but something about her infuriated him.

And what was even worse was that her ankle was still sore from her fight with Jin Hadeed. She visited the infirmary once more and received another pain-suppressing tincture. It had eased some of the pain, but she still had a slight limp. Glancing down, Devora studied the dark cloth wrapped snugly around her ankle, her cheeks flaring from the memory of last night. It was nice witnessing the gentler side of the captain. It reminded her of the small peek she had into his soul.

Devora shook her head, still feeling the tingles of Captain Blake's hands gently holding her ankle. Her injury had felt better since the captain had rewrapped it, but she would still need a miracle to win Round Three.

Devora attempted to quicken her steps as she hurried through Level Five. She hadn't visited the wolves since the contest began and was worried about the female wolf. Did she have her pups? Sir Jacques graciously offered to complete her duties so she could focus on training. Although the knight assured her the wolves were taken care of, Devora still wanted to check on them.

As she strode passed One Shot's cell, Devora stopped. The Level Five assassin slept on his side, his breathing steady as his shaggy black hair swept across his forehead. Devora peeked in further, studying his serene face. He looked so young, barely twenty summers.

Devora blinked and a blue and yellow swirl spiraled atop One Shot's chest. She narrowed her gaze. After using her soulsight on Captain Blake, she assumed blue meant sorrow, that meant yellow could mean the opposite. But she had yet to see a mixture of light colors.

Sorrow mixed with hope, perhaps? She thought. But when she tried to get a closer look, another memory slammed into her thoughts.

"You'll be safe, Mara. Just take the trade road during the day," a younger One Shot said to a girl with ebony ringlets and freckles.

"If you're sure," the girl said, her knuckles white as she gripped a wooden basket. She looked around the same age as Devora, maybe a bit younger.

The memory swirled and Devora heard the uncouth comments and whistles being thrown at the girl as she hastily sped up a wide dirt road. She went during the day as instructed by One Shot, but the townsmen still wouldn't leave her alone.

The men caught up to Mara and stole her basket before pushing her between them. They dragged her away and Devora's stomach lurched. Where was everyone? Why didn't someone help her?

The memory spun again, and One Shot sprinted into the scene, his creamy skin slicked with sweat as his head whipped back and forth.

"Mara!" he called, his voice laced with fear.

He ran with a crossbow tight within his grasp until he suddenly stopped. Devora watched as One Shot's body stilled to stone and he raised the weapon. Without another breath, he shot it. Four different screams and grunts came from the direction he aimed and, as the vision cleared, Devora saw four bodies slumped to the ground.

"Mara," One Shot gasped as he sprinted to the girl. Though she looked mostly unharmed, her eyes held more horror than any young girl's should.

Devora gasped and hung onto the bars of the cell to balance herself. Cold sweat rolled down her temple as she heaved from the horrible memory.

"Did you see?" One Shot asked quietly, now seated upright on the cot. He placed a hand over the yellow and blue swirl. It didn't look agitated like Captain Blake's had after Devora intruded. Instead, the swirl sagged, as if it carried the weight of a mountain. "I could feel someone searching."

Swallowing the knot in her throat, Devora nodded. "I'm so sorry for intruding on your memories. Is your sister..."

"I didn't want to go with her to deliver the baked goods my father made," One Shot explained, covering his eyes with his hand. "I can't even remember why I didn't want to go. I told her she would be fine."

He rose from the bed, his towering height exemplified by the shadows pulling from him. His face molded to stone as he said, "If I lied at my trial, I probably wouldn't be here.

But when the court asked me to apologize to all the men's families, I refused. I'm not sorry for killing them." One Shot rubbed the back of his neck. "When I wouldn't apologize, they locked me down here and said I deserved to rot for what I had done."

Devora took a step back. She wanted to run away and forget the terrible vision. But she couldn't. Now that she knew the truth, she would never forget.

One Shot ran a hand through his hair, looking down at his feet. "The last time the Fortress allowed me to write to my family, Pa said Mara had gotten married to a local farmer. He was a friend of mine, so I know he's a good man. He must have done a lot to earn her trust because after that day, Mara secluded herself from all of us: my father, our friends but mostly from me."

One Shot hung his head and leaned against the bars of his cell. "I'm not sure how you saw that, but I need to win this competition. I need to be pardoned of my crime and see my family again."

Tears pricked Devora's eyes as she gripped the cell bars. "Of course, I understand."

Her heart wrenched as she thought about not being able to see Mama and Papa.

Will I ever see them again?

"Devora, if it comes to a battle between me, you, and Conan, I refuse to kill an innocent."

Devora froze. The thought of a battle to the death never crossed her mind. When she focused back on One Shot, his dark eyes were wide, as if she would strike him down, condemning him for killing in defense of his sister. The blue and yellow swirl on his chest shook, frightened.

But how could she condemn him when she would've acted the same?

Reaching through the bars, Devora grasped One Shot's large, thin hands between her own. "Thank you, my friend. I will do the same." The swirl of his soul settled, now holding more yellow than blue.

Trying to forget everything she learned, Devora hurried to gather the buckets of meat before heading to the wolves. Though it was a struggle with her injured ankle, she managed to hobble to the doorway. Once she made it to the wooden shack, Devora placed one of the buckets down and opened the door, hoping she had gained the male wolf's trust. When the male wolf didn't stir, Devora quickly stepped inside, grabbing the pail before closing the door.

The male wolf growled at her then nestled next to the female. The poor female wolf laid on the ground, her eyes closed. Fear struck Devora's heart before she saw the wolf's steady breaths. She noticed the female wolf's belly wasn't as swollen as before. Devora searched around the hut.

Where are the pups? Did Warden Hazor take them away from their mother?

Anger ignited in her chest as Devora slowly placed the buckets of meat on the ground. If the warden harmed the wolves, Devora didn't know what she'd do.

Minding her ankle, she crouched to the hay-ridden floor. The wolf followed her descent, baring his teeth, but not coming closer. It was then she noticed another gray wolf lying in the corner, away from the couple. It focused on her, watching her movements closely. There was something striking about the wolf's gray eyes.

Devora waited until high-pitched yapping broke the third wolf's glare and a litter of pups scampered out from beneath the mother wolf. Devora gasped in surprise before a smile split her face. The pups squealed and barked at the father wolf, then barreled into the gray-eyed wolf in the corner. They jumped on top of him and nipped at his ears. The wolf shook a few of them away but did so gently.

Devora chuckled to herself. *Not so tough now, are you?*

The wolf turned to her, as if he had heard her thoughts, but he didn't growl.

With a steady hand, Devora pushed the meat bucket closer and scooched to the edge of the shack. The wolf pups jumped and yipped all around, excited to have a visitor.

After she had stayed with the pups, parents, and additional wolf for a little while, the rising sun between the cracks of the shack told her that her time was up. Standing, she pulled the pieces of straw from her uniform and carefully stepped around the pups that had gathered at her legs.

"I'll come back soon," Devora whispered before slipping out of the shack.

Her heart ached at the sight of the dilapidated hut. Maybe, when she won Regulus Protecti, Devora could ask the warden to give the wolves more room.

Breathing in the cool morning air, she slowly trudged back to the Fortress, ready for whatever Warden Hazor had planned.

Chapter Twenty-Eight

The Theater, The Fortress

Folding her arms across her chest, Devora tapped her fingers on her bicep as she limped around the training room. Sir Jacques had instructed that she wasn't to know what the final round held until she was in the Theater. But whatever Round Three was, each participant was to face it alone. Devora ran her hands over her head to her tightly pinned bun at the nape of her neck. Waiting was always worse than facing the challenge head-on.

After speaking with One Shot, the fear of a battle to the death stayed plastered in her mind. But when she heard stomping and cheers above her, the fear lessened.

Am I going to be facing another giant like Babshee?

She had never felt the Fortress quake other than when the angry giant was barreling through it.

Devora stopped pacing and stared at her wounded ankle. Her arm was still sore from the attack, too.

Only with Tunri's help am I going to win in this condition.

The rumbling vibrated her training room again, followed by gasps.

Maybe Warden Hazor wanted One Shot and Sir Conan to fight and then the winner would battle her. Devora brought her hand to her mouth and began biting her fingernails. But that didn't explain the thundering noise.

Devora's mind reeled.

Can I defeat Sir Conan?

Sure, she had learned the moves of hemna and could wield the mech almost as well as any other soldier, but Sir Conan had years of experience on her. *And* he wasn't injured.

"Calm down," Devora scolded herself, her panic tightening her chest. Letting her arms fall to her sides, she closed her eyes and sucked in a deep breath through her nose. After a moment, she slowly let it out.

"Tunri, be with me," she whispered, keeping her eyes shut. "Guide me on what to do. Help me complete the vision you sent me."

Devora breathed in and out a few more times until her pulse returned to a steady rhythm. When she opened her eyes, she saw Captain Blake standing before her. She jerked back.

"Oh, I didn't know you were here," she explained, the words jumbling out of her mouth. *How had he gotten in here without me hearing him?*

Captain Blake's voice was as cool as the air had been that morning. "I'm glad you prayed. You're going to need it."

The captain assessed her, his shoulders rigid. His lips stayed pressed in a firm, thin line as they had been the first time Devora met him. By the way he stood like the stone surrounding them, she knew he wasn't joking.

The fear Devora had just vanquished crept upon her again, poking and prodding her thoughts. Scenarios of her death piled into her mind before she stopped them. Tunri was with her. He wanted her here. He would help her through whatever waited for her. He had to.

Squaring her shoulders, Devora met Captain Blake's gaze. "I'm ready."

The crowd roared as soon as she entered the Theater. Arms flailed in the air as prisoners and gambling noblemen whistled and hooted, trying to get her attention. Devora gave them all a nod and a quick wave, trying to stay focused.

As soon as she and Captain Blake reached the middle of the Theater, the captain spun around. Devora peered up at him, noticing the fear and concern keeping his features taut. She wondered—hoped— his emotions were for her.

The captain started to reach out to her but thought better of it and brought his hand back to his side.

"Try to avoid putting too much weight on your ankle. Remember what I told you in Round One: dodge and deflect as much as you can." His throat bobbed, as if he wanted to say more. "Be smart, Medee."

He handed her a real mech. Not a wooden training sword, but a deadly metal weapon. With a nod, he marched away.

Devora held the sword to her chest, watching the sturdy shoulders of the captain as he strode up the stairs of the arena. Once Captain Blake seated himself, Warden Hazor stood, and the crowd immediately silenced.

"Congratulations, contestant," the warden announced, extending his thick arms as he focused on the crowd and not Devora. "You've made it to the third and final round of Regulus Protecti. If you succeed with your final challenge, you will receive a pardon and win an audience with me—" he motioned to himself— "and our courageous king." The warden gestured to King Atol and Queen Leza seated at the top of the Theater.

Devora's throat went dry. *The king and queen are watching the competition?*

Didn't King Atol have more pressing issues to deal with, like the unending war with Kadesh or the possible capture of his daughter? Why were they wasting time watching a tournament?

The crowd clapped quietly, scared to interrupt the warden.

"But if you fail, you will spend the rest of your days as my personal servant."

Devora refused to cower at the mischievous gleam in the warden's eyes.

"For your final challenge," he continued, "You will have the honor of facing the creature from the darkness, the monster in the shadows, the Behemoth!" Terror rocked Devora's limbs as the crowd erupted into cheers. "Succeed where your competitors failed! Subdue this beast and you will be victorious!"

A wheel of chains clanged to her right and the giant iron door slowly lifted. Large black hooves stomped impatiently on the other side as the door crept upward.

Fear paralyzed every nerve in her body. Her mind yelled, "Run!" but her feet stayed planted in the sand. Devora gripped the hilt of the mech, the weight of it heavier than its wooden counterpart.

"Tunri is with me," Devora encouraged herself as blood rushed between her ears. "Tunri is with me."

The door creaked higher and higher, revealing four hairy, mud-covered legs and a huge, white torso. Giant white antlers protruded from the Behemoth's head, so wide that the giant elk-like creature had to turn its head sideways to stomp into the arena. Devora took a few steps back as the door finished its ascent and the Behemoth fully entered the Theater.

Terror coiled around her core as she stood still, not knowing what to do next. The Behemoth reared back on its hind legs, unleashing a guttural growl from its snout. It held similarities to an elk, but its frame was too large and its antlers too wide to be an ordinary one. As it kicked out its legs, its antlers almost grazed the domed top of the Theater. Devora wobbled backward, trying to steady her shaking hands as she pointed the mech at the giant creature.

The Behemoth stomped on the ground, bellowing a roar that stifled her courage before jumping to its hind legs again. It raised its front hooves in the air and roared. The crowd gasped; some people even hid behind their hands and cloaks. Devora wished she could do the same.

Though, as she readied her stance, a pained voice fluttered through her mind.

Help me.

Devora paused, her eyes darting to the creature as it thrashed against the chain tightened around its neck. The stone collar gleamed, and she instantly recognized the imperial opal.

Does the Behemoth possess some sort of power as well?

The Behemoth strained against the chain, its cry sorrowful as it tugged and pulled. Devora's heart broke. This creature was a prisoner just as much as the rest of them. But were its crimes true, or was it provoked to violence, like One Shot?

Devora raised the mech, circling the Behemoth. When she first came to the Fortress, the creature had spoken to her. And it spoke again when she had seen its giant purple eye.

But why me? Devora thought, slowly pacing in front of the Behemoth. *Can no one else hear the creature's cries?*

She stared at the animal, now noticing the cuts on its head and neck, the patches of fur missing from its torso. The outline of its ribs protruded from its side, as if it hadn't been fed in months. Fury swelled in her heart. Even the worst prisoners in the Fortress received nourishment. Why was this creature being tortured and starved?

The Behemoth bore down on the chain, whipping its head left and right, its antlers barely missing the cowering crowd.

Help me, it pleaded against her thoughts.

The desperation in its voice weighed on Devora. It would do anything to be free. She had felt the same way only a day ago.

Holding the mech high, Devora knew what she needed to do. Without another thought, she hobbled to the chain secured in the center of the Theater. The Behemoth's large purple eyes followed her. It stepped back and pulled the chain tight. Rearing back, Devora raised the mech above her head and brought it down on the rings of metal with all the strength she had. The loud chink echoed through the Theater, stunning the crowd to silence.

With a grunt, Devora lifted the mech again and slammed it against the chain. No creature should be treated this way. The clang vibrated up her arms, awakening the pain in her wounded bicep. Sweat beaded at her brow, and she raised the mech a third time, wincing as she bared down on the metal. But the chain wouldn't budge.

Tunri, Devora cried. *You know this isn't right. Help me!*

A swirl of lavender power coated her hands and wrapped around the sword. Holding the mech above her head, Devora hurled the blade into the rusted links. The crack of metal bounced against the walls before the Behemoth roared. It jerked its head to the side, whipping the chain around its neck before it reared back. Devora dove out of the way, dodging the black hooves that quickly descended.

The Behemoth stilled, its violet eyes studying her carefully as the rest of the imperial opal collar disintegrated to dust.

You're free, Devora urged the beast.

Crouching down, she laid her mech beside her and placed her forehead to the ground.

The Behemoth took a step forward and sniffed her hair. Its warm breath tickled the nape of her neck, but Devora didn't move. The giant creature nudged her head then stepped away.

Thank you, it whispered inside her mind.

The Behemoth circled the Theater, snorting at Warden Hazor before it faced the exit. With a huff, the elk-like animal rammed its antlers through the stone wall.

Devora's head whipped up before she shielded her eyes from the flying debris. Cries of horror escalated through the Theater as the Behemoth stepped back and trampled more stone. Seconds later, its clomping hooves echoed through the Fortress' stone corridors.

Grabbing her sword, Devora hesitantly stood and faced the crowd. She knew she just forfeited her life for the Behemoth, but she wouldn't allow that beautiful creature to be tortured any longer. Though she may be killed in a few moments, peace descended upon her, knowing she had done what was right.

But to her surprise, Warden Hazor's guards weren't waiting to slash her throat. Instead, the king, queen, and the entire crowd stared at her with their mouths agape, not knowing what to do. When Warden Hazor didn't announce her victory, it was the deep, crisp voice of Captain Blake that broke the silence.

"Your champion of Regulus Protecti, the new Defender of Tenton, Lady Devora Medee!"

Chapter Twenty-Nine

The next few hours spun by in a fury. Devora was swept from the Theater to a special bathing room in one of the towers of the Fortress.

A team of seamstresses and handmaidens flocked around her, their identical silver circlets glinting as they rushed back and forth. The circlets reminded her of Master Riggs' silver. Had he made these, as well?

The handmaidens cleaned every inch of dirt off her body while taking her measurements and styling her hair. Devora assumed she couldn't have an audience with the king and queen covered in the filth of the Fortress. Still, a part of her wanted to be presented in her grimy state. Like the flames beneath Master Riggs' silver vat, the Fortress was her fire. And though she still had much to learn, the Fortress had begun to refine and fortify her into who she was meant to be—grime and all.

As the maids flocked around her, Devora sat still, unsure of how to act. She hadn't been doted upon in weeks. It was so strange to be fawned over and told how amazing she was by the chittering ladies. If this had been months ago, Devora would've joined in and agreed that she was spectacular. But instead, she sat quietly as her long hair was brushed. While the maids held different necklaces up for her to try on, Devora wondered where the Behemoth had gone.

One petite maid with blonde braids held up a shimmering lilac dress. Where the handmaidens had gotten it, Devora wasn't sure, but it fit her like a glove. Though the fabric was smooth, she found herself missing the comfortable pants of her training uniform. The dress was immaculate, but how could she defend herself in it? Devora smiled at how much her thoughts had changed.

Her ebony hair was softer than it had been in weeks and was swept up in several intricate braids that wove through one another at the back of her head. Hestia would've loved the style. Where were her friends now?

Her old self would've had no problem ordering the head handmaiden around. But the deep shadows and wrinkles collecting around the handmaiden's eyes stung Devora's heart.

What is this woman's life like? Does she have a family? Children?

Taking a breath, Devora held up Nadia's pin. It had been taken from her hair and placed on the table in front of her. "I would like to wear this, please."

The elderly handmaiden paused, her wrinkled hands hovering above Devora's head. She glanced down at the pin. "Yes, of course, my lady," she replied, before taking the pin and placing it in Devora's hair.

Devora's gaze then darted around, searching for her violet sash she had worn for the tournament. "I had a purple sash..."

"Yes, it was torn and ripped to shreds. One of the girls is mending it. It will be ready in a moment."

Devora glanced up at the woman. "Really?"

The handmaiden nodded before motioning to Devora's gown. "We thought you would want a dress to match it. The girls have been keeping up with the tournament ever since it started." The elderly handmaiden put a finger to her temple. "They've talked nonstop about you since Round One." She shook her head and smiled. "My lady doesn't enjoy the gossip, but I don't mind."

"Your lady?" Devora questioned. She assumed Warden Hazor hired servants to bath and clothe whoever had won Regulus Protecti.

"Queen Leza."

Devora's jaw dropped.

"My lady offered her personal handmaidens before Round Three began. I have a feeling she knew you'd win." The handmaiden winked at Devora before beginning to paint her face.

Devora sat in silence as the woman primed and coated her skin. When she was finished, the younger maids held up a gilded oval mirror. Devora blinked, hardly recognizing herself. Dark kohl lined her eyelids, making her violet eyes look bigger and brighter. Her lips had been stained the color of red roses. She reached up to her face, feeling the white powder layer over her bronzed skin. Though she was lovely, she looked nothing like herself.

Twisting her head, Devora admired the intricate braids cascading down her back with Nadia's pin holding half of them in a beautiful swirl at the center of her head. She loved what the head handmaiden had done with her hair, but the paint on her face was too much.

Glancing to the side, Devora noticed the rag the elderly handmaiden used to wipe her hands off on. Devora grabbed the rag and gently wiped the powder off. The girls gasped but didn't stop her. When she turned back to the mirror, Devora smiled. Though she still wore the kohl and lip stain, she would not cover her face for the king.

"I'm here to escort Lady Medee," Sir Jacques' voice rolled against the smooth stone walls of the bathing room.

Relief washed over her. It felt as if it had been ages since she last spoke to Sir Jacques before the beginning of Round Two. Lifting the hem of her silk dress, Devora turned to see the knight's jaw drop.

"What?" she frowned, looking down at the smooth fabric. She ran her fingers across the gemmed belt hugging her waist, making sure it was straight before meeting Sir Jacques' stare.

He cleared his throat, quickly averting his eyes with a bow. "You look like the leader you are, Lady Medee.".

"Wait, don't forget this!" A young handmaiden, no more than Devora's age raced up to her. She curtsied before holding out the purple sash. The fabric had been mended well, but the rips and tears were still visible. But Devora enjoyed the scars the sash held—reminders that the broken can be mended.

Devora wrapped her fingers around the silk. "Thank you for fixing this. It means more than you know."

The girl gave her a wide grin and glanced at the other handmaidens. They curtsied and clasped their hands behind their backs. A few bounced on their toes, trying to contain their excitement.

Devora placed the sash over her shoulder and secured it across her chest.

"My lady," Sir Jacques said, offering his arm.

With a nod of thanks to the handmaidens, Devora slid her hand into the crook of his arm, and they padded down the hallway. The clanging of Sir Jacques' metal armor echoed between the stone walls until Devora asked, "It's too much, isn't it?" She motioned to the shining lilac dress.

Sir Jacques peered down at her with a smile. "I meant what I said."

Devora ran a hand over her styled hair as they continued toward a peaked door.

"King Atol, Queen Leza, Warden Hazor, and the King's Council are inside," Sir Jacques whispered. "Be ready for them. They're worse than the prisoners downstairs."

Devora swallowed the knot in her throat and nodded. Sir Jacques opened the door, bowing again. "Good luck."

Holding her breath, Devora strode through the threshold, her soft, silk slippers gliding easily across the smooth floor. They felt so frail and vulnerable compared to the thick leather boots she had grown used to.

A circular wooden table occupied the center of the large room. Around it sat various members of the King's Council, all dressed in the latest fashions of bright colored fabrics.

Devora scanned the room. There were representatives from all the regions of Tenton except for Grenly. Fear clenched her heart. Although Captain Blake said Papa was headed back to Grenly, he was still a member of the King's Council. Shouldn't he be here?

"Our champion," Warden Hazor commented.

Devora focused her attention on him.

Warden Hazor tented his fingertips and pressed them against his straight lips, disturbing his thick white mustache. "I didn't think you'd even make it past the first round."

"I'm glad she did," a nasally voice chimed in before Devora could answer. She turned toward a short, thin man with a hooked nose and beady eyes. He smiled widely at Devora. "I bet a good wager on her."

"You should've informed me of your bet," a deep voice interceded. "Phineas assured me his competitor was sure to win."

Devora spun back to where Warden Hazor sat, but it wasn't him who spoke. Next to him, dressed in rich reds and golds sat King Atol. His maple brown hair curled around his simplistic golden crown as his light emerald eyes watched Devora closely. His large, tanned hand grasped a petite pale one.

Devora shifted her gaze to the woman next to the king. Queen Leza. Silky straight hair rolled down the queen's slim shoulders, black as night. A delicate crown winked as Queen Leza turned her head toward Devora.

The silver strands of metal braided around one another in a circle until they peaked, surrounding an imperial opal. Devora lifted her brows, recognizing the gem.

Why does the queen have an imperial opal in her crown?

Queen Leza's skin was whiter than the powdered sugar on a cocoa cake. But as Devora faced the queen fully, her stomach clenched. Two piercing black eyes stared back, wide and hard. It was as if the queen could see straight into Devora's soul. Blinking, Devora engaged her soulsight. What greeted her wasn't a blue or yellow swirl, but a black hue, twisting with rage.

Devora stifled her gasp. Why did she feel a familiarity between the hag who had given her the vial and Queen Leza?

Bending her knees, Devora performed a gentle curtsy before standing upright again, blinking the dark swirl away. "King Atol, Queen Leza."

"Lady Devora Medee," the king replied, assessing her carefully.

Devora caught the sardonic undertone as he announced her former title. She swallowed the retort on her tongue as she watched the king release his wife's hand and pull out a small leather pouch. The navy bag looked miniscule in the king's thick fingers. After opening the pleats, he poured out the Categorization Call stones. Each one tumbled out easily before King Atol lined them side by side on the table.

"If I'm not mistaken, you were meant to attend Vlacklear Academy. Is that right?"

Devora watched carefully as the king ordered the stones in Vlacklear's original categorization: blue, yellow, green, red, purple.

Heat rose up her neck. *Is he mocking me?* It was *his* law that sent her to the Fortress in the first place. She had never wanted to come here.

But, even in the short amount of time she had been here, she had learned so much. She had met so many people she never would've met at Vlacklear. When Devora scanned the room earlier, she was hoping to find Captain Blake. But he was nowhere to be found.

Taking a steady breath, Devora focused back on the king. *Give me the words Tunri because I don't trust myself.*

"You are correct, sire," she began. "I originally categorized the order for Vlacklear Academy. I categorized for it perfectly. Every time."

The king leaned back in his chair; his features stern as he grasped his wife's small hand again. His light green eyes darted between Devora's, as if expecting a different answer.

"Do you blame your kingdom for your time here at the Fortress?" A threat lingered beneath his question.

Devora paused. This was definitely a trap. But a cool aura wrapped around her, reminding her of her visions. Tunri had sent her here to inform the king and his council about the creatures in Kadesh's army and the location of Princess Haden.

Before she could respond, quick heavy footsteps pounded from the hall. In a matter of seconds, Captain Blake appeared in the doorway. His shoulders heaved before he quickly straightened. After adjusting his formal attire, he entered the room. His gray eyes widened at Devora's dress but were soon back to their usual cold demeanor.

"My king and queen," the captain said, bowing deeply. "Forgive my tardiness. I was instructed that our meeting would be held elsewhere."

King Atol's eyes flashed at Captain Blake's presence, but an easy smile soon crept across his thick lips.

"Ah, Matthias, I'm glad you're here. I was just asking Lady Devora about her time at the Fortress. Sit and join us." The king's voice pierced the air like needles as he motioned to the empty chair beside Warden Hazor.

Captain Blake stiffly marched to the chair and sat, his eyes fixed on Devora.

The king turned back to Devora and waved his hand. "Please continue."

Devora's heart pounded at the sight of the captain. She was thankful that he was here but also confused as to the exchange between him and the king.

Tunri, she prayed. The cool confidence wrapped around her again, instructing her on the correct response.

"While I was surprised at the kingdom's new law, I actually must give you my thanks." Devora held back her grin at the king's look of surprise. "Because of the new law, I have gained new abilities I never would have learned at Vlacklear."

Captain Blake's lips twitched while Warden Hazor slapped the table and laughed. Devora flinched at the sudden outburst.

"See, Atol? I told you my prison would make amiable soldiers. Aren't you pleased you moved the military here?"

"Yes," the king mused, running a thumb over his wife's hand. "But is Lady Devora a true soldier?"

"She won Regulus Protecti," Captain Blake replied nonchalantly. The council members whispered to one another as he spoke without permission. "I believe that means she's now Tenton's Defender and will help you in controlling its armies."

Devora's heart swelled at the compliment, and she risked a glance at the captain. He gave her a slight nod before continuing, "I also believe that means she receives one pardon. Isn't that what you promised, Warden?"

Warden Hazor stroked his white mustache, seeming to not hate Devora as much as he used to. "I could pardon her for releasing the Behemoth and destroying my prison. She was meant to kill it, not set it free."

Devora clasped her hands in front of her. She did her best to impersonate Mama's graceful demeanor. When, in reality, she was holding herself back from clawing the warden's eyes out.

"There was no penalty for setting the creature free set forth in the rules," she answered calmly.

Warden Hazor's neck reddened as he opened his mouth to reprimand her, but the king held up a hand.

"Peace, Phineas. The lady is correct. You should write the rules more precisely next time." Devora tried to ignore the hairs standing up on her neck at the king's smooth, condescending tone. "What is it that you want, Lady De-vora?"

Devora paused. This was it. Everything Tunri had guided her to was happening right now. Sending up one more prayer, she began, "I know General Sage has captured Princess Haden and I know where she is. My Sight from Tunri has granted me this vision to tell you. He has also given me a prophecy of a new creature Kadesh plans to unleash upon Tenton. Vicious monsters with razor teeth and iron armor are coming for our eastern border. They plan to cross through the Edo desert and fully invade the capital. If we don't prepare soon, Tenton, as we know it, will perish."

Silence blanketed the room as the King's Council gaped at Devora. The king blanched and the queen curled her free hand into a fist. The only person who wasn't surprised at her reply was Captain Blake. He gave her a firm nod, a gleam of admiration in his eyes.

Devora hesitated before adding, "I would also like to use my pardon for One Shot."

The councilmen gasped. Even Captain Blake looked taken back.

"The assassin from Level Five?" a man with feathers on his collar cried.

"Surely, you can't allow that," a long-nosed man interceded, directing his comment to the warden as he fanned himself.

Warden Hazor stroked his chin. "I will grant your pardon."

The man with feathers fainted as the rest of the King's Council erupted into protests. But King Atol held out his hand, silencing them.

Warden Hazor stood and faced the king. "Sire, I would personally like to send a team to rescue the princess. I can also command a battalion to hold off Kadesh's creatures from invading Juro."

Devora gawked at the warden. He had accepted her word without any evidence. She glanced at Captain Blake, who tilted his head and gave her a knowing look.

By winning the tournament, she had finally proven herself, and now the warden respected her. Devora's tense shoulders relaxed slightly, thankful to have finally delivered Tunri's message.

"No," the king responded, snapping out of his daze. "I need you to continue to watch over the training of our soldiers. No one can keep them in line like you can."

"Then I will send my best man to do the job," the warden replied.

Warden Hazor raised his hand, and Sir Conan came forward from his position in the back of the room. Bruises covered the knight's hands, and he limped toward the king and queen.

Devora lifted her brows at the knight's injuries. He must have fought the Behemoth before her in Round Three. *What did the Behemoth do to him?* She thought of One Shot and hoped the giant creature hadn't harmed him as well.

"Sir," Sir Conan said, placing a fist over his chest. He bowed slowly and winced as he stood straight.

"Conan, ready your best men," Warden Hazor commanded. "You will be sent to the front lines as commander." He paused before adding. "Medee will accompany you."

Captain Blake shot up from his seat, a vein popping from his forehead as Devora choked.

"What?" they both exclaimed.

"Absolutely not," Sir Conan seethed. "I'm not taking orders from a bloody Seer."

Devora's voice cracked as she tried to speak, but words wouldn't form.

"Sir, I must protest," Captain Blake started, but stopped when Warden Hazor lifted his hand.

Warden Hazor's eyes darted from Sir Conan to Devora, his brows furrowed. The air weighed with anticipation as they waited for his answer.

After a moment, the warden sighed. "Medee will go."

Devora's stomach lurched. *The front lines?*

"Understand that if you succeed," Warden Hazor continued, turning his back on them. "The honor of victory for this battle will be because of Lady Devora and her Sight."

Rage burned across Sir Conan's face, but he bowed before hobbling out of the room.

The warden locked his gaze onto Devora. "Prepare yourself. You leave at dawn."

Chapter Thirty

The Council Room, The Fortress

Devora stood paralyzed. She only thought she was meant to deliver the message from Tunri, not go to war. She had done well in learning how to fight within the walls of the Fortress. But how would she fare on the battlefield?

Will I survive?

"Lady Devora," King Atol said coolly. "I would like you to rescue my daughter. You said you knew where she was, so I trust you to find her." He flicked his hand to Captain Blake. "Matthias will go with you, as he is an expert at vanquishing the enemy."

Captain Blake's jaw clenched as he placed a fist over his chest and bowed. "It would be an honor to accompany Lady Devora on this mission, Your Majesty."

"Take the girl from Yekel with you also," Warden Hazor added. "She is inventive and fights well. But for this mission, you can have no more in your squad than four. I suggest you convince One Shot to use his freedom wisely if you want to survive the oncoming battle."

With another curtsy, Devora replied, "We will leave with Sir Conan at dawn."

After they were dismissed, Devora raced out of the suffocating room, trying to wrap her mind around everything that had happened. She finally delivered Tunri's message, but now *she* was going to the frontlines.

Devora glared at the ceiling. *Why did you leave that part out, Tunri?*

Darting around a corner, she leaned against the wall, her pulse thundering. She thought Warden Hazor hated her. Why would he choose her? Yes, she was now the Defender of Tenton, but that didn't mean the warden should instantly like her. It was strange.

Queen Leza's black soul rose to her thoughts. Devora shivered. There was something odd about that as well. She couldn't ignore the nagging feeling that the hag and the queen were one and the same. But how could that be possible?

Devora placed her back on the cool stone and slid down, bringing her knees to her chest. She knew she could do anything with Tunri's help, but would He want her to be victorious?

Resting her chin on her knees, Devora closed her eyes. Tunri had been with her all this time. He wouldn't leave now. Everything she had been through—being sent to prison and training for the tournament—had prepared her for this. *This* was why she had been sent to the Fortress.

The cool aura wrapped around her again, encouraging her to stand tall, to accept her destiny without fear.

Devora tilted her head up. *Thank you, Tunri.*

Standing, Devora lifted the hem of her skirt and hurried to Level Five.

"You're free!" Devora shouted between the bars of One Shot's cell.

The tall, thin man shuffled out of the shadows. A few cuts marred his arms, but other than that, he was unharmed.

The Behemoth didn't hurt One Shot nearly as much as Sir Conan. I wonder why?

"Congratulations on winning," One Shot replied with a sad smile. "I knew you could do it."

Devora frowned at his sagging blue soul. Had he not heard what she said? "Thank you. Didn't you hear me? You're free."

One Shot shook his head, his shaggy black hair falling between his eyes. "I don't deserve freedom."

"One Shot," Captain Blake's voice boomed from behind Devora, making her jump.

She spun around. *How did he follow me without me hearing?*

"Devora used her pardon to free you. Stop sulking around. We have a war to win." Captain Blake reached around Devora and unlocked One Shot's cell.

The prisoner's shoulders straightened as he took a few steps out into the corridor. Though Captain Blake was a tall man, One Shot towered over him.

"I won't kill any innocent people for this corrupt kingdom," One Shot replied, peering down at the captain.

Captain Blake shrugged, keeping his stance firm. "While Tenton has not been just, the Kadeshians are hardly innocent. They've ravaged our lands, stolen our crops, and have taken our women and children. I would've thought an avenger like you would enjoy stopping them from doing more harm."

Devora glanced between the two men, realizing the captain must know One Shot's story, as well. He had chosen his words very carefully, saying exactly what needed to be said to encourage One Shot to their side.

One Shot ran a hand through his hair before peering at Devora. "Are you going?"

She nodded. "The king has asked us to find Princess Haden. Tunri granted me a vision of where she is."

The free man looked between Devora and Captain Blake, his eyes blazing. "I'll need a crossbow."

Chapter Thirty-One

"I've modified this crossbow so that you can shoot four arrows before you have to reload it," Nadia explained as she handed the weapon to One Shot with a grin.

One Shot cautiously took the crossbow and analyzed it, his dark eyes running over every crevice. His long, pale fingers gently patted the four arrows locked and ready to shoot.

"Why don't you give it a try?" Nadia encouraged with bright eyes, her leather notebook open. She had her charcoal stick poised on a blank page, ready to take notes.

Devora held back a laugh at the eagerness in Nadia's voice. If she didn't know better, Devora would have thought Nadia wanted to shoot the crossbow.

It was amazing to see a real Tinker at work. Since Yekel was burned years ago, all the Tinkers had been captured or gone into hiding.

"Give him time, Nadia," Devora said as she strode inside her tent and unpacked the metal armor from the trunk.

Warden Hazor had given each of them a set of armor before arranging carriages for their journey to the front lines. As soon as the carriages stopped, Devora sprang from the small space, ready to be in the fresh air.

The heat of the Edo desert was unlike Grenly's rich and nourishing weather. Even in the late afternoon sun, the desert was dry, sucking the life out of everything in it.

Earlier, when the soldiers assisted in setting up their tents, Devora searched for Captain Blake. But after an hour of scanning the rows of dark red tents camped along the desert, she gave up. He said he would try to see her before they departed the Fortress, but he never came.

Devora held up the breastplate and frowned at the kingdom's crest winking back. Her audience with King Atol had not gone as she anticipated. He had accepted everything so easily. For someone who had slaughtered all the Seers years ago, he didn't bat an eye at her prophecy. It was almost as if he *wanted* her to go to battle.

Devora placed the breastplate on the ground with other pieces of armor. She wasn't sure whether Warden Hazor wanted her dead or not, but an uneasy feeling crept up her spine about King Atol. Because she hadn't died in the tournament, was the king hoping she would die in battle?

"If he doesn't shoot it soon, I will," Nadia huffed through the tent flaps, interrupting Devora's thoughts.

With a laugh, Devora exited her tent and rejoined them outside.

One Shot gave Nadia a blank look before extending his arm to the side. Keeping his dark eyes on the inventor, he shot the first arrow of the crossbow, landing it in the dead center of a palm tree fifty yards away. A group of soldiers seated nearby jerked at the whoosh of the arrow zinging past them.

Placing her hands on her hips, Devora studied the anxious men seated around the various fires. She didn't blame them for their fear, but Tunri was with them. All of them. He wouldn't let them fail.

In another blink, One Shot released the other three arrows into the trees next to the first one. A soldier carrying a bowl of gruel shrieked and dove to the ground, his bowl landing on his head.

"Whoa!" Nadia exclaimed, throwing her arms in the air. "My design worked!"

One Shot broke his gaze from Nadia and studied the weapon again as a black horse sidled up to Devora.

"I don't think it's wise to shoot rogue arrows in a group of soldiers anticipating battle," Captain Blake chided.

As the captain dismounted, Devora's heart fluttered. Sleek metal armor covered his entire body. The king's crest shone in the evening firelight as he sat upon a midnight-colored horse. He looked commanding, intimidating...*extremely attractive*.

"Maybe you can practice more later," Devora suggested, keeping her focus on One Shot. But she knew there wouldn't be time later. They would be heading to battle at first light.

"This is a work of art," One Shot commented, still enamored with the crossbow. "Thank you for giving it to me."

Nadia waved her hand in the air. "It's nothing," she said, before explaining to him the different angles he could shoot the crossbow.

One Shot nodded here and there, quietly asking more questions.

"Dev-er-Lady Devora," Captain Blake corrected as he dismounted the large horse. He placed a fist across his chest and bowed. "I wanted to make sure your journey was fair, and you had everything you needed for tomorrow."

Devora sucked in a breath, taking in the muck covering his horse's feet and the dust swept over his armor. Hope fluttered in her chest. She wasn't sure why the captain had been delayed, but he had traveled for two days straight, and the first thing he did was find her.

"The journey went as expected," Devora answered, striding back into her tent. She scanned her eyes over her suit of armor as she remembered the cramped carriage that rolled over every rock in the kingdom. The smooth metal of Captain Blake's gait sounded behind her. "Although—" she glanced over her shoulder, sizing up his attire— "is there a different type of armor to wear? This is very..." She gestured down to the armor, not able to find the right words.

"Loud? Unflattering?" Nadia called from outside.

Devora bit her lip as Captain Blake's eyes narrowed.

"This is the official military armor of Tenton, Lapith." He turned to find Nadia sticking her blonde head through the tent flaps. "It's an honor to wear it."

Nadia rolled her eyes before fully joining them. After circling Devora's armor, she tapped the piece of charcoal on her thin nose, leaving black dots on her tan skin.

"It'd be an honor for a clunky man. But this is completely wrong for Dev. It's hard and unmoving." Nadia clicked her tongue after she crouched down and banged on the breastplate. "No, no. This won't do. One Shot, come help me," she called as she started gathering up the pieces of armor.

The lanky man entered the tent, gave Captain Blake a bow, and started collecting the pieces of Devora's armor.

"Give me a few hours with it, Dev," Nadia said with a wink. "I'll make it work for you."

"Thank you, Nadia," Devora said, glad she had a Tinker as a friend. She then faced the captain. "I believe that's it. We'll be ready to move at dawn."

Captain Blake shuffled, his armor screeching as he moved.

"Loud," Nadia mouthed behind his back as she pointed to his armor before exiting the tent with One Shot.

Devora diverted her eyes from her friend and focused on the captain. His stance was tight and rigid, as usual. But there was something lurking behind his cool, gray eyes. Fear. But fear of what? Of battle?

Captain Blake had been to battle before. She had even heard his heroic tales of defeating giants and saving captured soldiers. But if he wasn't fearful of the oncoming battle, what was he so afraid of?

"Captain," she started before he held up a hand.

"Matthias, please," he corrected gently.

Butterflies flew through her stomach. "Matthias. Do *you* have everything you need for tomorrow?"

His gaze moved over her slowly, as if memorizing every feature of her face. "Yes. Conan will meet us at dawn. We'll convene on the boundary of the eastern region and Edo. Once there, we'll wait for Kadesh."

"And then it begins," Devora whispered, staring down at her hands.

Matthias took a step forward, his shoulders relaxing. "Devora, I need you to know—" Her gaze shot to his and he froze, his lips parted, ready to say more, but no words came out. After a few painful moments of silence, he coughed and said, "I just wanted to say thank you, and I'm sorry."

Devora furrowed her brows, confused.

Why won't he just tell me what he's thinking? And what is he sorry for?

"Anyway," the captain said, squaring his shoulders. "You better get some rest." He turned abruptly and exited the tent.

Devora watched his shining armor disappear before Nadia sauntered back into the tent. She bent down and scooped up the last lingering pieces of armor when her eyes followed Devora's gaze.

With a metal gauntlet in each hand, Nadia asked, "Do you think he knows we named our crow after him?"

The sun broke through the horizon and the camp imme-diately sprang to life. Though the soldiers had been up for hours already, they acted as ghosts wandering through the tents before the light brought them to life.

Devora had been up too. Already donning her leather pants and tunic, she ran a hand over her braided bun. Securing her hairpin, Devora searched for Nadia. Nadia promised Devora's armor would be done before dawn, but dawn was here, and Nadia wasn't.

"Excuse me," Nadia shouted over the crowd of men shuf-fling about. "I need to get through. Move it!"

Nadia barreled through the armored soldiers until she broke through with a huff. "I'm here." Shadows rimmed Nadia's lower lids, but she grinned and held out Devo-ra's battle gear. Clad in her own customized armor, Nadia asked, "What do you think?"

Devora's eyes went wide as she took in Nadia's work. It was the same armor the men wore but morphed to Devora's size. No longer was it squared and hard, but the metal curved delicately to fit Devora's figure.

Devora brought a hand to her mouth as she saw the outline of a sash branded into the metal. Purple ink dyed it the same shade as her family's color. Tears pricked her eyes.

"Oh, Pahga," Nadia cursed at the armor. "You hate it."

"No, Nadia," Devora said, quickly, reaching out to take the armor. "It's incredible."

She grasped the metal plate for her chest. The metal was thick, but it felt lighter than air. Carefully, Devora traced her fingers over the purple sash. For Mama and Papa. "It's perfect."

Nadia's eyes glistened. "Really? I wasn't sure about the sash, but..."

Before she could finish, Devora rushed forward and hugged her tight. "Thank you, my friend."

Nadia's sturdy arms came around her and hugged her back.

Once the two women broke away, Nadia sniffed. "There's no time for this," she gestured to her watering eyes. "We need to kick some Kadeshian butt."

Nadia helped Devora strap on her armor. Like the dress she had worn days ago, the armor fit her perfectly. But, unlike the vulnerable silk fabric, the armor fed her confidence and assured her that she was where she was meant to be. No longer was she the governor's daughter. She was a warrior.

"One more thing," Nadia said, reaching into a canvas sack slung over her shoulder. She pulled out two identical weapons. "These are for you. I've sculpted the hilts so they fit better in your hands, since you don't have big, meaty man claws. I've also made this." Nadia pulled out a thick leather sheath. "I've laced one of your mechs with the lethal poison of the gumberry tree." She held out the sword in her right hand. "Keep this mech sheathed until you are absolutely ready to use it." Nadia wrapped the poisonous blade in the leather then handed it over.

Devora hesitated, remembering the soldier who had been poisoned by the gumberry tree in the infirmary. She would never forget the boils sprouting from his skin. Shuddering, she took the barbaric blade, praying she wouldn't have to use it.

As she strapped her weapons to her armor, Devora saw a solider come before her with a copper-colored horse, speckled with white spots. He bowed and handed Devora the reins. "From Captain Blake."

Devora gasped at the beautiful horse. Its shimmering mane glistened in the morning sun as it shook its spotted white snout. "What?"

The soldier saluted. "Because of your Seeing gift, study of military and war tactics, and victory in Regulus Protecti, you've been promoted from lieutenant to captain. All higher-ranking officers are required to travel on horseback so the soldiers can hear your orders."

Devora stared blankly as she grasped the leather straps. *My orders?*

The horse whinnied and nudged her shoulder.

Nadia gave a low whistle. "Captain Blake is definitely Mister Pants and Soap. He has to be. Now he's given you a horse!"

"Soldiers need to report to their stations," the soldier barked at Nadia.

Nadia stuck out her tongue as the soldier marched away.

As soon as Devora straddled the horse, Nadia clasped her hands in front of her. "You look incredible. I did an amazing job. Let's go slay some monsters."

Devora laughed before reaching down and squeezing her friend's hand, praying they would see each other again soon.

Devora led the copper horse to where Sir Conan and Captain Blake waited to head the attack. The captain rode a black horse, dark as coal. The horse was beautiful yet terrifying at the same time. Just like its rider.

Devora looked into the crowd of anxious soldiers. One Shot explained that he could aim better from afar, so he planted himself a few rows back, hidden within the soldiers. Nadia joined him.

"Captain," Devora said calmly, hiding her jittering nerves.

The captain twisted his head around before his scrutinizing gaze fell on her. "If we make it through this, tell Lapith I want to hire her for a new battle armor design."

Devora grinned, her tense shoulders relaxing. "She'll be thrilled."

"Captain Blake," Sir Conan's voice boomed.

The captain faced the burly knight. Sir Conan's armor had been thoroughly shined and covered every inch of his body. He had already secured his helmet on his head, making his voice echo every time he spoke. In one hand, he held the reins to a sleek brown horse. With the other hand, he balled his fingers into a fist and placed it to his chest, bowing deeply to the captain.

Sir Conan's armor scraped as he straightened and focused on Devora, bowing again. "Lady Medee." He paused and took off his helmet. Beneath, his skin was slicked with sweat and whiter than the clouds rolling by. "I trust Tunri will guide your orders."

Devora's lips parted at the statement. No snide comment or degrading remark? What had happened to Sir Conan?

As the knight replaced his helmet, Captain Blake leaned over and whispered, "Apparently, Conan experienced a vision from Tunri last night."

"What?" Devora gasped.

The captain shrugged. "That's the rumor."

Just then, a deep horn blared in the distance, rumbling like the roar of a tiger. A thick wave of fear blanketed the soldiers, silencing their early morning chatter. Devora twisted her neck to see the outline of Kadesh's army. Several orange banners, looking like scraps in the wind, stood tall among the endless lines coming toward them. Though the enemy only seemed to be black dots on the horizon, Devora knew the iron-armored beasts were coming.

"Our soldiers are ready to move out," Sir Conan said, his voice wavering at the end.

"Excellent," Captain Blake answered, unfazed by the encroaching enemy. He assessed the lines of troops behind him then turned back to Sir Conan. "Are you going to say any words?"

Sir Conan took a step back and Devora could imagine his face paling at the thought. Captain Blake gritted his teeth as he waited for the knight's reply. But after more than a few moments of silence, Devora spoke up.

"I will."

Sir Conan's shoulders relaxed while Captain Blake spun to her, his horse twisting to face her own.

"*You* will?" he questioned with a quirked brow. "And what will you say?"

Devora lifted her chin. "You'll see." She shifted her weight on her horse, then squared her shoulders and faced the soldiers, hoping the right words would come to her quickly.

The number of Tenton soldiers was vast, but from what she had seen in her vision, the Kadeshian army was far greater.

Her violet eyes roamed over the men. In this crowd were brothers and sons. Fathers and uncles. She and Nadia came to mind. Daughters were included now too. The thought weighed on her heart.

Devora gripped the reins of her horse tighter. In a blink, the lights of the soldiers' souls appeared. Some swirls shivered while others sat still, but they were all blue and filled with sorrow. Devora's heart wrenched. These men had been forced by the kingdom to fight this never-ending war. Fear and defeat already made a home in their eyes.

A chilled aura spun around her, building her confidence. Closing her eyes, Devora sent up a quick prayer.

Thank you for your guidance, Tunri. Continue to guide me to do what is right.

Though she had no idea what to say before, her mind soon filled with the words she needed to speak to encourage the soldiers.

"I am Captain Devora Medee, daughter of Governor Cusha and First Lady Glance Medee." All eyes focused on her. "I was raised in the southern region of Tenton in the citadel of Grenly."

Her voice rang strong and sure, commanding the presence of all the soldiers before her. A shaky breath escaped her lips. Hollow, defeated gazes stared back at her. How much death and destruction had these soldiers witnessed?

"Six weeks ago, King Atol abruptly changed the laws of Categorization, and I was sent to the Fortress. I didn't know why I had been sent there, but later realized it was Tunri's hand guiding my path."

Murmurs dispersed across the crowd at her mention of Tunri. Devora's mind pulled at the memory of her and Nadia talking about the goddess, Pahga, the Queen of Heaven.

As she scanned the crowd, Devora watched some blue swirls fade to yellow, but the majority stayed the same shade of azure. She knew not everyone believed in Tunri, and maybe they never would. But she did, and she would never retreat from that belief.

"But what I didn't know was that Tunri was preparing me. By sending me to the Fortress, I learned how to fight and defend myself." She glanced to where Captain Blake sat regally on his horse.

He cradled his helmet under his arm, his lips set firm, but his eyes gleamed with pride.

"I met incredible people with life-changing stories." She found One Shot standing to the side of the soldiers, blending in with the tent shadows. He leaned out ever so slightly. Beside him stood Nadia, who whistled and waved.

"But I also learned that with Tunri, anything is possible. With His help and guidance, I survived an assassination attempt, freed the Behemoth from the basement, and won Regulus Protecti."

Devora's chest swelled. She couldn't believe all the things she had accomplished by trusting in Tunri. Five weeks ago, she was a silly little girl, upset that a boy had replaced her with a prettier version. Now, she was a warrior in Tunri's army, ready to defend and protect her people.

"Without Tunri," she continued, "I would have never succeeded. So, I ask you all today, will you trust in Tunri to bring us victory?"

Carefully, Devora reached for the mech on her right. The rising sun glinted off its smooth tip as she pointed the blade to the sky. She raised her voice.

"Will you trust in His guidance to defeat this evil that has plagued our kingdom for too long?"

Devora held the sword higher as silence responded. Sweat dripped down her spine, the dry air swirling around her. Blank eyes blinked back at her. A few more lights had changed to yellow, hopeful in her words, but the majority were still blue.

Did I say the wrong thing?

Heat seared her neck and she started to lower her sword when the sound of metal scraping rang through the air.

"I will," Captain Blake answered, pointing his mech to the sky.

He kept his piercing glare at the soldiers before him, staring them down from his giant steed. And though he didn't break his gaze to look at her, Devora knew he would be with her until the end.

"I will," One Shot's deep voice rang from the middle of the crowd. A few of the soldiers surrounding him jumped at his sudden appearance.

"I will," Nadia screamed.

"I will," Sir Conan joined in, his voice strong and determined as it had been in the Fortress.

Devora's hope soared as more voices shouted from the crowd, solidifying their allegiance not to Tenton, but to Tunri. Soon, the entire battalion of soldiers responded, each unsheathing their weapons and declaring victory to Tunri. As more souls lifted from sorrow to hope, the chant increased in tempo until the soldiers were pumping their swords in the air.

"For Tunri!" she cried, thrusting her blade a final time in the air.

The soldiers erupted into cheers, pounding their armor, and pointing their swords. A swirl of light surrounded Tenton's soldiers, as if Tunri had created a wall of protection around them.

Blinking the light away, Devora shifted her horse toward the oncoming battle. Tunri was with them. They would not fail.

Chapter Thirty-Two

Devora did her best to ignore the growls and gnashing teeth as the iron-armored beasts marched toward them. But she still flinched every time one of them howled.

"Not the same as the warden's wolves, are they?" Captain Blake muttered.

"No," she replied, keeping her eyes forward. "Not the same at all."

Sweat covered her gloved palms as she gripped the mech. Devora tried to calm her racing heart, but the beat of the horses' hooves and the snarls of the beasts kept her pulse elevated.

Tunri is with me. Tunri is with me.

"Are you ready?" Captain Blake asked, his gaze trained ahead as they marched.

Devora didn't respond, her stomach flopping with each step. Tiny black dots appeared in her vision. Her mind sped through the thousands of terrible outcomes when the captain reached out and grabbed her hand, clenching it tight.

"I'll stay with you. No matter what."

Devora's rapid thoughts froze and her vision cleared. She cast a glance at him, her chest squeezing. How had he known those were the exact words she needed to hear? Not knowing what lay ahead, she slid her fingers through his.

"And I, you."

The captain peered over at her, his gray eyes softening before the horn of the Kadeshian army blared across the desert. The beasts howled in the morning air and charged.

Sir Conan raised his sword high and yelled, "For Tunri!"

He gave his horse a hefty kick, and the steed took off, galloping straight toward the snarling monsters. The ranks behind him cried out and followed, brandishing their mechs and shields.

Captain Blake secured the faceplate of his helmet before releasing Devora's hand. Planting his heels into his black horse, the steed whinnied and sprinted forward as the captain screamed a battle cry. Devora snapped her faceplate into place, thankful for the riding lessons Papa had made her take all those years ago. She squeezed her legs around her copper horse and took off.

Her heart thumped against the smooth armor as heavy breaths escaped her lips. Trying to focus on everything at once, Devora peered through the slits of her helmet. The iron-armored beasts didn't waste time in attacking Tenton's army. Wails erupted from the battlefield as their wolfish snouts bit and clawed Tenton's soldiers. Devora raised her mech, swinging at any beast that came near her. Her hands shook at the cries of death surrounding her.

Tunri is with me. Tunri is with me.

"Devora!" Nadia cried, kicking a Kadeshian soldier in the face. His bronze helmet pinged under her blow, smashing against his dark-skinned nose. "Look out!"

Devora spun her head to see an iron armored beast barreling toward her. Her body stiffened at the horrific sight. Pointed yellow fangs grew from black gums. Thick saliva flew from its jaws. Its face resembled a wolf's, but the features were larger. Shined, black armor lined its head and torso, clanging as its huge paws pounded through the sand. She had never seen anything like it.

Before she could make a move, the beast slammed into her horse, sending her sprawling. As soon as she landed in the dense sand, Devora scrambled to rise. Her head whipped all around, searching for her mech, but she must have dropped it when she was tossed from the saddle.

The iron-armored beast found her and snarled as it stalked closer. Cautiously, Devora extracted the poisoned gumberry blade from her other sheath, thankful Nadia had thought ahead. Taking a breath, Devora readied her stance. As soon as the monster lunged, she swung her blade. The poisoned sword met its mark and the growls instantly ceased. A high-pitched yelp pierced through the battle cries as Devora lobbed off the beast's front paw. Blood spurted from the wound, and the creature fell to the ground, snarling. It flailed its other three legs before the gumberry poison began its work.

"Nice," One Shot said, coming up beside her. Nadia wasn't far behind.

Devora's stomach lurched as she took in the convulsing body of the creature before her. Yips and cries escaped from its fanged mouth. It was a terrible way to die.

Her heart twisted with grief. "I will not allow this torture to continue."

Striding forward, Devora lifted her mech and pierced the beast's heart, ending its suffering.

Lifting her faceplate, she turned toward One Shot and Nadia before a scream roared behind her. Whipping around, Devora flung out her blade to stop the encroaching enemy when, suddenly, the Kadeshian soldier froze. Once he fell backward, Devora saw the arrow protruding from his chest.

"Thank you," she breathed to One Shot.

"You mean, thank me," Nadia said, admiring her weapon in One Shot's hands. She spun around and jabbed a Kadeshian soldier in each shoulder. The soldier's arms went slack then Nadia kicked him in the head, knocking him out.

One Shot aimed his cross bow and unleashed all four arrows at once. The arrows whooshed through the air, flying through twelve different Kadeshian soldiers.

Devora stumbled back. "That was incredible." *Does One Shot have a special gift from Tunri, as well?* Devora had never heard of someone shooting with such accuracy.

One Shot gave her a stiff nod, then reloaded and lined up his shot again. The battle raged around them, soldiers crying and screaming as they fought the iron-armored beasts and one another. The thick stench of blood and death coated the morning air.

Though there had been hundreds of iron-armored beasts, Tenton's men had been victorious in slaying more than half of them. But as the Kadeshian horn blared again, she knew the battle was far from over.

After fending off three Kadeshian soldiers, Devora spun toward the noise to see another round of soldiers advancing. Her hope all but disappeared. Though Tenton's army was fighting strong, she knew they would never hold up against Kadesh's endless lines of soldiers.

Tunri be with us. Give us the strength to endure.

Devora scanned the soldiers until she found Captain Blake battling two iron-armored beasts. He had been knocked from his black horse and was barely holding both creatures back.

"Shoot there," Devora instructed One Shot, pointing at the creatures.

"Mhmm," One Shot murmured before he positioned his crossbow and shot two arrows.

Devora's jaw dropped as she watched the two arrows fly next to each other before splitting and piercing an eye of each creature. The beasts reared back and howled, smashing their heads on the ground to extract the arrow.

"A beautiful shot," Nadia commented from the side.

Captain Blake took no time in slicing his sword through the beasts' thick necks. Bright red blood gushed onto the desert sand and Devora averted her eyes.

Captain Blake whipped around and immediately found them. Wielding his blade, he knocked out at a few Kadeshian soldiers before sprinting in their direction.

"What's our next move?" he heaved. He lifted his face-plate and scanned the battlefield. Sweat beaded at his brow and rolled down his cheeks as he faced Devora.

One Shot silently extracted his arrows from fallen soldiers and reused them to shoot down any enemy who came within fifty feet of them. Nadia joined another group of soldiers that were rounding up the iron-armored beasts and subduing them in pairs.

"We need to find Princess Haden," Devora answered, gripping her mech. She extended the sword, preparing to stop a Kadeshian headed toward them. But he was cut off by an arrow protruding from his neck.

She glanced at One Shot.

"I can shoot and listen," One Shot said calmly as he loaded another arrow, his eyes surveying the battle.

"Where's the princess?" Captain Blake asked.

Devora closed her eyes, trusting One Shot to protect her as she searched through her previous vision. A dark tent, stacks of barrels, the strong scent of ale and wine. She continued through the vision, trying to find anything that could help her locate the princess. A tall palm tree slammed into her thoughts before everything went black.

Devora's eyes shot open. "We need to find Kadesh's camp. The princess is being held there. She's in a tent by a palm tree."

The captain nodded. "Are there any guards?"

"I don't know."

"Iron-armored creatures?"

She clenched her jaw. "I don't know."

Captain Blake took a breath. "Is there any other information you'd like to share that would help us?"

Devora cut her eyes to him. "I know that we'll win if you trust me and trust Tunri."

His lips twitched. "Of course, my lady."

Devora turned back to the battle. Only a few iron-armored beasts littered the field. Tunri was helping them. He had to be. Most of their soldiers were still standing and fighting.

Give them strength, Tunri, she prayed.

Looking beyond the battle, the cool confidence cocooned her again, directing her to the east.

"That way." She pointed before snapping her faceplate into place. "Come on."

Holding her mech high, Devora readied to remove anyone who tried to stop her, but One Shot had already cleared a path.

"Right behind you," Captain Blake replied as One Shot stepped into place behind him.

Wary faces glanced at her as she ran by. Devora engaged her soulsight to see the hope draining from their spirits. She had to do something to keep them encouraged, to keep them fighting.

A Kadeshian soldier riding an iron-armored beast rushed toward her. Devora felt all the skills she had learned over the past few weeks kick in as she sliced the strap off the soldier's saddle. He swung off the iron-armored beast, his head slamming through the sand. The iron-armored beast howled as it spun around and charged at Devora. Dodging, Devora swung her mech again, slicing clean through the beast's belly.

Tenton's soldiers around her stood in shock until she lifted her mech, she yelled, "We will prevail!"

Yellow light surged in her soldiers' souls, and their faces now bore determination and strength. The soldiers yelled their battle cry again and continued fighting the enemy.

Hope hugged her own soul as she and Captain Blake wove through the crowd. Maybe the battle would be over soon. They would find the princess, return her to the king, and everything would be well. Maybe she could go home and see Mama and Papa again.

The thought only stayed in her mind for mere seconds before the Kadeshian horn blared again, crushing her plans into dust.

"Oh, no," Captain Blake grunted.

Devora stopped in her tracks.

A line of giants replaced the iron-armored beasts. Upon each of their chests laid the gilded Kadeshian crest, mocking Devora's thoughts of victory. The giants chanted in unison as they spun their hands, engaging their earth manipulation power. The sand of the Edo desert rose before compacting into shards of glass.

Devora took a step back, gripping the hilt of her poisoned mech. She had seen Babshee manipulate the stone of the Fortress before the guards put the imperial opal shackles on. But she didn't know the giants' powers were this strong.

Between the giants, a regular-sized man sat atop an iron-armored beast. He didn't wear a helmet, allowing his cropped black hair and thick black beard to be seen. Devora knew that if she could look close enough, she would see the jagged scar running across his eyes. Though he wasn't the size of the giants, his reputation was large enough.

"General Sage," Devora breathed, remembering the vision she had of him gagging Princess Haden.

"Devora," Captain Blake said, placing a hand on her shoulder. "We need to find the princess. Now."

Devora bobbed her head. If Tunri wanted her to slay the general, she would. But first, she needed to save the princess.

"One Shot, come on," she yelled over her shoulder.

They took off in a sprint before the horn blasted again, and the giants shot the glass shards into the air.

Chapter Thirty-Three

The Edo Desert, Kadesh

"What's that noise?" Erza asked, peering out of the tent.

The clanging in the distance had been echoing for a while now. It sounded like a battle was encroaching on their new home. Erza glared at the horizon. She had finally gotten everything where she wanted it and didn't want a sandstorm of brutal soldiers disrupting her shabby tent of a home.

Although I wouldn't mind the excuse to go back to Renta, she thought before turning back into the tent.

Her beautiful pottery and fine rugs lay sprawled along the coarse desert sand. If she ignored the rippling canvas walls, she could almost say she liked the small space.

"I'm sure it's nothing, my dear," Jarrick answered, wrapping his arms around her waist. He gave her a kiss on the cheek and peered through the tent flaps. "Who's that?"

Erza shielded her eyes from the blazing sun. How she hated the early morning heat. As she squinted, a small figure appeared in the distance. Nausea bubbled up in her throat.

As the figure sprinted closer, Erza recognized Kadesh's seal on his chest. Her lungs tightened as her hand balled into a fist. A messenger from General Sage, the snake.

"Sir Jarrick," the liaison huffed, his shoulders heaving as he knelt before Jarrick on all fours.

The boy looked no more than fifteen summers; the exact age her Josef had been before General Sage forced him into battle. Erza swallowed the fury boiling in her chest as she watched her husband take the note.

"Rise and rest," he said to the boy, gesturing to their tent.

"Come." Erza ushered the boy in, not wanting another mother to go through the pain she endured. She offered the boy a jug of water and a plate of dried figs, meat, and bread. "Drink and eat before you return. The journey is long and the desert is not kind."

"Thank you," the boy breathed before he sucked down the water and inhaled the plate of food.

Erza allowed herself to smile, remembering how Josef ate the same way. Young boys always acted as if each meal was their last. Her smile fell. If only she had known that day it would be Josef's last meal.

"My love," Jarrick said, rushing into the tent. "General Sage needs more weapons immediately. I must go." He quickly filled a satchel with food, cloth, and his tools before giving her a kiss. "I will be back soon."

Erza clutched her stomach as she watched her husband disappear with the young messenger. She prayed it would not be the last time she saw him. Erza balled her hands into fists. Jarrick better return, or it would be General Sage who would pay.

Chapter Thirty-Four

Devora wove through the crowd, praying Captain Blake and One Shot were right behind her. The sickening sound of glass impaling Tenton's army rang through the battle-front.

Tears formed in her eyes. How could they win against this?

Tunri, where are you?

The captain's quick, heavy steps matched hers as they trudged through the thick sand.

"Take cover!" Sir Conan screamed over the battle cries.

Tenton's soldiers lifted their shields in defense while try-ing to battle the remaining iron beasts and the Kadeshian troops littering the desert.

Devora's chest tightened as she scooped up the nearest shield she could find and crouched beneath it. Her arms shook from its heavy weight. Soon, the weight lifted, and she glanced up to see Captain Blake holding not only his shield, but hers as well.

"Keep running," he grunted.

Focusing ahead, Devora ran as fast as her legs would take her. She wheezed, wishing for more air as she pushed her body.

The giants continued to mold and make the glass. Crystalized spears rained on Tenton's army, impaling the white sand and the soldiers. Screams and wails of the dying men rattled her bones, but there was nothing she could do. Not only had the giants struck Tenton's army, but they had also taken out a number of their own Kadeshians, as well.

How could General Sage treat his soldiers in such a way? Were they really so disposable to him?

But Tenton wasn't much better. It was King Atol's law that brought her here in the first place.

As they sped through the fighting soldiers and falling men, a guttural cry erupted behind them.

Devora's blood went cold, and she spun around. A giant shard of glass protruded from One Shot's left leg. Bright red blood pooled from the wound, staining the glass as it dripped to the ground. Devora dove to the sand, placing an arm under One Shot as she gently lifted his head onto her lap. His skin was paler than usual as beads of sweat formed across his brow.

"It's okay," One Shot breathed. "This is an honorable way to die."

"Not while I'm around," Captain Blake barked. "You—" he pointed to the nearest Tenton soldier—"take One Shot back to camp, to the physician." He bent down and assessed the wound. "Do not move this glass if you can help it."

The soldier placed a fist over his chest and bowed before calling another man to help him. As Devora helped secure One Shot between the two soldiers, she noticed his crossbow lying on the ground.

Grabbing it, she handed it to one of the soldiers and said, "He may need this."

The soldier gave her a confused look, but One Shot let out a breathy laugh. "Thank you, my lady."

Tunri, keep them safe, she prayed as she watched the soldiers and One Shot disappear into the desert.

Devora realized she hadn't seen Nadia since earlier in the battle. With her expertise in hemna, Nadia fought the enemy well, but worry still twisted Devora's gut. She didn't know what she would do if another one of her friends were injured.

"We need to keep going," Captain Blake commanded.

Devora nodded and they ran. But before they could get twenty yards, the giants chanted again, creating more raining glass shards. The captain grabbed Devora's arm and spun her around, smashing her against his hard chest as he held his shield over both of them. His long arm pressed into her back, squeezing her against him.

The glass shattered on the metal shield like iron bells in a storm. Devora curled herself against the captain, trying to become as small as possible so neither one of them would get hit.

As soon as the glass stopped, the ground vibrated beneath their feet. Devora held on to Captain Blake as the sand rumbled around them. Ceasing their chants, the giants were now sprinting toward Tenton's soldiers.

"Fall back!" Sir Conan cried at the sight of the wall of giants barreling toward them. "Fall back!"

Tenton's soldiers scrambled backward, trying to retreat while keeping their focus on the death coming for them.

Fear constricted Devora's throat. Babshee had easily injured her that first day in the Fortress while chained. These giants were twice the size of Babshee. They would slaughter Tenton's troops in the blink of an eye.

"This isn't good." Captain Blake tightened his arm around her waist. He focused on her, desperation glinting in his eyes. "Any ideas? Visions? Anything?"

Devora shook her head, tears building in her own. She didn't know what was going on. *Has Tunri sent us here to die?*

"Then we need to retreat," he decided, grabbing her hand before fleeing.

Devora's mind went numb as her steps mechanically followed the captain's. Tunri had never failed her. Her visions of Regulus Protecti and Princess Haden had been true.

Did I misinterpret my visions? Did I lead all these soldiers to their deaths?

Before she could think any further, a loud roar pierced the air and Devora froze. What other creatures could Kadesh have to slay them?

But as she peered into the distance, it wasn't a Kadeshian giant or an iron-armored beast. It was the Behemoth from the basement, galloping across the desert. Its once filthy fur had been washed clean, now shining a brilliant white like a blazing beacon in the desert. It tilted its head back and bellowed again before lowering its wide, white antlers to the ground.

Hope reignited in Devora's heart as she watched the Behemoth ram into the line of giants. Three of them fell, toppling over one another before the giant animal trampled them into the dunes. Once they no longer moved, the Behemoth roared to the sky and charged at the rest.

Tenton's soldiers froze, not knowing if the giant white creature was a friend or an enemy. They looked to Sir Conan for guidance, but he turned to Devora.

"Captain Medee," he yelled, his gaze darting between her and the beast charging at them. "Orders?"

Devora's mind quickly rifled through all of her previous lessons and everything she endured at the Fortress. Learning *hemna*, how to use the mech, Regulus Protecti, and then she remembered One Shot's advice: *If that giant gives you trouble, shoot right between the eyes.*

"Aim for the giant's faces, right between the eyes," she commanded, her voice growing louder with each word. "Use anything you have to take them down."

The soldiers yelled in agreement. Archers notched their arrows and sent them flying. The Behemoth had taken out half of the giants, but a dozen continued their march.

"Release!" Sir Conan yelled, and the archers sent a second volley of arrows at the giants.

"Right when we needed One Shot," Captain Blake muttered, holding his mech high.

The ground quaked as the giants homed in on them.

The captain turned to Devora, agony lacing his features. "Find Nadia and go back to camp. Get out of here." His steely eyes glistened as he pleaded. "Live, Devora."

Her heart almost burst at his heartfelt words. Unsheathing her poisoned blade, she stood next to him. Tilting her chin up, she answered, "We live together, or not at all."

Captain Blake's eyes darted between her own before he wrapped his arm around her waist. Pulling her against him, he crushed his lips to hers. Devora's stomach flipped as blood raced between her ears. Before she could reciprocate the kiss, the captain released her. He gently cupped her face, his eyes drinking in hers before he spun around and raced toward the giants.

"Matthias!" she called.

But he didn't stop.

With a growl, Devora held her mech high and sprinted after him.

The lead giant swung his bronzed, hairy hand, barely missing Captain Blake. The captain dodged and pierced the giant's shin. It stumbled a few feet back but regained its balance easily.

Devora pumped her legs. Of all the infuriating things this man had done, this was the worst. Passionately kissing her and then trying to die heroically?

"I don't think so," she said out loud as she reached the battle between Captain Blake and the giant.

The giant clapped its hands, summoning stones as large as Devora's body to rise from the sand. Levitating above the ground, they soared toward the captain. Devora dove out of the way as a boulder landed a few meters from the captain and almost hit her.

Do all giants have terrible aim?

More rocks plummeted around her and Captain Blake. Devora lifted her arms over her head, deflecting the rain of pebbles falling from the stones. What should they do now?

Her thoughts raced to the giants' first attack, how the glass had impaled not only Tenton's soldiers, but Kadeshian ranks as well. Devora's lips parted in realization. One Shot's advice finally made sense. Giants could barely see. That's why he said to shoot between the eyes. They wouldn't see it coming.

As if a confirmation of her thoughts, a string of arrows zinged behind her, each one making its mark between the giant's wide, brown eyes. It flopped forward before falling prostrate onto the sand.

Devora whirled her head around to find One Shot standing between the two soldiers who had taken him away earlier.

"What are you doing?" Devora demanded, rushing toward him. The glass shard still protruded from his leg. His skin was deathly white, but a weak grin split his face. "You need to see a medic."

"It was too good a shot not to take," One Shot wheezed, stumbling back.

"Apologies, Captain Medee," the soldier on the right said. "He threatened to use us for target practice if we didn't bring him back."

One Shot gave a throaty chuckle.

"Take him all the way back to camp. Do not bring him back, no matter what," she commanded, and the soldiers nodded. Before they took One Shot away, she reached out and grabbed his shoulder. "Thank you, my friend. But I need you alive."

He gave her a slow nod before his head hung between his shoulders.

"Hurry!" she ushered them, and the soldiers rushed away.

"Devora!" Captain Blake shouted, pulling her attention to him. "Run!"

Spinning around, Devora's eyes widened. She tried to retreat, but it was too late. A thick giant hand snatched her around the waist and hoisted her off the ground.

Chapter Thirty-Five

The Edo Desert, Tenton

Devora's mech and shield fell from her grasp as the giant threw her into the air. Her stomach launched to her throat, and then she fell. Screams poured from her lips but silenced as the giant caught her in his sweaty palm.

Her head whirled as the giant flung her back and forth. Devora knew she had to pierce the giant between its eyes, but with her arms pinned to her sides, she couldn't move. There was no way she could reach for the hairpin Nadia had given her. And with her mech on the ground, not even the poisoned gumberry blade could help her.

"Devora!" Captain Blake yelled.

She could hear his blade chop the flesh of the giant's leg, but the monster held her tight, crushing her between its pale, sweaty fingers.

The giant bellowed with laughter, as if Captain Blake striking him were a game. He hopped to one foot, then the other, toying with the small captain. All the while Devora was flung back and forth in his grasp, trying her best not to vomit from the jerky movements.

Tunri, Devora prayed, trying to squirm free. *Keep my parents safe, keep Nadia, Reese, Hestia, and Ida safe. Keep One Shot and Sir Jacques safe. And please, please keep Matthias safe.*

The giant tossed Devora again, this time higher. Hot, sticky air surrounded her as her body went up, up, up, before plummeting. The giant caught her again, but this time Devora had flung her arms above her head, keeping them out of the giant's grasp. As the giant held her close to his face, Devora yanked the hairpin from her head and plunged it between the giant's large green eyes.

The giant screamed and flailed. He clawed at the small hairpin protruding from his forehead with one hand, refusing to release Devora in the other.

Devora thrashed against the giant's grip, but it was no use. When the giant fell to the ground, she would go with him.

Just then, a shining light shimmered in the corner of her eye. The Behemoth had squashed the final giant in the line and was coming toward them.

An idea sprang into her mind. The large elk-like creature had spoken to her before, maybe they still had a connection. Closing her eyes, Devora sent the Behemoth the same thought it had sent her.

Help me.

When she opened her eyes, she saw that the giant animal hadn't stopped its charge.

Growling, the Behemoth scooped up the giant still holding Devora between its thick, white antlers. The giant flung its long limbs, trying to escape the bone prison. But the Behemoth wouldn't relent. It shook its head until the enormous man opened his fist and released Devora.

Devora screamed as she fell to the sand, pinching her lids shut. She didn't want the giant's backside to be the last thing she saw before she died.

But her fall was broken by two strong arms. As soon as she landed, her eyes flew open to see Captain Blake peering down at her in disbelief. Falling to his knees, he cradled her against his chest.

"Thank Tunri," he whispered into her hair, holding her close.

Devora wrapped her arms around his neck, enjoying the closeness until he released her.

The Behemoth roared behind them, causing Devora and the captain to jump and face the beast. The giant scrambled between its antlers, cursing in a different language.

The Behemoth shook the giant again and turned its violet eyes on Devora, as if waiting for her command. Taking a breath, Devora nodded. With a flick of its head, the Behemoth launched the giant several hundred yards away. The giant soared above the battle, bellowing and flailing until its body smacked on the ground in front of General Sage.

Snorting, the Behemoth knelt before Devora.

"Thank you," Devora said, rubbing the top of its silky-smooth nose.

The Behemoth nuzzled her chest then faced Captain Blake. The captain's rigid stance returned as the Behemoth sniffed him up and down. It blew in his face, causing the captain to stumble back a few paces.

"He's retreating!" a soldier shouted.

Devora lifted on her toes to watch General Sage abandon his army and flee into the desert on his iron-armored beast. The ranks behind him stopped their advance, unsure of how to respond to their leader surrendering.

A coward after all, Devora thought before her previous vision slammed into her thoughts.

"The princess," she breathed, turning to Captain Blake. "What if the general isn't retreating, but going after Princess Haden?"

Sir Conan trotted over on his horse. Sand, blood, and sweat covered his face, but relief lit his gaze.

"I'll capture the general, Captain Medee. You save Princess Haden." He placed his fist over his chest and bowed before kicking the side of his horse. It whinnied then galloped in the same direction as the fleeing general.

Captain Blake gripped his sword. "I'm right behind you."

A wide grin came to her face as she remembered the vision Tunri had sent her about her and the captain riding a giant white creature. This was it.

After she found her poisoned blade and picked up a discarded shield, Devora ran to the Behemoth. It laid on its belly, allowing Devora to jump up and straddle its back. Soft white hair spread through her fingers as she extended her hand to the captain.

"Come on," she said. Captain Blake scanned the Behemoth, his face paling. Devora held back a laugh. "You said you were right behind me."

The captain's eyes turned hard at the challenge. He marched up to the large creature and grabbed Devora's hand, climbing behind her. The Behemoth rose to all fours, and Captain Blake latched his arms around Devora's middle, squeezing her tight. Devora's breath hitched at their closeness, but she didn't mind the embrace.

"I didn't know I was agreeing to it literally," he growled in her ear, sending pleasant chills down her neck.

Devora grinned again and patted the Behemoth's shoulder. With another roar, the giant animal surged forward, causing her to clutch the smooth white hairs on its back.

The desert wind spiraled around them as the Behemoth galloped through the dunes. Kadeshian soldiers fled in every direction, not knowing where to go or what to do. General Sage had left them leaderless.

Urging the Behemoth forward, Devora feared the Kadeshian troops would return for the princess and take her elsewhere. Princess Haden would be huge leverage for Kadesh. Devora had to find the princess quickly before it was too late. Feeling the urgency, Devora patted the Behemoth's neck again and the animal quickened its pace.

As the outline of the Kadeshian encampment came into view, a cool aura guided Devora to the left. She gently veered the Behemoth and Captain Blake held her tighter as the creature jerked to the side.

The Kadeshian guards spotted them in the distance, their screams followed only by their retreating footsteps at the sight of the Behemoth. Devora assumed the news of their commander's surrender had reached them, for the soldiers didn't fight but dropped their weapons and ran in the opposite direction.

Devora scanned the tents, searching for the large palm tree. Hidden in the farthest corner of the camp sat a gray tent, secured to the towering palm tree from her vision.

Just like Tunri said.

"That one," she said, gesturing to the tent.

Devora patted the Behemoth's neck, and the giant animal easily smashed the other tents of the camp as it trotted forward. Once they arrived, the Behemoth shook its antlers and lowered to the ground.

Devora kept a firm grip on the thick white hair until the Behemoth had stopped moving. Yet as she tried to slide down the animal's side, she found that two arms were still clamped around her waist. With a smirk, Devora gently placed her hand over Captain Blake's.

"Matthias, we're here."

The captain lifted his head from its burrowed position in her shoulder.

"Thank Tunri," he breathed, detaching himself from Devora and sliding off the majestic elk.

He took a few wobbly steps then regained his balance. Snapping straight, the captain unsheathed his mech and searched for enemies.

Devora's skin cooled from where the captain's head had been pressed against her neck. Her stomach swirled, but she shoved the feeling down as she slid off the Behemoth.

"Thank you," she said to the Behemoth, gently stroking its side.

It nuzzled her stomach, then stood. Sniffing around the Kadeshian tents, the Behemoth happily trotted through the barren camp. More Kadeshian troops fled while the Behemoth enjoyed slurping up barrels of food.

Devora unsheathed her blade and turned back to the captain, pointing to the tent next to the largest palm tree. "She's in there."

Holding her blade high, Devora entered the tent first. Though the other soldiers fled, that didn't mean the ones guarding the princess had. Her eyes surveyed the space before she felt confident there was no one else.

Captain Blake entered after her, took one look around, and said, "We're alone."

Towers of barrels filled the spacious rectangular tent. The scent of ale and wine weighed the air, reminding Devora of the vision she had before. This was definitely the right place. She crept through the tent, searching around the barrels.

"Princess Haden?" Devora whispered, hoping the princess could make some sort of sound to alert them of her location. She tried calling a bit louder. "Princess?"

A muffled groan sounded from the center of the tent, and they hurried toward it. Bound and gagged to a wooden chair sat Tenton's only princess.

Throughout the kingdom, Princess Haden was known for her beautiful, shining white- blonde hair. But now, grease and mud matted her locks as they hung limp at her shoulders.

Devora rushed to the princess. *Are we too late?*

"Princess Haden?" she asked cautiously, taking a step forward.

Just then, the princess kicked her foot out, attempting to trip or injure Devora. But Devora's training took over, and she lurched away, simultaneously grabbing the princess' foot and holding her long leg in the air.

Princess Haden's jade green eyes flew open as she tilted back in the chair. The gag around her mouth was still secure, but muffled exclamations came from her lips.

"We're here to help," Devora said, impressed with the clever tactic as she lowered the princess' foot.

A garbled response came from the princess before Captain Blake untied the gag and unbound her hands from behind her back. Princess Haden shot the wad of fabric out of her mouth, coughing and spitting before she peered up at Devora, her eyes wide.

"A Seer? How are you still alive?"

Devora scoffed. A thousand replies flittered through her mind in an instant: *Who were you expecting? A giant? Yes, Princess, it's my honor to rescue you. No, I'm not a Seer, I just have bright violet eyes for fun. What about a thank you?*

Devora shook her head at her snarky replies before giving a slight bow and saying, "Yes, Your Highness."

Princess Haden analyzed Devora, but not with repulsion as others had, but fascination, like Devora was a rare creature.

Devora sheathed her mech, remembering that if King Atol, this young woman's father, had succeeded in his decree sixteen years ago, she would be dead. Devora pursed her lips. She *was* a rare creature and wondered how long it would be until she, too, was extinct.

The princess swallowed. "I didn't think my father would send anyone." Her voice was quiet, defeated, as if she had given up hope long ago.

Striding forward, Devora untied the princess' bonds. The leather straps came free, and Princess Haden stood, stretching her long, thin arms to the sky. Devora didn't realize how tall the princess really was until she stood at almost the same height as Captain Blake.

"The king had no idea where you were," Captain Blake answered, coming next to Devora. "Tunri sent Devora a vision of your location." The captain bowed. "It is an honor to rescue you, Princess Haden."

Devora pressed her lips together as the captain oozed formality. All men ogled the princess. But when the captain glanced back at Devora, she was reminded of their kiss and knew Captain Blake wasn't as easily swayed by a pretty face as some other men.

Princess Haden studied Captain Blake then looked back at Devora. "But you're a woman."

Captain Blake snapped straight. "What?"

Devora laughed and placed a hand on his arm. "Yes, I am."

"And a Seer?"

Devora quirked a brow. Maybe the princess wasn't as clever as she thought.

"Yes," Devora repeated. "In fact, I am a Seer, a woman, and the Defender of Tenton."

Princess Haden blinked, unsure how to respond.

After a quick search of the tent, Devora found a skin of water and some dried meat. Offering them to the princess, she asked, "Are you hurt in any way?"

Princess Haden examined her mud-caked hands. "No, but I could use a bath." She rubbed them ferociously on her tattered yellow dress, leaving two large brown streaks before taking the food.

"I'm sure we can arrange that," Devora replied with a grin. Maybe she and the princess had more in common than she thought.

Chapter Thirty-Six

Erza stood outside the tent, gripping the coarse material in her fist. The horns stopped blaring long ago and Jarrick hadn't returned. An uneasy feeling crept along her skin. Jarrick was never away for so long without sending a messenger to her.

She took a deep breath and closed her eyes, allowing the afternoon breeze to brush across her bronze skin. Maybe she was overreacting. Jarrick hadn't been away that long. And the army's horns ceasing could mean that Kadesh was victorious, and her husband would be home soon.

Erza forced the thought to take root in her heart, but it wouldn't stick. Something was wrong.

A snarling echoed in the distance, and her eyes jolted open. Just beyond the horizon, a figure rode straight toward her. Dropping the tent flap, Erza rushed outside, joy and relief filling her heart. Jarrick was okay. He had returned safely from the battle.

But as the figure closed in, her excitement vanished. Riding on a hideous beast covered in iron armor was General Sage.

Erza swallowed the terror and fury building in her throat. Spinning around, she placed her hands on her ebony braids.

Why is General Sage coming to our tent? Is he here to bring news of the death of Jarrick? Has this atrocious man taken someone else away from me?

The sound of the beast's claws beating on the sand came closer and closer, matching her pounding pulse. Erza's eyes sped around the tent, her mind filing through every possibility before the general's deep voice called.

"Lady Erza," he said confidently.

Erza whipped her head around, her gaze narrowing as the general dismounted his beast and bowed low. Sweat rolled down his tanned temples, glistening in the setting sun as it ran down his thick beard. Mud and sand caked his armor.

Is he coming from the front lines? Is the battle over?

Erza smoothed the fabric of her azure dress, forcing her heart to calm. Maybe this meeting was an opportunity for her. She could finally have her revenge.

A welcoming smile spread across Erza's face, and she curtsied. "General Sage. To what occasion do I owe this honor?" She kept her head bowed a moment longer than necessary. It was better for the general to think of her as a simple woman; an ordinary, humble servant to her husband and all men.

The general offered a smug smile as he sauntered toward her. His eyes roved over her face, and she knew he had bought her lie.

"I've come from the battlefront and am in need of nourishment and rest," General Sage said, stretching his thick arms above his head. "Will you grant this request?"

Erza stepped back and opened the tent flap, making sure to look away at the last moment. "Of course. Our home is your home, general."

She ushered the general in, gesturing to the pile of plump pillows and blankets before she did her best to seem flustered at his presence. General Sage stretched out on the pile, releasing a sigh of contentment.

Erza choked, smelling the awful odor coming from his sweaty skin. But she covered it with a delicate cough. With her heart pounding, she searched through her jars until she found a strong wine she and Jarrick used for medicinal purposes. After popping the cork, she poured the deep red liquid into their best chalice before fluttering to the general. Erza batted her lashes, handed him the cup, then turned away, feigning shyness.

Out of the corner of her eye, she watched the general roam his gaze up and down her body, making her want to crash the wine bottle into his head.

Patience, she told herself, swallowing her fury. *Soon.*

As Erza prepared a platter of bread and fruit, General Sage's deep gulps filled the tent. Erza held back her snarl as she placed the plate before him.

"Make sure you don't drink it all," she playfully scolded with a sweet smile and refilled his glass to the rim.

"You're so beautiful," the general replied, his words sloshing together as he took another swig of the hard drink. He reached out to her, and she swiftly dodged his filthy hand.

"Thank you, general, but I'm a married woman. Those compliments are inappropriate. Jarrick would not approve."

General Sage barked out a laugh before emptying the contents of the chalice and throwing it to the ground. "What that second-rate weapons master doesn't know, won't hurt him," the general slurred as he stood from the pillows. "We should be quick before he returns."

Fear pierced Erza's heart and she scurried away. But as she watched the general sway back and forth, her panic subsided. Within a few moments, the wine fully consumed him, and he thudded on the ground.

Erza's fury flared as she studied the large man before her. First, he killed her son. Then he insulted her husband. That was the final straw. The general had been given to her on a gilded platter, and Erza wouldn't waste it.

Carefully stepping over the burly man, Erza searched the tent until she found what she was looking for. A twisted grin crept across her face as she grabbed the cool metal tent stake and hammer Jarrick used to pitch their tent only weeks ago.

"This is for Josef and all the innocent blood you've shed," she whispered before she positioned the stake at General Sage's temple, raised the hammer, and pierced the general's skull.

Chapter Thirty-Seven

The Edo Desert, Kadeshian Camp

Once the Behemoth had finished destroying the Kadeshian camp and eating all of the rations, it lowered itself to the ground.

"What is that?" Princess Haden gasped, her emerald eyes the size of the moon starting to show in the darkening sky.

Devora opened her mouth, but closed it, not wanting to call her animal friend "the Behemoth from the Fortress." She had yet to learn its name.

Vinn, a soft voice whispered in her thoughts.

Devora turned her gaze to the giant animal, who blinked back at her.

"This is Vinn," Devora introduced before climbing on the creature's back. She offered a hand to the princess. "He's our ride home."

Princess Haden gave Vinn a once over before shrugging. "Works for me." She grabbed Devora's hand and hopped behind her.

The two women peered down to find Captain Blake planted in place. He sheathed his sword and assessed Vinn. Taking three large steps, he strode to the animal's face. Cautiously, the captain reached out and placed his hand on Vinn's nose. Vinn blinked at him before nuzzling into his chest. The captain released a deep chuckle as he rubbed the creature's snout.

Devora smiled, her heart warming at the sight. She loved seeing the gentler side of the captain. His military side was admirable and respected, but this was far better.

Captain Blake then leaned down and whispered something into Vinn's ear, too soft for Devora to hear.

The captain quickly stood and patted the animal's snout before stiffening once more. "Let's try not to throw everyone around this time, okay?"

Vinn flapped his lips before pushing against the Captain Blake's hand, and Devora could imagine the elk-like creature rolling his eyes.

Captain Blake climbed up the silky, smooth hair and sat behind the princess, careful to not hold on to her like he had with Devora. Instead, he clutched Vinn's thick hair so tight his knuckles turned white. Bowing his head, he squeezed his eyes shut.

"I'm ready."

Devora suppressed a grin as she faced forward and patted Vinn's neck. The giant animal lifted and took off.

"Whoa!" Princess Haden exclaimed, gripping Devora's shoulders.

Devora peered back to see a wide smile adorning the princess' dirtied face. Princess Haden quickly found her balance and lifted her hands to the sky. With a laugh, she tilted her head back and let the rushing wind twirl through her muddied hair.

The princess exuded a certain freedom and independence that was contagious. But it wasn't just her freedom from captivity—she was free to be herself, free to be anything she wanted.

Devora focused her gaze ahead. She prayed the princess would use her freedom to better their kingdom rather than destroy it like her parents had.

The moon shone brightly when they arrived at Tenton's camp. Fires blazed and songs of victory rang through the cool night as mugs clinked in unison. As soon as the trio and Vinn were spotted, cheers erupted from the soldiers' mouths. They lifted their mugs of ale as Vinn approached. The Kadeshians had retreated from the Edo desert back to Kadesh, accepting their defeat.

"Praise Tunri and His Seer, Captain Medee!" The men hooted and shouted, their faces light and joyful from their celebrating.

Vinn knelt down and allowed Devora, Princess Haden, and Captain Blake to slide off. The giant creature then stood and trotted to the edge of the camp. Devora kept her eyes glued to the stark white animal, fearing her friend would leave. But as soon as Vinn lowered his head and closed his eyes, Devora knew he would stay.

Rest, my friend, Devora thought to Vinn. *You've earned it.*

When Devora turned back to the soldiers, their cheering ceased, their eyes wide as they looked beyond Devora to the princess.

"Um, hello," Princess Haden said, giving a quick wave as she hunched behind Devora.

"The princess," a few men whispered while the rest gawked.

Devora clucked her tongue then shook her head, rolling her eyes. Though Princess Haden's beauty had been plastered all over the kingdom for years, she was currently caked in mud and grime. What was alluring about that?

"There's nothing to see," Captain Blake boomed as he blocked Devora and the princess with his body. "Captain Medee and Princess Haden need rest. I expect you all to give them the privacy they deserve." The captain shot a deathly glare at the men. The soldiers went rigid before bowing. They slowly started shuffling away, peeking over their shoulders at the princess before they left.

"Devora!" Nadia's loud voice shouted through the crowd.

Devora stood on her tiptoes to peer over Captain Blake's sturdy frame. A tan hand waved with a tall, pale figure behind it.

"Why is everyone just standing around?" Nadia said. "Move!"

"Please," One Shot's deep voice added.

Tears welled in Devora's eyes as Nadia and One Shot hobbled through the crowd. As soon as Nadia broke through, Devora rushed over and hugged her friend. Nadia returned the embrace before stepping back. Pursing her lips, she paced around Devora, stroking her invisible beard.

"Yes, the steel seems to have held up a lot better than the iron. Of course, steel has iron in it, so that makes sense, but the quality and shine are exceptional," she muttered to herself, running her eyes up and down Devora before pulling out her leather notebook. She scratched a few lines then secured it back in her pocket.

"You did it!" Nadia exclaimed, throwing her hands in the air. "I knew you would."

Devora jumped at the sudden shift and laughed.

"I'm glad you remembered my advice about the giants," One Shot said. Using crutches, he limped over and tried to bow. A large white bandage covered his leg from where the glass shard had been. "Thank you for giving me the chance to do good."

"It wasn't me who saw the good in you, One Shot, but Tunri," Devora answered.

"So, the princess?" Nadia said, sauntering up to the tall female.

Princess Haden took a step back as she assessed Nadia and One Shot and then focused back on Devora.

Nadia slapped Devora on the shoulder with a wicked grin on her lips. "Does that make you her knight in shining armor?"

Captain Blake scoffed. "If that were true, Lady Devora is everyone's knight in shining armor. She saved us all with her quick thinking." He gave her a firm nod. "Please make sure the princess receives everything she needs." With a deep bow, the captain turned and marched away.

Devora's heart dropped.

Has he already forgotten about our kiss? Or that he was willing to give his life to save me? Why has he returned to the rigid captain after everything we've been through?

"Good to know that the battle didn't faze the cap," Nadia snorted, gesturing to Captain Blake's silhouette disappearing into the camp.

"No, it didn't," Devora replied slowly, trying not to think of his embrace or how safe he made her feel. Shaking her head, Devora turned back to the princess. "There's an oasis not too far from here. Nadia and I will take you there." She turned to One Shot. "Will you keep guard to make sure no curious soldiers wander over?"

A mischievous grin came to One Shot's lips as he held up his crossbow. "No one will even come close."

Chapter Thirty-Eight

The return journey to the Fortress was easier this time. For one, Devora had Vinn to ride on and didn't have to be stuffed into a tiny carriage. She breathed in the chilled air as they made their way to the northern region. Though she missed the tropical heat of Grenly, the crisp breeze had grown on her.

Vinn trotted in stride with the first carriage that held Captain Blake and Princess Haden. A twinge of jealousy pricked Devora's heart as she thought of the two of them alone together, but she pushed it away. The captain could be with anyone he liked. And after he had stayed in his tent and not spoken another word to her since the battle, he obviously didn't care about her. Just like his brother.

Vinn and Devora soon led the caravan of carriages and soldiers and arrived at the Fortress first. Once she dismounted Vinn, Devora sent him to graze among the few patches of trees along the edge of the Fortress' land. Vinn was free and Devora would do everything to make sure he stayed that way.

Wiping her hands on her pants, Devora strode toward the Fortress. As she took in the hard, dark stone, it didn't look as daunting or terrible as it had when she first arrived. Devora smirked and shook her head. Maybe it was the morning sun or the victory she had just experienced, but she was happy to return.

"Captain Medee," Warden Hazor called, meeting her at the front gate. "I hear you're our savior." He gave a deep bow that Devora took to be genuine.

"Thank you, Warden. But I'm not your savior. Tunri is."

The warden grunted as he peered over her shoulder to the approaching caravan. "Regardless, there are a plethora of people waiting for your return. Apparently, there's a ball in your honor tonight."

She took a step back. "What? Why?"

Warden Hazor stroked his mustache. "I'm not sure what goes on in our king's obtuse mind, but he has demanded it. Follow me."

Sucking in a breath, Devora followed the warden inside. Cheers erupted as she made her way through the different levels of the prison. How different it was from the first time she fled through these halls. Only Tunri could have changed her horrible circumstances and used them for good. But as she searched for Ida, Hestia, and Reese, she found they weren't there.

"The king's banquet is in a few hours," the warden huffed over his shoulder. "Queen Leza has been generous enough to leave trunks full of dresses and jewelry in my office for you to choose from."

Devora chuckled at Warden Hazor's displeasure but flattened her smile when he scowled.

"Her handmaidens are waiting for you." He gestured to his wooden office door.

"Thank you, sir," Devora replied with a bow.

As she grasped the metal knob of the door, Warden Hazor grabbed her wrist.

"Be careful of the friends you make in the palace, Medee. There are worse wolves in the king's court than the ones outside." His glower penetrated into her, rising the hairs on the back of her neck.

Devora gave a hesitant nod. "Thank you, sir," she whispered before he released her.

The sturdy man marched down the hall. With his back to her, he lifted his hand. "Good job, Medee. You made the Fortress proud."

When Devora entered the room, the queen's handmaidens immediately flocked around her, paying her endless compliments about the victory over Kadesh. Devora smiled politely, but Warden Hazor's warning rang in her thoughts as the women prepared her for the banquet.

Four forest green trunks hunched against the stone walls of the warden's office. Holding a golden key, the head handmaiden opened the first trunk. A heap of bright-colored fabrics burst out. Devora gaped at the brilliant blues and alluring reds. The young handmaidens gawked at the beautiful dresses, trying to lure Devora to their favorites. As the head handmaiden moved to the next trunk, more dresses poured out. In a matter of moments, all shades of purple, pink, and emerald decorated Warden Hazor's office.

The light jade dress peeking out of the side made Devora think of Princess Haden and her bright eyes. Her carriage had been sent straight to the palace with Captain Blake escorting her.

Devora sighed, trying to push the memory of their kiss from her thoughts. Maybe he thought they were going to die, and he didn't want to spend his last moments alone.

Her mind settled on that thought. She didn't like it, but it was rational and fit with the captain's personality. It was better that there was nothing between them. Tristan had already scarred her heart; she didn't want to give Captain Blake a chance to.

While the other maids pulled the dresses out of the trunks, fluffing and draping them over any piece of furniture they could find, the head handmaiden unlocked the final trunk. Devora gasped as glittering jewels pooled out, shimmering and shining like a delicate stream.

"The queen is too generous," Devora breathed, reaching toward the jewels. Her fingers grazed a beautiful strand of pink pearls. They would have matched Nadia's hairpin perfectly.

"My queen wanted the Savior and Defender of Tenton to choose anything she desired," the head handmaiden replied with a soft smile.

Devora glanced at the handmaiden before peering back at the jewels. Though they were all stunning, she couldn't forget the pink pearl necklace. Grasping it again, she studied it closely.

"I'm not Tenton's savior. Tunri sent me the visions." Devora strode to the tall, rectangular mirror the handmaidens had propped against the wall and held the pearls to her neck.

It wouldn't be long before Kadesh regrouped and attacked Tenton again. Why was everyone acting like the war was over with one battle? Yes, General Sage was dead. She had received the report from Sir Conan that nomads in the desert had killed him. But Captain Blake said Kadesh had two more generals: Generals Yada and Beta. Would they come for Tenton next?

"An excellent choice, my lady," the head handmaiden commented, coming behind Devora. She took the pearls and layered them around Devora's neck. The handmaiden undid Devora's hair, allowing her thick waves to spiral down her shoulders and back.

Devora's breath hitched as she touched the pearls, staring back at herself. She looked like Mama.

Mama, I pray you and Papa are safe.

Although Captain Blake had intervened for her parents and they were still alive, Devora had no idea if Papa had made it back to Grenly or if Mama was okay. Maybe they would be at the banquet tonight.

One of the younger handmaidens with soft blonde curls brought a chair and Devora sat. Closing her eyes, Devora relaxed as the head handmaiden combed her tangled hair. The captain's face flashed through her thoughts: his strong jaw, steely eyes, and furrowed brow. Her heart skipped.

Why do I care for this infuriatingly confusing yet wonderful man?

When she opened her eyes, the head handmaiden had made her hair into a work of art. Twists and braids piled atop her head, all pinned with matching pink pearls.

"Thank you for your kindness," Devora said, giving the handmaiden's hand a squeeze.

The handmaiden fluffed Devora's hair with a grin as the other maids collected the paints for her face. Devora noticed how they only pulled out red and black, not the white powder from before. She raised her brows in surprise. They remembered everything she disliked.

The handmaiden smiled at Devora in the mirror. "The queen's handmaidens are the best. Now,"—she ushered Devora to the dresses— "It's time to choose a dress."

Chapter Thirty-Nine

Devora's ribs tightened with each breath as she hurried down the hall. If she had known the beautiful scarlet gown was going to suffocate her, she wouldn't have chosen it. She spared a glance to admire the shining red fabric, her purple sash glistening with each rushed step she took. She looked every bit a princess and she loved it. The dress was worth the pain.

Outside the Fortress, the king's elegant, gilded carriage waited. Devora laughed at the strange fairytale she was in where she was the knight in shining armor *and* the princess.

"Lady Medee." The footman bowed, his black velvet coat scraping the ground.

He offered her his hand and Devora took it before stepping into the carriage. From what she remembered, Maldove Palace wasn't too far away. She had easily seen it many times during her job with the wolves. But still,

Devora was thankful for the carriage. She couldn't imagine riding Vinn to the palace, especially in the poofy dress.

What a sight that would've been, she chuckled to herself as she ran her hand along the plush green upholstery surrounding her.

The carriage bobbed and weaved steadily over the cobblestone streets, not jostling her once as it made its way to the palace steps. As soon as they arrived, the footman hopped off the front and opened the door, offering his hand again.

"Thank you." She nodded, carefully stepping out of the carriage, wary of the hem of her dress.

The footman released her hand and bowed again before climbing on the carriage.

As soon as the carriage disappeared, Devora faced the palace and sucked in a breath. The white marble of the king's castle gleamed in the moonlight, as if it had just been polished. Large white columns lined the entranceway, making anyone who entered feel like royalty. Devora gently gathered her dress and ascended the large stone steps.

People bustled around her, rushing up the steps in their elegant clothing. Her chest constricted as she thought about all the nobility that would be waiting. She let out a breath and kept walking. She had faced giants and ironed beasts; why was she scared of a party?

Devora tried to control her breathing as she finally made it up the steps. Though her ribs squished her lungs, her breaths eventually returned to normal. As she approached the gilded doors, a short, plump man wearing a large scarlet hat with a white feather stood at the doorway.

"What is your name, my lady?" he questioned, his eyes big and bright, as if he genuinely cared who she was.

"Lady Devora Medee," Devora announced, clasping her black-gloved hands in front of her.

The man's eyes widened even more. "Our guest of honor." He bowed deeply, his hat almost falling off his head. "I am honored to welcome you to Maldove Palace, Lady Medee."

Heat tinged Devora's ears as the people gathering behind her started murmuring. Waving a quick hand at the herald, she said, "There's no need for that."

The man straightened. "And do you have an escort? Is Captain Blake with you?"

Devora's smile faltered, but she quickly composed herself. She didn't know where Captain Blake was, but she made the best excuse she could.

"I'm afraid Captain Blake was unable to make it tonight. He had other business to attend to."

"Fortunately, I was able to finish my other business," Captain Blake said, coming up beside her.

Her stomach lurched at the sound of his voice. Devora spun around and her jaw dropped. Gone were his battle armor and weapons, replaced with a smooth black shirt with a black jerkin strapped over it. Black pants and boots finished the captain's monochromatic look, but Devora couldn't tear her eyes away.

Captain Blake grinned as his eyes quickly traveled the length of her and flashed with excitement before they focused on the man. "Lady Devora Medee and her escort, Captain Matthias Blake."

"Captain Blake!" the man squeaked in excitement, bowing so low his nose touched the floor.

He was obviously a fan of Captain Blake's.

"Rise, herald," the captain commanded, giving Devora a wink. "We are ready to enter."

"Yes, sir, I mean captain, I mean sir," the man flustered before grabbing the silver horn latched to his belt.

The herald stood in the now open doors and blew the horn. The nobles below silenced, and Devora faced the crowd, her pulse increasing by the second.

"Announcing our guest of honor, the Defender of Tenton: Lady Devora Medee and her escort, Captain Matthias Blake."

There was a pause.

Once they see my eyes, will everyone...?

A gentle touch pulled her attention away from the waiting crowd to the softened gaze of Captain Blake. He offered his arm. Relief relaxed her tense shoulders as she slid her arm through his.

"I'm right beside you," he whispered in her ear, his warm breath tickling her neck. Goosebumps lined her flesh, but she didn't mind.

As soon as she and Captain Blake appeared, the king's court erupted into applause. Devora's steps faltered, but the captain pulled her close.

"Just smile," he said out of the corner of his mouth. He preceded to nod at the people with a polite grin. As he nodded, the chain that held her ring peeked out from beneath his collar.

Devora wondered why he still had the imperial opal ring before she smiled at the excited crowd. Women in vibrant colored dresses waved their fans as men in frocked collars and silks clapped loudly. Besides the Regulus Protecti tournament, Devora had never seen so many noble people.

She searched the crowd, hoping—praying—she would find the familiar faces of Mama and Papa. But as she and the captain reached the center of the large room, Governor and First Lady Medee were nowhere to be found.

Devora bit her lip, trying not to think the worst, when the king and queen of Tenton entered the throne room. The room applauded again, but with less vivacity than before.

Dressed in a deep forest green cloak with a matching tunic, the king strode confidently through the crowd. His gilded crown sat firmly on his thick curls as he surveyed his court. Devora could've sworn his eyes narrowed and a scowl formed on his thick lips when he saw her. But when she blinked, his charming, kingly smile had returned.

An uneasy feeling crept up Devora's spine as she watched the royal couple. Queen Leza was striking in her dark green dress, a perfect match to the king's ensemble. Her pale skin glowed in the chandelier light. Two golden combs held her hair back, defining her slender neck and the deep neckline of her dress. The silver crown laid upon her ebony waves, perfecting her regal appearance. As the queen strode by, the imperial opal in the center winked at Devora.

The king and queen nodded and greeted everyone who surrounded them as they made their way to their thrones on the opposite end of the vast room.

Devora didn't know why, but she felt as if she was being watched. In a blink, she engaged her soulsight. Yellow swirls fluttered on the chests of most of the nobles. Yet as she focused on the queen, her soul was still blacker than midnight. Devora shuddered and averted her gaze to the king. Though his soul wasn't as dark, it was still a dingy gray.

Devora willed the swirls away and subtly turned her head to the side. There were guards spaced evenly throughout the perimeter of the room, but why wouldn't there be? This was the palace. The king probably received hundreds of death threats and assassination attempts daily. Plus, they had only won a battle, not the war.

Still, her unease didn't waver.

"My friends," King Atol boomed, extending his hands to silence the chattering crowd. The nobles shut their mouths immediately, leaning forward to absorb every word from the king's lips. "Tonight, we honor not just one victory, but two. The return of our princess,"—The crowd interrupted the king with loud applause. He stared them down and they silenced immediately— "And the defeat of Kadesh at the battle of Edo."

The nobles applauded politely this time. Devora shifted her gaze around the crowd again, clutching onto Captain Blake's arm.

Where is Princess Haden? Shouldn't she be here?

Devora's anxiety grew, and she tapped her fingers nervously on the captain's arm. Something wasn't right.

Leaning over, Captain Blake whispered, "What's wrong?"

Devora glanced up at him, ready to reply, but stopped. A thin sheen of sweat glistened on the captain's forehead, and his face had turned a deathly shade of white.

"Matthias, are you all right?"

He glanced at her before tugging at his collar. "I'm just having second thoughts about coming tonight."

Devora's heart dropped to her feet. "Oh."

Have I said or done something to make him want to leave? She quickly reflected on their previous conversation, finding nothing offensive.

He placed his hand over hers. "What were you searching for?" he asked, changing the subject.

Devora trained her eyes forward. King Atol had finished his speech and was now seated next to his wife, stroking her hand as members of the King's Council danced to a soothing tune. It may have been the lighting of the room, but Devora could've sworn she saw the queen scowl at her. Yet, as soon as Devora did a doubletake, the queen giggled angelically at something her husband said.

"Princess Haden," Devora whispered to Captain Blake as he directed them to the dance floor. "Where is she? Shouldn't she be here?"

Captain Blake wrapped his arm around Devora's waist and, before she could protest, they were swept onto the dance floor.

"What are you doing?" she hissed, trying not to step on his feet as they glided through the other couples. He was a surprisingly good dancer.

The captain twirled her around, moving them smoothly with the soft melody. When he twirled Devora again, she saw that a guard was speaking to the king. While King Atol nodded to what the guard was saying, he kept his gaze fixed on them.

"Blending in," Captain Blake muttered, pulling her closer.

The hard muscles of his toned chest pressed against her as he clutched her waist and Devora's nerves heightened to a new level.

"Why do we need to blend in?" she whispered, feeling the line of tension in his broad shoulders as she placed her hand on them.

"Devora," he breathed in her ear, his cheek resting against hers. He pulled back, the storm in his gray eyes returning as his gaze roamed over her face. "Forgive me."

Devora stopped, furrowing her brow as the clicking of marching footsteps sounded behind her.

"Matthias." She started to reach out to him when he snapped an imperial opal manacle around her wrist. Her pulse raced as he secured another one around her other hand.

"What's going on?" Devora cried, staring at the chains.

They were the same shackles that bound Babshee and Vinn. The stone that forbade any power from being unleashed. The stone that would kill her if she wore it for too long.

Immediately, her energy waned. Devora's head felt like a boulder as she looked up at Matthias. His gaze held a fury of emotions before he focused on his shined boots.

"Lady Medee," King Atol's voice rang through the throne room, drenched in arrogance and condemnation. "Is it true you rescued Princess Haden from the Kadeshian camp?"

Devora's body went numb as she mechanically turned to the king. Her limbs felt so heavy it was difficult to stand.

The king pounded on his throne. "Answer me!"

Devora blinked, confusion clouding her thoughts. "Yes."

"And is it true that you allowed the princess to return to the palace unguarded and alone?"

Devora's vision became hazy as her eyes shifted between the king and the queen then to Matthias. "I—" she started, but the king interrupted her.

"It was reported that Princess Haden had returned, but when my dear wife went to check on our beloved daughter, she found this instead." The king held up a piece of parchment. Delicate cursive scrawled along the page, but Devora couldn't read what it said.

"'Upon my return to the palace, Lady Medee's assassin followed me and forced me to write this ransom. If you do not give Lady Medee ten thousand crowns, they will kill me in one week.'"

"What?" Devora exclaimed, trying to bring her chained hands to her spinning head. Her arm felt heavier than a mountain. She could barely lift it.

Trying to regain some energy, Devora's mind quickly filed through the statement. She hadn't ordered anyone to capture the princess. And who was her assassin? Devora's heart stopped. One Shot. Someone had framed him. Someone had framed *her*. But why?

"This is Princess Haden's handwriting," the king stood, showing the crowd who gasped and scurried away from Devora. Nasty glares and whispers soon followed. "The note was later confirmed by Captain Blake," the king continued. "He tried to stop the assassin but was too late. And now the princess is gone."

The crowd roared with anger, shaking their fists and shouting insults at Devora while she slowly turned toward the captain.

Captain Blake wouldn't meet her eyes.

"Look at me," she gritted her teeth, fury, rage, and betrayal churning in her heart.

He slowly met her glare, tears building in his eyes.

"How long?"

"Dev—"

"How long?" she growled at him, lunging forward with the last bits of strength she had left. "Was it you who planned to give me the poison, too?" she screamed. "Why did you stop me from taking it?"

The guards reined her back. Shrieks came from the retreating crowd. Some even fainted.

"Take her to Level Five of the Fortress," King Atol ordered. "She will be kept there until the princess is found."

Tears clouded Devora's vision as the guards dragged her away. Her chest heaved as she tried to control the tears, but she failed. Waterfalls gushed out of her eyes, streaming down her face.

And Captain Blake turned away.

Chapter Forty

Level Five, The Fortress, Tenton

Three days passed and Devora hadn't received any news of Princess Haden or One Shot. What she did receive was a lump of stale bread and a cup of muddied water. She stared at the meal, the desire to eat nonexistent since she had been imprisoned. The dining hall gruel was a lot more appealing than this.

As soon as the guards locked her in Level Five, Devora immediately missed her cell just a few levels above. While her cell in the prison wasn't luxurious, it was at least clean. Level Five smelled of rotting flesh and decay. She wasn't even sure if the pile of ash in the corner was dust or the remains of a previous prisoner.

How could One Shot live in these conditions?

She couldn't believe One Shot had endured this horrifying place for years.

For hours, Devora tried to finagle the stone manacles off her wrists. She tugged and pulled with every ounce of strength she had left. She even yanked a pin from her hair, which was now a mess of tangles and pearls, and wedged it between her reddening skin and the stone. A spark of her power returned, and hope plunged into her heart. But when she wiggled the pin a little more, nothing else happened.

Devora brought her knees to her chest. The beautiful red dress seemed so out of place in this terrible chamber. Even with her minimal movements, the pristine fabric had already been sullied by the filthy floor.

It hurt to stare into the darkness, so she closed her swollen eyes. She couldn't remember the last time she had cried so hard and for so long. Tears didn't afflict her eyes often. But when they did come, they came full force, barreling down her cheeks like waterfalls that would never end.

How could I have been so stupid?

Captain Blake had used her, just like he said he would when they first met. *She's young and moldable. If we train her correctly, we can use her to our advantage within the court.*

How could she have believed everything he said, the compliments, the training, the kiss...

Devora balled her hands into fists. Her sadness and hurt diminished after the first day the captain hadn't come to explain himself. Now there was nothing left but bitter fury. Twice, she had been made a fool by the same family. Her heart hardened. It would never happen again.

Her muddled thoughts tugged toward Tunri. Leaning her head against the frigid, stone wall, Devora looked up.

Why is this happening, Tunri? I thought I had done what you wanted. I thought I had done what was right.

The door leading to Level Five shrieked, its hinges rusted from neglect. The guard's usual clomping footsteps echoed against the dismal walls. He was meant to check on her five times a day.

Devora scoffed. *Where do they think I'm going to go?*

Before she tried to use the pin to unlock the manacles, she tried to use it to pick the lock. Unfortunately, the pin was too short. If it had been a bit longer, Devora would've had no problem maneuvering it through the simple lock into the iron bars caging her.

Another set of footsteps followed the guard's, and the flicker of two torches glinted from the hall. Devora lifted her head at the familiar heavy march, wondering why Captain Blake thought she would ever want to see him again.

"Five minutes," the guard growled before placing a small hourglass in front of her cell. He flipped it over and continued down the shadowed tunnel.

Devora watched the white sand fall into the lower chamber, thinking back to the battle in Edo and everything she had been through to get there. It was all for nothing. She had started in a prison and now she would end in a prison.

Captain Blake stood outside her cell, outlined in the light of the torch in his hand. He didn't say anything and neither did Devora.

What could she say? *I trusted you and you betrayed me? I thought I meant more to you. How could you do this to me? I thought I was beginning to fall...* Devora slammed the door on that thought. She wouldn't fall. She would *never* fall for anyone.

"When the king changed the categories," Captain Blake started, keeping his gaze fixed on the hourglass at his feet. "We were notified that nobility would be coming to the Fortress." His voice was rough and scratchy, as if he had been screaming. "Warden Hazor recognized your name. Apparently, he knew your father and mother when they attended Vlacklear." He took a shallow breath. "The warden charged me with watching you to see what kind of daughter Governor Medee had raised." The captain slowly lifted his head, his gray eyes bloodshot. "When I watched you stare down the warden, unafraid of his knife at your throat, I knew I couldn't let him kill you."

Devora focused on him, her jaw clenched, but she remained silent.

"I never intended for this,"—he motioned to the cell—"to happen."

Captain Blake turned his head to the left, checking the empty hall. Reaching in his pocket, he pulled out an iron ring of keys and slid a thick skeleton key into the lock of her cell. The captain turned it slowly and a click rang through Level Five. Once the cell door opened, he hurried inside.

Devora stayed seated on the ground, keeping her gaze hard as he came near. He slowed his steps, holding up the key, as if she would bite him if he came closer. Maybe she would.

Devora turned her head away. He betrayed her. Was he really trying to rescue her? But why?

Silently, she held her wrists toward him, making sure to keep her gaze on the floor. She couldn't trust her heart against those stormy eyes.

"One Shot is waiting outside with Vinn," Captain Blake whispered, clicking the key into place. "You need to get as far away from here as you can."

Her stone bonds snapped open, and Devora ripped them off, massaging her swollen wrists. Cool power wrapped around her, embracing her in a tight hug. As if a spring had been unleashed, her energy instantly returned, and Devora felt more alive than she had in days. She never thought she would miss her gift so much.

Captain Blake tried to help her stand, but she wrenched away from him.

"Don't touch me," Devora spat, standing on her own. She smoothed the wrinkles of the red ballgown and lifted her chin. "Don't come near me."

Guilt and hurt flashed across the captain's face, but he nodded. "Understood."

He marched out of the cell, keeping the door open until she exited.

Captain Blake turned, his mouth open, ready to speak when a metal rod whacked him over the head. Devora stifled the squeal that wanted to escape. She was still partially in her cell and had to decide if she would try to run or stay put.

But before she could decide on either, a large arm wrapped around the captain's waist. Captain Blake's body hung over the arm like a sack of potatoes until the stark white head of Warden Hazor appeared.

"Warden?" Devora questioned, taking a cautious step out of the cage.

The warden grunted before heaving the captain over his shoulder. Devora's eyes went wide. Captain Blake wasn't a small man. For Warden Hazor to haul him on his back like he was nothing was impressive.

"Let's go, Medee," Warden Hazor growled before taking a torch off the wall and striding down the dark hall.

Questions piled on top of one another in her mind as Devora quickly padded behind him. She finally settled on one.

"What's going on?"

Warden Hazor shifted the captain's body so he could peer back at her. "When you first came to the Fortress, Blake took an interest in you. I knew that if he was willing to talk me out of killing you, you were something special. I didn't like your father when we were at Vlacklear and I don't like you, Medee. I don't like nobles, and I don't like things that can't be explained rationally. And you're both. But that doesn't mean you should be murdered."

Devora blinked rapidly as she tried to keep up with the warden's long strides.

What is he saying? He didn't want to kill me that first day?

"Why did you try to kill me then?"

Warden Hazor paused. Keeping his back to her, he said, "A test. I wanted to see your reaction. Were you like your father or your mother?"

Warden Hazor knows Papa and *Mama? How?*

"And?" she asked.

The warden readjusted Captain Blake on his shoulder. "Defiant like your father, diplomatic like your mother. You have the best of both of them."

Speechless, Devora stood in the dark corridor until Warden Hazor continued down the hall.

"I have no respect or tolerance for our idiot of a king. I never have," he said. "But I'm willing to play his games so that we can eventually win this war over Kadesh and place a new king on the throne." He glanced at Devora. "Since your parents were freed, the king has been trying to find a way to arrest you. Blake held him off for as long as he could, committing terrible acts to keep His Majesty satisfied."

"What?" Devora exclaimed, the memories of the captain leaving on short notice all the time. The piece of parchment with names listed. "But why?"

"And here I thought you were a clever one," Warden Hazor snorted, stopping in front of a small metal door, barely large enough for Devora to squeeze through.

He slid Captain Blake off his back and laid him face down on the floor before rifling through his pockets. After a moment, the warden pulled out the iron key the captain used to free her. Devora stared at the key as the warden placed it in the lock to the door.

"Sixteen years ago, Queen Leza received a prophecy from a Seer. A prophecy that frightened her. She was so terrified that King Atol ordered for every Seer to be killed. Every Seer but the one who delivered it. That Seer was Kanna Blake, Matthias' mother."

Devora's gaze whipped up, her mouth dropping open. "Does Matthias know?"

His name tasted sweet on her tongue. Though it had only been a few days, she missed it. Curse her treacherous heart.

"Why do you think he's been under the king's thumb for so long?" Warden Hazor asked, stroking his white mustache. "Like his mother, you were another piece of leverage the king used to keep Matthias leashed. He's a powerful soldier with a quick mind that can easily run circles around His Majesty. Atol knows this, too." Warden Hazor glanced down at Captain Blake's crunched body. "I told him to give you the stables to see if you could be trusted in freeing him from the king's grasp. Would you flee or stay? I knew he wouldn't tell you all this, but if you're going to survive, you needed to know. It has to look like you knocked him out or he'll be executed."

Devora gasped. She was furious at Captain Blake for not explaining things to her, but she didn't want him to die.

"What do I need to do?" she asked.

Warden Hazor looked up. "Find Kanna. The king has hidden her somewhere that Matthias can't find. Find out what the prophecy was. It's been stricken from Tenton's history books. And, if you can, find where the princess is. Rumor is she fled from the palace right after Matthias secured her in her room. No one knows why, but there's talk that she knows information that can end the king's reign."

Devora took in a breath, trying to process all the information being thrown at her. Warden Hazor then turned the key and opened the door. The crisp night air welcomed Devora into its embrace. As she stepped through the threshold, the outline of Vinn's gleaming hair shone in the moonlight, a tall rider seated upon his back.

Devora whipped around. "What about Nadia? She came to the battle, too. And my other friends. I don't want any more people being hurt because of me." She cast a final glance at the captain's body, still sprawled along the dismal dungeon floor.

"Don't worry about the Tinker," Warden Hazor said, crossing his thick arms over his chest. "She's off on a special mission along with Ida Shabawn and Jacques and the twins. I've sent them different places and won't tell you their whereabouts to keep them safe. But if they're wise, they'll stay away for as long as possible."

Devora studied the tall stance of the brutal warden before giving him a deep bow. She was thankful she had earned his respect, but he had earned hers, as well.

"Thank you, sir."

"Medee," Warden Hazor said, his voice heavy. "Only a Seer can find another Seer. So, no matter what happens, make sure you stay alive. In order to save Matthias and this kingdom, you need to live."

Devora's heart twisted in her chest as she remembered Captain Blake telling her the same thing on the battlefield. The moment they shared felt like decades ago.

Taking in a breath, she took one last look at the captain before grabbing the purple sash adorning her chest.

"I will," she proclaimed and fled into the night.

The Author

V. Romas Burton grew up bouncing up and down the East Coast where she wrote her first story about magical ponies at age seven. Years later, after studying government and earning an M.A. in Theological Studies, V. Romas Burton realized something even bigger was calling out to her--stories that contained great adventures and encouraging messages. Her debut novel, Heartmender, has won several awards including: First Place in Young Adult for the 2020 Next Generation Indie Book Awards, Second Place in Juvenile/ Young Adult for the 2021 Illumination Book Awards and tied for Third Place for Young Adult Fiction-Fantasy/ Sci- Fi in the 2020 Moonbeam Children's Awards. You can find future updates and news on her website: www.vromasburton.com

Quill & Flame Publishing House

Find other Quill & Flame titles at www.quilland-flame.com or
@quill.and.flame.publishers on Instagram.
Stay tuned for more short stories as well as future releases from Quill & Flame Publishing House.
Join Quill & Flame Book Tours by emailing quillandflame publishinghouse@gmail.com.

Find other Quill & Titles releasing soon!

Making Magik: A Magik Prep Academy Anthology January 2023
Fortified by V. Romas Burton February 2023

Of Flame & Frost by AJ Skelly March 2023
By Light & Love by Anna Augustine April 2023
R.E.M. by Ashley Schaller May 2023
Hearts by Brittany Eden June 2023
Heart of the Sea by Moriah Chavis August 2023
By Blade & Blood by Anna Augustine September 2023
Shadowcast by Crystal D. Grant October 2023
Magic & Mistletoe: A Quill & Flame Christmas Anthology
December 2023

Acknowledgements

These acknowledgments are a testament of God's faithfulness. There was a time not long ago where I thought my writing career was over. After writing a debut award-winning series, I accepted that I had an excellent experience and set my writing to the side.

However, God is always full of surprises. First and foremost, I thank Him for seeing me fit to continue sharing the stories He places on my heart.

To David, Matthew, and Thomas, thank you for reminding me that our little family is my number one treasure.

To my family who never stops supporting and encouraging me, even when I don't believe in myself.

To Courtney, it was chatting with you long ago that inspired me to write this version of Fortified.

To my college gals, my favorite fan girls!

To April (AJ Skelly) and my Quill & Flame Publishing family (including my wonderful editors!), thank you for reigniting my love for writing and loving my thick, crazy plots.

To Burton's Booklovers, you've supported me since the beginning, thank you for still supporting me now!

Lastly, to my wonderful readers. Without you, there is no one to tell a story to. Thank you for being willing and ready to dive into another world, always ready for a new adventure.